POPPY McVIE

SAVING ANIMALS

ONE BOOK AT A TIME

BOX SET 1-3

POPPY McVIE
SAVING ANIMALS
ONE BOOK AT A TIME

KIMBERLI A. BINDSCHATEL

Turning Leaf Books · Traverse City, MI

Published by Turning Leaf Productions, LLC.
Traverse City, Michigan

www.PoppyMcVie.com
www.KimberliBindschatel.com

Print ISBN-13:9780996189071
Print ISBN-10:0996189076

Thank you for purchasing this book and supporting an indie author.

The greatness of a nation can be judged by the way its animals are treated.

~Mahatma Gandhi

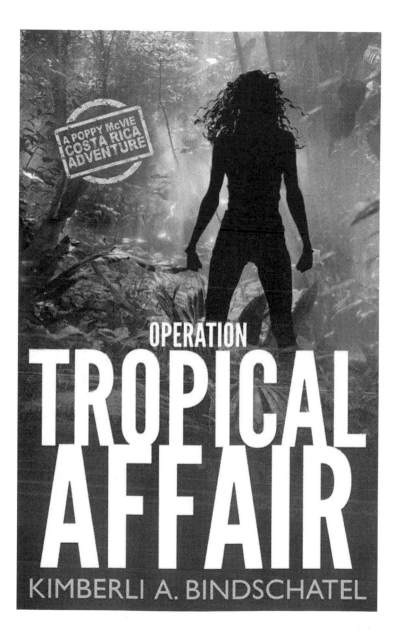

A POPPY McVIE
COSTA RICA
ADVENTURE

OPERATION
TROPICAL
AFFAIR

KIMBERLI A. BINDSCHATEL

OPERATION
TROPICAL AFFAIR

a Poppy McVie adventure

CHAPTER 1

I knew they'd come for her. The poor thing. Wandering in unknown territory trying to shake a disorienting drugged-out haze. She was easy prey for a couple of two-bit rednecks. Goes to show how things are bass ackwards in this world.

Well, they weren't going to get away with it. Not on my watch.

Honey Bear—as she'd been christened by Sally Newberry, the second grader who'd won the naming contest run by *The Mining Gazette*—had been caught rummaging through the trash cans of some downstater who didn't know any better than to throw her chicken bones into a black plastic bag and set it right out on her back porch. Might as well hang a neon welcome sign. It was the bear, of course, who needed to be *rehabilitated*. Dubbed a "trouble" bear, she'd been trapped, tranquilized, poked and prodded, then released yesterday afternoon here on the north side of the refuge. Now she was an easy target.

The sun hadn't poked up over the horizon yet and there they were. Just as I thought. The Lawson boys. Coming down the two-track in their souped up purple Geo Tracker. It was outfitted with a state-of-the-art antennae mounted on the roof, makeshift kennels built into the back, and two greasy haired, grinning idiots inside. The true genius of their bear poaching contraption was the blue tick hound dog straddling the hood, his collar chained to an eye hook mounted where a hood ornament would go, his long ears flapping in the wind. This way, his nose was right out front to catch bear scent. I shook my head. Rednecks. I aimed the video camera and pushed the record button.

The dog's name was Brutus. I'd met him a few weeks ago when I'd pulled them over and demanded they take him off the hood. They were just outside the refuge and claimed they were training the dogs for the legal season. Not my jurisdiction, but I couldn't help it. The heat from the engine could burn his paws and being chained to a moving vehicle was dangerous, not to mention absurd. They promised to glue some carpeting up there, give 'im something to grip, they'd said. Assured me that'd do the trick. Jackasses.

Roy, my SAC, (that's special-agent-in-charge), told me to choose my battles. Hell, it's not illegal and besides, we have bigger fish to fry, he'd said after he'd eased out of his pickup and went through his usual routine of tugging at his belt, pulling up his pants, first on one side, then the other, then sauntered over to stand beside me and ask what was the matter.

At first, I didn't know what to think of Roy. Michigan's Upper Peninsula was my first duty station and Roy the experienced officer I was assigned to do field training under for my first forty-four weeks on duty. Soon enough I'd realized Roy's kinda lovable in a grandpappy kind of way, what with the green flannel jacket he wears everyday and the old red plaid Stormy Kromer hat covering his bare head, ear flaps up in the summer, down over his ears in the winter. He's got that easy, laid back disposition that makes you feel like time's an illusion and tomorrow's just as good a day as ever to do whatever it is you might be pondering doing.

I got him some snazzy suspenders for his birthday. He gave me a half-grin and a genuine confused look, asked whatever in the world I'd done that for, the belt he had worked just fine. I wasn't sure if I'd made a serious faux pas, or as they say in *da* U.P., if I'd *stepped in it*. There was a long, awkward moment, the kind which I've come to accept as a common reaction to me, before he'd chuckled and snapped on the new suspenders. Course he still adjusts the pants in the same old routine.

Brutus let out a yowl and the little Jeep-wannabe came to a halt. He'd caught Honey Bear's scent.

I shoved the last of my granola bar in my mouth and hunkered down in my blind. I was sure the Lawson boys were planning to dart Honey Bear and sell her live to an illegal bear bile farmer where she'd spend the rest of her life barely conscious, crammed into a cage no larger than her outstretched body to restrict her movement, a metal catheter implanted into her gall bladder to withdraw a continuous supply of bile. The cruel practice causes excruciating misery for the bear. But poachers don't care. Bear bile sells like liquid gold. 250ccs fetches around US $1000 in China to those who believe in traditional medicine. They say it's a cure-all for hepatitis, hemorrhoids, hangovers, and chronic diarrhea. Maybe it is. But torturing a bear to get it, well, I'd take on the PLA to stop it if I could. Right now, in my corner of the world, I'd have given my right eye to see these bastards fry, but sending them to prison would have to do. I just had to bust them first.

And today, that's just what I was going to do.

The boys got out of the car. The dogs were going ape shit, yipping with excitement. I had about ten seconds to call it in. Roy answered the phone right away. "What now, McVie?"

"Listen, I'm in the northwest unit, off the Old State Road. The Lawson boys just pulled up in their hound wagon."

"What the hell are you up to?"

"They released Honey Bear yesterday."

Roy sighed. I could tell he was rubbing his temples, like he always does. "You been out there all night?"

Roy had an annoying habit of asking the obvious.

"Listen to me now, girl. Don't you go underestimating them boys. Out there alone in them woods, that badge ain't gonna protect you."

"What good is this badge if I can't protect the animals?"

I tried to pull the phone from my ear to hang up, but it was stuck in my hair, all matted and tangled with a gob of pine sap. Roy was still yammering on the other end. "You wait for me to get out there." I yanked it free, punched the end button, and put on my USFWS hat. At least I tried. Somebody had the bright idea to require us to wear these things. Whoever it was has never tried to tame my mop. I shoved my ponytail through the opening in the back and called it good. I was ready.

Bear hunting with dogs works like this. The dogs catch the scent. The hunter (if you call it hunting) sends his pack of dogs to chase down the bear, tree the poor thing, then the men track their prey using GPS to the location sent by the remote contraption on the dog's collar. The dogs might run for several miles before they corner the bear. So the Lawson boys will tool along in the little Geo, watching a blip on a tiny screen until they get the signal that the lead dog has stopped. Then they'll saunter over to the bear, all puffed up and proud of themselves, and shoot the helpless creature out of the tree.

Unfortunately, in Michigan, this is perfectly legal. In fact, letting your dogs chase a bear in the off-season, terrorizing it for training and practice, is also legal. Darting a bear and capturing it live isn't.

As my grandpa always said, come hell or high water, I was going to catch them doing it.

The problem was, they had the advantage of a dedicated GPS unit. If I followed them, they'd see me and bail, claiming they were just out letting their dogs run. I had one choice. Do it the old-fashioned way: keep up with the dogs.

The good thing is a pack of hound dogs will yip and yap, making a ruckus as they race after a bear. When they close in on their prey, they start baying, a low bawling that can be heard from a distance. The bad thing is they can run about twenty miles per hour. Good thing I wore my wilderness running boots.

The kennel doors were flung open, Brutus was unchained, and

the pack took off through the woods, yapping with excitement. I waited for the boys to latch the kennels closed and mosey to their seats then drive off before I left the blind. I strapped on my running pack and slipped my hand into the strap on the video camera. With a deep breath, I touched the bracelet at my wrist. *I know you're with me, Dad.* And I took off after them.

The dogs headed southwest and kept a steady pace for about fifteen minutes, gaining distance ahead of me. Twice, I slipped in the mud on wet leaves, but for the most part I managed to keep upright and moving forward. Then their vocalizations changed. They were close to the bear now and had her on the run.

I slid down the edge of a ravine, sprinted up the other side, barreled through a patch of brambles, and tripped and fell flat on my stomach. The video camera went tumbling. I got up and shook it off. I needed a moment to regain my bearings.

The pack had headed into an old logging area where the pines grew in rows. I picked up the camera, made sure it was still working, and sprinted down a fairway until I ran out of steam. I bent over, my hands on my thighs, my chest heaving. These dogs were fit. After I caught my breath, I continued on. They weren't far off. Must have her treed already, I realized. *I'm coming Honey Bear!* I approached with caution in case I was wrong; a terrified bear wasn't someone I wanted to stumble upon.

I homed in on the yowls. They came from an open area covered with moss and grass that had been trampled by deer bedding down overnight. Sure enough, on the far side was Honey Bear. She'd shinnied up an old oak tree, all four paws clamped on. She was grunting and growling while the dogs whined and scratched at the base of the tree. Brutus had his head tilted back, howling for his masters.

I quickly scanned the area. I needed a place to hide. My own prey would be along soon. My best option was a small spruce pine on the edge of the clearing. I set the video camera in the crook of a branch, pointing toward Honey Bear, double checked it was recording—I didn't want any mistakes on this one— then crawled beneath the pine boughs and checked my phone. No cell service here. Using the handheld radio was too risky; anyone could be listening in. I texted the GPS coordinates to Roy, hoping a text would make it through, then hunkered down to wait.

It seemed like an eternity. Poor Honey Bear was frothing at the mouth. For successful bear poachers, they sure were slow. There was no doubt, though, that's what they were. Word around town was, last winter, they'd showed up at the Buckhorn Bar with brand new snowmobiles, acting like big shots, buying all their buddies Budweisers and running their mouths about hitting it big time. They were tight lipped about details, though. Come spring they had new four-runners and shiny new Remington shotguns. It didn't take a seasoned Special Agent to figure out they were doing something illegal. Since they had no common sense and couldn't hold a regular job, it wasn't hard to surmise they were making money on the only thing they were good at. Poaching.

My father and I had run into poachers a few times over the years. Spend enough time in the wilderness and it's bound to happen. I'd rather face down a tiger than an angry, gun-toting poacher. The image of my father, facing down a poacher was too much—I heard their voices. Then I caught sight of them ambling into the clearing. Jed, the longer haired one, held the GPS tracker in his left hand, and—*I knew it!*—a dart gun in his right. His cousin Larry was right behind him, a shotgun slung over his shoulder. They both wore Carhartt coats, blue jeans, and the requisite baseball caps, always sporting either some beer logo or a silhouette of a woman, the kind that commonly adorns the mud flaps of an eighteen wheeler. I'd seen them all.

I could arrest them right now for carrying a loaded shotgun with the dogs off-season, but the penalty was a slap on the wrist. No. I wanted them for poaching a live bear.

Jed nodded to his cousin, a shit-eating grin on his face.

Leaving Brutus on point, they called off the other five dogs and tied them to nearby trees. Then Jed took the shotgun from Larry, handed him the dart gun, and grumbled something I couldn't quite make out.

Larry beamed with pride.

I looked up at Honey Bear. My heart clenched. *Sorry girl, I have to let them do it. It's the only way. You'll be all right.*

Larry raised the gun and pulled the trigger. The dart flew wide and stuck in a tree limb low and to the right.

Jed yanked the dart gun from Larry's hands. "Gimme that, you dumbass," he said. "We don't got none to waste." He shoved the shotgun at him. "Hold that."

Jed zeroed in and let the dart fly. It struck its target. Honey Bear flinched and dug in with her claws. Soon her head started to droop and she slid halfway down the tree trunk, ripping bark off in tiny strips, until her claws let loose and she flopped to the ground with a thud. Larry let out a hoot.

"That's how it's done!" Jed shouted and gave Larry a high five.

The dogs bounced around, barking themselves hoarse, yanking to the end of their ropes.

Jed leaned the dart gun against the tree and while Larry tied up Brutus, he took some twine from his pocket and hogtied the bear. He slipped a muzzle around her mouth, cinched it tight, then punched something into his cell phone. Texting the GPS coordinates, I assumed. He wasn't stupid enough to drag this bear out of here right now, with the dogs and the dart gun. Someone else was the pickup crew.

I crawled out from under my tree, brushed off the pine needles, and straightened my hat. Then I walked right up behind the cocky bastards. "Howdy boys." Jed spun around. Larry's head bobbed over his shoulder, his mouth hanging wide open. He blinked twice, his eyeballs bulging like a bullfrog in a murky swamp. He wasn't sure if I was real or an apparition.

He still had the shotgun slung over his shoulder. I kept my weapon holstered. Provoking an armed idiot wasn't a good idea. I was glad it was Larry who had the firearm, though. He wasn't a killer. He'd hesitate. Besides, his aim sucked.

Jed, the smarter of the two, screwed up his face, trying to figure out how I'd gotten all the way out here in the middle of the woods. He spit a glob of black goo out the side of his crusty lip. "Who the hell are you?"

"Special Agent McVie. You're under arrest."

"Really?" He smirked and glanced at his cousin. "And who's gonna arrest me?"

Cousin Larry's eyes darted back and forth, eyeing every tree another agent might be lurking behind. "Yeah, who?" he muttered.

"Wait, I know you," Jed said as he took a step closer to me.

Good. Keep coming closer.

"You that new duck cop. Pippa, ain't it?"

"Special Agent McVie. Now step back. Turn around, put your hands up, and lace your fingers behind your neck."

"Pippa, huh?" said Larry. "Like that princess a' England. Dude, she's hot."

"Shut up, Larry." Jed took another step toward me.

That's it. Keep coming.

"Now what you doin' way out here all by yerself?" His eyes traveled down to my waist and back up, settling on my chest. "Ain't it kinda dangerous? A sweet young thing, all alone in the woods?"

He took another step closer, just beyond my arm's length. He wore steel-toed boots. That was to his advantage. And he stood a foot taller and had at least a hundred pounds on me, too. But his Carhartt coat would restrict his movement. I looked up at him. "I can take care of myself. Now turn around."

He grinned. "You hear that, Larry." He turned his head to spit. At least he was that polite.

Larry scratched his neck. "Jed, I think we oughta just go."

"Well, Larry, that's the thing. We can't *just go.* She seen us."

I nodded. "It's true, Larry. I did."

Honey Bear moaned and tried to get up, licking her lips like an old drunk. *Hold on, Honey Bear, just a bit longer.* I turned my gaze back to Jed. "You see, Larry," I said, my eyes locked with Jed's. "That beautiful bear is going to stay right here where she belongs, in the wild. And you and your cousin are the ones headed for a cage."

"Sheee-at," Jed said. "Ain't you a feisty little thing?" His toned changed. "Larry, go get the dart gun. We gonna have us some fun."

"Larry, don't you move a muscle," I said, my eyes still on Jed. I could handle these two, but if they got a dart in me…

Jed howled with laughter. "Woohoo, this is gonna be fun!" he shouted. Then he made a mistake. He took one step closer and grabbed me by the shoulder. I planted my foot, flung my arm up over his, and dropped. His elbow made a crack as it broke. *That's for Honey Bear, you son of a bitch.* I butted him in the back of his knee and took him down. He landed on his belly, bellowing like a pig in heat. I rammed my boot into the small of his back, grabbed his broken arm at the wrist, twisted it to meet his other wrist, and slapped a twist-tie around both.

"Holy mother!" said Larry. He tossed his shotgun to the ground and took off running.

I kept my boot rammed in Jed's back while I unclipped my radio from my belt. "Suspect is on foot, heading north-northwest from my location."

"Yeah," was all I heard. I looked up to see Roy at the edge of the clearing. Larry was backing away from him. He tripped and fell on his ass. "Got him," Roy yelled with a wave.

I leaned over and whispered to Jed. "Tell me who you're selling these bears to."

"Screw you," he growled and spat.

I rolled him over, sat him up, and just as he drew in a breath, I smacked him on the back. He coughed and hacked.

"How's that chew taste?" I asked.

"Bitch, I ain't telling you nothin."

"That's okay," I said. "Something tells me he's on his way. We'll just wait here for him." Jed closed his eyes and put his head down.

Roy had Larry handcuffed and leaning against a tree. He stomped toward me.

"What the hell were you thinking?" he snapped. "I told you to wait."

"I had to catch them in the act."

Roy closed his eyes and rubbed his temples with his left hand. He looked over at the bear, then down at Jed who was moaning, his right arm twisted at the wrong angle. "What am I gonna do with you?"

I clenched my teeth together. I knew when to keep my mouth shut. Well...most of the time. Roy shook his head and walked away.

I went to Honey Bear, knelt beside her, and stroked her head between her ears. *You'll be all right. Just sleep for now. It will all be over soon.*

Roy had gotten about four paces before he turned around. "While you've been out here galavanting around, the CO's been trying to get you on the phone. I didn't want to use the radio."

"What's he want?"

"Dunno. Said to call right away."

"As in right now?" Our CO, head of the Midwest region, was headquartered in Minnesota, an hour behind. "He's up early." I had to walk about two hundred yards to get a signal. Three missed calls. *Crap.* I punched the call back button. "This is Special Agent McVie, I—"

"Hold the line," I was told. Then seconds later, "McVie?"

"Yes sir, what's—"

"Pack a bag and get to the Detroit airport by six p.m. You're booked on a flight to Georgia."

"Georgia?" The federal law enforcement training center, FLETC, is in Georgia. "I just had my FLETC training. Wait, did you say six p.m.? But, sir, Detroit's an eight hour drive from here."

"Yeah, you better get moving. Leave your badge and firearm with Roy."

"My badge, sir?" Why would he ask me to leave my badge? "Have I done something wrong?"

"Temporarily reassigned."

"Reassigned?" I'd been a field agent for only four months. I was still doing field training. This was unheard of. This couldn't be good. "Where?"

"Uh—" There was a long pause. "Actually, I don't know."

"What do you mean, you don't know?" *What the hell is going on?*

"I was told to tell you to wear civilian clothes."

"I'm not sure I understand."

He huffed. "It's above my pay grade. Alls I know is you've been specifically requested. That means they ain't askin."

This wasn't making any sense. I glanced back toward Roy and the Lawson boys. "I can't leave now. I just busted a couple poachers taking a live bear. We've got to stake out—"

"Roy can handle that."

"Yeah, but Roy—"

"Poppy." He sighed. "Just get your ass on the damn plane."

CHAPTER 2

As I exited the jetway in Atlanta, I ran smack into an airport employee holding a paper plate with McVie scribbled across the back. Nice. I followed the young man but started to get the feeling I was getting punked, like I was being walked onto the set of a seventies horror movie—the long, confusing corridors, the lone flickering fluorescent bulb, all the closed, unmarked doors.

He finally came to a halt in front of what looked like a broom closet. Porn movie then? He gestured for me to go on in. "Thanks?" I managed.

I gripped the door knob and flung open the door. "Hi, I'm Poppy McVie."

A balding man in a crumpled white shirt and a tired striped tie looked up from his desk and frowned. His left hand lay atop a briefcase that looked like it had been issued during the Vietnam War. It was crammed full of manila folders. Definitely from headquarters.

"Poppy!"

I turned. It was Mr. Strix, my favorite instructor from FLETC. What was he doing here? He bowled me over with a bear hug. This was new. "I'm so glad you were available," he said. He gestured toward the stuffed shirt. "This is Stan Martin, head of Special Operations."

I snapped to attention and glanced back to Mr. Strix, my

eyebrows raised in a did-you-just-say-what-I-think-you-said question. The head of Special Ops? Mr. Strix gave me a quick wink.

"It's nice to meet you, sir," I said. *Holy crap, Special Ops! Special Ops! Okay, calm. Stay calm.* I pasted a professional smile on my face—not too wide, no teeth.

Mr. Martin was staring at me with that look. The oh-my-god-she's-just-a-girl look. He frowned. I frowned. The thing is, I'm five foot two and all of one hundred and four pounds. I have unruly red hair and freckles and in high school, kids called me Pippity-Poppity-Poo, as in Pippi Longstocking, the precocious Swedish children's book character who has no manners and—this is my favorite part—can lift her horse with one hand. Not exactly the moniker of which a teenage girl dreams.

In college, I wore fake glasses for a semester, the kind with clear lenses, thinking they'd make me appear older, more sophisticated. Damn things gave me headaches.

Now, at age twenty-four, on looks alone, I could probably pass for Pippi's older sister. I've learned to accept people's reactions to me. Well, mostly. Okay, sometimes. When I'm in the mood. Like when I'm meeting the head of the organization of which I've dreamed of working since—well, forever.

"Why don't you have a seat?" said Mr. Strix, his hand on my back, gently guiding me toward a chair. I dropped my duffle next to the door and sat down. He perched on the side of the desk and adjusted his thick round glasses. "We don't have a lot of time, so why don't we get right to it."

"Yes, sir," I smiled and turned to Mr. Martin. "So I'm being promoted to Special Ops?"

Mr. Martin harrumphed. Actually harrumphed. *Oops. Apparently that wasn't the thing to ask.* He crossed his arms and shook his head. I looked to Mr. Strix for help. He cleared his throat and put on a smile. "Temporarily reassigned. An Ops team is in need of a, well they need some help, an agent with your—" He sat up straighter. "Unique skills and talents."

"Okay," I said. What else could I say? No one knew what I was capable of better than Mr. Strix.

Mr. Martin closed the briefcase. "Jim, I'm not sure she's—"

Strix held up his hand. "Now Stan, you asked for my recommendation. Poppy is as bright as a whip. She was top of her class." He beamed with pride. "I have every confidence in her—"

"I got the resumé," Mr. Martin said. "But for Special Ops, an agent needs—"

"Balls," I said.

Their heads snapped in my direction.

"That's your concern, right?" I sat up straighter and looked him in the eye. "What exactly do you need me to do?"

Mr. Martin regarded me with skeptical eyes for a long moment. His lips puckered and unpuckered. Twice. Finally, he sighed and said, "We're nine months into a long-term investigation." From the briefcase he plucked a folder, flipped it open, and handed me a photo. "Our target: George Hillman. An ex-pat living in Costa Rica. He sells legal species for the pet trade, frogs, snakes, whatever. We know he's the contact for the sale of some exotics, CITES class I and II species, but the offer to sell always comes anonymously, so we can't pin it on him. More importantly, we think he's the connection to the kingpin of shark fin exports. Shark fins are big business and the Costa Rican government has asked for our help."

I knew a bit about shark finning. In a few short years, fishermen had decimated ninety percent of the shark population off the coast of Costa Rica. The black market price for shark fins soared up to $700 a kilogram. Shark meat, which is legal to harvest, has remained inexpensive and, therefore, not worth carrying for the fishermen. To maximize the space in their holds, they'd begun hacking off a shark's fins while they had it on the hook, then tossing the still-breathing creature back into the sea, unable to swim. It's heinous.

"This George is the target for shark finning? You said he

deals in exotics for the pet trade."

Mr. Martin shrugged. "We know he's connected. But he's slippery. We don't know much else."

"What *do* you know?"

His eyebrows narrowed. Lips puckered.

Oops. "I mean, what else can you tell me?"

Mr. Strix shifted his position on the desk. His head pivoted around so he could see me through the narrow vision of his glasses. "Poppy, you must understand, the guys on the ground are undercover. It can be risky to make contact with headquarters and when they do, they don't always have time to tell us much."

"So what are their assignments then?"

"That's the thing," said Strix. "They—"

"This is an elite team. The best of the best. I don't give these men assignments," said Mr. Martin with impatience. "I give them objectives and they work independently." He closed the folder and frowned. "You'll be briefed when you get there by the SAC, Joe Nash."

Joe Nash! Joe Nash was a legend. A super legend. He practically wrote the book on Special Operations. In as indifferent a voice as I could muster, I said, "I heard he has his years in for retirement."

"He does, but he says he won't file until he nails this guy."

I nodded. I could relate.

"He's posing as a rich collector. We have another man on the ground, Special Agent Dalton." I hadn't heard of him. "He's a buyer. Then there's a third agent on the case, Special Agent Tom García. We've had no contact from him in weeks." He looked concerned.

"What was his objective?" I asked. They were throwing a lot at me at once, probably to see if I could keep it straight.

Mr. Martin said, "He was working the poaching side, trying to identify the buncher." He paused. "A buncher is—"

"I know. The middle-man. He buys from the poachers, tends

the inventory, then sells to the smuggling kingpin."

Mr. Martin gave me a respectful nod. He handed me a post card. "His last correspondence." The image was of a palapa bar on the beach called The Toucan. On the back García had scribbled a message: *Having a great time. Have my sights set on a beautiful butterfly. Paco.*

"What's that mean?"

Mr. Martin shrugged. "Dunno. Butterflies are a big black market species. When you talk to Nash, give him the info. Maybe it makes sense to him."

I tried to read the postmarked date. "When did you get this?"

"Two weeks ago. Nothing since. It could be he's too deep to make contact."

Mr. Strix shifted to the edge of the desk. "It's a dangerous operation, Poppy. When you work Special Ops, you're on your own."

I sat back. I could handle that. In fact, I preferred it. "Is this typical protocol? To bring in another agent right in the middle of an investigation?"

The two men looked at each other, tight-lipped. Mr. Martin leaned back in his chair and crossed his arms. "Undercover work isn't like you've read in your textbooks, young lady."

Young lady? I could feel my teeth involuntarily clenching together.

Strix drew in a breath. "Poppy, listen. This op is vital. We've had very short notice to find someone, the right someone, to send in." He leaned forward and adjusted his glasses. "I believe that someone is you."

"So how do I fit in?"

Mr. Strix grinned as if he were about to hand me a winning lottery ticket. "You're going to choose your own pet monkey."

I looked to Mr. Martin, then back to him. "I've always wanted a monkey?" The Barenaked Ladies tune started playing in my head.

Mr. Martin picked up a pencil and tapped it on the folder. The beat didn't match the rhythm of the tune in my head and it was aggravating. "You'll be partnered with Special Agent Dalton. His cover is the owner of a chain of pet stores in Texas." He handed me a business card with the info. "He spends about ten days in Costa Rica once a month. He's built a rapport with George and recently hinted at wanting to buy class II species. Specifically," he cocked his head to the side, "he mentioned how his wife wants her own pet monkey."

He paused, waiting for my reaction. The fluorescent tube above, as if on cue, flickered and hummed. As he had said, Special Ops is an elite group. Those guys were seasoned agents. The legendary Joe Nash was in his late sixties. Thinning hair, arthritis. Dalton must have been about the same. *Probably has dentures.*

"So I'm the trophy wife," I said. *The things I do for animals.* I held out my hand for the folder. "How long do I have to study my cover?"

Mr. Martin put out his hands, palms up. "That's it."

I looked to Mr. Strix. "What do you mean, that's it? How do I make contact? Where do I go?"

He reached into a sack that had been tucked beside the desk and produced a wide-brimmed straw hat and a god-awful handbag—gold lamé with a giant buckle studded with sparkling bling. It was large enough to carry a poodle. "Seriously?" I asked.

He examined the handbag, innocently perplexed by my reaction. "It's my wife's," he said, as if that made it unquestioningly perfect.

I zipped my lip.

Mr. Martin looked at his watch. "Your flight's in one hour. You connect through Dallas where you'll switch to first class." He eyed my duffle. "Make sure you pick up a new carry-on bag that's appropriate to your cover."

Mr. Strix took my hand and slipped a diamond the size of

Montana onto my finger. I shook my head. "Whoa."

"Yeah, well, you'll be running with the big spenders. Besides,"—he gave me a wink—"Brittany's worth it."

"You've got to be kidding. Brittany?"

Mr. Martin harrumphed again. "This from a girl named Poppy."

My eyebrows stretched upward so far my eyeballs hurt. In a soothing voice, which from anyone else would seem condescending, Mr. Strix said, "Dalton had to pick something. He didn't know at the time we'd be sending someone in."

I tried to smile, wondering if the next trick he'd pull from the bag was a voucher for a boob job.

"Dalton will be at the airport in San José to pick you up. He'll be wearing tan slacks and a light blue polo shirt. Make sure you wear this hat." He plopped it on my head.

I flipped through the folder again. "Where's a picture of Special Agent Dalton?"

The two men looked at each other, blank faced.

This was starting to feel like some kind of back room, cold war, clandestine mission. Flick the lighter twice, knock once. It was going to be fun. I wanted to rattle off a *I'm your Natasha* in my best Russian accent. Instead, I said, "It's all right."

Mr. Martin leaned forward on the desk. "Listen, I know this situation isn't ideal. But Jim assures me you're up for it." He set his jaw. "You need to understand the serious nature of the op you're walking into. One mistake could mean your life or the life of a fellow agent. Got it?"

I took off the hat. (It was going to be a full-on job to get my mop to fit in that thing.) "I got it."

"I mean it, Agent McVie." He paused for a beat. Then huffed and shook his head. He glared at Mr. Strix. "I hope I don't regret this." He turned his glare on me. "Rule number one of undercover work: always keep your cover. The thing is, undercover work is like improv. Don't take anything personally. You've gotta roll with it. You two are newlyweds, so smooch it up. You never know who might be watching."

"I understand, sir." I had the urge to ask if I should pick up some Viagra on the way, but I was already pushing my luck and Mr. Martin didn't seem to have much of a sense of humor.

"Rule number two: tell as few lies as possible. Makes it easier to keep things straight. If you liked Barbies when you were seven, then Brittany liked Barbies when she was seven. The key is to be yourself, to act natural. Got it?"

I nodded. "Barbies. Got it."

"Three: if something doesn't feel right, don't proceed. Walk away. Be patient. You don't want to push a relationship. Better to take another day than to blow it. And four: if you suspect you've been made, get the hell out of there. Notify your SAC right away."

"Yes, sir."

"If you get the chance to meet George, be cautious. He's likely going to test you. He'll scrutinize everything you say and do."

"George. Test me. Got it."

He stared for a long moment as though it were his last chance to change his mind.

"Is that all, sir?"

He heaved a sigh. "Good luck."

Mr. Strix rose to his feet. "I'll walk you out."

I slung the rich-bitch bag over my shoulder and gave Mr. Stan Martin a nod.

After two right turns and three to the left, Mr. Strix handed me a cell phone. "A Michigan number is programmed under Mom. It will transfer to me. Call if you need anything."

"Michigan?" I asked, but as the word came out of my mouth I realized. "No Texas accent. I grew up in Michigan. Got it." I stopped and turned to him. "Thanks," I said.

He smiled.

"Has there been any news on my dad's case?"

He shook his head. "I'm sorry. Nothing."

I walked a few more feet, turned and—nope. I was going to let it go.

He lifted his glasses to rub his eyes and sighed. "What is it?"

"Nothing, sir." I turned to continue on.

He gently grabbed my arm. "It's Special Ops. That's what you've always wanted."

"Yes, sir. Thank you for recommending me, sir."

"I was glad to do it. You'll make me proud. Just promise me you'll be careful."

We continued on, another left turn. I stopped again. "The wife? Really? I was *specifically requested* because they need a woman? That's it?"

"Listen to me." He took me by the shoulders like my dad used to do to make me face him. "It's an opportunity. Take it." He gave me a hopeful smile. "When you get there, listen to your SAC, follow protocol, and I'm confident, in no time, they'll see your potential." He gave me another hug. "Trust me, Poppy."

I gave him a smile of thanks and winked. "You can call me Brittany."

Juan Santamaría International Airport in San José, Costa Rica is the second busiest airport in Central America. This was an advantage. Even someone I knew, like my own husband, might be easily overlooked in the bustling crowd.

At Customs and Immigration, I presented my new passport. Under my mug was the name Brittany Katherine Fuller. It even had my actual birthday, April 3, 1990. Someone was really thinking when they tucked in an immunization card with an emergency contact: my husband of three months, John Randolf Fuller.

I ran through some memorization routines. *Hi, I'm Brittany, John's wife. So nice to meet you, George. This is my husband,*

John. John, John. I need to go to the John with John. John the baptist. John Lennon. Johnny. Johnny be good. Johnny Depp. Oooooh yeah. Johnny Depp. I could be married to Johnny Depp.

I couldn't think of any thing else to prepare. During my flight from Detroit, I had rummaged through the handbag and found a pack of gum, a tin of aspirin, two emery boards, several maxi pads, a bottle of hand lotion (half used), a mini-pack of tissues, a pair of cheesy, goggle lens sunglasses, and a change purse that looked like it was handmade by someone's grandma. Everything a girl could need and all courtesy, no doubt, of Mrs. Strix. I'd have to remember to send her a thank-you note. Without the typical items, I was at risk of someone realizing that stunning fashion accessory was a prop. There was no time to shop for a poodle.

The most important item I'd found in the bag was a wallet with cash and a credit card in Brittany's name. It worked at the luggage store in the Dallas/Fort Worth International terminal where I found a shiny white leather carry-on bag. (I'd never buy leather, but I figured Brittany would love its rich, supple feel.)

The U.S. Fish and Wildlife Service could pull some strings pretty quickly, it seemed. I hoped they were as good at wardrobe assignments, because that's all I had to go on. Tan slacks and a blue polo shirt. I was about to find out.

I flipped the straw hat onto my head, pulled it down, hoping it would stay, and moved with the crowd toward the ground transportation area, scanning for my new hubby. It felt like a freak blind date, only I couldn't fake a migraine and slink out the back door. I kept telling myself, no matter what, I was going to smack him with a big kiss, right in front of everyone. No one was going to accuse me of blowing an op.

As I approached the exit, I knew I was in Central America. The cool of the air conditioning mixed with waves of humid, tropical air and exhaust fumes wafting in from the street where cars honked and engines ran, all maneuvering for the best spot.

I caught sight of someone waving. He wore tan slacks and a blue polo, but it couldn't be him. This man was young, tall and lean—one of those guys who crawls under razor wire and bounds over ten foot walls for exercise. I quickly scanned the luggage claim area for a balding man in the same get up. No one. I turned back. The guy was walking toward me, waving. I faked like I hadn't seen him the first time. "Hi Honey!" I called.

He walked toward me, his arms outstretched. I dropped my bag and lunged into his embrace. He lifted me up and spun me around. Wow, he was strong. I tilted my head back and he kissed me, long and hard. "I missed you," he crooned as he set me down.

Man, was he ripped, pecs firm as a ham hock. I lingered a moment with my hands on his chest, looking into his deep, brown eyes. He was my husband after all. I gave him my best Texas sweetheart smile. "I've missed you, too, darling." *Like, my whole life.*

Dalton gave me another peck on the lips, then, his eyes warning me to be careful, he nodded toward a man who hovered a few paces back. "George sent his driver. Wasn't that nice?"

I pulled away from his embrace and flashed my best Brittany smile at the man.

"He's invited us to dinner," Dalton added.

"Fantastic, I'm starving." I reached for my carry-on bag but Dalton grabbed it before I could.

"Let me get that," he said.

Maybe this marriage could work out after all.

CHAPTER 3

The drive from the airport was breathtaking in more ways than one. Costa Rica's countryside is lush with the dazzling greens of the rainforest and, as we got further west, occasional vistas overlooking the Pacific Ocean. It made me itch to go exploring. This tropical paradise has the highest density of biodiversity in the world. Nearly 500,000 species live here, hundreds of which exist nowhere else on Earth. With tropical rain forests, deciduous forests, Atlantic and Pacific coastline, cloud forests, and the coastal mangrove forests, the possibilities were endless for a nature lover like me.

The driving on the other hand was a free-for-all. Typical Latin America. Stop signs, yellow lines, no passing zones—all trivial suggestions only tourists take seriously, meaningless to the average tico, as the locals call themselves.

Dalton and I sat with his arm around me, snuggled up together, saying very little other than an ooh or ah at some vista and banal chitchat about the comfort of my flight and such.

At last, we arrived. George's palatial hacienda was tucked into the jungle a half-mile from the main road. Actually, it was more like a compound—three barns, a fenced horse pasture, surveillance cameras rigged at every corner.

Our car approached the main house, a sprawling ranch of typical Central American design—white stucco walls, red-tiled roof, expansive, open porch with a thatched overhang. The drive encircled a white marble fountain and led right up to the edge of the porch.

Four dogs, some kind of German Shepherd mix, came tearing around from the back of the house. Dogs will naturally guard a home, but their level of training speaks volumes about their effectiveness. The driver got out of the car and with a quick hand command, they retreated. Hm. Well-trained. The driver opened the back door of the car and offered me his hand to get out. One firearm in a shoulder holster, and one, I was sure, at his ankle.

I was ready to do my job, but honestly, I could have spent another hour snuggled up next to Dalton in the back seat.

I kept a grip on my handbag. My carry-on, in the trunk, would no doubt be ransacked while we ate. No problem. Nothing but clothes and my toothbrush in there.

George stood on the porch, his arms wide with welcome like Ricardo Montalbán in Fantasy Island. Now here's what I pictured. Old man with a potbelly, yellow teeth, and the dark leathery skin of one who's lived in the tropics for years. He'd combed his hair from one side of his round head, up and all the way over the top in an attempt to cover a shiny bald spot.

I tried not to stare as we crossed the porch. The white sport coat was just too much. He took my hand in his with a smile that beamed with delusions of being a rich and attractive playboy. All financed by exploiting animals. I hated him instantly. "Nice to meet you," I said.

"You must be thirsty, my friends. What can I get you to drink?" He turned toward a wooden cabinet stocked with bottles and glasses.

Dalton didn't miss a beat. "Scotch, if you've got it."

"And for the lady?"

"Oh, my. It's been a long day." I put my hand on my tummy. "I'd better eat first."

"Suit yourself," he said and splashed some Scotch into a glass for himself.

I stepped to the edge of the porch and scanned the grounds. One of the barns must have been where George housed the legal species. Snakes and frogs and such. Must have been where Dalton came to make buys.

Another car came up the drive, black, nondescript. It rolled to a stop and waited for the butler to emerge and call off the dogs before a tall, grey-haired man in his late fifties got out. Apparently, we weren't the only guests for the evening. George's driver got behind the wheel and drove the car away.

"Ah, Felix," George waved him in. "He's from Germany," he said with no further introduction. He dropped a few ice cubes into a glass, filled it with gin and a splash of tonic, then handed it to the man as he stepped onto the porch. So they were already well acquainted.

I moved next to Dalton and slipped my hand in the crook of his elbow, shyly hiding behind him the way a Brittany would do. Dalton introduced himself, then me. He obviously didn't know the man. Interesting. He didn't look like a henchman. He looked like someone's opa in a wrinkled polyester suit. His eyeglasses were made some time circa 1964, thick lens, greasy around the edges. Probably another buyer. When he shook my hand, I noticed a nasty gash notched in the fleshy webbing at the base of his thumb. Snake bite.

We settled into rattan chairs facing the fountain. I smiled. Felix smiled. Dalton took a swig of his Scotch.

The sun was setting fast, I noticed, and the drum of the rainforest insects increased, filling the awkward void. Soon, I heard the rumble of another car coming up the drive. Again, the dogs came running and were called off. A stocky man in his late fifties (early sixties?) got out, smoothed his white shirt, and took a cigar from the pocket. He took his time puffing to get it lit before crossing to the porch and barging in like a bull through the gate. "Where's my drink?"

It was Joe Nash. I was sure of it.

"Carl, you old bastard. You know Maria hates cigars in the

house," George said with a chuckle.

"I'll eat out here with the dogs, then," he said with a grin, took another puff.

"Carl, is it?" Dalton was on his feet, shoving his hand out. "John Fuller. Nice to meet you."

Nash nodded, his eyes immediately on me, looking me up and down. "And who do have we here?"

"My wife, Brittany." Dalton gave me a pat on the butt, nudging me toward Nash.

I suppressed my impulse to twist his arm off at the shoulder socket. Somehow I managed a grin and stepped forward to shake hands with Joe Nash, the legend. And called him Carl. Surreal.

George handed him a drink. Bourbon maybe. "Pura vida, mi amigo," Nash muttered, the cigar twitching with each syllable.

Carl, Carl, Carl. I drilled his name into my brain. The rich collector. So all three guests were buyers.

Headlights shined through the trees—another car coming up the drive. This time a hunky, cowboy-looking guy got out and sauntered our way. Introductions were made. Kevin, from Australia. Around thirty. Deep, husky voice. Easy on the eyes. Nice fitting jeans, white T-shirt. His wavy hair was cut short with a tiny curl at the back of his neck. He started talking about the weather, the ride over, how beautiful the rainforest was. My mind drifted in the direction of adultery, my fingers gripping that curl. Something about that Australian accent.

It seemed he was the last of those expected. The men made small talk, the boring small talk of those who aren't sure why they're together. They sipped their drinks, Nash absentmindedly chewing on the cigar, until finally the butler arrived with news that dinner was to be served.

"Shall we?" George gestured toward the entrance to the main living area and the dining room, I presumed. The guests filed in. Joe—I mean Carl!—stepped to the edge of the porch, clipped the burning end off his cigar, and stuffed the chewed end back into his mouth. He gave me a wink.

The house had an open layout with white marble floors and oversized leather furniture. Ceiling fans slowly circled overhead. As we moved toward the dining table, a door opened and closed down a corridor toward the back of the house and two toy spaniels with oversized ears scampered toward us— clickety, clickety, click. "Ah, my wife Maria and her—" George glanced down at the dogs and curled his lip "—entourage. Frick and Frack."

Maria glided into the room, steady and comfortable on four-inch heels. Gobs of jewelry dangled from her neck, wrists, and ears. A beauty, and at least fifteen years George's junior, she was definitely a native tica. Wavy dark hair and creamy skin. George didn't make an effort to formally introduce her, so I knelt to pet the dogs.

"Look at those ears," I said. "They're so cute."

"Papillons," George muttered as he gestured for us to be seated.

"French for butterfly," I said as I rose.

He didn't respond so I turned to Maria. "The ears, like a butterfly."

She gave me a blank look. Perhaps she didn't speak English? Without thinking, I said, "Mariposas—" Then it hit me. It would be an advantage if they didn't know I spoke Spanish. (Or German for that matter. Or French.) Too late. Or was it? I looked right at Maria. "Did I pronounce that correctly?"

Maria smiled at me. "Sí, mariposas."

I shrank into a timid shrug. "I thought it would be fun to learn some Spanish while I'm here."

She gave me an amused grin and said nothing. She turned to her other guests.

We were seated around a table the size of my apartment. The place settings were bone china and real silverware. Our first course, a plate of cheeses and fresh fruit—mangoes, red bananas, starfruit—was already placed before us. The butler popped a cork on a bottle of Sauvignon Blanc. I recognized the label. "Excellent choice," I said to George. "You have impeccable taste." Doesn't hurt to butter him up.

The butler circled the table filling our wine glasses, the ladies' first, then back for the men. Dalton declined. Both elbows on the table, he shoved a hunk of cheese in his mouth. I thought to myself, would a Brittany scold him for his table manners? Probably not. I smiled at him. "You really should try this, honey. It's Kim Crawford." I handed my glass to him. His face was frozen in a blank stare. He grabbed it by the rim, like a beer glass, took a gulp, and swallowed. Cretin.

Kevin, the conversationalist, piped up. "What's so special about Kim Crawford?"

"Indeed," said George, his eyebrows raised. "What's so special about her?" His question sounded like a challenge. He flashed his toothy smile. Felix and Kevin gazed my way. The butler paused, waiting to hear what I had to say. I could feel Dalton tense up next to me.

I hate Barbies crashed into my thoughts. And I'm charming, dammit. Except when I'm not. Like when I try too hard to be charming. I wasn't raised in some rich family with uppity parents and nannies with British accents who taught you the proper fork to use or how to properly compliment your host. I've seen the world, though, just not from a Lear jet. My dad and I lived out of a backpack. I slept in a hammock. I had no idea there was such a thing as silk sheets. (And, man, would I love a set.) But wealth and prestige wasn't the only way to know wine. It was about sheer passion. And I have a passion for wine. If Poppy loves wine, then Brittany loves wine.

"Not her," I said to George. "Him. He's a winemaker from New Zealand's Marlborough region. He's known worldwide for this very wine." I turned to Kevin the Australian. "From down near your neck of the woods."

"Yeah, those Kiwis sure know how to squeeze a grape." He winked and took a swig.

"So do you own a pet store in Australia?" I asked, trying to direct attention from me.

Kevin glanced at George and shook his head. He crammed a piece of mango into his mouth.

"How about you, Felix? What brings you to Costa Rica?"

"Business," he said as though he were oblivious to any expected social nuance.

Okay. Shutting up now.

"Brittany," George said. "May I call you Brittany?"

I nodded.

He gestured toward my wine glass. "Please, tell me more about this vintage."

He's testing me, like Mr. Martin said he would. Am I really the rich Texas wife? The tiniest thing can give you away. Well, it ain't Barbies but here goes... I swirled the golden liquid around in the glass, then tucked my nose into the glass to take a sniff and savor the bouquet. I drew in a long sip, slurping so it would aerate on my tongue. Then I swallowed. "Bold fruit with a hint of melon. Finishes with a crisp acidity." I set the glass down. George was grinning. "My compliments," I said. "With its unique herbaceous flavor profile, it pairs quite well with the mango."

I thought Dalton was going to swallow his tongue.

George let loose a bellowing chuckle. "John, that's quite a lady you've got there."

Dalton grinned. "Don't I know it." He squeezed me to him and kissed me on the temple.

The kitchen door swung open and the chef came in pushing a rolling cart, atop which sat a silver domed platter. He wheeled the cart up next to George and with the sweeping gesture of a magician, lifted the lid, revealing a giant slab of prime rib, floating in its own bloody juices.

My stomach flipped. The thing is, I don't eat meat. Ever. Mr.

Martin's words rang in my head. *Keep your cover. Roll with it. Crap! What do I do?* I was prepared to kiss an old man. To play the rich, trophy wife. To carry a leather bag even. But I cannot, will not, swallow a piece of meat. *Oh my god, I'm going to blow this op right now. And I just got here.*

The chef sawed away at the hunk of flesh, cutting it into slabs a size no man should consume in one sitting. Of course, being the visiting lady, I was served first. The thing lay limp on the plate in front of me, visions of my eighth grade biology class banging in my head. Thirty-two thirteen-year-olds dissecting a cow lung. For some twisted reason, the others thought it was great fun to saw off spongy pieces and fling them at each other, to see if they'd stick. I promptly barfed on Sonny Davis' shoes, then spent the rest of the afternoon in the nurse's office, searching for a new career goal as my dream of being a veterinarian had vanished in one hands-on lesson.

I tried to vanquish the thoughts as I politely waited for everyone else to be served. I searched for ways to bow out. A coughing fit? Sudden case of indigestion? A phone call? How could I get the cell phone to ring right now? This moment was always awkward for me. *Thanks, but I'm a vegetarian. What? Are you crazy? Just try it, you'll love it.* People never got it. There was no way I could bring it up here, now. It would raise too much suspicion. Brittany was from Texas. A genuine beef-fed American.

Dalton had his fork in one hand, his knife in the other, sawing off another bite as he chewed an oversized hunk he'd already shoved in.

You have to do this, I told myself.

I got a piece on my fork, forced myself to open my mouth, shoved it in and clamped my mouth shut before I could change my mind. George hovered over his plate and gnawed off a piece, the juices dripping down his chin. He used a white cloth napkin to slop up his face. I was inspired. I picked up my napkin and, in a swift move I'd perfected as a child, as I wiped, I spit the meat into the napkin, then eased it into my lap. *Tah dah!* I only had to do that about twenty-seven more times without attracting attention.

Like angels descended from Heaven, two little butterfly-faced pups appeared, drooling on my shoes. My saviors. I slipped one bite to the floor at a time where it disappeared instantly.

Dalton must've sensed something was up. "Sweetheart, how are you doing? That's an awfully large portion."

"It's absolutely delicious," I grinned and took a gulp of wine, a fine Tempranillo the butler had poured while I had been distracted. "But I am getting full."

He stabbed it with his fork and dragged it to his plate, leaving a few drips on the table. I drew in a breath. "Honey, you're making a mess." I used my napkin to wipe it up.

He gave me the don't-embarrass-me-woman look.

I smiled and shut up, secretly thanking him.

At least I was now left to enjoy the rice and beans.

The conversation lulled while everyone chewed. Not that it had been a robust sharing of ideas before the meat arrived.

"So, Brittany," George managed to say through a full mouth. "I saw you looking at the horse barn when you arrived."

I halted mid-chew. "Yes?"

"Do you have an interest in horses?"

Horses. Not illegal, not a typical black-market species. My brain synapses fired away, crackling in my skull, searching for the right answer as I slowly chewed what was in my mouth before answering.

"Would you like to go horseback riding?" He glanced at Maria. "Perhaps you ladies could go tomorrow while John and I discuss business."

"Well, I—"

Dalton interrupted. "Brittany isn't really a horse person." Why was he saying this? Shouldn't I take any opportunity to connect, even if it was with the wife?

"Oh, I'm sure she'll love it." George turned to Maria, the first he'd spoken to her since we sat down at the table. "Le llevara a caballo mañana?" *Will you take her horseback riding tomorrow?*

She shook her head. "Tal vez en unos días," she said with a forced smile. *Perhaps in a few days.*

George turned to Dalton with an authoritative nod. "We'll make it work."

I finished my rice and beans in silence, my intuition buzzing. Something wasn't right. Something wasn't right at all.

CHAPTER 4

After a cordial drive through town, George's driver dropped us at our room—some rent-by-the-week kind of place. Individual thatched-roof bungalows dotted the property amid typical tropical landscaping, complete with roped walkways.

As we got out of the car, we were greeted by the on-site manager. He took my bag and led us to bungalow number eight. My spidey-sense tingled. This guy was too eager to help.

His uniform was a crisp white shirt with a tie striped in bold, tropical colors. His dark hair, cut into a terribly executed mullet, resembled a long mane and I instantly pictured Yipes, the zebra mascot for Fruit Stripe gum. (Yipes was my greatest hero for about four months when I was six because he donated five cents from each pack sold to the World Wildlife fund for the preservation of endangered species.) I had a feeling this Yipes wasn't such a good guy. He was probably being paid to spy on us. I'd have to keep my eye on him.

Dalton had his key in the lock and I got the feeling Yipes intended to follow us right in. I gave him a wink and told him to leave the bag. For good measure, I grabbed Dalton by the hand and swung him around for another kiss. After all, we were to make a good show, right? Like a good undercover agent, he went with it. He slid his hand around my back and pulled me up against him. "Feeling feisty, are you?" he said, his voice husky, his eyes drinking me in.

I wrapped my arms around his neck and we held there a moment, looking into each other's eyes with a playful tease. He leaned in to kiss me, then just as our lips met, he pulled back. *What are you waiting for.* His hands slid down from my back to my ass and with a gentle pull, I was pressed against him and the hard bulge in his pants. A warm heat rushed through me. He pushed the door open with his foot, kicked my bag inside, then pulled me with him as he backed into the room. I had the feeling he wanted to consummate this marriage post haste. Good thing Yipes had turn and fled.

As soon as the door shut, I heard, "So, you're Special Agent Poppy McVie?" I spun around. Special Agent Joe Nash stood there with his arms crossed.

"Yes, sir." I straightened my blouse, feeling as though I'd been caught kissing behind the school bleachers. "Reporting for duty, sir." I glanced around the room. "How did you…"

He nodded to Dalton. "I swept for bugs."

Dalton plopped down in the only chair in the room. "Nash, look at her. She can't be two months out of training." He gritted his teeth. "I told you this was a bad idea. This is too risky."

Joe held up his hand. "Now hold on—"

"You were there." Dalton got up from the chair, one hand gesturing in my direction. "She can't keep her mouth shut." His gaze swung around at me. His hands dropped to his hips. "My god, girl. What the hell was all that? I mean, who uses the word herbaceous? When you run off at the mouth, making stuff up, that's how people get killed."

I let him fizzle a moment. Calmly, I said, "First of all, I'm not a girl. Second, Martin told me to keep my cover as close to the real me as possible." I gave him a moment to ask. He didn't. "I was a sommelier in college."

Dalton shook his head and rubbed his eyes. "Well, you didn't have to make me look like an idiot. We're supposed to be married. You know, act like we like each other. It needs to be realistic, believable."

Nash grinned.

Dalton glared at him. "What's so funny?"

"Oh, trust me, it's believable."

Dalton threw up his hands. "I'm supposed to be able to trust her with my life." He glanced my way. "Do you even have any tactical training?" He looked back to Nash, but pointed at me again, his finger inches from my face. "I bet she can't even—"

I hooked my hand under his thumb, clamped down on his elbow with the other, and in one swift move, I twisted, collapsing him to the floor. I shoved my knee in his back. "Can't even what?" Holding him in the thumb lock, I leaned down and whispered in his ear, "Make you believe I'm actually hot for you?"

"Jesus Christ. All right already. You got something to prove. I get it."

"You should never let your guard down."

"What the hell? I shouldn't have to be on my guard with you. That's the point."

I looked over at Nash. He was shaking his head. I released Dalton.

"Strix recommended her," said Nash. "I trust his judgment. Deal with it." He gave me a stern look. "Work this out."

Dalton plopped back down in the chair. "Yes, sir."

Nash crossed his arms. "I don't need to be playing referee for God's sake. I shouldn't even be here. I wanted to make sure you were fully briefed and the two of you have a game plan. "

I sat down on the edge of the bed. "Sorry, sir. I do have some questions. Mr. Martin knew very little. He said you'd brief me."

Nash nodded. "About nine months ago, we nailed a smuggler in Miami with a primate. The intel from that bust led us to George. Our ultimate goal here is to identify the kingpin. For now, he's the target of our investigation, but we're not sure it's him. We think he'll lead us there." He grinned. "Tug on one hair and you'll find it's attached to the whole beast.

He went on. "I've been posing as a rich collector, having been referred by a friend, a guy we busted last year. George has been chummy, but not giving anything up yet. He's shifty. He mainly likes to drink and golf. Dalton's been working his way in as a wholesaler from the states. He makes regular buys, all legal species. He's been trying to take it to the next level. He can tell you about it. The point is, we know George is involved. All the connections lead to him. But he has a very sophisticated system of avoiding any direct communication. He doesn't make the offer to sell. He's too smart. He knows that's what we need to nail him. Dalton has been doing excellent work, though. We figure it's imminent."

"But so far you have no hard evidence?"

"This is Special Ops," said Dalton. "We don't gather evidence, we gather intelligence."

"What about the other agent, García?"

Nash shrugged. "He's working the poaching side alone, trying to identify the buncher. A buncher—"

"Is the middleman, I know. Buys from the poachers."

Nash nodded.

"García sent Martin a post card from a palapa bar down on the beach, The Toucan. On the back he scribbled a message: Having a great time. Have my sights set on a beautiful butterfly. Mean anything?"

Nash shook his head.

"Is this bar connected to George in any way?"

Nash shrugged. "Not that we know of."

I looked at Dalton. "Maybe we should check it out."

He shook his head. "No. Don't you get it? We can't stick our noses in on his op and risk being recognized. We stick to the plan. As soon as I get the call, you choose your monkey. Then you're on your way home."

"That's it?"

Nash held up his hand. "I need to get some shuteye." To Dalton he said, "You two need to get to know each other tonight.

Make sure she's prepared. Read her in on anything you've told George about the two of you, your life, your history." He smiled at me. "Welcome to the team. Let's nail these bastards."

"Thank you, sir." I rose. "One more question. Who are Felix and Kevin?"

"Never met them before. As far as I can tell, they're potential buyers as well."

"Why would George bring us all together for dinner? They seemed just as perplexed."

"Maybe he wants us to know there's demand," said Dalton. "So he can get a higher price."

Nash shrugged. "Another thing we need to figure out."

Dalton went to the porch door. He scanned the grounds before gesturing to Nash that it was safe to leave.

Just like that, we were alone.

I plopped my bag on the bed and sifted through it for my toothbrush. "So start from the beginning," I said. "How'd we meet?"

Dalton rubbed his eyes. "You came into one of my pet stores one day, looking for a cat, and it was love at first sight. Whirlwind romance, married two months later. That was three months ago. We live in Dallas, Texas. Our stores are called The Pet Corner, which is a real business by the way. The owner works with us." He took a business card from his wallet and handed it to me. "Here. Memorize this."

I scanned the card. "I've already—"

The bathroom door slammed shut.

Seriously? I plopped down on the bed. This was not going as I'd hoped. The shower started running.

I got up and opened the door and went in and sat down on the edge of the sink. His shirt and pants were neatly folded and stacked on a tiny table in the corner. "Why the attitude?"

He poked his head out from behind the curtain. "What the

hell, woman?"

I grinned. "It's alright. We're married."

He groaned. "Unbelievable." He yanked the curtain shut.

"What's with the monkey?"

Dalton didn't answer. All I could hear was lathering soap and splashing water.

"Strix said I was here to pick out my own monkey. Why wouldn't you just choose one? You're the buyer."

The water shut off and he reached out from behind the curtain for a towel. A moment later he slid back the shower curtain. He was standing there half naked, the towel wrapped around his waist, wet hair, water dripping down his chest. I swallowed. He was ripped. Not an ounce of fat.

He raised his arms to comb his fingers through his hair and I noticed the tattoo, the SEAL Trident.

"You were in the Navy."

He glanced at the tattoo and frowned.

"My mother was in the Navy. I recognize the symbol. You were a SEAL."

He turned toward the mirror, ignoring me.

"Unless you rang the bell."

He glared at me.

"No, of course you didn't."

He took a long breath as though contemplating whether he wanted to make me disappear without a trace. He was a SEAL; there was no question whether he could. My mother warned me against dating SEALs. They're crazy, she'd said. Every last one of them. No daughter of mine, blah, blah, blah. That's all I remember actually. But if Dalton was a SEAL, at least I knew something about him. Something significant. It takes a certain kind of man to be a SEAL. A man of honor, loyalty, and integrity, not to mention grit, tenacity, and discipline.

"White-faced Capuchin."

"What?" I snapped back from my thoughts. He was lathering his face with shaving cream.

"I was testing the waters, asking for a class II species, see how he'd react."

"And?"

With an old-fashioned straight razor, he shaved one side of his face, taking one swipe, then another before rinsing it.

"And he asked about the buyer." He scraped the razor under his chin and up to his lip, then rinsed it and started up the left side of his face. "See, you have to understand, these guys get nervous about new people in the pipeline. They don't like surprises." He splashed water on his face and used the hand towel to wipe it dry. "He was getting squirrelly."

"Squirrelly?"

He flipped up the toilet seat, waited. When I didn't move, he turned to me. "Do you mind?"

I crossed my arms.

He rolled his eyes and reached under his towel.

"Fine," I said and backed out of the bathroom, shutting the door behind me. I stared at the queen-sized bed. It had been awhile since I'd had a man in my room. Suddenly I was imagining him naked, the lights off, the—the door swung open and Dalton came out of the bathroom wearing the same pants, no shirt. He strode over to face me.

I swallowed hard, getting my head back on straight.

"I didn't want to lose the ground I'd gained. So—"

"So you said it was for your wife."

He thrust his jaw forward and nodded ever so slightly.

"And he suggested you bring her down here, implying she could pick it out herself." So that was it. Dalton screwed up. He had given George an open door to call his bluff.

He leaned forward, his face close to mine. "I don't need you to tell me how to do my job."

"I didn't say anything." I could feel his hot breath on my face. I tried to keep my voice non-confrontational. "Now here we are. In this whirlwind romance."

He held my gaze for a long moment. Then smirked.

"Yeah."

I broke away and went back to my suitcase. "What was all that about horseback riding with Maria?"

Dalton shrugged. "What do you mean?"

"It seemed like an opportunity to get close to George. Why wouldn't we do it?"

"You need to follow my lead, not question everything." Before I could respond, he screwed up his face, annoyed. "We just need to be cautious, that's all, not seem too eager. This is a delicate thing."

"All right," I said, staring at him. What was that all about?

"When the time is right," he said. "You can chat and do whatever it is women do."

"Whatever women do?" Wow, he was a piece of work. "And what was that outside the door a few minutes ago? Is that just what men do?"

He glanced at the door and I could read his thoughts. "I was playing a role."

"Really?" I said. "You weren't the slightest bit into it?"

His eyes lit with fire. "Hey honey, I'm a healthy, virile man. You were rubbing up against me."

Two could play this game. "Just playing my role, *hubby*." I crossed my arms. "Speaking of that, I don't get Maria. She doesn't seem like a woman who would go for someone like George. She was too—"

"You need to work on your observation skills. Didn't you notice his fat wallet? A lot of women find that pretty darn attractive."

"I know, it's just that—"

"That's what women do. Act all aloof and independent, suck you in, then whine when the dough dries up."

I shook my head. "You don't have a girlfriend, do you?"

He huffed. "Divorced."

"Shocking," I said. With those strong arms and his boyish grin, he oozed sex in an all-American kinda way. "I bet you were a football player and made all the cheerleaders swoon. She was the prom queen, right?"

"Listen, you're here for one thing. Until then, your job is to look pretty and keep your mouth shut. Go shopping, go to the beach. Get your hair done." He threw up his hands. "I don't care."

"Let me get this straight. I'm to do nothing, say nothing? Even think nothing?"

"Now you're getting the idea."

"You don't care about my experience, my abilities, my skills." I slammed my hands down on my hips. "I'm only here because I have boobs."

His eyes dropped to my chest. "And you've come with very fine assets." He ripped the cover from the bed, plopped down in the chair, and drew it over his head. "Goodnight, sweetheart."

CHAPTER 5

I took a cold shower. I still didn't sleep well. Too many things about this whole situation bothered me. Namely, Special Agent Dalton. What the hell? He practically had me panting for him and then claimed it was all an act. Asshole. My mother was right. What really bothered me was that I couldn't decide which was worse—him or my mother being right.

I rolled over but couldn't get the image out of my mind of him standing in the shower with the towel wrapped around his waist. I really needed to get out of the north woods. I loved the boreal forest, but the boyfriend prospects up there were nonexistent. I contemplated a second cold shower, forced my mind elsewhere.

Why had George brought all the potential buyers together for dinner at his house? What would be the advantage? If anything, you'd think a savvy business man would want to keep his associates from talking to each other. There had to be a logical reason.

And the postcard from García. He must have thought Nash could put it together. A beautiful butterfly. What in the world did he mean by that? Butterflies were big business on the black market. But he hadn't mentioned one species specifically? I needed some knowledge of local butterflies.

When dawn rolled around, Dalton grunted something about going to do his job, to have fun at the beach.

Like hell. I wasn't going to sit on my hands and do nothing. I was going to the palapa bar, see what I could find out. I know how to blend in, be discreet. Unfortunately, it wouldn't be open for several hours, so I had time for my morning yoga. After that, I decided to check out the butterfly garden. Worth a shot. Maybe I could get an idea of what García might have been referring to on the postcard.

I brushed my teeth, tied my hair back into a ponytail, threw on a t-shirt and shorts, grabbed Mrs. Strix's handbag, and headed out.

The valley surrounding our bungalow had a mix of tourists, ex-pats, and snowbirds. A nice walking path had been slashed through the edge of the jungle for ease to the shopping district where one could find all the modern conveniences yet still feel as though in a tropical paradise.

The morning air was cool. I took my time, enjoying it. This close to the equator, afternoons could be oppressively hot and muggy. I've never understood the phrase "tropical paradise." It's an oxymoron, if you ask me. Heat and I don't mix.

There was no denying though, this truly was a nature lover's paradise. The trees were filled with birds, squawking, chirping, chattering. An iguana scampered off the path where it had been basking in the morning sun.

From above, I heard a distinctive swish in the canopy. Two white-faced capuchin monkeys scampered across a limb like a couple of squirrels. The way these two could romp through the treetops was breathtaking to watch. They dropped down, one at a time, to swing on a hanging vine, then flip over onto the next limb, keeping balance with their prehensile tails. One seemed to notice I'd stopped. He sat back on his haunches, his arm around a branch, his round, black eyes lit with curiosity as he chittered at me with his high pitched call.

He reminded me of the Philippines and the tarsiers I loved as a kid, though the tarsier's ultrasonic call is inaudible to the human ear. With large, bug-like eyes and long, bony fingers, they grasp a branch in a pose that always makes them look like they're hugging it.

My dad would get me up before dawn and we'd hike into the forest, to a blind he'd placed the day or two before, and we'd wait for one to come along and then hope for the light to be just right for the perfect wildlife photo.

I wished I had a camera with me right now. The capuchin was so close and seemed unafraid in my presence. I lingered for a while, watching the two watch me. This is why I'm here, I thought. This is how it should be.

Before I moved on, I glanced behind me and caught sight of Yipes, several paces back, trying to act nonchalant. So I had a tail. Hm. Good to know.

I continued down the path toward town and found the butterfly garden tucked away on a side street, a tiny educational building serving as its entrance. I went inside and wandered for a few minutes, taking in the layout, before I was greeted by a guy about my age, an American with movie-star good looks. "Bienvenida al Jardín de Mariposas," he said in greeting.

I understood him perfectly, but I had to keep my cover. "Um...hello to you, too. Do you speak English?"

He gave me a smile that made me smile involuntarily in response. "Welcome to the butterfly gardens." His voice had husky, earthy notes, a sound that belonged in the bedroom. My bedroom.

"Oh, thank goodness," I said. I stared a moment too long.

He stood with his weight on one leg, his hand on his hip, exuding an easy confidence. He knew he was hot. His long hair was tied back in a ponytail at the base of his neck. His square jawline and scruffy stubble made me want to tug him into a dark back room and go crazy. *Damn Dalton for getting me all revved up.*

I shoved my hands into my pockets to hide the monster diamond on my left hand, thinking how ridiculous it was to have to hide my fake ring because of my fake husband that I wasn't getting any action from anyway, fake or otherwise.

"Would you like a tour?"

Um, with you? Yeah! I glanced down at my shoes. *Poppy, get it together. You're a federal agent for god's sake.* "Yes, I think so," I said with a shrug, trying to act indifferent. *Wait. Maybe this guy has some information. And flirting will get me a lot further, get him talking, won't it?* "When's the next one?"

"Oh, we aren't that busy. I can take you right now, if you'd like."

As I ransacked my purse for the ten dollar fee, I slipped the ring off and let it drop to the bottom.

"We're a non-profit, supported completely by donations and volunteers."

"You're a volunteer then?" I said, stating the obvious. *Geez. My hormones must be eating away at my brain cells.*

"A couple days a week."

I glanced around. "Are you the only one here?"

"Yeah, we're a pretty small operation."

"And what's your name?"

"Oh, I'm Noah. Glad to meet you. And you are?"

I stared at him, my mind blank. For the life of me, I couldn't come up with my cover name. "Noah, that's a nice name," I said, stalling. "I get it. As in the guy with the ark." His expression changed. *Oh my god. I'm such an idiot.* "Oh my gosh, I'm sorry. That's really your name, isn't it?"

He cocked his head to the side, a look of confusion on his face.

"I figured you must get a lot of children and"—*kill me now*—"that was part of your, you know…"

He gave me a genuine smile. "Naw, we don't get a lot of kids. Wish we did, actually."

I extended my hand. "Well, I'm Brittany. It's nice to meet you, Noah. "

"Likewise," he said, and led me to the insectarium, a room rimmed with glass aquariums, each housing some exotic native insect—beetles of all sizes and shapes, scarabs with iridescent green shells, spiders that would make my mom vow to never set foot in this country. Posters adorned the walls showing comparable sizes of insects, butterflies, and moths, as well as paintings from local artists, and a large case of pinned insects.

Noah patiently told me about each live insect—its lifespan, eating habits, predators—while taking it from its tiny habitat and holding it out for me to see. "Half of the species on Earth are arthropods," he said.

"That's a lot of bugs. I'm glad they're not all as big as that one." He was holding the Hercules Beetle, a bug the size of an Idaho potato with horns. He assured me it was harmless and offered to let me hold it. He looked surprised when I took it and held it in the palm of my hand.

He grinned. "Wow, most ladies won't touch him."

I looked right into his eyes. "Well, I'm not like most ladies."

His eyes turned sultry. "I can see that."

We moved out of the building to the gardens, several of which were designed to replicate different natural habitats from low-elevation forest to cloud forest, a habitat rare on Earth save for a few specific locations, one being right here in Costa Rica. Each was enclosed with netting to keep the butterflies in.

In the first, I learned about the Blue Morpho butterfly, the pride of Costa Rica. One lighted on his hand and I swear its wings spanned eight inches. When it opened its wings, it shined a brilliant iridescent blue, but the underside of the wings was a dull brown color with swirls and eyespots. Noah told me that in flight, the contrasting bright blue and dull brown colors flash, making it appear as though the butterfly is magically appearing and disappearing, inspiring countless tales in local folklore.

As we moved on through the other gardens, Noah told me about the unique glass-winged butterflies that don't rely on bright coloring, but rather use pheromones to attract a mate. I could have told him a thing or two about the effect of pheromones right now.

The last stop was a giant leafcutter ant colony. Noah seemed to come alive as he spoke about it. Next to humans, he said, leafcutter ants form the largest and most complex animal societies on Earth. Deep within their nests, the ants work collectively to cultivate a fungus that grows on their chewed leaves—gardening to produce their own food.

Through observation, scientists realized that certain species of leaves, avoided by the ants, tend to possess compounds called terpenoids, a breakthrough discovery of antifungal chemicals now used for medicinal purposes or fungicides.

Noah relayed this information to me as though it were the most amazing discovery of mankind.

The tour ended back in the tiny building in which we had started. Noah gestured toward the items for sale in the room—artwork, jewelry, books, nature guides. "All the proceeds from our gift shop support our conservation efforts and the upkeep of the gardens here, the care of the butterflies, that kind of thing." He pointed to a jar near the cash register. "And if you can, we're asking for donations for our capital campaign to build a wildlife sanctuary here for animals that have been injured or orphaned. Our goal is $200,000."

Normally, I'd empty the bottom of my handbag of all its loose change for such a thing, but I couldn't risk my cover.

I stood there, trying to search my rational mind for insight. Could Noah be involved somehow with the smuggling? After all, I'd come to the butterfly garden to poke around, see if there was any connection to the clue from Agent García's postcard. It certainly would be an excellent cover. No one would suspect. I glanced at Noah. No way.

I chose a book, *The Birds of Costa Rica*, and paid cash. "Do you know of any good birding trails?" I asked.

He gave me a free map of the area and pointed out a few of his favorite spots. I thanked him, stuffed the map in my purse, and lingered. I didn't want to go. He had some kind of gravitational pull.

He leaned on the counter. "What brings you to Costa Rica, anyway?"

I smiled. I could stay and talk with him all day. Maybe he'd take me by the hand and lead me into that back room. "The birds, actually. I'm kind of a bird nut. I was hoping to see a keel-billed toucan. And the resplendent quetzal, of course."

He nodded. He understood my obsession. "I know a tree cavity where I've seen a family of toucans. You interested?"

My eyes lit up. "Yeah!" I yanked the map back out of my purse and opened it on the counter. "Where?"

"I'm done here in an hour. I could show you." His eyes had that hungry-for-me look. My breath caught in my throat.

"Well, I, uh." Darn, I had work to do. "I really have to get back right now. But, maybe later?"

He nodded, looking disappointed. "Sure."

My gaze lingered on his lips. "No, I'd really like that," I stammered. "I'll stop back by." I scooted out the door before I could spontaneously combust.

For my next stop I needed to be sure to ditch Yipes. He wasn't that difficult to spot, but I had to be careful. There are two tried-and-true ways to lose a tail: the covert maneuver or the distraction. Yipes seemed like the type who'd fall for a good old-fashioned distraction. I walked back to the bungalows and knocked on his door.

"Buenos días, Señora Fuller," he said. "How may I help you?"

"Would you please call a taxi for me and point me in the direction of a drug store. I need, well, some woman things."

His cheeks burned and he nodded. "Uno momento." He slipped back into his room. That ought to do it.

I had the cab drop me at the drug store in town where I picked up a new beach bag, yellow flip-flops, and some cheap sunglasses, then went around the block, rented a moped for the week, and headed for the beach.

Most people would be thrilled to spend the afternoon sipping pineapple drinks on a sunny tropical stretch of sand. I am not most people. I hate the sun. Or I should say, the sun hates me. Red hair, freckles, pasty white skin. While my high school girlfriends strived for the tanned little bunny look, I worked hard to avoid the crispy lobster imitation.

The Toucan palapa bar was more my style. Its giant thatched roof was nestled among the palms, providing glorious shade. Brightly-colored, hand-painted signs directed beach-goers down a roped path toward shrimp skewers and ice cold margaritas. (Obviously for tourists who have no knowledge or interest in true local fare.)

I tucked my hair under the hat, donned the sunglasses, and strolled in.

The place was packed. Jimmy Buffet blared from speakers mounted at every corner. Waitresses bustled about delivering metal pails filled with Cerveza Imperials. The mixed scents of stale cigarettes and spilled beer hung in the open air.

Every inch of wood in the place—supporting posts, table tops, chairs—had names and dates crudely engraved, testaments to memorable drunkenfests. At the bar, a group of six college kids simultaneously tipped a bamboo log with shot glasses attached while their friends pounded on the bar, making memories of their own.

I sidled up to the bar and elbowed in. A young tica with her hair pulled back in braids hollered, "What can I getcha?" as she hustled by, her arms loaded with fried fish baskets. Her name tag read Isabella.

"Do you have a local IPA?"

She dropped the baskets in front of the bamboo shot meisters, grabbed a bottle from the cooler, and popped the top as she headed back toward me. "Eight dollars," she said, but kept walking. I pulled out a ten and before I could drop it on the counter she was back, plucked it out of my hand, and was off again.

"This place always this busy?" I asked the guy holding down the bar stool next to me.

He leaned over. "Cruise ship lunch rush." His lip curled up on the left side in an attempt at a grin, his blood alcohol content apparently causing partial facial paralysis.

I looked in the direction he was making a valiant attempt to point. The shipping dock jutted out into the ocean directly to the south of the bar where a large white vessel with bright orange lifeboats was docked.

I ordered some gallo pinto, Costa Rican style rice and beans. I was going to be here awhile.

At the other corner of the bar, a couple college boys posed for a picture holding a six-foot boa constrictor. One of their drunk pals held out a twenty to take his turn to look macho holding a snake that was probably nearly comatose.

A sign hanging behind the bar read: Animal photos, $20 - Birds, snakes, monkeys. Above the sign, two scarlet macaws perched in the rafters. Scarlet macaws are highly intelligent, and with their bright red, yellow and blue plumage, they make popular pets. For that reason, they're endangered in most of their habitat, making them a CITES class I species. One bird can sell for thousands of dollars on the black market. Someone in possession really should have a permit, but in Central America, keeping animals like these is culturally ingrained and rarely prosecuted. The Costa Rican government concerns itself primarily with illegal export. At this point, these two birds couldn't go back to the wild anyway. They'd probably been in this bar their entire lives.

I sipped the beer, killing time, watching the staff. This seemed like an unlikely place for a wildlife poaching connection. A lot of money was being passed over the bar, though. I watched one of the bus boys put every third bill into his front shorts pocket. Interesting, though not my concern. I was keeping an eye out for anyone named Paco. Maybe I'd get a glimpse of my fellow agent.

Every once in awhile, a man came from the back, went straight to the cash register, took out some cash, then went back out. Some buying of something was going on out back.

After about an hour, most of the patrons staggered toward the boat gripping plastic souvenir cups in the shape of pineapples in their sweaty hands. The music was turned down and I could actually hear the surf as it rolled on the beach. The bartender came back by. "Another IPA?

"Sure, why not?" I dug out another ten spot.

A young couple lingered at the end of the bar. Newlyweds. The girl pointed at the rafters. I glanced in the direction she was looking. A white-faced capuchin swung from a rope. The girl giggled and nodded and her pink-cheeked husband tossed a twenty on the bar. The monkey swooped down with a screech, snatched up the bill, and raced back to his perch. The newlyweds frowned. "Hey," the husband called.

Isabella whistled and gestured to the monkey. He skittered and chirped, then reluctantly descended to the bar. The wife opened her arms and the monkey curled up in her embrace. He cowered, his eyes darting from her to her husband. How could no one see how terrified he was? She cooed at him like he was a baby.

I had to admit, he was cute with his round, black eyes set in that adorable little human-like face. That's what made them highly sought after for pets. Unfortunately, it's often people like this, animal lovers, who do the most harm. They don't stop to think; these are wild animals. Sure, they look like cute little babies when they're young, their faces and hands so much like ours, but once they hit puberty, they can be aggressive. Wild animals are meant to stay in the wild, not interact with people. If I wasn't undercover, I'd be over there explaining all that to them right now.

Isabella kept a close watch on the monkey. She knew. The

husband snapped a few pictures, no doubt for their honeymoon Facebook page. That's when I noticed the monkey's right hand was missing. Poor thing. Often, monkeys are caught in primitive snares which can do all kinds of damage as the monkey freaks out trying to get free. Most likely that's what had happened to this little guy.

The monkey loped across the bar where Isabella provided a treat, then he scampered back up to his ropes. So sad. "How long as he been here?" I asked her.

"Clyde? Oh, dis one a few years." She ran a wet rag down the length of the bar. "De owner has had many, all named Clyde. You know, from de Clint Eastwood movie."

"That was an orangutan," I said.

With an eye roll, she said, "I know." She headed for the beer cooler, but made an abrupt turn, headed back toward me and quickly started restocking the plastic cups. A tico in his fifties, his dark hair slicked back, entered the bar area carrying a black satchel. He reminded me of an old, washed up Hispanic version of Vinnie Babarino.

"Who's that?" I asked.

She kept her head down. "Oh, dat Carlos. He de owner."

Carlos grabbed handfuls of bills from the cash register and stuffed them into the satchel. He called Isabella over to him. Her shoulders turned inward and, with her eyes downcast, she obeyed. He whispered something to her and glanced around the bar. I turned to the side and tipped up my beer so he couldn't see my face. Then he was gone.

Isabella returned to the bar. "Another?" she asked.

I shook my head. "He looked familiar. I think he's a friend of my brother. What's his last name?"

She glanced his way as though she wanted to be sure he was gone. "Mendoza."

"No, not him," I said. "Oh well." I shrugged. "How long have you worked here?"

"Too long," she said and moved away. I finished my beer, set the empty bottle on the bar, and gave her a wave. That's all I was going to get for today.

I took a walk down the beach and punched up Mom on my cell phone. It rang five times before Mr. Strix picked up. "Everything okay?"

"Yeah. I was hoping you could look someone up for me."

"I'll do my best."

"Carlos Mendoza. He owns The Toucan, the bar on the postcard."

"How'd you get his name?"

"Long story. Could you also scare up a picture of García?"

There was a pause. "I'll see what I can do. Hey, Roy called. He said to tell you they nailed the guy."

I smiled. "And Honey Bear?"

"Roaming free."

I smiled wider.

"So, Mendoza. How'd you—"

"Sorry. Gotta go." I hit end and headed back toward the bungalow. I didn't want to have to explain.

Within ten minutes, I got a text with a photo. It could have been the man who'd gone to the cash register, but I wasn't sure. Mr. Strix called back. "You're not going to believe this. The Mendoza family is quite large. Most live in Nicaragua. Besides the bar, a few years back, the family purchased a coffee plantation in Costa Rica. It's no longer producing, but get this: it borders George's property."

Bingo.

Chapter 6

If Carlos was the buncher, he needed a remote location to house the illegal animals, keep them fed, alive. It needed to be far from the eyes of the law or meddling neighbors. Like an old coffee plantation.

After a quick exploration with Google Earth, I had a pretty good sense of the lay of the land. Only one structure still stood on the property, one that looked large enough to house animals—the old roasting shed. That had to be it. But I needed to find out for sure.

Field trip!

The farm sprawled across a steep hillside, quite rugged terrain compared to some of the larger plantations, leaving few locations for coffee trees. The rest appeared to be wild jungle. A river ran through the property from the northeast, meandered through the east quarter, then exited its boundary just north of the southeast corner.

The driveway, a rutted two-track, would likely be under surveillance. The best place to enter the property unnoticed was at that southeast corner, south of the river. It was going to be a trek.

I strapped my binoculars on my chest, tossed my new bird book in my backpack, laced up my boots, and was out the door. What better disguise than a bird nut, hopelessly lost in search of the resplendent quetzal?

From the edge of the dirt road where I stashed my moped among the tangle of jungle, I followed a power line for about five hundred yards, then headed up the side of the hill. I was in pretty good shape, but the humidity was stifling. My T-shirt was soaked in minutes. Flashes of color flitted through the trees—motmots and trogons, parrots and toucanets—birds I'd loved to have the time to stop and identify.

I did keep a sharp lookout for snakes, though. Central America is not a place to underestimate when it comes to poisonous creatures, especially the slithering kind. I didn't want to stumble across a fer-de-lance. There was a reason it was known as the ultimate pit viper. Most snakes will avoid contact. When threatened, the fer-de-lance rears up and advances. The darn thing can strike above the knee cap. It produces an overabundance of deadly venom and isn't afraid to use it. Forty-six percent of snakebites in Costa Rica come from this guy and they aren't pretty. Symptoms rival that of simultaneously stepping on a land mine and being sprayed with poison gas. Yeah, I was watching my step.

I turned twenty-five degrees and walked another four hundred yards figuring I'd arrive just south of the shed. When I got to within one hundred yards, I stopped dead. Good thing I'd been watching so diligently for snakes. About six inches above the ground ran a primitive tripwire—a thin cable stretched horizontally through eye hooks that had been drilled at the base of trees, then upward to an iron bell that hung about twenty feet in the air. Clever. Simple, yet effective. I stepped over it and crept forward more cautiously. Someone was definitely guarding something.

I found a perch in a banyon tree with a decent view of the shed. On the southwest corner, a guard paced back and forth in a way that was clear his training came from watching Schwarzenegger movies. Not good. He could be unpredictable, therefore dangerous. He carried an old rifle of some sort, its barrel wrapped with electrical tape.

The sturdy old structure he guarded was tucked into the hillside, longways. Corrugated tin walls supported a split-style roof that provided a three-foot gap at the peak for air circulation and natural light. Large bay doors stood open on either end, east and west. The driveway came up from the east.

On the open, flat land south of the shed, large, flat concrete slabs had at one time been used to spread coffee beans to dry in the sun. Beyond that was jungle. Two more guards with similar technique to the first paced at the edge of the clearing.

Using my binoculars, I scanned the eaves of the shed. No video cameras. In fact, looked like there was no electricity. I thought I heard the faint hum of a generator. Perhaps for lights at night?

I slipped back into the cover of the jungle and, keeping to the harsh, late afternoon shadows, I headed up the hillside on the west side, avoiding the driveway, to get a look from the north. I came across three more trip lines, the same setup, each attached to an old bell.

About five hundred yards from the northwest corner of the shed, I crossed a path that disappeared into the dense foliage. I followed it to a ravine where a cable stretched across from which a metal basket hung, large enough to carry two people. It was rigged with a pulley system that allowed the basket to be moved by hand in either direction. On the far side, all I could see was an outhouse. I hadn't noticed it on Google Earth, but it was small and tucked under a tree. It would be too risky to get in the basket to check it out. If someone came along, I'd have nowhere to hide and nowhere to go. Besides, it might squeak and rattle and bang. I slipped back among the leaves and headed toward the shed.

I stayed on the north side, uphill of the shed, and crossed all the way to the east to a vantage point where I could clearly see the main entrance. Two guards posted there carried 9mm submachine guns, looked like MP-5s. There was definitely something of value in there. I crouched down on my haunches and wondered how I was going to get inside to find out.

And how I was going to tell Dalton.

I had to assume that if the place was guarded, it was guarded twenty-four hours a day. I could set up a diversion to draw the guards away, but, working alone, that would likely provide very little time to get inside and back out. I could do a stake out, see what comes and goes. But that kind of operation took more time than I had and required constant surveillance, which I couldn't do alone, nor could I make excuses for the time away from Dalton. Bribing one of the guards for information was way too risky; I could blow my cover.

I decided to pack it in. This was all I was going to get today. I circled back around to the south side of the shed and dropped into the thick brush when a bell rang somewhere to the west of me. *Crap.* I looked down. I hadn't tripped a line. I was sure the closest one was a good twenty paces to my left.

Shouts came from the shed. The guards were scrambling. I had to get out of here. And fast.

A second bell rang. This time closer. Someone was coming my way and closing in fast. If I ran, I'd be spotted. I dropped to the ground and rolled under some ferns. A man went barreling by, laughing as he went. I pushed up on my elbows to get a glimpse of him. He went straight for the next tripwire, jumped up and down on it, causing the bell to clank back and forth. When he turned to listen for the guards, I got a good look at him.

It was Noah. I blinked. From the butterfly gardens. What the hell was he doing?

He took off, heading south, then dropped with a thump. He let out a moan.

Crap. I couldn't afford to get caught here. But I couldn't let him get shot.

I scanned the jungle for pursuers, then left my hiding spot and sprinted to him. He was rubbing his right shoulder. "Is it broken?" I whispered.

"No." He got up and brushed mud from his shorts. It took a moment, but I could see recognition set it. "What are you doing here?"

There was movement behind him. I held up my hand in a gesture to be quiet. He turned to look and I slipped behind a tree. A guard burst through the brush and skidded to a halt, aiming his weapon at Noah. "Ah, ha! Te he cogido," the guard muttered. He turned his head and drew in a breath to shout. I pounced, slamming him to the ground. I knocked the rifle from his hands and with a quick punch square on the temple, put him out cold.

"Holy crap! Where'd you learn that?" Noah said, his eyebrows arched all the way to his hairline.

"Self defense class?" I shrugged, trying to look surprised myself. "Ha, who knew it would pay off?" I grinned.

"Yeah," he said, staring at the guy.

"I think there might be more coming," I told him. *Four to be exact. Two heavily armed.*

"Yeah." He turned east. "Follow me."

I hesitated. I had no idea what Noah was up to or why he was here.

"C'mon, trust me," he said and flashed his adorable smile. "You don't want to stick around."

I glanced down at the guard. At this point, my fate was tied to Noah's anyway. He launched into a full-out sprint, crashing through the brush. I followed as he ran down a shallow ravine, up and over a ridge. Shots rang out behind us and a bullet went zipping by my head. And Noah was headed toward the river. We needed to cut south.

"I think there's a river ahead," I said. "It's whitewater. Too strong to cross."

"I know," he said and kept running.

"But—"

"Trust me," he hollered over his shoulder.

The land sloped downward and we burst through some thick

foliage at the edge of the river. "Go, go, go!" Noah shouted as he plowed into the water. I glanced around. In a small eddy just downriver, a young woman sat in a two-man inflatable kayak, a paddle in one hand, a rope loosely tied around a tree trunk in the other. She let loose the line and dug in with the paddle, shoving off. "C'mon," he shouted to me as he launched himself into the kayak. I hit the water and in two strides I was straddling the edge of the kayak, one leg in, one dragging, as it caught in the main current and sent us spinning.

He grabbed me under my arms and heaved me up and into the kayak. "Hang on," he said. "Whatever you do, stay in the boat. Listen to Claudia. She's a world-class rafting guide."

Water gushed and roared as it propelled us downriver in a turbulent, angry fury of white foam. I glanced back at Claudia. She looked calm and capable, focused on calculating the flow of the rapids. "Sounds goo—" I managed to say before we rammed a wall of water and white froth crashed over my head. I gripped the sides of the narrow boat with both hands and blew water out of my nose.

Noah dug in with his paddle at Claudia's commands. "Forward, now back paddle," she hollered over the thunder of the rapids as we spun sideways and rolled up one side of a crest and down the other. "Duck!" Our boat scraped under branches that jutted out from the bank. "Now hard left!" Noah obeyed and no sooner were we facing downriver than we hit a rock and the front of the kayak shot upward, stalling on the rock, jolting us to a halt as water roared past.

The back end slowly caught in the current and spun us around, lifting us off the rock, shooting us downriver facing backward, bobbing in the waves. Claudia looked over her shoulder. "Get ready," she said. Ready for what, I wondered, and we were airborne. Claudia dropped down, clinging to the back side of the kayak, as it flipped. Noah launched into the air. I rolled into the churning maelstrom, my arms flailing, grasping in the air for anything. Then the boat was there and I grabbed hold and heaved myself up onto it, coughing water from my lungs.

"Where's Noah?" His head popped up to our right, then got sucked under again.

"Grab him!" she shouted.

I reached out and when he popped up again, I grabbed ahold of his T-shirt and hauled him onto the overturned kayak. He coughed and sputtered.

Claudia managed to get us into a backwater at the edge of the river and we got the kayak flipped back over. "It's not over yet," she said.

Noah and I got back into the boat. Claudia gave it a shove into the current and crawled onto the back. The kayak bucked and tilted as we hit some big swells, then just as Claudia got her paddle in the water, we slid into a white hole of swirling water. The kayak jerked and spun in a white vortex, water pounding over us from all directions, pummeling us with surge after surge while Claudia shouted commands to Noah. I felt helpless, hanging on to the sides. Finally, the bow tipped upward and we shot out of the hole.

The kayak rolled sideways, then with a jolt, rolled the other way as Claudia shouted, "Lean left! Now right!" We countered our weight and managed to keep it upright as we squeaked through a narrow gully, water smashing into boulders on either side of us. "Hold on!" Claudia warned. The nose dipped downward and we plunged over a waterfall. Wham! We rammed into the water, slamming us forward. We hit the water so hard my eyelids yanked wide open and my eyeballs were washed inside and out. I let go to give them a rub and the kayak dipped and spun sideways, tipping to starboard. Somehow, Claudia kept us upright.

Then finally, the kayak slowed in a stretch of riffles. Noah got up on his knees, held the paddle over his head, and shouted, "Ha! Take that, you bastards!"

Claudia paddled us around another bend to where the river crossed under the road and they'd stashed a beat up old VW bus. We hauled out, strapped the kayak to the roof, and after three attempts to get the engine started, sped away, Claudia at the wheel and me and Noah on the floor in the back.

As soon as we caught our breath, Noah asked, "What were you doing up there?"

"I was out birding and kinda got turned around, I guess." I conjured some surprise and added a helping of fear. "Then you ran by and scared the crap out of me. Who were those men? They were shooting at you! At us!" *And why were you purposefully ringing the bells to get them to chase you?*

Claudia glanced back at Noah and something passed between them.

"I guess I'm lucky you came along," I said.

"I'm pretty sure it's the other way around." He shook his head. "Claudia, you should have seen her take down that guard."

I winced, but he didn't notice. That was an unfortunate complication and could be a problem. "He's making it sound like more than it was," I said, trying to produce a blush. "He scared me is all. I just reacted."

"Sounds like he got what he deserved."

Noah gave her a quick shake of his head. He looked at me and grinned.

If they were organized activists, they'd be cautious. Too many questions right away would cause suspicion. But I had a thousand. What did they know exactly? How had they found out about the shed? Did they know who was involved? I had to be careful. I wouldn't force him to give me an explanation. Better to act the flirt, see how things played out.

"All I know is we stumbled onto something." But I didn't want to look like an idiot. With narrowed eyes, I looked to Claudia and back to Noah. "Wait a minute. Are you cops or something?"

"Ha," he huffed. He shifted his weight and leaned forward. "Do we look like cops?"

I smiled and shook my head. He was looking mighty scrumptious with wet hair and his damp T-shirt clinging to his chest. If Claudia was his girlfriend, I needed to be extra cautious. I think he read my mind because he said, "You're shivering." He held out his hands, gesturing for me to scoot over and lean against him. "C'mere." I flipped around and cuddled into his embrace. "You should come to the bonfire tonight, meet the gang. Claudia's boyfriend will be there and Jack's doing a fish boil."

I grinned. "I'd like that." *And all the intel you can give me.*

CHAPTER 7

I wondered how the agency governed undercover affairs, what was allowed, how one handled *relationships*. I fully understood the risk in becoming emotionally involved, but a little fun while getting information couldn't hurt, could it? The agency had no authority over my sex life anyway. Maybe some fraternization clause, but civilians were none of their business. Besides, I needed to work this informant for all I could, right?

All this flashed through my mind when Claudia hopped out of the van, leaving me alone with Noah, his warm breath on my neck. He ran his hands up and down my arms. "We should get you out of those wet clothes," he whispered in my ear, his voice husky. My breath caught in my throat and all I could manage was to nod.

The back doors of the van flung open. "Looks like Jack's already got the fire going," Claudia said.

"We'll be out there in a minute," Noah said as we piled out of the van.

The sun hung low on the horizon. The surf rolled on the beach, its lapping mixed with the happy sounds of friends gathered near the crackling bonfire.

Noah took me by the hand and led me down a narrow sandy path, swatting palm leaves out of the way. He came to a halt at a clearing and spread his arms wide. "My humble abode," he said. Nestled in the branches of a tree was a tree house. An actual tree house. Okay, it was partially supported by poles, but it was the coolest house I'd ever seen.

Tiny solar powered lanterns lit a spiral staircase leading up to the rail of the balcony where a hammock hung.

"Nice digs," I said.

"Be my guest." Noah gestured for me to climb the stairs.

As I reached the top, my mouth dropped open at the view. I leaned on the railing and took it in. An amber glow lined the horizon. Pink clouds streaked across the sky. The bonfire below us sent rosy sparks into the air, soaring skyward.

Noah came up behind me and wrapped his arms around my waist. "You like?"

"It's beautiful," I said, steadying myself.

He nuzzled my neck. I held my breath.

He pressed his lips to my ear. "Your heart's racing."

"Yeah, I just, you know, I'm just a little on edge. It's not everyday I get shot at."

"I know." He flashed a conspiratorial smile. "Isn't it invigorating?"

He gently turned me around to face him. One hand on my hip, he reached up and caressed my cheek, then slipped his hand behind my neck. He paused, inches away, his hungry eyes lingering on my lips. I ran my hand up his arm, across his shoulder to his neck and pulled him toward me. Our lips met. His tongue touched mine and made my insides twinkle.

"Mmmm, I like your style," he said with a grin and kissed me again. His hand slid down from the small of my back, sending warm pulses up my spine. I twirled the hair at the base of his neck in my fingers, gently tugging. He pulled me closer and nuzzled my ear, then my neck. His stubble rubbed against my flesh and made me shiver.

"Where's the beer?" someone called from below. I backed into the rail. Noah held me, his strong hands keeping me pressed against him.

"The cooler's by the shed," he said. "Should be full."

"Right on, bro," the voice called back.

I pulled away from his embrace. This was getting too hot, too fast. I had to keep my head straight. "I should get changed," I said.

He hesitated as though trying to read my thoughts. "Sure." He padded across the wood plank floor and soon candles lit the room with a soft glow. To one side, comfy rattan chairs, a coffee table, and a bookshelf stuffed with paperbacks made a cozy living room area. At the edge of the railing stood a bar with two barstools. On the other side, drawers and a wardrobe were built into a solid wall, to the right of that was a wooden door. Beyond, a roped bridge led into the darkness, to another tree house possibly. A ladder reached upward to a tiny loft where I could see the edge of a queen-size mattress. The ceiling was part thatch roof, part plastic sheeting. A single fan slowly turned overhead.

He took a T-shirt from a drawer and handed it to me. "Bathroom's there," he said and pointed to the wooden door.

"Thanks." I couldn't get away fast enough. I splashed cold water on my face. What the hell was I thinking? I quickly changed into the T-shirt, stuffed mine in my backpack, looked in the tiny mirror, and took a deep breath. *Keep your act together, McVie.*

I shot a text off to Dalton: Will be late. Don't worry.

"Much better," I said as I emerged from the bathroom and sashayed toward the staircase. I could smell something roasting on the fire. "I'm hungry."

"All right then," Noah said.

I felt a twinge of regret.

Noah's friend Jack had the fire stoked enough to run a steam engine. To the side, atop a huge pile of coals, a makeshift pot, some kind of sawed open half metal barrel, bubbled with boiling water. Jack tended a basket, pulling it out to check the contents, then dunking it in again, each time causing the water to run over, sending up a whoosh of steam. The gang (I counted eight friends plus Noah) was gathered around the fire, watching Jack's elaborate show. Each time he dunked the basket, they stepped backward for fear they'd singe eyebrows.

My throat started to tighten with the familiar anxiety. "What's for dinner?" I asked, trying to get myself prepared. I have this thing about mystery food.

"Wisconsin fish boil," Jack said. "Sans the fish, of course." He yanked the basket upward again, poked at a potato with a stick, and nodded with satisfaction.

He carried the basket to a picnic table that had been covered in newspaper and flipped it upside down. Potatoes, corn cobs, onions, and what looked like chunks of squash tumbled onto the surface. "Grub's up!"

Noah handed me a plate, then whistled. Everyone turned their attention to him. He pointed to me. "This is Brittany." He made a vague gesture and said, "The gang." I smiled. Some nodded, smiled. That was that. I was accepted. Either Noah was their indisputable leader or they were a pretty easy-going group.

I waited my turn to take a helping of the vegan fish boil, then as everyone settled into places around the fire, their plates balanced on their knees, bottles of Cerveza Imperial propped up in the sand, I tried my best to chitchat. Not my specialty. But I wanted to have a good sense of who these people were.

Claudia and her fiancé, Matt, guided rafting tours on the Grand Canyon in the summers and spent about three months a year in Costa Rica. "It's affordable and gorgeous. What more could a couple of river rats want?" Matt said.

Dan and Sierra guided kayakers in Alaska for four months, then helped run a zip-line tour here in the winter.

Doug was an actor/part-time bartender. "Between jobs," he grumbled.

Amanda and Colette were a lesbian couple who sold handcrafted jewelry in the summer art show circuit. Amanda did freelance computer work, so they would travel with an RV chock full of jewelry, then park it at her parents' place in Silver Springs, Florida to take two months off in Costa Rica every year.

Jack cleaned windows on skyscrapers in New York City and made enough cash to hang the rest of the year "surfin' the CR, livin' the pura vida."

"What's your story?" Jack asked, then promptly shoved an entire red potato into his mouth.

"I'm kinda between semesters," I said. "Trying to find my way, you know."

This brought a lot of sympathetic nodding around the fire.

From the darkness, a monkey came scampering across the sand, leaped onto the table, grabbed a potato, and ran off, chittering with glee, the potato tucked under his arm like he'd been trained by the Green Bay Packers offensive coach.

"Clyde!" someone yelled.

"Hey Isabella," Noah called. Coming up the path was the waitress from the palapa bar. *Crap.* What was she doing here? What was their connection?

"Hola de nuevo," she said and went right for a plate. Clyde followed on her heels. She plopped down, cross-legged in the sand next to the fire and stabbed an onion with her fork. Clyde cowered behind her. Apparently he wasn't fond of fire.

"C'mon." Sierra slapped her thighs and Clyde leaped into her lap. She stroked his head and he cuddled against her.

Isabella swallowed her onion and looked at Claudia. "Did you get anything?"

Claudia glanced at me and shook her head.

Isabella looked at me and in a moment, recognition showed in her eyes. I had a choice. Claim a coincidence and hope they weren't too skeptical, or hit the thing head on, making them believe I'm one of them. Easy enough, but I had to have an explanation for being at the shed. A good one. Now.

"You must be wondering why I'm here. Hell, I'm wondering why I am here." I turned to Noah. "I wasn't birding today." I clenched my teeth together in a please-don't-be-mad-at me grin. "I was snooping. I think something illegal is going on up at that coffee shed." I turned to Isabella. "And I think your boss has something to do with it."

Next to me, Noah set down his fork. "What do you mean?"

"Well, I *was* out birding, a few weeks ago, and I saw these men. They had a bunch of animals in cages. Not chickens, but monkeys and other birds." I shook my head. "That's not right. So, I know it was a fool-hardy thing to do but—" I shrugged "—I found out who owns the property and that he also owns The Toucan. I'm not sure what I thought I was going to do when I found out the truth. I just couldn't stand to see animals being hurt like that, you know." I leaned forward and raised my eyebrows to show how scared I'd been. "I wasn't expecting to get shot at!"

It was subtle, but I could see nods around the group. They were accepting me. Noah finally said, "You're right. Something is going on. Those men are poachers. The worse kind. They capture live animals, snatch 'em right out of the forest, enslave 'em and sell 'em like plastic toys."

"No way," I said. "I knew it. That's awful." *Interesting.*

"It's big money. Right under our eyes, wildlife is being plundered and sold on the black market."

"How do you know all this? You said you aren't cops."

"No. We actually make a difference."

"So you're like some animal justice vigilantes?"

He laughed. "Yeah, something like that."

I smiled at him with eyes that said, *that's sexy,* which it was. "Cool."

That was it. I was part of the gang.

Isabella turned back to Claudia. "So how'd it go?"

"We're going to need a better camera. It's just too dark in there." She frowned at Noah. "I'm sorry. You did a great job distracting them. I had plenty of time."

So that's what they'd been up to. In the U.S., it's not uncommon for activists to try to expose cruelty and wrongdoing via videotaping. PETA has been quite successful with that approach, bringing some lawsuits or government action against the perpetrators. But in those instances, animals were being held legally. The video tapes revealed cruelty and abuse. Carlos's activity was obviously illegal, so I wondered what exactly this group was planning and what they thought they'd accomplish.

I nibbled on my cob of corn, trying to act interested, but not too much in the details.

"We'll get the footage," said Noah. "We just need to be patient."

"We should storm the place, set 'em all free, and burn it to the ground," said Matt, the river guide.

"Yea-ah!" said Jack. "Bring it on, baby!"

Colette shook her head. "It's a holocaust that's never going to stop."

"They sell a product like any other business," said Noah. "It's all about the money. We hit 'em in the pocketbook and they'll take notice."

"Yeah, but how do we do that?" Amanda put her arm around her girlfriend. "Meanwhile, innocent lives are at stake."

"I know. I know," Noah said. "We've talked about this. To beat them, we have to think like them. Find their weakness. Wildlife trafficking is big business, but it's got to be volatile."

Claudia piped up. "You mean supply and demand. But every time we set some animals free, they just go back into the forest and trap more. Demand is the problem."

They nodded in shared frustration. Claudia frowned. Amanda hugged Colette tighter. Jack and Matt took chugs of their beers. I feared the conversation was fizzling. "So why the video?" I asked.

"Sun Tzu," Noah said with a grin. "Know thy enemy."

"So you're surveilling the buncher, trying to find a way to

destroy his business, that it?" I said.

Noah looked at me and smiled. "That's the plan."

"But what might you learn from the video?"

"Schedules. When they have inventory of what. To sustain a business with live inventory, they must be hedging somehow, probably selling futures, but that involves its own kind of risk. If they can't deliver, they'll lose their clients."

Interesting approach. I wanted to ask more about it, but it didn't feel quite right to push any more than I already had right now. One thing was sure, Noah wasn't a typical activist. He had significant intel and would be a valuable asset. There was more to him than I had first thought.

"We could use someone like you on the team," he said with a wink as he rose to his feet and brushed sand from his shorts. "Hey, throw me another beer," he said to Doug, the actor, who was at the table getting seconds.

Sierra spoke up. "As long as you agree, wildlife belongs in the wild."

I secretly thanked her. She had given me another opening to drive home that I'm one of them. "You say that, but what about Clyde?"

Isabella answered. "He can no go back now. He never survive."

"But isn't he your pet?"

"No me." She seemed insulted. "Carlos. He don care nothing bout him. I take care him."

"Oh, sorry. I didn't mean anything."

"You should meet him." She gave Clyde a hand command and he leaped off Sierra's lap and scampered over to me. "Go ahead, pick him up."

I reached down and picked him up like a toddler. He snuggled into my lap. I couldn't help myself. He was adorable. I scratched his ears and, he snuggled closer. Cute little bugger.

Noah grinned at me. "Clyde's kinda our mascot. He's one of the gang." He chuckled. "He's even helped with the cause."

Balled up napkins started flying Noah's way. One walloped him on the side of the head.

"What's this about?" I asked.

Noah pointed at Jack. "See, Jack had this brilliant idea—"

"Hey, it was brilliant. It worked."

"Right," he said through a chuckle. "He rigged up Clyde with a GoPro camera, strapped it right to his chest."

"Monkey-cam!" roared Jack.

"Hear, hear," shouted Doug, raising his beer.

"Hear, hear," everyone responded and tipped their bottles.

"We were up there at dawn. Clyde was all fired up. We'd been working with him on drills, commands, you name it."

Clyde stirred in my lap. He knew they were talking about him. He buried his head under his arms.

"Hey, you're embarrassing him," said Dan.

Noah continued. "They only had one guard at the time. He was sound asleep. We sent Clyde in."

"So, what, Clyde was supposed to walk through the barn with the camera running?" I asked.

"That was the plan." Noah threw his head back and roared with laughter.

Jack plopped down in the sand, resigned. "The little shit. He ran straight to the first cage with a female, flipped the latch, and went at her like a dog in heat."

"Yeah, chicka-baum-baum," said Doug, grinding his hips. "Making his own monkey porno." He put out his hand, palm up. "Gimme five."

Clyde pounced from my lap, climbed up Doug's leg, and slapped him on the hand.

"Sure, you've got that mastered," Jack said.

Matt nudged Jack. "Hey, a guy's got his needs, man."

Claudia elbowed him in the gut. "Exactly. We should have sent a girl monkey."

"Hear, hear," said Colette, raising her bottle of beer.

"Hear, hear," chanted everyone.

More beers were passed around. Claudia got up and headed for the tree house.

I told Noah I needed to use the bathroom and followed her. A little girl talk was in order.

When she came out of the bathroom, I plowed forward, head on. "I really like Noah." I managed a blush. It was true. "What's his story, anyway?"

"We all love him. Great guy, but—" Claudia shrugged "—he's a bit of a mystery. Trust funder maybe." She grinned. "He's single though. But one thing I know for sure, you'll need a bull whip and a prod to tame that boy."

When I got back down to the fire, Noah had a guitar balanced on his knee and he was entertaining the group with a Woody Guthrie tune. A joint was passed around. I faked a drag. Noah covered Bob Dylan, Joni Mitchell, and even some John Denver while the others lazily sang along.

Soon, couples started retreating into the darkness and Noah and I were left alone at the fire.

"I like your friends," I said. *If only the circumstances were different.* "I feel comfortable here."

"Yeah, they're a good bunch."

"How'd you meet them?"

"Oh, you know. We share interests."

I wanted to know more about them, about him, about the smugglers, but I couldn't figure out a way to ask right now without being obvious. I stared into the smoldering coals.

"You're welcome to stay," he said. "I promise to keep my hands to myself."

"Now, why would I want you to do that?" I crawled toward him across the sand and hit him with a kiss that made his toes curl.

"Mmm, exactly," he moaned.

I pulled back. "But I really have to go." My mom always said, leave 'em wanting.

I caught a taxi, found my moped where I'd left it, and hurried back to the resort.

I didn't want to wake Dalton, so I slid the door open and quietly stepped into the dark. A flashlight beam blasted me in the face. My hand flew up to cover my eyes. "What the hell?"

"What the hell is right? Where have you been?"

"Following a lead."

"A lead? A lead!" Dalton flicked on the lamp and stood with his arms crossed. "What did I tell you?"

"Didn't you get my text? I did what you told me. I went to the butterfly gardens. Absolutely amazing what they're doing over there, by the way. You should stop in. They have an insectarium and four gardens, each dedicated to—"

"What's your point?"

"A guy who works there knows about the smuggling operation and—"

"What? Seriouisly, Poppy. It just happened to come up in conversation?" He nodded, mocking me.

"Well, yeah, one thing led to another, and the next thing you know, I'm invited to a bonfire with him and his friends. I found out that—"

He held up his right hand for me to stop and rubbed his forehead with his left. "I don't want to hear it."

"But—"

"I don't care what some civilian renegades think they might know."

"But they've seen things. They have evi—"

The hand went back up in my face. "I have been here for nine months. Nine months working this case." His eyes crinkled with worry and frustration. "Do you have no respect for what I've worked so hard to build here?"

"Of course I do. But you weren't there."

He turned away from me and lowered himself into the chair. "Stay away from them."

"Listen to me," I said. "The information they have, I know

it's valid."

"Oh, and how do you know?"

I hesitated. I couldn't tell him I'd been there. "I just do. I trust them—"

"Are you listening to yourself?" He got back up from the chair and got in my face. "Trust them? They're civilians. There's a reason we don't include civilians in our operations." His eyes were on fire. "You're going to blow everything."

"That's not fair. Just because you don't know me yet—"

"Don't you understand? This isn't a game, little *Poppy*."

I crossed my arms. "How dare you?"

"You're gonna get us killed." He threw up his hands and plopped back down into the chair.

"You don't trust me."

His eyes snapped to me. "Damn right I don't trust you! I don't know you. As far as I can see so far, you're a serious liability." He lay back in the chair. "I don't care if Joe likes you. One more stunt like that and I'll send you packing."

"Yes, sir," I said and turned on my heel and headed for the bathroom. I brushed my teeth, taking my frustration out on my gums, and when I came back out, Dalton was stretched across the bed. The blanket was piled on the chair.

CHAPTER 8

Dalton tried to slink out without a word.

"Wait, where are you going?"

"I'm going for coffee."

"Aren't you going to have breakfast with me?" I asked. Maybe I could get him to listen to me this morning. "We don't want them to think we're fighting."

"Why not? We are fighting. Spouses fight."

"Fine."

"Fine."

As soon as he shut the door, I threw the pillow across the room. *Dammit!* I had risked getting caught, ruining my career, blowing this op, everything, to get that information, and all for nothing. He wasn't going to listen to me. I stomped around the room, threw a few more pillows and kicked the bed before I slumped into the chair. *Dammit!*

A few minutes later he was back with two cups of coffee. He handed me one. "Get ready. I want to stroll around the shopping district, look like tourists," he said. "I could use a new pair of sunglasses anyway."

Shopping? Really? What would we learn there? I had to admit, though, it did seem the logical thing that John and Brittany would do. I grabbed my hideous handbag and we headed for town.

The old-town shopping district was a hodgepodge of tiny

stalls where local craftsmen hocked their handcrafted wares. I preferred it over the glitz of shoe, handbag, and perfume counters. This was a group of real people with real lives, trying to make a living for their real families. Not some faceless corporation from a foreign land.

Brightly colored sarongs and dresses livened the spaces with reds, yellows, and greens. There were hand tied hammocks and straw hats, wood bowls, cutting boards, trinket boxes, and hair pins made from exotic native woods.

We wandered through, looking for nothing in particular, Dalton holding my hand. It was hard to stay mad at him while he was holding my hand. I bet some marriage counselor had figured that out.

As I came around a corner, I spotted Yipes in the crowd. I spun around, wrapped my arms around Dalton's neck, and gave him a big kiss. "We have a tail," I whispered.

"Ah, you noticed," he said with a grin, his eyes on me.

"It's Yipes, the guy from our bungalow."

"Yeah, he's been—" He drew back and looked at me with a baffled expression. "Yipes?"

I started to open my mouth.

"Forget it," he said. "I don't need to know." He ran his fingers through my hair and pulled me toward him for another kiss. Dammit. Why'd he have to be so yummy? Jerk. This Jekyll and Hyde thing was going to put me into a tailspin.

"We should split up. You keep shopping, keep him busy. I'll meet you back at the bungalow for dinner."

I nodded and watched him walk away.

I exited the other side of the shopping area into a fruit market. Boxes of ripe bananas, mangos, watermelons, and coconuts were stacked on plastic crates. I selected a banana and paid. An Afro-Caribbean beat pulsed through the streets. I wandered toward the performers, then stopped and looked around. Head slap. Dalton had ditched me.

Fine. Two could play that game. I would take advantage

of the time to get better prepared, make sure I was ready for anything. Mrs. Strix had hooked me up with some realistic girly items, but she'd never been an agent. I needed a hardware store.

Around the corner and down the street, I found what I needed. A Leatherman tool, matches, lighter, heavy-duty string, tiny mirror, mini-mag flashlight, and assorted other items. I thought about a hand-held recorder, but like a gun, if I got searched, it could get me killed.

Now that that was done, what to do? I started toward the butterfly gardens then stopped. I needed to be careful. Dalton had been right about one thing, I had been reckless. Noah set me on fire. I could get burned. But oh my god, that kiss. A warm sensation came over me thinking about it. What's wrong with working an informant? Male agents do it all the time.

I sat down on the curb. Dalton made me want to scream. Noah made me want to scream, but in a different way. My head was mush. I went back into the store, grabbed a pre-paid phone card, then found a pay phone around the corner and punched in the country code and the number. After three rings, he answered. "Yo."

"Chris, it's Poppy."

"Girl, what's going on?" Chris is the only guy who gets to call me girl. We've known each other since sixth grade in the Philippines. When we ran into each other again in high school, half way across the world, we figured we were destined to be friends for life. Now he's a flight attendant for Delta airlines and I see him every few months or so, depending on how many layovers he spends with his latest flame.

I hesitated. I shouldn't have been calling him while undercover.

"Wow, silence. Something must really be wrong. Talk to me."

"I'm all right. Just frustrated. I wanted to hear your voice is all."

"Honey, what have I been telling you? You've gotta get out of redneckville and get properly laid. Come with me next weekend. I'm on a five-day Shanghai right now, then I've got four off. We could pop down to the Caymans. Drink some margaritas, watch those tight-assed college boys play beach volleyball. What do you think?"

"I can't. I'm in—" *Crap.* "I can't get away right now." I sighed. "I've been reassigned."

"What do you mean, reassigned? Poppy-girl, that doesn't sound good?" He paused a beat. "What'd you do?"

"Nothing! I busted the Lawson boys. But this is…Listen, I can't tell you. I just wanted to say hey."

"Well, now you've got me worried."

"Well don't. I can handle the job. It's just—"

He drew in a quick breath. "Oh my holy-hell. It's a man."

I blushed. Only Chris could make me blush. "It's complicated."

"Oh my holy-hell, it's two men. I just talked to you last week. You were bellyaching about rednecks and lumberjacks and now you got a love triangle going on?" I heard the rustle of blankets and his hand over the phone. It was the middle of the night in Shanghai.

"I'm sorry. I didn't realize what time zone you were in."

"No, no, no. I picked up, didn't I? Now tell me everything. I want every juicy detail. Like what are you doing in Costa Rica?"

Crap. Double crap.

"You think I don't know the country code? It's on my caller ID. Hey, are you on the Pacific side? There's a great hotel with a swim up bar that—"

"No, some bungalow in the valley, Arenal Gardens or something, and—never mind, I can't talk about it." I glanced down the street, one way, then the other. A random pay phone wouldn't be tapped, but being on it might cause suspicion. "You know, sometimes my work, I can't talk."

"Um, sweetheart, you called me."

"I know."

"This is much more than guy trouble, isn't it?"

"I'm sorry, love. I gotta go." I hung up. *Crap. What was I thinking?* He'd understand; I'd explain it all to him at Christmas. But that was a dumbass thing to do. I gritted my teeth. *That was a rookie move, McVie.* If I didn't watch my step, Dalton would boot me before I could stop my head from spinning. I needed to be more careful.

I circled back through the hardware store. I'd forgotten electrical tape. *Definitely not on my game. I need to step it up.*

I found a little cafe serving Costa Rican fare that had several vegetarian options. I sipped an iced tea and went over what had happened so far in my mind. Mr. Strix had told me to follow protocol, to listen to my SAC. But Dalton was so damn aggravating. My mother always accused me of having issues with authority. Damn, I hated when she was right.

After I finished my meal, I decided to take a walk, look for birds, at least I could add a few to my life list while I was here, when my phone rang. It was Dalton. "Where are you?"

"Why, I'm shopping, darling. Where else would I be?"

"Get back to the bungalow. I got the call."

Hot damn! Lights, camera, action. I'm going to pick a monkey.

The call came as an email. Anonymously, of course. We were to be ready at the bungalow for a white panel van to pick us up at seven o'clock.

"Are you ready for this?" Dalton asked.

"Bring it on. Let's do this thing."

"You understand, the van is so we can't see where we're going. They'll want us disoriented. And we'll likely be in an isolated location. We're on our own. It could get ugly."

"I can handle it."

He paced.

I said, "Somehow I don't think a Navy SEAL would get so nervous about a simple covert action."

He glared at me. "I don't like wild cards."

I shrugged. "I'm your loving wife, wanting a pet monkey. Nothing more. Nothing less. It's simple."

He grimaced. "Why do I get the feeling nothing's simple with you."

Seven o'clock rolled around. No van. At seven-twenty-two, a white, solid sided panel van rolled into the parking lot. The back door opened and Dalton and I hopped in. One man drove while another man in the back motioned for us to sit on the floor and stay there. There was no confusion about it. The men were both native Costa Ricans, nothing particularly notable about them. They were delivery men. That was all.

We made a right out of the parking lot, drove about two miles, then made a left, then an immediate right, then we were in a roundabout. *Crap.* Or a parking lot, though driving in circles might bring unwanted attention. The van circled several times. Difficult to keep north from south, but I kept my head down. I was sure we straightened out again heading in the same direction we'd started—north.

After seven minutes of driving, two lefts and a right, we slowed and turned onto a gravel road or driveway. The van bumped and rocked over potholes for about two miles, then turned left again, this time immediately heading uphill, crawling along on what must have been the driveway. We were getting close and I had a pretty good idea where we were.

The van came to a stop. They made us wait inside for something, then the back doors creaked open and we got out.

It was dark, but there was no doubt—we were at the Mendoza family coffee plantation. I recognized the shed. *I was right. I knew it—oh crap!* I dropped my head and stared at the ground.

What if the guard I clobbered is here? What if he recognizes me?

A man approached from the shadows. "Bienvenida," he said. It was Carlos. I smiled and tried to act excited. "This way please." As soon as he turned, I scanned for others. If that guard was here tonight, I was screwed.

There was no breeze. Musty smells hung in the stagnant humid night air. As we approached the dark shed—Carlos, me, then Dalton—the animals started to stir and make noise. "So you have those cute monkeys with the white fur face, right?" I said, trying to sound like the snooty Texan wife I was there to play. "I don't want one with a black face, looking like he's dirty all the time." Carlos stepped inside the shed, flipped a switch, and the tired fluorescent bulbs flickered to life.

I stopped mid stride.

Cages were stacked wall to wall, the stink unbearable. Flies buzzed everywhere. The cages near the top were stuffed with birds—yellow-crowned parrots and keel-billed toucans. One toucan squawked and fluttered, banging its huge bill against the walls of the cage, feathers flying everywhere, its raw flesh exposed, ninety-percent of its feathers gone. A lump formed in the back of my throat.

Another cage was full of tiny chicks. Stolen right from their nest. I clenched my teeth together.

Below that were the monkeys. Some shook the doors to their cramped cages, their cries high-pitched shrieks. Others cowered in the corners. One pulled at its fur, patches of red skin exposed where it had yanked out handfuls. My stomach churned, bubbling up angry acid at the back of my throat. *Calm down. Take a breath.*

A three-toed sloth lay on top of one of the crates, hog-tied, his little arms pulled behind his back. My own voice screamed inside my head. *How can you be so cruel?*

One of Carlos's men took a stick and rapped on the cages, hollering for the monkeys to shut up. If one let out a shriek, he'd poke it through the bars, jabbing at the sorrowful creature.

For a moment, I lost all sense of orientation. I was sure I'd descended into the depths of hell. How could this be happening? Why? I reached for Dalton to steady myself.

Carlos was oblivious. He went straight to a cage which held a tiny white-faced capuchin, opened the door, and grabbed it by the scruff of the neck. "Like this one?" he said and held it up. It squirmed in his grip, its tiny, round eyes lit with terror. "This one's a female," he said. Her fur was matted and caked with grime. He held her out for me to take. The lump in my throat grew larger. I reached for the monkey and faltered. My throat started to constrict. *No, no, no. Poppy, keep it together.* I took the monkey in my hands and the poor thing shook with fear. "No, this one's no good," I managed to say.

Carlos shrugged, took the monkey from me, shoved her back in the cage, and slammed the door shut. He moved to another one, reached in and grabbed this one by the tail, dragging it out as it screamed. I couldn't breathe. No air. Not enough air. "He's a feisty one, but he already knows some tricks," he said and shoved the monkey at me. It grabbed hold of my hair and tried to climb over my shoulder. Dalton snatched it from me and handed it back. "Too active," he said. With his steady hand on my shoulder, I drew in a breath.

Carlos nodded. He went for a third one. "I've got just the right one for you," he said. He reached into a lower cage and tugged out a baby capuchin, still docile and trusting. He held it out for me to examine, its body cradled in one hand while he had ahold of it by the neck with the other, the way a sommelier would display a bottle of wine for the buyer to read the label. A baby girl. Her little arms flailed, her tiny, human-like hands reaching for something to grip.

By the grace of some patron saint of undercover agents, I managed a smile and took the baby monkey in my arms. She looked up at me with wide eyes, her little nose twitching. Her tail curled around my wrist. I thought of Clyde, how he had snuggled against me just last night, how he too had been taken from the wild, snatched from his mother, robbed of his beautiful, natural life. I swallowed, trying to be rid of the lump in my throat.

This baby monkey mewed, a high-pitched whistle, calling for its mother. A tingling sensation pressed behind my eyes. *Tears coming. No, no!* I blinked, trying to hold them back. Blood thrummed in my veins and my lip began to quiver. My breath started to expose me. I sucked in air and shook as it rumbled into my lungs. I turned to Dalton. "Oh, John," I managed before the dam broke open and tears streamed down my face in a warm, blinding flood. I snuffled and brayed and snot came out of my nose. "I'm so sorry about the baby," I cried. "If we hadn't lost the baby."

He put his arms around me. "It'll be all right, my darling," he said. "I'm sorry, guys. My wife, she's had a tough time of it." He rubbed my back. "I thought she was ready, but, you know."

"Yeah, whatever," said Carlos. He took the capuchin from me. "Let's go."

We were led right back to the van and it was over. My one job to do here and I failed miserably. I couldn't handle it. *All those animals... I leaned into Dalton and let him hold me all the way back to the bungalow.*

I went straight for the bathroom and slammed the door behind me. I leaned against the wall and slid to the floor and cried. For the animals. For the suffering in this world. For the fact that the smuggling will go on because I just screwed up. Dalton eased the door open and poked his head in.

"Go away," I said.

He sat down on the floor next to me and wrapped his arms around me. "It's all right," he whispered. "It'll be all right."

"I'm so sorry," I cried. "I screwed up big time. I blew

everything. I'm so sorry." My tears wet his shirt.

"Don't worry. I think they actually believed you. I think it'll be okay." He stroked my hair and I let loose and sobbed until I couldn't cry anymore.

"I just couldn't," I whimpered, my breath ragged as I tried to regain control. "I just couldn't—"

"I know," he soothed and rubbed my back. "I know."

"Oh my god, the horror. They were sitting in their own feces. The birds, their feathers ripped out."

"I know."

I sat back, rubbed my nose with the back of my hand, and faced him. "I was the top of my class. Hand to hand combat. I won the firearm medal. I aced the law exam, for chrissake. Why can't—" My eyes teared up again and the words caught in my throat. "Why can't I handle this?"

He didn't say anything. Not a dig, not an admonition, or even how to fix it. He just took me in his arms and held me some more.

"How do you do it?" I sniffled.

"You keep your mind focused on the big picture." His fingers twirled in my hair. "You play for the long game."

"But meanwhile, all those animals suffer."

He nodded. "We can't save them all."

"How can you stand it? We've gotta stop it. We've got to."

"We are." He patted my back. "Every moment we get closer."

"We've gotta go back." I jerked from his embrace. "We need to choose a monkey we can document, can identify, right? So when he smuggles it, we can bust him."

Dalton was shaking his head. "Listen to me. I told you before, we're not here to bust anyone. We're here to gather intel. Taking down someone so low on the totem pole will gain nothing."

"It'll gain something for those animals!" I huffed. "I memorized the route we took in the van. I can draw a map to that barn. We can stake it out."

"That's not our call to make. Do I need to remind you, we're not on U.S. soil? We're here under a special agreement. These are Costa Rican citizens. We have no authority for that."

"Then we call in the Fuerza Pública."

"It's not our mission."

"But we can't just ignore the, the horror of it."

"I know it's hard, but that's exactly what we do." He smiled at me, the smile of someone trying to make someone else's pain go away, then took me by the hand, pulling me to my feet, and led me out of the bathroom. We sat down on the edge of the bed. "We made a huge step forward tonight. This is the closest we've gotten." He rubbed a tear from my cheek with his thumb. "Smile. We did good."

"How can you say that?" I couldn't stand it. My teeth clenched involuntarily and I started to shake.

"Poppy, listen to me. If you want to work Special Ops, you have to accept the fact that this is what we do. It's not all about saving fuzzy bunnies. This is syndicated, organized crime. We slowly work our way in. We have to pass up the small players to go after the big fish. Sometimes it takes years."

I huffed. "Meanwhile, millions of animals suffer."

"Yes, millions of animals are suffering. But we can't save them overnight." He sighed. "You seem like a really passionate woman. With all respect, I'm not sure this kind of work is for you."

"Not for—" I held my breath. I wanted to scream, to gouge his eyes out, to set something on fire. "I've dedicated my life to this!"

Dalton held his hands up. "Whoa, hey."

"I could kick your ass."

He smirked. "No doubt."

"Now you're being an asshole!"

"I—" He threw up his hands. "I give up."

I crossed my arms and flopped back on the bed. The steam

fizzled from my head and I was spent. "All I've ever wanted to be, for as long as I can remember, is a wildlife cop."

He eased back onto the pillow beside me. Smiled. "Because you love animals so much."

I nodded. "My father—" I sniffled "—my father said I was born with a love for every creature on Earth." I closed my eyes. "He used to take me with him on photo shoots. He was a wildlife photographer."

"He sounds like a pretty cool dad."

I swallowed hard. I missed him so much. "He was."

Dalton said nothing.

"My mom was always gone, out to sea or somewhere. My dad homeschooled me. We lived wherever mom was stationed or in the forest near the animal he happened to be obsessed with."

"He did a fine job raising you."

In a faked stern voice I said, "Not a proper upbringing."

He grinned.

"I speak five languages. Learned them all from subtitles watching eighties reruns in whatever country we were in. My dad, he wanted me to be…" I held back the tears.

Dalton took my hand. "You're all that and more."

The damn tears started again. "People are so cruel."

"Listen, there's no shame in it." He cupped my face in his hands and made me look him in the eyes. "No shame in feeling what you're feeling." His eyes brightened and his lip turned up at the side. "It's beautiful, actually."

He pulled me toward him and I snuffled in his chest and cried some more.

I came awake slowly, with a warm, snuggly, safe feeling, like I was emerging from a cocoon. Too warm actually. I wasn't alone. I was cuddled against a man, my arm draped over his naked chest, my leg entwined with his leg. I sat up. *Crap!*

"Sorry, sorry," I babbled.

He smiled lazily and his eyes opened. "You're beautiful in the morning, you know that? With those rosy cheeks."

"Are you trying to make me feel better?"

His eyes turned lustful. "I'm trying to tell you that you're beautiful."

"Oh," I said. I didn't know what to do. "Thank you?"

He grinned. "You don't like compliments, do you?"

"I don't know. You could have mentioned my skill when I pinned you down with the thumb lock. Now that'd be a worthy compliment."

He shook his head. "You really are something." He rolled over and sat up on his side of the bed. He combed his fingers through his hair and rubbed his eyes. He was wearing boxers. I sneaked a look.

I went into the bathroom and stared at myself in the mirror. I was a mess. Dark circles under my eyes. My pupils ragged like a madman's. My red mop needed an overhaul with a professional pair of scissors. I grabbed handfuls of my hair. "Arrrgh! You need to get your head on straight," I said to my reflection.

I washed my face and ran a comb through my hair. Then I went back out and plopped on the bed next to Dalton. "I suppose you're going to send me home now."

"Actually, I was thinking, maybe this will be a good way for you to connect with Maria, you know, the lost baby thing."

"Now the wife?" I glared at him. "What is it with you?" *Damn, why am I being like this?*

He frowned. "Or yes, you can go home."

"I'm sorry," I said. "It's just that…well, just because I, last night I, you know, doesn't mean I'm not capable of helping with the real work here. I have skills. I'm as good as any man." I launched from the bed. "I bet you're one of those guys who thinks women shouldn't be in combat."

"Uh, yeah. Women shouldn't be in combat."

"I knew it. You think we aren't strong enough, aren't smart

enough. You think we can't handle it."

"I never said that."

"You got this macho frogman ego. Elitist military crap. You know what I've got? The element of surprise. No one suspects little 'ol me. I can sashay right in and bam, knock you on your ass. I can outshoot you any day. Line up some cans, buddy."

"You know what I'm picturing right now," he said. "Me with my hand on your head and you swinging in the air."

"You are such an asshole!"

"You're so cute when you get all riled up."

"Cute? I'm cute!"

"Yes, my lovely, beautiful, cute little bride." He smirked. "Get it? I know you don't like it, but you're the wife. That's your role here. Take it or leave it."

I clenched down on my teeth so hard I thought my molars might shatter. "Yes. Thank you," I said. I'd rather stick an icepick in my eye, but there it was. My directive—be a good wife. *Shoot me now!* "Maybe I can learn to play bridge and make a positively delicious soufflé."

"Now you're talking," he said. He shuffled around the room, looking for his phone. He called George and all I heard on this end was an occasional yeah or uh-huh. He hung up. "He wants me to play cards tonight. I'll be late. Take the time to get your head together. Go to the beach, go to a spa. Whatever."

Like hell. I had something else in mind.

CHAPTER 9

I stopped by the butterfly gardens. He wasn't there. I went straight to the tree house. Noah was stretched out in the hammock, playing his guitar, an old Johnny Cash tune. I called up. "May I come in?"

He glanced down at me and my insides went squishy. God, he was yummy. He flashed a grin and I steeled myself. No kissing this time. I took the stairs two at a time. He eyed me from the hammock, but didn't get up. "Wasn't sure if I'd see you again," he said, matter-of-fact.

"Yeah, about that. Sorry?"

"I'm glad you're here now," he said and leaned forward and set down his guitar. "You look like you've got something on your mind."

"Haven't been able to get it off my mind actually. What you were saying, about the wildlife poachers."

"Oh, you were listening. Your first mistake," he said with a grin. He wiggled his empty beer bottle at me. "What can I get you?"

"Um, I'm not really a beer for breakfast kinda gal."

"Wine then?"

"Ah, sure." One glass wouldn't hurt.

Noah slipped across the hanging bridge, which I now saw led to a kitchen. He came back with two stemmed glasses in one hand and a corkscrew and a bottle of red in the other. "I figure you for a red kinda gal. Am I right?"

I smiled. He was right. I did a quick double take. The bottle in his hand was a $150 vintage. "So what's your story?" I asked. "All I know about you is that you volunteer at the butterfly gardens and in your spare time you like to dodge bullets."

"Yeah, well, don't let the Superman costume fool you. That was a pretty foolish thing to do." He handed me a glass (poured one-third full, the way it should be done) and held his up to mine. By the stem. "Here's to a little foolishness," he said.

"Indeed," I said, my eyes meeting his as we clinked our glasses together. Oh, what the hell. I leaned into him for a kiss.

"Mmmm," he said. "I like this vintage." He kissed me again until I was breathless, then pulled away. "You know what I think?" he said.

I held my breath.

"You're trying to woo me with your sexy wiles."

I grinned. "Woo you? Seriously? Who says that?"

"My grandma." He shrugged. "Of course, she was bat shit crazy."

"So you got it from her?"

He raised his glass as if to salute her in thanks. "You got it, babe," he said and took a sip. "Every bat shit crazy chromosome."

"How crazy are you?" I asked.

His gaze turned heavy. "What'd you have in mind?"

"I want to set those animals free. Every one of them. I don't care about video tapes and ticking off the guards. Supply and demand be damned. I don't care about the law either. It's all bullshit anyway. I want those animals out of that barn and back in the wild where they belong."

"Okay," he said. "I like a woman who knows what she wants."

"I'm serious."

"I am, too." He poured more wine. "So what did you have in

mind? I can call the gang, get them over here."

"No," I said. The more people involved, the more risky it would be. "Just me and you. Tonight."

He raised his eyebrows. "I like the sound of that."

"So no more wine." I set my glass down.

His lips turned up into an exaggerated pout. "What about one more kiss?"

I drew in a breath. He had my kryptonite. He set down his glass and moved toward me, his eyes on my lips. My pulse leaped into overdrive. Why'd he have to be so hot? His kisses so, damn, wow—I tilted my head back and he nuzzled my neck. He looked up at me and my eyes flitted toward the bed. "We could always storm the shed tomorrow night," he whispered, his hand moving from my waist to my backside and down.

"No," I said, pulling away. "Tonight. They can't be in those cages one more night."

"All right, all right," he said. He took a step back and held up his hands in surrender. "Tonight it is."

Our plan was simple. Sneak in under the cover of darkness, deal with the guards, release the animals. We agreed—violence wasn't acceptable. Taking out the guards needed some finesse. Distraction? Perhaps. Deal with them one at a time, tying them up? Could get dicey.

"I have an idea," Noah said. He picked up his phone. "I need a favor," he said when his call was answered. "Where are you?" A moment later he disconnected and said to me, "I'll be back." And he was gone.

I reclined in the rattan chair with my glass of wine. Why let it go to waste, right? Especially a Chateau Montelena. I stared at the label. What twenty-something year old guy, who lives in a tree house in Costa Rica and volunteers at the butterfly garden, can casually serve a $150 bottle of wine? He hadn't given any other indication of trying to impress me with money.

If anything, he'd been doing the opposite. His friends were all down to Earth, good-hearted folks. No one was knocking down six figures back in the States. They'd all freely talked about their jobs. Except Noah.

My heart was all in, but my head, or more specifically my training, urged me to find out more.

I wandered down the rope bridge to the kitchen. It was a wooden platform surrounded by a half wall about eight feet above the ground. A propane cooktop, oven, and chopping block lined one side, a sink built into the home-made counter top on the other. Nothing unique or extraordinary. I continued down the stairs to the shed below. An open padlock hung from the door latch. I eased the door open and stepped inside to find a state-of-the-art refrigerator, the kind that's highly energy efficient, a critter-proof cabinet stocked with gourmet foods, and, built into the sandy ground like a bunker, a wine cellar that could grace the pages of *Wine Aficionado*. At least two-hundred bottles lined the walls.

I backed out of the shed and pushed the door back to the position in which I had found it. Back up the stairs, I poked around some more. Clothes, shoes, underwear. Boxer-briefs. I paused, imagining him in them. I shoved the drawer shut. Beside the bed, a tiny built-in door hung askew. It seemed out of place. I eased it open to find a solid door to a safe behind. I snapped the door back shut, making sure it hung in the same crooked angle and went back to my glass of wine.

He could be a trust-funder like Claudia had suggested. That would explain the modesty. But generally, in my experience, someone who spends that much on a bottle of wine does so because he feels he's earned it. It didn't fit.

Noah came bounding up the stairs with a tiny travel case in his hands. He popped it open to display the contents, a sneaky grin on his face. "What do you think?" Eight sedative injection darts were clipped into the case, each large enough for a big predator. "The dart gun's in the van."

"My god, that dose looks like enough to take down an elephant. That's crazy."

"Jaguars, actually. I like to think of it as poetic justice." He flashed that grin again and my heart skipped a beat.

It wasn't ideal, but it was a non-violent approach. "I guess we're all set then," I said. "Now we just have to wait for dark."

He reached for his guitar. "I take requests." A monkey zipped up the railing and into the hammock. "Hey Clyde," said Noah. He turned to me. "Watch out. He likes the vino."

I tipped my glass and downed the last sip. Clyde leaped to the railing, wrapped his tail around it, pulled the hammock up to him, then leaped on. As it swung back and forth, he chittered and peeped with glee. When the hammock slowed, he jumped up and got it swinging again.

"His favorite toy," said Noah.

I looked down the stairs. "Where's Isabella?"

"She lives in one of the houses here on the property. Clyde comes and goes." He went to the bathroom and came back with something in his hand. He tossed it into the air and Clyde caught it with the skill of a miniature wide receiver. "It's a monkey biscuit. They're like Flintstones for monkeys. He loves 'em. I have to keep them in there, though, because it's the only place he can't get. He can't work the round door handle with only one good hand."

"Sounds like he can be a little stinker."

"That's putting it mildly."

Clyde held the biscuit in a tight grip, his one nimble little hand against the tiny stump of his right, as he gnawed away, crumbs cascading to the floor. His eyes flitted about, looking for other monkeys I assumed. Crunch, crunch, crunch and it was gone. He bounced up and down, flailing his little arms and chittering.

"Clean up your crumbs," Noah told him. "He wants another one." He pointed at the pile of crumbs on the floor. "Clean 'em up."

Clyde chittered away, whining like a toddler.

"Not until you clean up that mess," Noah said, shaking his head.

Clyde slunk to the floor, swept up the crumbs with his hand, licked them off his fingers, then sprang back up to the edge of the hammock and squealed for another biscuit.

"All right, one more," Noah said and went to the bathroom. Clyde spun around, jumping up and down with excitement. Noah lobbed the biscuit into the air and Clyde scrambled up the hammock line, up the support post, grabbed a ceiling truss, and flung himself into the air, catching the biscuit in mid air before he landed on the coffee table.

"He's too cute," I said. After he finished his second biscuit, he crawled onto my lap and curled up into a ball. "Wow, I can't get over how he's a completely different monkey than the one I met at the bar."

"Yeah, drunk people can be unpredictable and cruel. He knows he's safe here."

I gently petted him and he cooed.

"He's been a good bar monkey, though. He's never bit anyone."

I held him in my arms, enjoying him cuddling with me, and thought of the newlyweds at the bar. How was I any different? It was a cruel catch twenty-two. People who love animals are the ones who drive the industry. They simply don't understand that for their two minutes of enjoyment with the animal, that animal endures a lifetime of subjugation and, often, cruelty. The brutal truth is that breaking a wild animal's spirit to a point that it will accept interaction with people usually means beating them, or worse. It's not the natural way of things.

I rubbed Clyde under his muzzle. "I'm so sorry, little buddy," I whispered. I thought of the monkeys I'd met last night and my pulse quickened. I shook my head. "I won't let it happen to them," I said to Clyde. "Your cousins are going to be free."

I turned to Noah, my mind back on the plan and getting

prepared. Yesterday, when I was at the shed, I'd been too focused on my purpose—to choose the monkey. But now, as I recalled the scene and the layout of the shed, I remembered that besides the stacks of cages, there were two large iron contraptions in the shed. They looked like rusty old exploding mines from World War One. "What can you tell me about the layout of the shed? Have you ever been inside?" I asked. "I'd like to know what's there."

"We've only made the attempt a few times. We have Claudia's video. And Clyde's. Both are not very good footage."

"Can I see them anyway?"

"Sure," he said. He opened the safe in the wall and pulled out a laptop. (So that's what was in there.) He fired it up and found the videos right away. They were too dark, difficult to see the animals at all, but the contraptions were visible. "Pause right there," I said. "What are those?"

"Old ball coffee roasters. The huge iron ball is filled with coffee beans and slowly turned over a hot fire, to roast them evenly, kinda like a rotisserie popcorn popper. See the crank and the turning wheel? Underneath here"—he pointed—"is where they'd build the fire."

"Looks like a giant version of the little buddy burner I made with my dad when I was a girl."

Noah got a silly grin on his face. "You were a Girl Scout?"

I ignored him. "Is this some kind of heat shield then?" The second one must have been the same roaster with the shield closed. It looked like a giant oil drum with the turning wheel sticking out the side.

"Yeah. The heat shield surrounds the whole thing like an exoskeleton."

My turn to grin. "You're really a bug guy at heart, aren't you?"

He raised his hands in mock surrender. "Guilty."

We left the van in the same pull off, which meant we had a two-hour hike up the side of the mountain. Noah carried a GPS unit but seemed to know exactly where he was going. I followed, carrying the dart gun. I wasn't sure if he'd ever shot anything before, so I convinced him to let me do the shooting.

The jungle was alive with the incessant chitter of countless insects mixed with the occasional low-pitched thrum of nocturnal creatures bounding through the canopy. "Costa Rica is home to more than 500,000 species of critters, about 300,000 of which are insects," said Noah. "894 birds, around 175 amphibians, approximately 225 reptiles, and nearly 250 mammals, including the elusive jaguar—a nocturnal hunter."

"Yeah, I'd like to avoid each and every one of them," I said. "Especially the snakes." The key was watching our step and making our presence known. Unfortunately, this conflicted with our goal of a surprise attack.

As we approached the compound, we moved silently and cautiously. Then Noah motioned for me to halt. "There's usually a guard at that corner," he said. "Something's up."

An important rule of the tactical ambush is to know your enemy's movement and positions. An unaccounted-for guard is a serious problem. He could be in the latrine, changing shifts, or standing behind you with a gun aimed at your head. "Let's check the other positions, then circle back," I said.

We moved single file through the jungle, avoiding the bell alarms. Of the usual five guards, we could see only two who paced at the entrance looking bored. "Maybe they're taking the night off," Noah said.

I shook my head. "I don't like it."

"What do you want to do?"

Maybe they only kept two guards at night. That didn't seem out of the realm of possibility.

"I say we go for it," he said. "We're here now. And all those animals are in there."

I moved to get a better look. One guard was tipping a bottle to his mouth, then handed it to the other. Perfect. You don't share your Coca-Cola. Moonshine plus a jaguar-size dose of sedative ought to do the trick for sure.

"At least they're standing near each other," Noah said. "You can hit them one right after the other."

I waited until both were turned and facing the other way, then raised the dart gun, aimed and fired. The first guard reached for his butt cheek and started to crumple. I reloaded and fired again. The second guard slowly slumped forward.

We waited in the shadows for a full five minutes, watching for another guard to come along. I told Noah to wait where he was and circled the entire shed one more time to be sure no one else lurked about, then we crept out into the open, toward the men.

While Noah plucked the darts from their butts, I checked their pulses. Snoozing like babies. We propped them up beside each other with the bottle in the one man's hand. Not the first time a bad jag on moonshine made for a foggy memory.

The shed was dark, normally a sign that no one was inside, but we needed to be extra cautious. With the dart gun reloaded and at the ready (the only weapon we had), we slipped inside the door. Noah reached for the switch, gave it a flip, and the tubes flickered to life.

I stared in disbelief. The shed was empty. Every animal. Every cage. Gone.

I spun around and shined my flashlight on the ground outside the door. Fresh tire tracks in the dirt. "Dammit! A shipment must have gone out today."

"No wonder there were only two guards."

I turned back around and more slowly scanned the shed, my brain not fully accepting the situation. It was empty save for two folding chairs, a large workbench along the wall, and in the back corner, the two large coffee roasters.

"We need to get out of here. Now," I said.

"Wait," Noah said. "Check this out."

Strewn across the top of the counter where he stood were

tiny pieces of rubber or plastic. I picked one up and twirled it between my fingers. A burst balloon maybe or a condom. One side was coated in a white powder.

Crap. This complicates everything.

Then we heard a sound outside. Noah and I looked at each other. It was the sound of hoofbeats.

We were standing in the center of an empty shed, with the lights on. Sitting ducks. I glanced at the coffee roasters. It was our only option. I gestured for Noah to follow.

"¿Qué es esto?" *What is this?* A woman's voice outside. "Levántense, hombres perezosos." *Get up you lazy men.*

Hiding behind the roaster wouldn't provide enough cover; a simple walk around and we'd be caught. We gently opened the heat shield on the roaster furthest from the door, squeezed inside, and as we pulled the shield shut the hinge creaked, the rubbing of rusty iron on iron. My heart pounded in my chest.

Footsteps crossed the concrete floor. Then the clickety, clickety, click of tiny dog feet. "¿Qué puñetas está pasando?" *What the hell is going on?*

Maria? What was she doing up here?

The dogs came straight to the roaster and yipped. I looked at Noah. *We're screwed.*

"Ya basta!" she hollered. *Knock it off!* The dogs retreated. The footsteps circled, then paced back. "Dammit!" Then the beeps of a cell phone being dialed. "¿Qué te he dicho sobre el tráfico de drogas?" *What have I told you about running drugs?* A pause. "Dammit!" The beeps of her dialing again. "Es un pecado, Carlos. Un pecado contra Dios!" *It's a sin, Carlos. A sin against God!* There was a long pause. "Tú no vas a poner en peligro mi operación de nuevo." *You will not jeopardize my operation again.* "¿Me entiendes, hermano?"

Hermano. Brother. Carlos was Maria's brother. But she said *my* operation. *Holy crap! Maria is the kingpin.*

The lights switched off and Noah and I were trapped in the roaster in the pitch dark.

CHAPTER 10

I waited a full two minutes before I whispered in his ear, "We have to get out of here before the guards wake up."

At least Maria had switched off the lights and we had the cover of darkness. We eased the heat shield back, slipped from the roaster, and tiptoed to the door. The guards were still out cold. I took one step and saw the horse, tied to a post. She was still here. But where? I backed up and stepped on Noah's foot. He stumbled backward but caught me and we regained our balance. I sidestepped away from the door, dragging him with me. "The horse," I whispered.

"Where could she be?"

I shook my head. There wasn't much here save for the shed. Then I remembered. The basket on the cable. I leaned out and peered into the darkness. I caught sight of a light beam among the foliage. "She's gone up the path," I whispered. "There's an old cable car up there."

"Yeah," Noah said. "To the outhouse. Could we be so lucky?"

"Let's get the hell out of here while we can."

"I agree," he said and darted across the yard into the jungle. I was right on his heels.

I needed to think, to regroup. I made excuses and left Noah as quickly as I could.

When I got to the bungalow, Dalton wasn't back from the card game yet.

I sat down in the chair and tried to settle my mind. Deep breaths. Ommmmmm.

I jumped up from the chair. That wasn't going to work. Okay. I paced.

All right. Maria's the kingpin. She's running the show. Not George. Why would she ride her horse all the way up to the shed at 11:30 at night? In the pitch dark? She would have known the shed was empty. Wouldn't she? Was she checking on Carlos? Maybe she had suspected the drugs and wanted to catch him?

That explains why George had all the buyers to dinner at the house. *So she could approve us without anyone realizing.* It made perfect sense.

How was I going to prove it? I needed to catch her red-handed. But doing what exactly? Dalton had made it very clear he wasn't interested in catching her offering a sale. He wanted confirmation she was the kingpin. That was it. How would I get that? She'd kept her identity hidden well.

The only thing I knew for sure: I couldn't tell Dalton any of this. He couldn't know I'd sneaked up there to that shed. He'd kill me. That also meant I couldn't get his help. I was going to have to figure it out on my own.

I'd play the wife. Make Dalton happy. See what I could find out. Maybe I could press for the horseback riding, or stop by to visit with no excuse. Women do that all the time, don't they? But Maria wasn't the type to tolerate a mousy wife coming around wanting to chitchat. I wouldn't get many chances.

And I didn't have much time. I would have to force her to come to me, to show her hand somehow. But how?

She certainly was arrogant, sure of herself. Maybe I could use that to my advantage. She was smart, that was sure. She'd come up with a pretty good arrangement to keep herself hidden. She'd been right under Nash and Dalton's noses. I needed some way to lure her out, to force her to expose herself. But what? How?

I went into the bathroom and looked in the mirror. "You can do this. You can do anything you set your mind to."

Then it wasn't my voice I was hearing, but my dad's. I was holding a salamander in my five-year-old hands, a smile spread across my face. I raised it proudly, showing off my new pet. *Oh Poppy,* he said. *Sweetheart, you can't keep him. He needs to stay in the wild.* But Daddy, I pleaded, already knowing he wouldn't be swayed. I've made a home for him. Look. I pointed to the shoebox with the mound of sand, the pile of leaves, the butter dish of water. He'll be happy with me. *C'mere,* he said and patted the top of his thighs. I sat down on his lap. He poked at my chest. *You've got a big, beautiful, loving heart. Right now, that's what you're thinking with. And that's okay. That's how we love. But taking care of Mr. Salamander here takes a lot more than love. You need to use your head, too. You see, he's not meant to live in a box. He needs the entire eco-system to survive. He can't survive without it, and it can't live without him. Do you understand?* My dad took me by the hand and we walked together, back to the muddy bank where I'd found the salamander and I set it down and watched it slink behind a moss-covered log, tears spilling down my cheeks. *Oh, don't be sad, Sweetheart,* my daddy said. *You just made him the happiest salamander alive. He's safe now, at home, with his family.* But I can't live without him, Daddy. *You can,* he said. *You can do anything you set your mind to.*

"You can do this," I said again to the face in the mirror. This was my way into Special Ops. I had to make it happen. "Find a way."

But no matter how I did it, Dalton wasn't going to like it. I crossed my arms. So be it. Sometimes it's easier to beg forgiveness than to ask permission.

"Tomorrow, Maria, I'm going to take you down."

"I'm taking the day off to spend with my visiting wife," Dalton said before taking a gulp of his orange juice.

"What? No. You were right." *Why is this happening now?* "I need to get over there and make friends with Maria. I shouldn't waste any time."

"Tomorrow," he said. "My wife came all the way down here from Texas. I need to spend time with her."

"Seems like a waste of precious time you could be spending with George. What if you miss something important?"

"It's more important to be true to our cover. We are going to the beach together, snorkeling, surfing, whatever you want to do." He picked up his fork. "And the best part—" he raised his eyebrows "—is I get to see you in a bikini."

I frowned. Men. *Dammit!* I had plans to make, things to do. I had to figure this out. And I was stuck with Dalton, sitting by the pool like a couple of tourists.

I watched the colorful finches and tanagers flit to and fro, devouring the fruit that had been set out on a platform feeder as I finished my yogurt trying to figure out how to thwart his plan.

"Relax," said Dalton, a greasy chicken thigh in his fingers. "Most of the time this job demands our all. We don't get to choose. Every minute of our day we're on, you know what I mean. Let's go have some fun. It's what John and Brittany are supposed to be doing today. Might as well enjoy it."

I nodded, trying to appear agreeable.

I got up to refill my coffee and stopped dead.

"There you are!" My friend Chris was coming across the patio, his arms wide. *Oh crap!* "Girl, you are hard to track down." He wrapped his arms around me.

I hugged him back and put my lips to his ear. "Call me Brittany," was all I could get out before I had to break from the embrace without causing attention. I wasn't sure if he heard me. I smiled. "What a surprise." I gestured toward Dalton. "Chris, this is my husband, John." Chris's eyes grew large. He looked at Dalton, up and down, then back to me, his mouth hanging open.

"So you ran off and got hitched, huh? Lordy, girl, I never would've thunk it. Well, that explains you being my bestie *in absentia*."

I glanced at Dalton. He looked so mad I thought his hair might catch on fire. He smiled through clenched teeth as he rose and reached out to shake Chris's hand. I glanced around the patio and saw Yipes. He seemed to just notice us. "Listen," I said to Chris. "This isn't a good time."

"What? I just got here." He grabbed the back of a chair and pulled it out to sit down.

Dalton growled, "I'll be in the bungalow. You've got two minutes," then lumbered away.

"What a grumpy, grump," Chris said. "I mean, I know I surprised you but—"

"Chris, listen to me—"

"Married? How could you not tell me?" He turned to me and I thought I had his attention, but he kept on. "No wonder you were in a tizzy." He held up his hands. "I get it. You wanted to tell me in person. Geez, and I thought my news was spectacular." He ran his hand down his silk shirt. "I got a raise. Check out my new duds. Genuine—"

"Chris, shut the hell up and listen to me."

He jerked back like he'd been slapped. "All right, already."

I leaned in close. "I'm undercover and you're going to screw it up. Do you understand?"

"No kidding?" He glanced around. "Are we being watched right now?"

"I need you to go. Now."

"Okay, okay," he said, smiling a fake smile and nervously brushing imaginary lint from his silk shirt.

"Are you staying at that place you mentioned, the one with the swim up bar?"

"Yeah, Coco-Cabana." He pursed his lips. "So you aren't married?"

"I'll call you there when I can, okay?"

"Yeah, sure. Of course you're not. Sorry, man. I didn't know." He shrugged. "I was worried about you."

"I'm sorry. This was my fault." I gave him a reassuring smile. "I like the shirt. But the chain and the white fedora," I cringed. "Too much. You look like a drug dealer."

He tugged at his collar, making sure it laid the way he wanted. "Yeah, well, that's the look I was going for." He turned on his heel and shuffled off.

As I stepped into the room, Dalton was hanging up the phone. "Pack your bag," he said with an unsettling calm.

"Dalton, I didn't—"

"Doesn't matter."

"But I—"

"It doesn't matter."

I stared at him. He wasn't going to budge. "How are you—"

"Your mother's sick. Needs you right away. I got you a seat on a plane this afternoon." He crossed his arms. "You'd better hurry to the airport."

I nodded. "Yes, sir." *Argh!*

I picked up the phone and dialed the cab company. "They'll be here in fifteen minutes," I said. "Will you please return the moped then?" I went to the bathroom and got my toiletries bag. Everything else was already in my suitcase. I sat down on the edge of the bed and sighed. All my dreams, devastated by one weak moment, one phone call to a friend. *Dammit!* At least I figured out who the kingpin was. At least I'd done that much. I glowered at Dalton. "It's Maria."

"What are you talking about?" he said.

"Maria. She's the kingpin."

He looked at me with skeptical eyes. "How do you know this?"

"The palapa bar, The Toucan. The one in the postcard. I found out Carlos Mendoza is the owner, he—"

"You went to the bar?" He threw up his hands. "Dammit, Poppy."

"His family owns the land that abuts George's property. It was him at the shed. "

"Yeah, so?"

"Maria and Carlos are brother and sister."

He stared at me. I could tell he was turning it over in his mind. "It's a connection to George. Doesn't mean she's involved."

How could I make him believe me? "But it all makes sense. You know George isn't—"

"Okay, enough. I've heard enough."

"It's her, Dalton. We gotta stop her."

"*We* aren't doing anything." He got up and grabbed my suitcase. "You're getting on a plane."

"But I—"

He flung open the door and shoved the suitcase at me. "Just go." He hustled me out and slammed the door behind me. The air left my body. So that was it. It was over. I slinked to a nearby bench and sat down to wait for the taxi. I wanted to storm back inside, tell him everything, tell him how I knew, but he probably wouldn't believe me anyway. I had no proof.

When the taxi pulled into the drive, I slid into the back seat, hugging my damn over-sized purse against me. "Aeropuerto, por favor," I said and slammed my head back.

The driver put the cab in gear, drove out of the drive and on to the main road and I felt everything slip away. All because, in a moment of frustration, I had needed a friend. *Dammit!*

The taxi moved along in traffic, then suddenly the driver jerked the vehicle to the side of the road.

I sat upright. "¿Qué pasa?" I asked.

"Meep, meep, meep!" Came the silly horn of a moped behind us. Why on earth would he pull over for a moped? I spun around in my seat.

Dalton was knocking on the side window. He opened the cab door, grabbed my hand, and pulled me from the back seat.

"I'm sorry, darling. I love you. Say you'll stay." He wrapped his arms around me and plastered me with kisses. "Let's not ever fight again."

"I'm sorry, too," I said and kissed him on the mouth. "Take me to bed or lose me forever." He dug in his pocket and tossed a few dollars at the grinning cabbie, grabbed my suitcase, and slammed the door shut.

"Pura vida, mis amigos," said the cab driver as he pulled away.

Dalton swung a leg over the moped and I tried to fit onto the seat behind him, my obnoxious white leather suitcase balanced on my knee. Dalton made a U-turn and we puttered back to the bungalow.

Once inside the room, I asked, "What's going on?"

He stared at me, paced, then stared at me again as though he was still trying to decide whether he should have left me in the cab. He thrust his hands on his hips and said, "I think you, well, my gut tells me…what I mean to say is, I think you might be right. I've had the same suspicions."

I assessed him for a moment. "Why? What have you seen?"

"It doesn't matter. What you say makes sense. And since—" He gritted his teeth. "Dammit!"

"Dammit what?" *He's not telling me everything. He's holding something back.*

"Brittany would want to connect with the wife, right? That'd be natural." He paused, then through clenched teeth, said, "We have to see it through."

I tried to hide my excitement. "I'm telling you, Dalton. It's her. I know it's—"

"Yeah." He had his hand up to shush me as he shuffled across the room, picked up his phone, and dialed George. After their hellos, he chuckled and said, "You know how women are. She's been on my back about horseback riding with Maria." I felt like we were kids and he was scheduling a playdate. "Yeah, uh-huh." There was a long pause. "All right. Thanks." And he disconnected.

"He said to come on over."

I grinned. "Dalton, I swear—"

"You've got three days to see what you can find out. Then we both get on a plane and go home. I'll be making the next run alone. Do you understand me? Three days." He made sure he had my attention. "But you listen to me, you better watch your step. This reckless behavior of yours has got to stop. From now on, you do as I say, do you understand?"

I nodded.

"You don't go anywhere, you don't do anything, you don't talk to anybody without my approval. You got it?"

"Yes," I said, my expression solemn. "I got it."

He eyed me for a long moment. He didn't believe me. It was all right. Neither did I.

"Sit down. We've got a half an hour to get you prepped."

I did as he commanded.

"Your first priority is to gain her trust. Don't ask her a lot of questions. You are the clueless, sweet, loving wife. You wanted a pet monkey is all. You have no idea it's illegal." He rubbed his chin. "But don't talk about that unless she brings it up. Understand?"

I shook my head. "No illegal monkey talk."

"Make it seem like we've got a lot of rich friends. Don't be blatant about it, but make it part of who you are, a wealthy socialite with filthy rich friends."

"Rich friends. Okay."

"It's all right to have different opinions, disagree with her, whatever. Don't ingratiate yourself. It could cause suspicion."

I nodded.

"Are you listening to me?"

"Every word."

He sighed and combed his fingers through his hair. "This op is turning to shit." He looked me in the eye. "Are you sure you can handle this?"

"I know I screwed up before. And I never should have called Chris. I just—I can do this. You can trust me."

"I hope so," he said. "Now, you're going horseback riding, so—"

I opened my eyes wide and let my mouth drop open. "Oh my god, I have to get on a horse?"

He closed his eyes. "Oh, we're screwed."

"Dalton, I'm kidding."

He glared at me. "If they don't kill you, I might."

CHAPTER 11

I left on the moped, Dalton in the car. He was going to golf with George.

I figured I could get away with a few extra minutes so I parked near the beach, two hotels down from the Coco-Cabana. I found Chris lounging by the pool with a piña colada in his hand, his eyeballs glued to a team of college boys in the pool playing volleyball over a tiny net.

When he saw me, he sprang to his feet. "Oh my god, girl. Did I get you fired? I am so sorry."

"Don't worry about it. I told you, it was my fault."

"Man. If I'd a known."

"I smoothed it over." I scanned the pool crowd. I didn't want to run into anyone else I might know. "How long are you planning to stay?"

His eyes traveled back to the bare chested guys in the pool. "Honey, I might never leave." A blond spiked the ball and it hit the side of the pool and bounced across the patio. "I've got it," Chris yelled and scurried to pick it up.

"You're incorrigible, you know that?" I said when he returned.

"Yes, but I get laid a lot more than you do, my dear." He smacked me with a kiss on the lips. "You look exhausted." He sat down in his lounge chair and patted the one next to it. "Take a load off." He hailed the waiter walking by with a tray full of tropical libations. "I'll order one with an umbrella. That way, as you sip it, you won't have to worry about burning that little pink nose."

Chris had that creamy olive skin of the perfect mix of genes. His mother was Egyptian, his father of Scandinavian descent. No one could guess where he was from. He fit in anywhere on the globe, sunny or otherwise.

I shook my head. "I can't. I've gotta go."

"At least tell me about that hunk of meat you are shacking up with. This fake husband. Is there any fake sex going on? Give me the juice." His eyes went back to the blond in the pool. "I mean, he's not really my type, but I can see why you got all flustered and had to call."

"He's my partner. And this job…" I slumped into the chair. "I've got a lot on my mind."

"Poppy-girl, you know how you are. You take on too much."

I looked at Chris, my best friend for as long as I can remember. His eyes were creased with worry. "I'm just frustrated really. This case." I took a deep breath. "At home, poaching, it's black and white. I catch you, you go to jail. But this." I shook my head. "It's complicated, organized crime. Even if I could catch someone red-handed, they'd get a slap on the wrist. That's why criminals choose it over running drugs. The risk is low, and for the big boys, the payoff high."

"Then the laws need to be changed." He held up his drink. "Maybe you should run for congress."

"Yeah, right. You've seen me in a suit."

"You'll find a way." Chris gave me a sympathetic frown. "Hey, they got Al Capone on tax evasion."

I stared at him, my mouth hanging open, recoiling from the jolt of an idea snapping into shape in my head. "You're a genius." *Yes, this could work.* Maria was one arrogant bitch who was used to being in control. But to do that, she required a lot of information. She had people watching our every move, had all the information about us at her fingertips. Or at least she thought she did.

I'd been so worried about Chris appearing, how it had looked to Yipes, I hadn't considered it might be useful in my favor. I ran over the scene in my mind, Dalton storming out, what Yipes thought he saw, different ways it could be interpreted. It was perfect.

"Hey, Earth to Poppy," Chris said, snapping me back to the now.

"I'm going to need a favor while you're here." Chris could do his part, then hop a plane out of here.

"So lay it on me."

"I need to get some information first, see if I can pull it together." I got up from the chair, my brain on fire, ideas spilling out. "But don't, whatever you do, come back by the bungalow, okay? I'll come here as soon as I can and fill you in." I took a step, then turned back. "And make sure you call me Brittany."

"Are you sure you're okay?"

"I'll be fine," I said and bent down and kissed him on the cheek. "Trust me."

"Yeah, right. The last time you said that I ended up with a shaved head and a case of the crabs."

The relative humidity had dropped. A cool breeze blew down from the mountain. The sky was dappled with big, white, puffy clouds. A beautiful day for a horseback ride.

Maria was filling a water bottle in the kitchen when I arrived. "Thank you so much for the invitation," I said. "I'm looking forward to a ride. It's been awhile since I've been out."

She forced a smile.

I shifted my weight to my other foot. "Have you been riding long?" I asked.

"Since I was a child," she said, in perfect Midwestern

English, no detectable Costa Rican accent.

"What a relief," I said, letting out my breath.

She looked at me quizzically.

"I thought maybe you didn't speak English."

She nodded as though that made sense. She handed me a water bottle. "The horses are being saddled."

I followed her and her little dogs to the barn. Once inside, I had to hide my surprise. The barn was immaculate. The floors swept clean, not one piece of straw out of place. Tack hung on hooks in front of each of eight sturdily built stalls. The horses looked clean and healthy. A hint of straw was the only odor I could detect. This was the barn of a wealthy equestrian who cared about her horses. It didn't fit the image I held of an evil wildlife smuggler—filthy cages, worm-ridden food. Interesting. As Noah had said: *Know thy enemy.*

A man I didn't recognize stood at the far door, arms crossed. The way his belt pulled tight at his waist, I was sure he had a firearm tucked at the small of his back.

Two horses were saddled, one with little saddle bags for Maria's dogs. Strange. Not an iota of guilt over the animals she tortures and sells, but she treats those little dogs like they're her children.

The horses were ready, but I had the sense we weren't going anywhere right away.

"I'm glad we are alone," Maria said. "I've been wanting to ask you something."

I shrugged. "Sure, shoot." *What is she up to?*

"Tell me, how do you say butterfly in Spanish?"

"Butterfly?" I asked. *Where is she going with this?*

"Yes, the beautiful insect with colorful wings."

"Um, mariposa?"

"Ah, yes, mariposa." The corners of her mouth curled into a devious smile. "It's funny. When my American friends try to learn Spanish, they always stumble on certain pronunciations."

Crap. Mari, rhymes with sorry. A newbie would pronounce it like Mary.

"You know what I think?" she said. She picked up a riding crop. "I think you are much smarter than you let on." Her intense gaze was intended to make me feel like a butterfly pinned to the wall.

I grinned wide and let out a sigh. "Oh thank god, you are a breath of fresh air," I said. Her eyes narrowed. She wasn't expecting this response. *Good.* "I thought I was going to be stuck with some woman who wanted to swap cookie recipes." I waved my hand in the air as if to dismiss her concern. "You know how men are—delicate egos." I leaned toward her as if to emphasize a secret. "Please don't tell John that I speak Spanish. He already feels like an idiot because he was an absolute dolt the other night when we got to talking about the wine." I rolled my eyes. "It's like he has to be good at everything or he doesn't feel like a man."

"Yes, well—" she smiled wide, a fake smile, and nodded to the man at the door "—your secret is safe with me. Shall we?" She moved toward her horse.

She was already dismissing me. This might be my only chance. *It's all or nothing.* "My husband, well, he doesn't exactly have a mind for business either. Oh, he's fine to look at, and oh my, in the sack—" I paused as if to savor a memory of our passionate lovemaking. "After awhile, a girl gets bored when there's not much upstairs, if you know what I mean. But in this misogynistic world, to do business, we women still need our men out front, even though we're the ones doing all the work. The brains behind the brawn, so to speak. If you know what I mean." I paused for effect, looked her straight in the eye. "But, of course, you know exactly what I mean."

She shifted her stance, ever so slightly. "Excuse me?"

I took a step closer to her. A subconscious sign of taking control. I lowered my voice. "I have no interest in one damn monkey. And I'm not looking for some amateur strap-a-bird-under-your-pants smuggler crap. I've got buyers, buyers with very big wallets. I want a source. A direct, reliable source."

Her eyes narrowed the slightest bit. Barely perceptible. She was good. "What you are describing sounds illegal. I think you have misunderstood. My husband's—"

"It's all right." I shrugged. "I'm sure I'll find what I'm looking for while I'm here in beautiful Costa Rica, nature's paradise." I winked. "Speaking of that. I must decline the ride. Enjoy yourself though. I've got business to attend to."

I turned my back on her and walked out the door.

I got back to the bungalow a couple hours before Dalton. Time to squeeze in some needed yoga.

"How'd it go?" he asked before the door was shut.

"Fine," I said.

"Fine? What does fine mean?"

I shrugged. "Fine. Nothing much to tell. She's cold. She didn't really want to take me. I think maybe George pressured her to, or she is covering her bases, keeping an eye on me. I don't know."

"Well, what'd you talk about?"

"Not much. We rode. Not a great situation for long conversations."

He stared at me as if he was trying to sort something out.

"Why? What's happened?" I asked.

"George got a call from Maria right before I left. He hung up and invited us to a fundraiser dinner. He wouldn't take no for an answer. No, it was more than that. It was the way he said it. It wasn't an invitation. It was more like a directive. I wonder what that's about."

"What kind of fundraiser?"

"For Manuel Antonio National Park. For conservation and preservation. Can you believe that?"

CHAPTER 12

Playa de Delfines, a private beach club a few miles north of the park, hosted the fundraiser. Tiki torches and glowing paper ball lanterns illuminated the beach and patio with a warm glow. A nice evening breeze carried the scent of salt. The surf unfurled unto the sand with a gentle, rhythmic gush that mixed with the easy Latin beat of the band. A temporary dance floor had been laid out on a deck where several couples swayed and twirled.

About two-hundred and fifty people were in attendance. Waiters in crisp white shirts casually moved about the crowd carrying trays of tropical drinks. A long table stretched the length of the patio, covered in white linens, its centerpiece a giant ice sculpture of a dolphin, and tray after tray of hors d'oeuvres—skewered shrimp, scallops wrapped in bacon, crackers covered in a dollop of ceviche, chorizo stuffed mushrooms. Nothing I'd eat. Once again, I'd be scrounging for a source of sustenance that didn't include animal flesh.

Dalton and I mingled, doing the only kind of intel gathering one can do at a party like this—see who's wearing what, or, in other words, who has money, who wants everyone to think they have money, basically who's maneuvering for power. You could easily identify the few couples who were actual donors. They sauntered about, arm in arm, gripping martinis, their lips permanently fixed with passive smiles.

I headed for a drink, but came to a halt. Isabella was behind the bar. I made a quick U-turn. If Isabella was working here tonight, that meant it was likely Carlos had his hand in this shindig somehow. I glanced around. There were several bars. At least I could avoid her.

I spotted Kevin, our new Australian friend, amid the crowd. Our eyes met and he immediately headed my way. I needed some information from him for my plan and was hoping to speak to him without Dalton overhearing, so I quickly closed the distance between us. "G'day, Ms. Brittany," he said. "Enjoyin' your visit?" The accent made me grin.

"Yes, it's a lovely country. The beach is gorgeous. I'm thinking of moving to a seaside room, maybe with a balcony. Our place is, well—" I curled my lip into an expression of dislike. "How about you? Do you like where you're staying?"

"Yeah, very nice little place to the north of here, the Casa del Mar. You should check it out."

"I will," I said with a wink. *Mission accomplished.*

Dalton appeared at my side.

"'Owdy, mate," Kevin said.

"Evenin'," Dalton said. They exchanged a manly that's-all-I-got nod. Charming conversationalists.

We stood in triangle formation for an uncomfortable moment before Kevin said, "Well, I's needing some grog. See yoos late-tah."

Dalton and I faced each other and casually scanned the crowd. Joe Nash was meandering our way, the cigar in his mouth. "There's Carl," I said to Dalton.

"John, right?" Nash said, offering his hand to Dalton as he approached.

Dalton nodded. "Nice to see you again."

"Likewise." He smiled at me. "John, my good man, mind if I take your lady for a spin around the dance floor?"

Dalton grinned. "Go right ahead." As I endured this old boy transaction I thought about my role and the plight of women everywhere, how women handle these situations with varying responses. Brittany would smile at Carl in a flirtatious way, enjoying the attention. Poppy would punch John in the nose and tell Carl to take a hike.

I flashed my Brittany smile and held out my hand to Nash.

Once we were on the dance floor, where the sound of our whispers would get lost in the music, he asked how things were going.

"Okay, I guess." I waited for a couple who seemed like they were hovering close by to pirouette in another direction before I added, "We've identified the kingpin." He raised an eyebrow. I whispered, "Maria."

"You're sure?"

I nodded. "Anything on your end?"

"Nothing that huge. But it gives me perspective."

I saw Dalton talking with Felix, the man from Germany. "Learn anything more about our foreign friends? I'm thinking the dinner was for her to assess potential buyers."

"It's a good theory. I'll see what I can find out."

The song was coming to an end. I wasn't sure how to ask Nash what I wanted to know, so I went ahead and said it. "Do you think she could also be running drugs?"

"Possible," he said. "Why? Any signs?"

I shook my head. "Just a hunch."

The song came to an end and I thanked him for the dance. "Be careful," he whispered in my ear before he sauntered toward the bar and I casually made my way through the crowd to Dalton and Felix. "Hello Felix," I said.

"Ah, Fräulein." He bowed in greeting, then pushed the greasy glasses up his nose. "How are you dis evening?"

"Very well, thank you." I wanted to find out, as quickly as I could, where he was staying, but he was going to be a tougher nut to crack than Kevin. "And you? What do you think of Costa Rica?"

"Zee veather is vonderful. Sun chine all day."

"Have you had time to walk on the beach?"

"Busy verking," he said, shaking his head.

I smiled and nodded like I was sympathizing. "Did you at least get a room with a view?"

"No, no."

I was getting nowhere.

The vibe in the party changed suddenly. All eyes turned toward the entrance where Maria strode in, George a couple paces behind her, which I'm sure was by directive. Of course, they were fashionably late, which was right on time for a grand entrance.

Maria demanded attention in a tight-fitting red bandeau dress, her girls pressed together and showing eight miles of cleavage, the skirt knee length, slit up the side to her waist with a black ruffled edge. As if that wasn't flashy enough, she wore purple and red sparkly earrings and wrist bangles. To top if off, she glided across the floor on red velvet pumps sporting four-inch heels.

I had on a cornflower blue sundress, cotton, sleeveless. Nice, cool and comfortable. I whispered to Dalton. "Do you find that attractive?"

"Um," he didn't take his eyes from her. "No comment?"

I almost sprained my eye socket doing an eye roll.

George and Maria worked the crowd before making their way to us. They thanked us for coming, for all the support, blah, blah. What a load of crap. Dalton and I smiled and nodded and acted the part as I tried to figure out why she wanted us here. Certainly to appear as though she had clout, as though she had the ear of big donors. Money and influence drove Maria, that was obvious. But why us?

She and George hobnobbed their way to the podium which had been placed at the side of the dance floor. A man in a white suit coat stepped to the microphone and hushed the crowd. Must have been the head of the nonprofit for which this fundraiser was hosted. After a rather boring overview, he launched into a glowing introduction of Maria Mendoza Hillman.

She strutted to the podium, taking her time while all the eyes were on her. "Good evening," she said in her perfect English. "Tonight is a celebration of all that is good and beautiful in Costa Rica. I don't have to tell you how vital it is that we keep it that way. Our heritage, the mighty rainforest, is at risk."

The crowd made a collective nod of agreement. I squeezed Dalton's hand and glared at Maria. *You lying hypocrite.*

"We must, all of us, do our part to support this organization and their good works. *Mis amigos*, please, open your pocketbooks."

My teeth had a firm grasp on my tongue. *Indeed, for if there is no rainforest, there are no animals to steal.*

"Together, we can keep our country lush and green."

Applause. I forced my hands together. Thankfully her speech was short and to the point. I don't think I could have stomached any more.

The band started up again in a hot, latino salsa beat, the volume cranked up two-fold. George and Maria took to the dance floor. I watched as they and other couples shook and bounced and twirled.

Dalton, standing next to me, said, "The trick is to swing your hips."

My head snapped in his direction. "You dance?"

He shrugged. "I like holding a lady in my arms. If I have to move my feet to do it, well, I know a few steps."

The tune changed to a slow waltz. He downed the rest of his beer, set the bottle on a tray, and held out his hand. "Shall we?"

I wouldn't call myself a great dancer, but I do all right with a strong lead. When I was a child, no matter where we happened to be in the world, my father would find an American oldies music station on the radio and I'd stand on the top of his feet and he would twirl me around the room. He taught me the fox trot, the mamba, the waltz, the rhumba, the cha cha cha. I haven't had another dance partner since and I was feeling a bit rusty.

Dalton led me to the dance floor, then turned to face me, his left hand held out to the side for me to take. "It's like sex," he said as he placed his right hand on the small of my back and pulled me tightly to him. "Move your hips with mine." He waggled his eyebrows. "On the beat, step back with your right foot. I'll take it from there."

I counted—one-two-three, one-two-three—then stepped back and we were in motion, moving as one, my body so close to his, it felt fluid, natural. I twirled, spinning round the axis that was Dalton as he led me around the floor. I didn't think about the steps, about the rhythm, it just was. Being in his arms was easy, letting him take control. He moved and I moved with him.

By the end of the song, I was breathless. He held my hand tightly and eased me backward into a dip. When he pulled me upward, I stopped inches from his lips, his hot breath on my face. He leaned forward and kissed me ever so gently. I was glad to have his arms around me because I thought I might melt.

Who said I couldn't look like the wife, hopelessly in love? *We've got this nailed.*

My hand held high in the air like a professional dancer, he twirled me around and led me off the dance floor into the crowd, where we ran smack into Noah.

For a moment, his presence didn't jive in my brain. What was he doing here? In a tux? My mouth opened to speak, but I couldn't. I couldn't acknowledge him at all. I'd blow my cover. But there was nothing stopping him from blowing it for me. Right now. *Please, Noah. Don't say anything. Please.*

He stared at me with an unreadable expression, then his eyes zoomed in on my hand and the diamond I wore. They refocused to assess Dalton, then shifted back to me. There was more than disappointment in his eyes; there was something that looked more like condemnation, as though he'd received an answer to a question he'd been purposely avoiding. My heart sank.

For a moment, I thought he might turn away, before anyone noticed, but his eyes were locked on Dalton. Noah offered his hand to Dalton. "You must be Brittany's...husband?"

Crap. Isn't there some unspoken code about affairs? You don't purposefully meet the husband.

Dalton quickly looked to me for an explanation.

"John, dear, I met this nice gentleman at the butterfly garden. You remember. I told you I had stopped by."

Dalton's hand squeezed mine. This was a problem. I needed to do something. Now.

I steeled myself. "This really isn't a good time," I said with emphasis, willing him to take the hint. "Perhaps we can discuss our donation to your cause another time." My eyes locked with his. *Please, just go with it, Noah. Walk away.*

Noah eyed Dalton, assessing him. His eyes shifted back to me and held for a long moment. *Please, Noah. Take the hint.*

He held up his hands and backed away.

"Forgive me," I said.

My words hung in the air as Noah disappeared in the crowd.

I turned and caught sight of Maria, staring at me through the crowd.

"Let's get a drink," I said and steered Dalton toward the bar.

We were steps away when Maria materialized out of nowhere. "Where have you been hiding?" she said to Dalton, a wicked grin on her face. I opened my mouth to speak but she had him by the arm. "I've been hoping for a dance."

I watched as she led him to the dance floor and pressed her body against his. He twirled her around while she shook her fanny and made an ass of herself. What was she thinking? Like he'd go for a gold-digger like her. *Wait, what do I care? I don't like him in that way. Sure he's hot but.... But he's my husband.*

When the song finally ended, he gave her a polite thank you

and what looked like goodbyes for the evening. He took me by the arm and practically dragged me out the door and into the car.

"What's going on?"

Dalton kept his gaze forward, his eyes on the road. "She knows something. I've been doing this a long time. I can tell. She's suspicious."

"Why? What did she say?"

"That kid,"—*kid?*—"you said he knew about her operation, that he had some evidence? What does he know?"

"I—" *Crap.* "I'm not sure. You told me not to talk to him again."

He glared at me. "And since you've been here, you've followed my every order?"

I frowned. "Is that steam coming out of your ears?"

We headed into the downtown area. "You need to fix this. Make sure this situation is neutralized."

"Neutralized? What the hell are you suggesting?"

He pulled the car to the curb at a busy block in town. "Go talk to him. Find out if she knows who he is. We need to get a handle on this."

"Right now? The butterfly garden isn't open at this hour. How do you expect—"

"You're going to lie to me now?"

I stared into those eyes. Those beautiful eyes. The same eyes that looked at me with loving sympathy when I'd sobbed into his shirt. "No, I'm not." I got out of the car. He drove away before the door was shut.

CHAPTER 13

The lights were on in the tree house and I could hear the slow, melancholy sound of a Joni Mitchell tune on the guitar. I ascended the staircase and sat down in one of the rattan chairs. Noah strummed his guitar without looking up, made no acknowledgement of my presence. I waited till the end of the song.

His eyes turned on me. "So are you a cop or something?" His words were laced with sarcasm and thrown at me with the same inflection as I had asked him that first day. He reached for his bottle of beer and tipped it up. I watched his movement for any sign of his intentions.

"Fish and Wildlife," I finally said.

"I suppose that guy's your partner then?"

"Yes. We are undercover as a married couple."

His lip curled up in a sarcastic grin. "Yeah, I figured."

"All right," I said, half relieved, half annoyed. "How'd you figure?"

"Well, for starters, when you first arrived at the butterfly garden, you were wearing a wedding ring." He exaggerated a nod. "Yep, first thing I noticed. Then it was gone. But there was something about you. I just couldn't make you for a player. Too..."

"Young and innocent?"

"Something like that." His eyes traveled down my body

and back up again. "Then your kung fu moves on the guard up there in the hills. And c'mon. Got lost birding?" He rolled out of the hammock, pushed a stack of magazines to one side of the coffee table, and sat down on the edge facing me. He reached up and ran a finger through my hair. "This is fiery red, not dumb blond."

"All circumstantial," I said. I couldn't tell if he was mad and toying with me, or amused and flirting with me. Either way, I was totally turned on.

"Ah, but the true tip off, the crème de la crème, the icing on the cake, the—"

"All right already."

"Only feds call the middleman the buncher."

I closed my eyes. "Damn."

His hand caressed my cheek. "It was so adorable."

I suck at this.

"I didn't realize you weren't working alone."

"Yeah, about that—"

"You and your husband—" he leaned in and kissed me on my neck, just below my ear "—looked awfully into each other on the dance floor."

My breath caught in my throat. "It's my job. That's my cover."

He moved farther down my neck.

I shook my head. "I thought you'd be angry with me."

"Angry?" He pulled back and looked into my eyes. "I don't know if I can keep my hands off you."

I smiled, relieved. I cocked my head to the side and matched his intensity with my gaze. "While we're being honest, what's your story?"

He sat back. "What do you mean?"

"I think you want your friends to believe you're a trust funder, but I don't buy it."

He flashed an innocent smile.

"At first glance, this is a modest tree house. But ocean front property? I bet you own it. You're not Isabella's neighbor, you're her landlord."

He kept his expression the same, but I saw the slightest flinch of acknowledgement.

"And the Chateau Montelena Estate Cabernet Sauvignon— nice taste by the way—that wine retails for nearly two-hundred dollars. Trust funders don't spend that kind of coin on wine. They go to Europe, ski the Alps. You earned your money."

He wouldn't nod, but I knew I was right. I placed my hand on his thigh and slid it forward as I leaned in. "But the true reveal, the final blow, the…" I paused. "Damn, I can't think of another idiom."

He grinned and shook his head. "Go on."

"Financial lingo. Hedging? Selling futures? My bet is Yale, left before you even graduated to take on Wall Street. Am I close?"

He ran his fingers through my hair. "I knew you were a natural red." He held my head in his hand, gently pulled me toward him, and nuzzled the soft spot right above my collarbone, then worked his way up my neck, leaving a trail of kisses that made me shiver with desire.

He pulled away from me again, leaving me breathless, his hazel eyes mischievously assessing me. "So we know each other's deepest secrets." He grinned. "Now what do we do?"

"Anything we want," I said and practically launched out of the chair into his arms, hungry for his lips on me, his tongue. I tugged at his T-shirt and yanked it over his head.

He wrapped his arms around me and spun us around. He surprised me with his strength; he held me with his left arm as he knocked the magazines to the floor. He lay me down on my back on the coffee table and slowly crawled on top of me, taking his time to enjoy the curves of my body, working his way back up to my neck. He buried his head in my hair and whispered in my ear, "God, you're hot."

I grabbed onto him, shifted to my hip, and rolled to straddle him. The table tipped and we fell to the floor with a thump, me sprawled on top of him. The table slammed to the floor with a bang. "I'm sorry. I'm sorry," I said. I pushed myself up on my hands but kept my body pressed against him.

He laughed, rubbing the back of his head. "Wow, you are feisty."

I had nothing to lose. "Yes, I am." I ran my hands down his chest to the button on his jeans.

He shoved the table out of the way. "Let's wreck this place."

I lay in his arms. "I'm sorry I lied to you," I said. "I had to. It's my job. Even though, obviously," I sighed, "I'm not very good at it." I shifted so I could see his eyes. "But it was for the greater good."

"Most honorable." He kissed the tip of my nose. "And you are good at it. I'm just really good at reading people." He gently stroked my hair. "I used to swindle people for a living."

"What? I don't believe that."

"Even if it was legal, that's what I did." He pushed himself up on the pillow. "But I wasn't always like that."

I propped myself up on my elbow. "I bet I know one thing for sure; you've always liked insects."

His grin was laced with nostalgia. "When I was a kid, I loved bugs. My Uncle Frank got me this really cool ant farm for Christmas one year. I'd watch them for hours. Fascinating, you know, how industrious they are. My father hated it, of course. Said it was a waste of time.

"One day, he was angry because I didn't have my homework finished or something, I don't remember. He was always mad at me for something. Anyway, I'll never forget how he stomped around my room in a rage and knocked it off my dresser. I swear it hovered in mid air, you know that defining moment, and I was helpless to stop it." He winced at the memory. "It was like time froze, just so I'd have to endure that agony. Then it smashed on the floor and shattered. Sand and dirt flew everywhere. The ants skittered around in circles. They didn't know which way to go. Their entire world had been destroyed in an instant, shattered to bits. My father stomped his foot right in the center of it, smooshing them to death."

"He made it clear. Nothing else mattered but perfect grades. I was going to business school. It wasn't an option. He didn't care whether that's what I wanted to do. My dream of being an entomologist was pointless to him. I couldn't have hobbies, play sports. Nothing that wasn't an *approved* extracurricular activity." His eyes traveled down my chest. "Girls were most definitely off limits."

He paused as though he wasn't sure he wanted to tell me any more of the story. He turned to look me in the eyes. "Yes, I went to Yale. Got a job in the secondary mortgage market. I was exactly what my father wanted me to be." He shook his head with disgust. "I was a selfish sonofabitch. I wanted to make money. Lots of it. And I did."

"What happened? What changed?"

"One day, this guy Mark, asked me to go for a walk. We were friends, I guess. As good of friends as two guys in finance can be. He wanted to get out of the office, tell me about an opportunity he didn't want overheard. Funny part about it was, I'd just bought this new suit, custom tailored. Three grand. Mark shows up in the same suit and gives me crap about finding my own style.

"Anyway, we walked to the corner of the block. There was this tiny park there, you know, a patch of grass, one tree and a bench. He was telling me about this company that was over leveraged, how he could take over, liquidate, some mom and pop outfit that held a patent of which they didn't realize the value. We got to the bench and there was a homeless man sitting there feeding the pigeons. Everything he owned in the world was in the bag on the ground next to him, but he was sharing what he had with the pigeons. I don't know why. The joy of their companionship maybe, maybe to feel like he was helping."

His eyes turned glassy with the memory. I didn't want to interrupt his story. So I waited.

"Mark wanted to sit on the bench, but he wasn't going to sit down next to some stinking homeless man—his words—so he walked up to him and told him to move along, get a job. The man didn't flinch, didn't acknowledge Mark."

He paused again. Closed his eyes.

"What'd Mark do?" I asked.

"He kicked a pigeon. Sent it flying into the tree trunk. It flopped around on the ground, its wing broken. The old man looked up at Mark. There was no fear in his eyes. Just pity. Pity for Mark." He clenched his teeth together and I was sure it was to hold back a tear. "The old man got up. Mark thought it was because he'd intimidated him into leaving. Mark plopped down in the seat without a second thought and starting talking strategy, about a partnership." He shook his head. "The old man shuffled over to the base of the tree and drove the heel of his boot down on the bird, putting it out of its misery. Then he poked around in his bag and pulled out a spoon and right next to where Mark sat, the old man dug a grave for that bird."

"Wow, that's…" I didn't know what to say.

"And I sat there next to him. In the same damn suit."

I gave him a moment before I asked, "What'd you do?"

"I went back to the office, packed up my things, and walked out. I've never been back." He shifted and met my eyes. "I like it much better here. Don't you agree?"

"Yeah," I said and as if he'd been cued, Clyde bounded up the side of the balcony. "You're in good company."

Noah got up and tossed a biscuit to Clyde. While the little visitor crunched away at it, Noah adjusted the pillows we'd piled up on the floor beneath us and eased back into place, his arms around me. "What made you want to be a wildlife cop?"

"Hold on. You don't just volunteer at the butterfly garden, do you?"

He grinned. "Don't go changing the subject. I asked *you* a question."

"Fine." I thought of my dad, but I couldn't go there. Not right now. "I can't stand to see animals being hurt. And I love being outdoors. I can't imagine a job in a city, in a cubicle somewhere. It'd be the death of me."

"No kidding. Tell me about it."

"I just don't understand how anyone can hurt an animal the way these criminals do and think nothing of it. The horror, the tragedy of it all. It's mind-boggling. I always wondered how these people can be so heartless. I'm starting to see it's more about the human capacity for denial. That combined with plain ignorance. I mean, anyone who's ever had a dog ought to see that animals have feelings. They feel pain." Clyde finished his biscuit and bounded across the room and jumped up and down at our feet.

"Did you clean up the crumbs?" Noah said.

Clyde scurried back and swept the floor with his tiny hand.

"I'll get it," I said and got up for another biscuit. I held it in my hand, wanting Clyde to take it from me. He approached without hesitation, his high-pitched whine as cute as can be. "See, he knows. Instinctively or otherwise, he knows I'm a friend. He's smarter than we are in some ways." I clenched my jaw, anger stirring in me. "But humans have the immense capacity to be deceitful. We have better traps, better weapons, better cages."

Noah sat up. "So you're a fed. What are you doing here in Costa Rica?"

"Not nearly enough," I said. "But you can help."

"Tell me how."

"Does Maria know you're the one who has been targeting her operation?"

"I don't know how she would."

"Would she recognize you for any other reason? Does she know you're an activist?"

He kinda half shook his head. "She might. If she went out of her way to investigate."

I nodded. She certainly would have done that. "I have an idea."

"Will it save animals?"

I smiled wide. "We could use the gang, too."

"Tell me when."

"Tomorrow morning, I'll be back. We'll plan our attack."

I had all day. After I'd assured Dalton that Maria couldn't possibly know Noah, not to worry, he left for his morning five-mile run and after that he'd planned a day of sorting through snakes and frogs, then going to play cards again, so he'd probably be late.

I stopped at the Coco-Cabana, dragged Chris out of his bed, and we headed for the tree house.

"Noah, this is Chris. He's a friend. Not a cop."

Noah shook Chris's hand. "Coffee's almost ready," he said and tromped across the rope bridge.

Chris raised an eyebrow at me and mouthed the word *wow*.

"He's straight," I whispered.

He raised the other eyebrow.

I grinned. "Very straight."

Clyde bounded up the stairs, Isabella not far behind him. "Buenos días," I said.

"Buenos días," she groaned, one eye open.

"Noah's coming with coffee," I told her, which caused a slight uptick in her step.

Chris and Clyde were making fast friends. Chris held his arm out and Clyde swung on it like a trapeze artist. "He's so cute," Chris cooed.

Jack and Doug arrived, Jack with a bag of doughnuts and

Doug carrying a watermelon. Noah came across the bridge with a pot of coffee and three mugs in his hands. "Grab some more mugs," he said to Jack. "And let's take this to the picnic table. This old tree house is pretty sturdy"—he winked at me—"but I'm not sure how many people it'll hold."

Matt and Claudia walked up as we plopped everything on the picnic table. "Amanda and Colette will be here soon. Dan and Sierra have to work."

The morning sun felt warm on my back. I dug my bare toes into the sand.

Their hands wrapped around warm mugs of coffee, the others sat down forming a circle around me. "This is going to be dangerous," I said. "If you don't want to be involved, I understand. Just say so now." They each looked around at the others, none of them wanting to bow out. "All right." I assessed my team, then turned to Chris, Jack, and Doug. "My plan is a bit, well, bold." I grinned. "I think its time Maria had a little competition. Chris, meet Doug and Jack, your bodyguards."

"What do I need bodyguards for?"

"You're a wildlife smuggler. A very successful one. And you're moving in on the competition."

Doug piped up. "I'm not trained for that sort of thing."

"You're an actor, right? It's all for show." He nodded, the concept slowly settling in.

"Your first task: go shopping."

Chris gave me his yeah-I'm-gay-but-c'mon look. "Seriously?"

"You need to dress for success." I turned to Doug and Jack. "You, too. Ex-military, green beret types. Can you do that?"

They nodded, excited.

I turned to the rest of the group. "They'll need a car."

Noah jumped to his feet. "This way." We all followed him into the trees to a structure built with corrugated tin panels. He lifted the latch on a sliding door and pushed it open. "This work?" Parked inside was a shiny new black SUV.

"Perfect."

Doug slapped him on the back. "You've been holding out on us, man."

"Nice ride, dude," said Jack.

Noah turned to Doug. "You drive."

"We'll need the VW, too," I said.

Noah shrugged. "Whatever."

As we walked back to the beach together, I explained that we'd be visiting some potential buyers. Chris asked, "How will we convince them to leave Maria and buy from me?"

"Oh, we don't have to convince them of anything. We go talk to them, about the weather, whatever. As long as we're seen doing it."

"But what if she asks?"

"She won't. But if she does, even better. They'll say we talked about the weather, because we did. Of course, she'll think they're lying."

"But I don't see what that does if there isn't a real threat," said Jack.

"The threat doesn't have to be real. She only has to think that it's real."

We sat back down in the sand. Noah said, "This whole plan depends on your judgement of Maria. That she has people watching, that she'll act on this. You're giving her a lot of credit."

"She didn't get to be a world-class wildlife trafficker by being stupid." I looked him in the eye. "And she's not going to let it go very easily either. That's our advantage. We know her goal and we know what she's afraid of. The key is to guide her in the direction we want her to go, without her realizing it. We do what fortunetellers do. We give her the right bits of information and let her connect the dots."

He shook his head. I wasn't sure if he was skeptical or in awe of my great insight.

I turned to Isabella. She likely had the best information I

needed for the other part of my plan. "Have you ever seen Maria come to The Toucan to see Carlos? The woman from the fundraiser?"

Isabella shook her head.

"Okay, just tell me what you know about Carlos, everything you know."

She made a disgusted face. "I don like heem."

Noah answered. "He owns The Toucan, a hangout for tourists who get off the cruise ships, mostly a lunch crowd. All regular deliveries, the food, alcohol, come in the morning, like any other bar. But it's a front for the smuggling. During the lunch rush, when the place is too busy for anyone to notice, locals show up, delivering boxes to the storeroom, a shed out back, behind the kitchen."

"Everyday, the same time?" I asked.

"During lunch. We figure they're the poachers. Carlos hangs out back with his right hand man. Whenever a poacher arrives with something to sell, he sends his man into the bar to get cash from the till."

"How big is the shed? Big enough to house these animals?"

He shook his head. "They load them right into the panel truck. Carlos just hangs out back there, smoking all day. At two-thirty, Paco drives away in the van and Carlos empties the till and leaves in his own car."

I turned to Isabella. "What about drugs? He running those through the bar?"

"I don know," she said. "I never seen no drugs."

"So it's possible they are in one of these mystery boxes, then?"

Noah said, "We didn't know there were drugs until you and I—"

"Right, got it," I said. Everyone didn't need to know about our escapade. "So if there are drugs, they'd be in the panel van, headed to wherever the animals are taken."

Jack piped up. "We rode the van once. To the shed at the old coffee plantation. That's how we knew about it."

"All right, what about—wait, what do you mean you rode the van?"

Jack grinned. "We roof surfed. You know, like hood surfing, only on the roof." He put out his hands like he was balancing on a surf board.

"You're kidding right?"

He stared at me, his brow knit. Like why wouldn't that be possible?

Amanda and Colette came walking down the beach, hand in hand. They filled coffee cups and joined us. "What's going on?" Colette asked.

Doug held up his mug. "We're going to kick some wildlife smuggler ass!" he said.

I thanked them for coming, but my head was still at The Toucan. "Does the van go to the shed at the plantation everyday? Or could there be multiple locations?"

Noah shrugged. He looked to Jack and Doug. They shrugged. Noah said, "We do know that the van comes back in the evening. They drive down on the dock. Everyday by five. That's when the shipments go out. Then the empty van gets parked behind The Toucan for the next day."

"All right." To Amanda and Colette, I said. "You two can impersonate drunk college girls, right? You have bikinis?" They nodded. "And Amanda, I have a computer question. We can chat about that in a bit. What we need to know right away is details about the whereabouts of the drugs. We need to know what day they ship. I need surveillance on the shed at the plantation." I looked at Noah. "It's not a fun job, but I can't be seen with you. Will you do it?"

He nodded and turned to Matt and Claudia, the river guides. "I'll need your help."

"Anything," they said simultaneously.

"Make sure you have enough supplies to camp out up there for a couple days if need be," I said. "Take your cell phones.

Make sure they're charged and keep them off until you need to contact me. There's no cell coverage up there. You'll need to hike out a ways to get service. So as soon as you see the van—wait a minute." I turned to Isabella. "Did you say Paco? Is there more than one Paco?"

"I don know."

Could it be? Could I be that lucky? Agent García had likely chosen Paco because it was such a common name but—"How long has Paco been with Carlos?"

Isabella shook her head. Noah, too. Isabella said, "This Paco, I haf seen him around, but only a few month does he get dee money and drive dee ban."

"Do you work today?"

"Sí, everyday at eleven."

To Chris, Jack, and Doug, I said, "Get shopping. Be dressed and in character and meet me at The Toucan at noon. Get a table close to an exit."

CHAPTER 14

I had to change my clothes, grab a few things, and, this time, make sure Yipes followed me to where I was going for lunch. I popped into the bungalow and ran into Dalton.

"There you are," he said. "I thought you were going up to the cocina for some coffee and you'd be right back."

"I went for a walk. What are you doing here? I thought you had frogs to sort."

"I'm taking the day off. Gonna spend it with you like we had planned for yesterday. I was just going to call you."

Crap. I had to get back to The Toucan. This would blow everything. I had to think. Fast. I smirked. "Yeah, you don't need to babysit me. I'm behaving." I made sure he heard the sarcasm and disappointment in my voice. "It's already getting hot out there. Thought I'd change and go shopping. Yay!" I snatched my khaki shorts and a tank top from my suitcase, waltzed into the bathroom, and shut the door.

I quickly changed, trying to think of what else I might need so I could grab it and go. I opened the door and Dalton was standing right there, blocking my way.

"I want you to know," he said, his jaw muscles tight, "that I'm sorry. I've been on your case since you got here. I haven't given you a fair chance." His eyes dropped to his hands. He examined his cuticles, then the backs of his hands. Finally his eyes came back to mine. "You were right. I screwed up and that's why they sent you down here and, well, I was ticked off."

"I understand," I said. "Don't worry about it." I pushed by him and headed for the door. He grabbed me by the arm and spun me around.

"Wait, that's it?" He looked hurt. "I'm trying to tell you I'm sorry." He threw up his hands. "God, women!"

I screwed my face into a smile. "I'm just saying, no apology needed. I get it. This op is important to you and you don't want anything to jeopardize it. I respect that."

"Thank you," he said. He actually looked relieved. God he was such a sweet guy. *Dammit. My plan better work.* He took my hand in his. "I'm actually glad you're here. The way you figured out it was Maria so quickly."

I blushed a little.

"I was thinking maybe…"

"Yeah, no." I yanked my hand away. "We've got a job to do here." I gave him a stern look. I had to be stern.

"Wow, you really don't like compliments, do you?"

"Do you compliment Joe?" I had to pick a fight.

"What?" He stepped back. "Why would I?"

"I bet you wouldn't spend the day at the beach with him. So you could *finally see him in a bikini*." The last words I spat at him, dripping with sarcasm. "I get it. I'm here on your turf. But you also made it abundantly clear who's in charge. This job's important to me too and I'm doing exactly as you told me. Shopping, going to the beach. Staying the hell out of your way. I'm being the good, obedient wife. You don't have to rub it in." And I was out the door, feeling like a heel.

When I got to The Toucan, the guys were already there, halfway through three baskets of fish fingers and a bucket of Cerveza Imperials. I had to take my time getting there to make sure Yipes could follow. I sat down at the table with them. My eyes on Chris, I said to Jack and Doug, "Remember, boys, don't talk to me. You're the muscle. My business is with Chris." They didn't flinch. Excellent. "We're going to chat. You look confident, comfortable. I'll shift in my seat a few times."

Chris nodded. Acted nonchalant, in control. He was good at this.

"Now, sit tight," I said. "And easy on the beer." I went to the bar and waved Isabella over. "Next time Paco comes in, point me out to him and tell him I'm also hunting a beautiful butterfly and that he looks like he could use a bathroom break."

She looked at me with a quizzical expression.

"Make sure you say exactly that."

"Okay," she said with a shrug and went back to work.

I leaned on the bar and waited, trying to blend in with the tourists. Finally, a man slipped behind the counter and went straight for the cash register. Isabella was so busy she didn't notice him. I got her attention and motioned in his direction with my eyes. She spun around and caught him by the sleeve as he was headed back out. She whispered to him and he looked right at me. *This better be him. Otherwise, this whole plan disintegrates fast.* He listened to her, his eyes on me, then with the slightest nod, he left. Isabella brought me an IPA and said with a shrug, "I toll heem."

"Thanks."

I moved through the crowd and around to the outside corner to the restrooms. I waited until the area was clear and slipped into the men's room.

Men's rooms, I've found, are a microcosm of life. When left to their own devices, men are simply pigs. God knows when the last time this place was cleaned. Paper towels were strewn on the floor, soap dispenser missing altogether. I slipped into a stall, prepared to stand on the toilet seat if necessary, but hoped it didn't come to that.

I didn't have to wait long. The door eased open and I heard it close and the click of the lock.

I slipped from the stall. "I'm a friend of Joe's." I watched his reaction. "Joe Nash."

"I don't know nobody name'a Joe." He wasn't going to blow his cover no matter what. He walked to the stall, looked inside, walked back and grabbed me by the arm and slammed me against the wall. He ran his hands up my right leg, then my left. He spun me around and checked under my arms.

"Who the hell are you?" he said.

"Martin showed me the postcard."

"What do you want?" He frowned. "And this better be good. Make it quick."

"Carlos running coke?"

"I think so. But on the side. Definitely not sanctioned by his boss."

I crossed my arms. "You think so or you know so?"

He shook his head. "Whenever we get a poisonous snake, Carlos takes the afternoon delivery on his own. I just figured. Only thing that makes sense."

"Right," I said. Drug dealers were known to use aggressive or venomous animals to guard their inventory. He probably hid the drugs in a secret compartment in the bottom of a crate. Snake on top. Border agents aren't likely to mess with it and the fine is minor for the snake. "Any particular day?"

"No. But we got one this morning, if that helps."

That didn't give me much time.

He crossed his arms. "Directive from Virginia is to stay the course."

"Right," I said. "We're just working another angle. What else can you tell me?"

"Not much really. These guys are amateurs." He glanced toward the door. "Amateurs with guns. I'm gone too long, I'm toast."

"I've got it covered. At the far table, three guys. Smuggler and his bodyguards. The competition. Make it be known you've just been solicited and turned him down. Solidify your loyalty, help our cause."

He pondered this a moment, then nodded slowly. "I gotta go." He moved toward the door.

"One more thing," I said. "How'd you know it was Maria?"

"Who?"

"On the postcard, you said you had your sights set on a butterfly."

"I always hear him on the phone. I figured it was a woman in charge because he calls her Mariposa. That's all I know. I was hoping Nash could connect the dots."

"It's his sister, Maria. She's the kingpin."

He nodded as if this made sense. "Good. We're getting closer. I'm getting tired of this asshole." He slid out the door, looked both ways, and nodded to me that it was clear.

I went straight to the table. "Carlos will be looking out here at you any minute now. Make sure he sees you, then get the hell out of here fast," I said and melted into the crowd where I could keep an eye on them.

Chris hailed the waitress. When she dropped the check on the table, he slapped her on the ass. I did an eye roll. He was getting cocky already. He looked up and hesitated. He whispered to Doug. He seemed to have caught sight of something. I spun around. Carlos and two thugs were headed toward him. *Oh no.* I moved closer.

"¿Qué te lleva a mi bar?" Carlos asked.

Crap! Chris doesn't speak Spanish.

Chris sat back in his chair, interlaced his fingers, and casually looked up at Carlos. "Nice place," he said. "The beer was cold—" he flicked his finger at the baskets on the table "—but the grouper was a bit soggy."

"What do you want?"

Chris grinned, his eyes traveled to a waitress who was bending over, wiping the table nearby. "Just enjoying the view."

Carlos shifted on his feet. "Well I suggest you find another one. Move on down the beach."

Chris slowly surveyed the scene, peering out at the water,

the beach, the cruise ship at the dock, the cargo ships docked along the pier. "I don't know." He turned back to Carlos and grinned. "I kinda like it here. You know what they say: location, location, location."

God, Chris, don't push it.

Carlos crossed his arms, his neck muscles pulled taut. His thugs moved in.

Chris pushed back his chair and rose to his feet. Doug and Jack rose on either side of him. Chris adjusted his shirt collar, then brushed down the front of his silk shirt, smoothing it out real nice. He made a show of looking around the bar, up at the rafters, from corner to corner as he pulled his sleeves at the cuffs. Then he winked at Carlos. "Yeah, I like it here a lot." He turned to Doug. "Shall we?" And he strolled out like he owned the place.

"That was awesome!" said Doug. He was at the wheel and we were speeding down the main road.

"Holy crap, Chris," I said. "That was risky. That could've gone south, fast."

He grinned at me. "Yeah, but it didn't."

Jack gave him a shove on the shoulder. "Dude, you're crazy. All I could think was how I was going to learn kung ku, like if I could get an instant download like in The Matrix. Dude, that was messed up."

"Where to next, boss?" Doug asked.

Chris pointed at me. "You'll have to ask her."

I gave him a head slap. "He meant me." To Doug I said, "Casa del Mar, a little hotel on the beach, north of the Playa de Delfines resort."

"I know it," he said. "What's the plan there? We going to rough up some poachers?"

"No!" I glared at him even though he couldn't see me with his eyes on the road. "Chris and I are going in to talk to someone.

You and Jack hang out at the door, looking around like Secret Service. Make yourselves obvious. But not too obvious. Know what I mean?"

"Sure, boss," Doug said.

"You don't have to call me boss."

"Hey, I'm a method actor. I'm getting into my role. Just go with it."

I rubbed my temples with my thumb and middle finger. Maybe this wasn't such a good idea, I thought. It made me think of Roy. And the Lawson brothers. I bet he enjoyed nailing their partner.

I texted Amanda and Colette to let them know to be ready, today was the day.

Then my phone rang. It was Claudia. "Dead!" she burst. "They killed a man. Killed him!"

"Take a breath. Tell me exactly what happened."

The connection was staticky. "They came on horses like you said, Maria and a man. They went into the shed. Then we heard gunshots. She left with the horses and—" Claudia whimpered "—the guards dragged the man's body out into the jungle."

"Noah and Matt are okay?"

"Yes," she said.

"All right. What did the man look like? Anything you remember about him?"

"He wore glasses. These ugly, old glasses, like from the seventies."

Felix. The German buyer. What had he done? "Okay, listen to me. This will be over soon. Everything's going to happen today. Tell Noah to mark the van somehow before it leaves. We need to know for sure we have the right van. Do you understand? We only have one shot at this."

"Okay, but I had to hike out to get cell service. I've got to hike back up there."

"As fast as you can. And be careful," I said then disconnected.

So Maria killed Felix. I felt a hole open in the pit of my stomach. I knew she was dangerous, but… Should I tell Dalton and Nash? No. Then I'd have to explain how I knew. I wondered what he had done. Didn't matter. I had to go on with the plan.

We pulled into the lot and I pushed it from my mind.

The Casa del Mar was a quaint little seaside motel with purple walls strangled by tropical foliage. I went into the office and asked for Kevin—*crap, I don't know his last name.* The staffer behind the desk was a sweet young gal with a cherub face, her long straight hair pulled back and pinned with wood barrettes. I leaned toward her and said in a whisper, "Australian guy. Very yummy." I tried to blush. The hardest thing to fake. "He, uh, left something in my room last night and I, uh, think he probably needs it back right away."

She nodded, enjoying the gossip fodder. "Room seven," she said. "But I think I just saw him out by the pool."

I winked and slipped out, Chris behind me.

We headed for the beach side and the pool area—me, Chris and his bodyguards. I rounded the corner and caught sight of Kevin, sprawled out on a lounge chair in his swimming trunks, a fruity drink in his hand. I told Chris to tell Doug and Jack to hang back and I walked up to Kevin and halted at his feet. He recognized me right away, I could tell, but he scanned behind me, quickly to my left, then my right. His eyes came to a screeching halt when he spotted Doug and Jack. "Miss Brittany," he said, sitting up on the edge of his chair. "To what do I owe the pleasha?"

"It's nice to see you," I said with a big smile. "This is my friend, Chris."

Chris acknowledged him with a curt nod.

"'Owdy, mate," Kevin said. I could tell he was running through scenarios in his mind, possible reasons I was here.

"Actually, I feel silly now that I'm standing here." I had planned on the bodyguards hanging outside his door, not having to explain them to him.

"Naw, it's awright." He leapt to his feet and grabbed the lounge chair nearby, spun it around, and offered for me to sit as he eased back into his chair.

"Thanks," I said. "But we don't need to stay and bother you." I quickly scanned the pool area. A waiter on the far side was lingering over a table, looking our way. Shazam. Kevin had his own Yipes. That meant he wasn't in with Maria and I'd accomplished my goal.

"Oh, you're no botha," Kevin said, smiling, his brow knit. I had him baffled. "No botha at-tall."

"Where are my manners? Here you are, relaxing by the pool, and we barge right in. It can wait until later." I nudged Chris. "We should go."

Kevin got to his feet. The gentleman. "No need."

"Maybe we could schedule a lunch?"

"What's this all about?"

"Oh, just a silly idea I had. Really, it's nothing." All I needed now was for him to nod. A reluctant nod. "So, lunch tomorrow then?"

He smiled. And then the nod. *Thank you, Kevin!*

As we headed back to the SUV, Chris whispered to me, "The pecs on that guy. And the accent. Oooooh. My god, girl, no wonder you're coming apart at the seams."

Chapter 15

We dropped Chris off at the Coco-Cabana. I told him to get packed and head straight to the airport. "But I could still—"

"No argument, Chris. You were a big help. I couldn't have done this without you. But it's too dangerous. Tell me you'll go right now. Get on the next flight out."

He nodded grudgingly. "You be careful, too," he said.

I checked my watch. It was four thirty-five. "I'll call you as soon as I get back in the States. I promise." I gave him a hug. "Thank you."

"Just get the bastards," he said with a grin.

I hopped in the SUV and slammed the door. "Get back to The Toucan. Now!"

In the short time Doug had been in Costa Rica, he had learned to drive like a tico. He weaved in and out of the lanes, passing on a double yellow line, up a blind hill. No problem. "Good way to blend in with the locals," I said, gripping the handle.

He turned into the parking lot, throwing sand and gravel as he skidded to a stop. We piled out and took off running toward the pier. "There's the van," Jack shouted. "Where's Amanda and Colette?"

A white panel van slowed to a stop, ready to make the turn onto the pier. I scanned the roadways. No sign of the VW. *Crap, where are they?*

The traffic cleared and the van made the turn. This was our

chance. I looked both ways, up and down the causeway. No VW.

"How do you know that's the right van?" Doug said. "Noah was supposed to make sure we knew which one it was, right?"

"If Claudia got the message to him. And he was able to. And if he did, how?"

"Look." He pointed with the tire iron he carried in his hand.

Another white panel van was coming down the causeway, headed our way. It was the van. No question. Noah was on the roof. I shook my head. I should have known.

I looked the other way. The VW was puttering toward the corner. *C'mon guys, we've got one chance at this.*

The van turned the corner onto the pier, Carlos at the wheel, and Amanda was there with the VW. She gunned it to get right in front of him, then slammed on the brakes. Crash! *Go team! We got him!*

The driver-side door popped open and Carlos was hollering before his feet hit the ground. Amanda and Colette eased out of the VW, clad in bikinis for extra attention, and staggered toward him, hollering back.

You can always count on the crowd to do what crowds do. Clumps of people started to form around the scene. I hid among the throngs. I couldn't be seen.

Doug and Jack closed in. They had to get that back door open before Carlos noticed. Amanda and Colette were doing their part, keeping him distracted. Before Jack and Doug reached the van though, Noah sprang down from the roof, flipped the handle, and swung the panel doors wide. Jack and Doug bounded inside, grabbed a wooden crate, and dragged it onto the road. These guys were good. Noah was prying at the lid with the tire iron. Within seconds, Jack had a second crate, and Doug a third, hauled out onto the road. From where I stood, it looked like that was it. Three crates total.

Carlos came around the side of the van. "¿Qué demonios crees que estás haciendo?" *What the hell do you think you're doing?*

Noah flipped over the first crate and a writhing pile of snakes slid onto the pavement. The crowd reacted with squeals and gasps. Carlos jerked his head toward the witnesses, panic on his face. He had an audience. He had to be careful.

Dan and Sierra materialized from the crowd, one on each side of the van, spray cans in hand, and went to work painting "LIVE FREE!" down the side panels.

"¡Esa es mi propiedad!" Carlos shouted. *That's my property!*

I glanced around the crowd. People stared, motionless. "¡Llame a la policía!" I said to a man standing next to me. *Call the police!* I moved through the crowd. "¡Llame a la policía!" I kept moving. *Get on your phones, people!*

Jack and Doug faced down Carlos while Noah pried the lid off the second crate. Carlos glared at them, then his expression changed as recognition set in. He looked to Jack, then back to Doug, wracked with confusion. I could imagine what was running through his mind. He didn't know what the hell was going on. But he was smart enough to know it was more than a group of harmless activists. His eyes grew large and flitted around.

Noah flipped over the second crate and another clump of slithering snakes wriggled to get free of each other. He immediately went to work on the third crate.

"Keep your hands off that crate," Carlos said in English. "Back off."

Be careful! Noah cracked the lid, flipped it open, and jumped back. That was the one.

Sirens wailed a block away. Noah glared at Carlos and I could tell something wasn't right. *Noah, wait for the police!*

Noah took a step back from the crate. "Screw you!" he said to Carlos. He slammed his foot into the top edge of the crate. It rocked, tipping on its edge. Carlos rushed forward to push it back. He grabbed hold of the open edge with two hands and a snake reared up and struck him on the wrist. He screamed out in pain and dropped to the ground, wailing. The crowd gasped. Carlos rolled around on the pavement, holding his wrist in his hand, blathering in Spanish.

Noah kicked the crate again and knocked it over. The fer-de-lance tumbled from the top and landed in an s-coil next to Carlos. Shrieks and cries of fear rippled through the crowd. The snake uncoiled and shot across the road, the crowd parting for it. It disappeared in the grass.

Left on the road next to Carlos was a tangle of boa constrictors, fat and sluggish. But no drugs.

Noah, Jack and Doug smashed the crate to bits looking for a hidden compartment. Something. But there was nothing else. They ripped apart the other two crates. Nothing.

The police cars came around the corner. Jack and Doug took off at a dead run. Dan and Sierra had already disappeared among the tourists. Noah picked up a boa, then another, scanning the pavement beneath them, shaking his head. There was nothing there.

Dammit! We'd been so sure. The poisonous snake was there. Carlos had been driving, not Paco. What had we missed? I held my head, a sinking sensation threatening to take me down. All this for nothing. *Dammit! Dammit! Dammit!*

I watched helplessly as an officer put Noah in handcuffs and another questioned Amanda and Colette.

This didn't make sense. Why was there a fer-de-lance in the crate if there were no drugs? One poisonous snake. One lousy snake wouldn't bring much on the black market. It was hardly worth the trip. We needed for him to get arrested. But now, especially since he'd been ambushed by activists, he probably wouldn't even get a slap on the wrist for possession.

I smirked. At least the snake had given him more than a slap. But it wouldn't help me catch Maria.

I stared at the boas lying on the ground. Why would he put a poisonous snake in with them? Legal species. The fat, lethargic things barely moved, as if they'd just been fed—*holy crap, that's it!* No wonder Carlos was so confident.

I looked around. Would they confiscate the snakes as evidence? Examine them? What if they didn't?

I stepped from the crowd. "Excuse me, sir," I said to the officer who had cuffed Noah. "I'm sorry to interrupt."

"Quédese atrás," he said, holding his hand out in the universal sign to stop.

"No, no, the snake, look at the snake," I said, pointing.

"I need you to stay back," he said in English, stepping toward me.

I held up my hands. "I understand," I said. "I'm a veterinarian. From the U.S. I just happened to notice, there's something very wrong with these snakes. Do you mind?" I stepped toward the boas.

"Get back," the officer told me, his voice stern.

"But they might die," I pleaded, giving him my best doe eyes. "Please. I just want to check on them. Please."

He looked to the other officer who shrugged.

"Gracias," I said. I got down on my knees and took the fattest boa in my arms. I ran my hands down the length of it until I felt the lump. The snake came to life at my touch and wrapped itself around my waist. Behind the lump, I squeezed, pushing the bulge forward, hand over hand like a tube of toothpaste, working the bulge toward the throat. The snake bucked in my arms. "C'mon, give it up," I told him. I kneaded and rubbed and shoved. I had to get my elbow into it, but managed to get the lump moving toward its mouth.

When it was close, I hollered for the officer to come over. "This snake was fed recently," I said and squeezed as hard as I could below its throat. The snake writhed and jerked, its mouth unhinged and spread open wide, and a red rubber balloon stuffed with drugs plopped out onto the ground.

The cop's eyes grew wide. He told me to drop the snake and back away. I did as I was told. He grabbed the radio from his belt and called it in. I backed away further, then a little further, and into the crowd.

Noah watched me go, a big smile on his face.

Once I was several blocks away, I took out my phone and punched the number for Mom. Mr. Strix answered in one ring. "Carlos Mendoza was just arrested for running drugs—"

"How in the world do you know that?"

"It happened right on the street. Everyone saw it." I had a short window. Carlos was in excruciating pain, so they'd take him straight to the hospital for the antidote, but eventually on to the police station. "Is there any chance you could keep him from making any calls? Have the customs authority hold him for questioning or something. Forty-eight hours would be great."

"I can try, but why—"

"I have a hunch."

CHAPTER 16

The cooler had been dragged out to the bonfire. Everyone was there, drinking in celebration. Everyone except Noah.

"Even though they saw the drugs, they still arrested Noah," I said.

Doug, tipping a beer, waved it off. He wiped his mouth with the back of his hand and said, "Noah'll be fine. He's been arrested before. No big deal."

Jack handed me a beer. "He'll be out in twenty-four hours."

I hoped they were right. I couldn't do anything for him without jeopardizing my job. I looked to Amanda and Colette. "Did you get the phone?"

"Right here," Colette said and dug it out of her handbag. "It was in the cab of the truck."

"Good," I said. I scrolled through the numbers to find Maria's. "Excellent. Amanda, you have the web thing ready?"

"Yep," she said and handed me a slip of paper. "Here's the URL."

I handed it and the phone to Doug. "You're up."

Doug took the phone and grinned. He drew in a long breath and his expression changed to one of a ruthless drug dealer. "Okay, I'm ready," he said.

He punched send and held the phone to his ear. We all waited, silent. After a few moments, he said, "Listen to me very carefully. Your brother has been a very naughty boy. If you ever want to see him alive again, you'll pay what he owes. Two hundred thousand dollars." He listened. "Well, you see, the thing is, my boss is not a patient man. By midnight. Or he dies." He looked at me as he listened, his eyebrows raised. Then finally, "Good. You'll transfer the money through a web site. I'm only going to give you this address once. Are you ready?" There was a long pause then he rattled off the URL. "And just in case he means less to you than we thought, we'll come for those sweet little dogs next." He disconnected.

I let out my breath.

"What'd you think?" he grinned. "What'd you think about the dogs? Nice touch, huh?"

I took the phone from him and ripped it open. I took out the battery and smashed the chip with a rock, then threw it into the fire. "Now we wait," I said. "You guys were fantastic today. I can't thank you enough."

Colette laughed. "I'm not sure the VW fared well, but it was worth it. Noah won't care."

"What if she doesn't pay?" Amanda asked.

"She will," I said.

"But I don't understand," she said. "Why'd you have her pay a ransom?"

"Pressure. I want to tick her off. A hit in the pocketbook ought to do the trick. Not to mention she wants to strangle Carlos herself right about now." I grinned. "But most of all, she's worried, wondering how much this new guy on the block will impact her business. I wouldn't want to be at her house right now."

"Yeah, she's probably pacing in circles, making her little dogs dizzy," Doug said with a grin.

"Now what?" asked Jack. "We storm her house?"

"Now we wait." I shook my head. I couldn't believe these guys.

Jack nodded and apparently felt waiting was a good time to be drinking because he flipped the top off the cooler and started passing cold bottles around.

My phone buzzed. It was Dalton. "Excuse me," I said and walked toward the tree house. "Hello?"

"Hey, it's me," he said. "What are you up to?"

"I'm, uh, at the beach. Enjoying a virgin margarita."

"Yeah, George cancelled cards tonight."

Interesting. "Did he say why?"

"No, but he seemed irritated about something."

Good. Very good.

"I thought maybe we could get dinner."

Are you serious? Just what I need right now. "Okay," I said. What else could I say? "I'll meet you back at the bungalow."

I shuffled back down to the fire. "I've gotta go," I said.

"What? What about Maria and the ransom?"

"You'll have to let me know."

Dalton was showered, shaved, and all dressed up. "Let's go someplace nice," he said.

I changed into the cotton sundress, the only remotely formal attire I had, and we headed for the restaurant at the Playa de Delfines resort. Dalton pulled up to the front door, got out of the car and ran around to open my door for me. He offered his arm and we entered the restaurant, happy newlyweds, as the valet drove away with the car.

Candles flickered atop tables covered with white linens. The aroma of fresh fish and seafood wafted on the sea breeze. The clink of silverware on fine china mixed with the murmur of intimate conversations.

We got to our table, a table for two on the deck overlooking the ocean, and Dalton pulled out my chair for me. He certainly was making an effort.

As he sat, he said to the waiter, "We'd like a bottle of wine. The lady will choose."

I smiled. "Your house red will be fine. Thank you."

I looked at Dalton and he looked at me. He seemed nervous. A Navy SEAL, nervous. "I was hoping…" He made sure he had my attention. "I was hoping we could start over."

He continued to surprise me. "How do you mean?"

"I tried to apologize today and, well, I blew it." He managed an uncomfortable grin. "Obviously."

I shook my head. "You didn't blow it. It was me." *Oh man!* "My mom always said I could hold a grudge."

"I didn't exactly give you a reason to like me," he said, his voice thick.

I smiled. "That's for sure."

He let out a short, half laugh, a sigh of relief really. "Yeah."

I grinned. The candlelight was warm, cozy. "You're kinda growing on me, though."

The waiter arrived with the wine. He poured the test sample. I sipped. It was fine. I gave him a nod, then he poured a glass for each of us. Dalton raised his, taking hold of it by the stem this time I noticed. "To a fresh start," he said.

I lifted my glass to meet his. "To a fresh start."

His eyes met mine and they softened. "I was an ass. I'm sorry."

"Yes, you were." I grinned. "But I've been a pain in the ass, too, so, you know."

He laughed, a light, easy laugh. I could tell he was already feeling relaxed. He smiled and his eyes seemed to light up. "I know what you're feeling. It's frustrating. But you'll make it to Special Ops someday. No doubt in my mind. You've got what it takes. I can see it in you. It just takes patience."

"Yeah, patience," I said. "Not exactly my strong suit."

"It'll happen." He smiled again and I noticed how the color of his eyes seemed to change from brown to a hazel-green, taking on the hue of the green shirt that fit snuggly over his shoulders. I pictured him in his dress uniform, crisp and cut. My cheeks flushed. I felt like one of those cheerleaders, swooning over the hot soldier who was home on leave.

"What?" he said. "I mean it. You'll be great."

"Thanks," I said. I glanced at my phone. No word yet from Amanda. "What made you want to be an agent? For that matter, what made you want to be a SEAL?"

"Oh, you know. Why does any SEAL want to be a SEAL?"

I nodded. They were a different breed, that was for sure.

"I knew I couldn't be a career SEAL, though. I mean, I loved the job, don't get me wrong. But I wanted to have another life, you know, kids." He shrugged, disappointment in his face.

"But your marriage…?"

"Navy wives," he said, matter-of-fact.

I grew up a Navy brat. I knew exactly what he meant. "I'm sorry," I said. "The crack about your divorce the other day crossed the line. I'm really sorry."

He nodded. "It is what it is." He shook his head. "And the girls back home…"

"Where's home?"

"Montana. I grew up hunting and fishing. Loved the outdoors."

I nodded. A lot of Fish and Wildlife agents had similar backgrounds.

He took another sip of wine. "As far as the undercover work, well, I've got no ties and I'm good at it."

I glanced at my phone. Nothing.

"Do you have somewhere to be?" he asked.

"What? Why?"

"The phone."

"Oh, no. Just checking the time."

His brows raised. He wasn't satisfied with my answer.

"Sorry, habit I guess." I tucked it under my thigh so I'd feel it vibrate if I got a text. "I just realized," I said. "I don't even know your first name."

His expression didn't change. "Everyone calls me Dalton."

"Isn't that your last name?"

He nodded slightly. "You can call me Dalton."

"All right." *Mental note. Dig into that story.*

I smiled. He smiled. There was a big awkward space you could steer a cruise ship through.

The waiter arrived to take our order. I chose the Pasta Primavera and Dalton ordered the Surf and Turf—tenderloin, rare, and grilled lobster.

I sneaked a peek at my phone. Nothing. I glanced at Dalton and suddenly felt like a complete fool. What if what I'd done backfired? What if I blew our cover to smithereens and everything he'd been working toward? Or worse?

I shook it off. *She'll pay. She's gonna pay. And then she'll come running to us.*

"So what's your story?"

He caught me off guard. "What?"

"You're a vegetarian." He gave me a sympathetic smile. "By the way, that first night, I felt bad for you, but you were a trooper, chewing away on that prime rib."

I smirked.

"Don't worry. No one else noticed."

"Yeah, but how'd you know?"

He cocked his head to the side. "I was sitting right next to you."

I sighed. Damn. I thought I'd covered pretty well.

"I know you're into yoga. But that's it. Oh, and you were a Navy brat. Overseas?"

"My mom was a physician on the Mercy. We were in the Philippines for awhile." I hesitated. He didn't need my whole life story. "High school in San Diego. Which SEAL team were you?"

"Three."

"So you were West Coast."

He nodded, impressed. "That's right. But you're changing the subject back to me. You're good at that."

I shrugged. It was true. I twirled my bracelet around my wrist.

"That's a beautiful bracelet," he said. "I've noticed you never take it off."

I nodded. "My father gave it to me. It was the last…" I looked into Dalton's eyes. "It was the last time I saw him." I shook my head. "I should have been there with him."

"What do you mean? What happened?"

I shook my head. "I was in school, my freshman year. I should have been there with him. If he hadn't been alone…"

Dalton waited, giving me time before finally asking, "What are you saying?"

"My father was killed by poachers. I know it. I was told it was an accident, but I know where he was. They'd threatened him in the past, but my dad, he was stubborn."

"Poppy, listen to me. If you'd have been there, you probably would have been killed, too."

I stared off into space, into the past, when my phone buzzed and I jerked in my seat. Dalton eyed me with suspicion.

"You know," he said. "Maria came out to the golf course this evening. She seemed agitated."

"Oh?" I said and took a gulp of wine.

"She talked to George, then he canceled the card game with no explanation, and she led him away by the nose."

"Really? What do you think that was all about?"

"I don't know, but we leave day after tomorrow. Maybe tomorrow morning you should stop in, make friends. See what you can find out. You can ride over with me."

"All right," I said. No way. I couldn't go there tomorrow morning. If I showed up on her doorstep, it would ruin everything I had going. She had to call me. I'd have to think of an excuse. "I should take something. I saw a bakery in town. We could stop on the way and get a torta chilena or something."

He eyed me and I couldn't read what he was thinking. "Okay," he finally said.

Our dinner arrived. As the waiter placed Dalton's plate in front of him, I stole a second to glance down at my phone. Text from Amanda read: Done.

I raised my wine glass and held it in front of me. "Here's to working with you," I said. "It's been, well, an experience."

He laughed. "Yeah, I'll say."

As we ate our meals, I decided I really liked Dalton. I was feeling more comfortable with him. Too bad I'd probably never see him again after we left Costa Rica in two days.

Neither of us wanted dessert, so he called for the car and we headed back to our room. He parked and got out to open my door again. "Let's take a walk," he said and took me by the hand. He led me down by the pool to a deck that looked out over the valley. Tiny solar lights lit the walkway and gave a warm glow to the night. The insects croaked away in the thicket, the warm air full of the scents of the floral garden. He leaned on the railing and turned to face me. "Nice view, huh?"

"Yes," I said. I could barely see him in the faint moonlight but the glow of Arenal Volcano stood out in the dark sky.

"Don't look now but," he whispered, "we're being watched."

"Oh?" I hadn't seen Yipes or anyone around when we got out of the car. How had I missed him?

"Kiss me," he said and pulled me to him. His lips met mine, a gentle caress, then he pulled me tighter, passion rising. It's too dark for anyone to see, I realized, mid-kiss. But I didn't care. I wanted his kiss. I wanted his arms around me. He pulled away for a moment, as if he were giving me the chance to back away, as though he knew that I knew no one was really watching. I hesitated. "I'm sorry," he whispered. "I—"

I wrapped my hands around his neck and pressed my lips to his and I was like a teenager, back in high school at the homecoming dance. My nerves tingled. Oh he could kiss! I leaned into him, pressing my body against his. He held me tight, his hands at the small of my back. I remembered how he'd lifted me up and twirled me around in the airport. Strong but gentle. His kiss was like that, strong but gentle. A flush of warmth came over me and I wanted to give into it. I wanted him to take me back to our room. I wanted to feel his hands on me, to—I pulled away to catch my breath.

"We probably shouldn't—" I bit down hard on my lip.

"I know," he said and nuzzled my neck.

"I mean, essentially, you're my boss and—"

"Yeah," he said, his head nodding in agreement. "You're right." But he didn't let me go from his embrace.

"We should call it a night," I said. "Head back to the room." I pinched my lips together. "I mean…you know what I mean."

I couldn't see his expression in the dark, couldn't tell what he was thinking, but his breathing changed and he held me against him as though he didn't want to let go. Finally, he nodded and we walked straight back to the room. He shut the door behind him and I was in his arms again. This time he pulled away. "I thought you said—"

"Shut up and kiss me," I said. He grinned. "No wait," I said. *Crap!*

I spun around and took a few steps away, then turned back to face him. His eyes had turned to a soft brown. He looked at me, waiting, his breath coming in short pants.

"I'm not sure we should—I mean, you and I—we probably ought to…"

He nodded.

"I'm going to take a shower," I said. I escaped to the bathroom and locked the door behind me. I looked in the mirror. My hair was all frizzed out. *This humidity has messed with more than your hair. Your damn hormones are on the fritz.* I cranked on the cold water.

CHAPTER 17

I left the bungalow early under the guise of wanting to get to
the bakery before they were sold out. I told Dalton to wait,
I'd be back. I didn't want him to catch me pacing and I didn't
want him going to the house. Maria hadn't called yet and I
was starting to wonder if she would. Either way, I was leaving
tomorrow, back to the U.S., back to the grind, back to working
my way up from the bottom. As Dalton had made clear, this
was a one-time deal, a necessity wrung from a senior agent's
mistake.

My plan had to work.

I climbed the stairs to the tree house. Noah hadn't been back
yet and the place had a lonely aura. So small, so primitive. I went
to the bathroom and gave the biscuit can a shake. I grinned with
absolute, unadulterated relief when Clyde bounded up the side
of the house and swung on the hammock, launching himself
into position to catch a biscuit.

"There you are," I said. I lobbed a biscuit into the air and he
caught it. I watched him gnaw at it, holding it in his little hand
and stump. I marveled at his ability to cope without his right
hand. He compensated well. After all, what choice did he have?
"Life is suffering," I said. "That's what the Buddha said." He
didn't look my way, didn't look up from his biscuit. He lived
in the moment. That peace for which we strive, he'd mastered.
Live for today. Live and let live. "If only others could share

your wisdom," I said.

I went out onto the balcony, leaned on the railing, and gazed out at the ocean. "Oh, Clyde, what if she doesn't call?" The morning sun streamed down into the water making it glow an aquamarine. "I'll never have this chance again." I turned back to Clyde. He was swallowing the last crumb. "Maybe I should have listened to Dalton. Maybe I should tell him what I've done. I think he'll understand."

Clyde jumped onto the railing beside me and bobbed up and down, chittering away, his way of communicating.

"I'm just trying to make a difference, you know." Clyde grinned at me, his round, black eyes looking into mine, like he knew. "You're lucky now, little buddy. You have Isabella. And Noah." I frowned. Noah. What was I going to do about him?

"I don't think I'll ever see you again, Clyde. This is goodbye, you know. Adiós." Clyde frowned, covered his eyes with his tiny hand, and shook his head. "Isabella must have taught you the word adiós, huh?" He shook his head again. "Oh Clyde." I picked him up, sat down in the chair, and cuddled him in my lap. "I'll miss you." I stroked his head and he cooed. I laid my head back, enjoying the warm morning scents, and warmth of another being, loving me. It was simple. "You're the perfect man, Clyde," I said. "Those other guys, complicated. But not you." I scratched behind his ear. "Not you."

The phone rang. I jerked in the seat. Clyde leaped from my lap. I looked at my cell. Unknown number. "Hello?"

"Brittany, this is George."

"Hi, George." Of course she'd have George call.

"Maria mentioned that you might be interested in looking at some animals yourself?"

"Oh that," I gave him a Brittany giggle. "No need. I'm all set. Thanks anyway." I hung up.

I gave Clyde a scratch on the head. "Time to talk to Dalton," I said and headed for my moped.

He was in the bathroom when I got there. I paced around the room, doubting, rethinking how I was going to tell him. The door opened. "We need to talk," I said.

"I know last night was—"

"What? No. This isn't about last night."

He looked confused. "All right, what then?"

"George just called me. He offered to show me some more animals."

"What? George? Called *you*? Why would he call you? What did he say?" He paused. "Are you sure it was him?"

"He said Maria told him to call me."

Dalton's brow knit with confusion.

I shifted on my feet. "Maria believes I'm the one making decisions on the big ticket buys."

He stared at me for a long, thoughtful moment, then his expression turned to annoyance. His temper in check, he forced out the words, "And why would she think that?"

I offered a don't-be-too-upset grin. "I kinda told her that."

His jaw tightened and he asked through clenched teeth, "And why would you do that?"

"She cornered me in the horse barn. She knew I spoke Spanish. She accused me of hiding something." I gave up on the grin. "So I went on the offensive."

He spun around, ran his fingers through his hair, and gripped a handful at the top of his scalp. "Please, tell me what you mean by offensive."

"Nothing really, I just tried to connect with her, you know, psychology 101. Since she's really in charge, and George is her lackey, I figured if I made her think I had really been faking the ditzy wife thing, give her a good reason, you know, the redirect, she'd understand and we'd bond."

"Bond?" He spun back around to face me. "You're not making any sense. And why didn't you tell me this before?"

I held his gaze. I had no answer. At least one I could tell him.

"Tell me everything."

"That's about it really."

"Why don't I believe you?" He paced toward the window and back. "So where did George say to meet and when?"

"He didn't."

"What do you mean? I thought you said he called with an offer."

"He did. I turned him down."

"You what?" He grabbed his hair again and laced his fingers together. He looked like he was holding the top of his head so it wouldn't blow off. "Why would you—"

"You don't bite at the first offer."

"Gee, don't tell me, Negotiation 101?"

"Actually, I saw it on an episode of MacGyver," I said, deadpan. He didn't need to be a total jerk.

He held out his hands like he wanted to grab me by the neck.

"Don't worry. She's going to call me herself."

His cheeks were turning red. "And how the hell do you know that?"

"Trust me. She will."

He plopped down in the chair, his mouth hanging open.

"I worked hard to make her think I'm a hard-nosed business woman. If I told George yes, she would suspect something was up. No good businessman would jump at the first offer." He stared at me, unblinking. "Only a cop would do that."

His expression turned to disdain.

My cell phone rang. "See," I said. "Right on time." I picked up. "Howdie," I said in a cheerful Brittany voice.

Dalton flopped back in the chair with a groan.

It was Maria. In a calm, clear voice she said, "I'm confident we can come to an arrangement that will suit your needs."

"I've already made arrangements that suit my needs," I said. Dalton covered his face with his hands.

"I tell you what," she said. "Hear me out. We already have an established relationship. Take a look at my merchandise. I will match any other offer or beat it. What have you got to lose?"

"Hold on," I said. I held my hand over the phone and winked at Dalton. He shook his head. I sang a verse of *Row, Row, Row your Boat* in my head. That was probably a good amount of time. I put the phone back to my ear. "All right," I said. "We might as well take a look."

Chapter 18

I mentioned to Dalton on the way to Maria's house that we should stop and pick up a torta chilena. I don't know why, but that seemed to irritate him more.

He felt the need to remind me of our goal. "We are to confirm she is the head of this operation. Nothing else. We don't reveal ourselves. We keep our cover. Nash decides what to do with the information. Do you understand?"

"Perfectly."

"I mean it, Poppy. We're not in the U.S. Our goal here is not an arrest. Our goal is intel. That's it."

"I understand." I got it the first time.

"Even if we get an offer to sell, we do not arrest, we do not hint at arrest. We don't warn, talk, sing. We do nothing."

"Got it. No singing."

He yanked the steering wheel to the right and skidded to a halt on the side of the road. He spun in the seat to face me. I instinctively pulled back from him. He was pretty fired up and I had no idea what was coming.

"Let me be very clear," he said, his jaw set. "I don't like this. I don't like how this has transpired. How you've—" He sneered. "I'm damn sure there's more you're not telling me. But we are going in there together. And there is no question about it, our lives are in danger. Do you understand that? Do you?"

I nodded. I did.

He stared ahead, his hands gripping the wheel for some time, then shook his head, reluctantly coming to some conclusion. "You got the invitation, however you did it. If she believes you're the one running the show, then—" he clenched his jaw, then let out a breath "—then we need to continue with that. You need to take the lead." He looked down, his tongue stuck in his cheek. "I'll act the clueless husband."

I couldn't believe what I was hearing. I had underestimated him. He was a true professional, dedicated to the mission—no matter what it took.

"Just remember," he said, his finger in my face. "My life is in your hands."

I nodded.

"I need to know you understand. I need to hear you say it."

I looked into his eyes. "I know this is not a game. I know it's dangerous. I promise to be careful."

He seemed somewhat relieved. "You better be."

I held his gaze, serious. I nodded.

He eyed me. "What else do I need to know?"

That I made her believe there's another kingpin in town, threatening to take over her business. That I tricked her into paying a ransom. That I put Carlos in jail for running drugs. "Nothing," I said. "I swear."

"All right." He seemed satisfied.

"I didn't mean to—" I sighed. "I just knew she was the kingpin and the opportunity was there and—"

"What's done is done." He stared ahead for a long time, thinking. It was as though some of the events of the past few days were clicking into place, making sense to him. "Believe me, I've been there. I just wish you would've told me before." He stared, thought some more. Then turned to me, his expression stern, as though to drive home the point. "Remember what I said? This whole business of working under cover is like improv. So now, whatever happens, whatever is said, we go with it. No matter what happens, we stay in character."

"I can do improv."

"Not just improv. The most important skill you can have—more important than any combat training, physical strength, or technical skills—is your ability to twist the truth to fit the situation, to shape it to your advantage. On the fly." He grinned. "And the ability to sell it. Which," he shook his head, "I have no doubt you can do."

He slammed the gearshift into drive and pulled out. "Let's do this thing."

As we pulled into the drive, the butler stepped onto the porch and called the guard dogs off. We parked and got out of the car. The butler greeted us. "She is waiting for you in the horse barn," he said with a smile, as if we were there for afternoon tea.

Dalton took me by the hand and, as we walked toward the barn, he leaned over and kissed me on the cheek. "For luck," he whispered.

As we entered the barn, part of me feared this was a farce, that she wouldn't be there. That all my work had been for nothing. But she was waiting.

If she hadn't been an evil wildlife smuggler, I'd have admired her poise. She carried herself with a confidence most women would envy. She was neither friendly nor stand-offish. She simply welcomed us.

Her little dogs circled, yipping their hellos. The same man was with her, the one who carried the gun. "Ramon will hold your cell phones," she said.

Dalton handed his over without reluctance. I dug around in the bottom of my handbag for mine. Fortunately, I'd erased all the texts and numbers already. "Search her bag, too," Maria said.

I shrugged and handed him the bag. "Keep it," I said. If he

searched it, some items might give him pause. This way, he'd be less likely to bother. I didn't like being without those items, but you do what you've got to do.

Maria gestured to three horses that had been saddled and were ready to ride. "Let's go then." Maria made it look easy. She seemed to float onto the back of the horse. Her man picked up each dog and they were placed in the saddle bags on either side of her, their little heads poking out.

Dalton helped me mount my horse. Not that I needed help. Then he heaved himself atop his.

We followed Maria out of the barn and down a trail, the trail that led to the neighboring property and the coffee-roasting shed. She wasn't hiding now. Maybe it was arrogance. Maybe she figured I knew now anyway. What was there to hide? Either way, she was taking us directly to her hidden lair and, I was sure, going to offer some class I species—scarlet macaws, howler monkeys, ridley turtles, maybe even a jaguar. If we were really lucky, she'd offer shark fins, but that was unlikely, since we'd established we were in the pet market. One step at a time.

I felt a divine sense of satisfaction. She was leading us to our goal, to confirmation. Yet, at the same time, it felt hollow. We'd get up to the shed, see the illegal animals, confirm she was the kingpin, then we'd smile and walk away. I wanted to see her in handcuffs, dragged off to prison for what she does. I couldn't help it; I wanted her to suffer for every animal she'd ever harmed.

At one o' clock in the afternoon, the heat was more than uncomfortable. The horses labored, huffing with sweat. Maria didn't seem to care. She pushed her horse up the inclines and we had to keep up. She said nothing. Simply led and we followed.

Finally, with my blouse soaked with sweat and my inner thighs raw from rubbing the saddle (of course I wore shorts), we came into the clearing where the roasting shed stood amid the concrete slabs. We dismounted and a guard led the horses to a shaded area with a trough.

I tried to hide my excitement. This was it. Once Dalton saw the class I species inside, there'd be no question she was the kingpin.

Maria led us around the corner of the shed and as we stepped inside I stopped short and my knees turned to jelly. It was empty. The two old coffee roasters stood in the corner and that was it.

She gestured toward a couple of folding chairs. "Have a seat."

What was this about? I glanced at Dalton. He acted the dopey husband, as he'd said he would. He happily grabbed a chair and popped it open, placing it in front of me, then set up another for himself. He plopped down as if he didn't have a care in the world.

"Before we go any further," she said. "I just want to clarify a few things." Her eyes bore into me. I met her gaze, as steely eyed as she was. "You came for a monkey, did you not?"

Dalton grinned. "Yeah, my sweetheart wants her own." He beamed at me, love in his eyes. At least *he* was following our plan. What was Maria up to?

Maria smiled demurely at Dalton. "John, dear, I hate to be the one to tell you, but your wife has been a very busy lady making some arrangements of her own." She stepped closer to him and ran her fingers through his hair. "And here, I thought we had something special."

"What?" My head snapped toward Dalton. "What's she talking about?"

He pursed his lips. "Nothing, honey bunny." He grinned wide. "Sweetheart." He glared at Maria. "She's trying to drive a wedge between us of mistrust." He shook it off. "It's an old business tactic. Don't fall for it." He looked her in the eyes. "Our deal stands. You know I'm willing to pay a fair price. Let's just see what you've got."

I eyed him, then looked back to her. She wore a sly grin.

Maybe I should give her what she wants. See where this leads.

"What's going on, John?"

"Nothing." He wouldn't look at me. "I said don't worry about it."

I drew in a sharp breath and covered my mouth. "You've been sleeping with her!" *Holy crap, I didn't see that one coming.*

"Oh, honey, can't you see? She's making you—"

"Don't you *honey* me." I turned my back to him.

"Oh, you're one to talk," he said.

I spun around and glared at him. *What the hell is he doing?* He crossed his arms and huffed, like he was trying to get up the nerve to say something. "You'll sleep with any young stud with a ponytail."

My mouth dropped open. "How dare you?"

"You think I don't know? You sneaking off during the day to get some action. While I'm working to put food on the table. You promised you'd stop. This trip was supposed to be for us." He managed a hopeful grin. "To bring us together."

I clamped my mouth shut. I didn't know what to say. I had to trust Dalton. He had just reminded me, improv was the cornerstone of undercover work. Go with it. But what the hell was going on? I looked to Maria. She stood with her arms crossed, a smug expression on her face, nodding approvingly. She was enjoying this.

I glared at Dalton and said through gritted teeth. "You have the nerve to accuse me. And you've been with"—I jerked my head toward Maria—"*her*."

He shrugged, a noncommittal, it-doesn't-matter-anymore shrug. "Can we just do some business here? Talk about this later?"

My mind went into overdrive. What does Maria think she knows? After I'd confronted her, had she tried to seduce Dalton to probe him for information about me? Or had he been sleeping with her all along? And if so, what had he been planning? Wait—he said ponytail. *Noah.* But why would he give him away? *Unless Maria already knows. That means—*

"Yes, let's get to business," said Maria. "I have just the right pet for you." She brought her fingers to her lips and whistled, one of those loud whistles that can be heard in the next county.

One of the guards came through the door carrying a cage with a cloth draped over the top. He set it down next to her and stood behind her, his hand on the weapon strapped over his shoulder. The cage was situated so the door faced away from me. I couldn't see what was inside. Maria opened the cage, reached in, grabbed hold, and rose to face us with a monkey in her grasp, her hand wrapped around its tiny neck. A white-faced capuchin. Squirming and squealing. It's little hands reached up to grip her wrist and I saw it. The right hand was missing.

Oh my god. It's Clyde.

Maria grinned with evil pleasure. She shook Clyde, tightening her grip around his neck, and he let out a shriek. "What do you think?"

My gut turned to water. *Think. Think! What the hell is going on?* Poor little Clyde. *She knows all about Noah and Isabella too! Dammit!* Of course she'd know who was targeting her operation. But Dalton must have known something, somehow. He covered with the adultery story. But how? Why hadn't he mentioned it to me?

She must think I'm an activist, an eco-terrorist. It was the only thing that made sense.

Clyde whimpered. Maria gave him another shake. "¡Cállate!" *Shut up!*

My breath came in short pants. *Not Clyde!* I wanted to grab Maria by the neck and shake her, shake her until her brains spilled out. But I couldn't. I couldn't move, couldn't act. Instead, I had to convince her I was a slutty, rich bitch who'd sleep with anything for sport. That Noah was a coincidence. If she thought I was an activist, here to infiltrate her operation, she'd kill us both. Dalton knew it, too.

I glared at him. "Are we still on the monkey kick?" I added

an eye roll. "I never wanted a frigging monkey. That was your idea. But you couldn't let it go." I crossed my arms. *"Oh, darling, let's have a baby,"* I mocked. "Don't you get it. I only married you because I got pregnant. And you were so—" I shook my head. "So damn sweet. Then we lost the baby anyway." I rolled my eyes again. "But Jesus, can you be any more boring in the bedroom? The lights always have to be out, really? Always on top? My god, screwing a Hobbit would be more exciting than you." I blew out my breath. *Where do I come up with this stuff?*

His bottom lip quivered. "You always have to do that, don't you. Emasculate me in front of other women."

"Emasculate? Wow, been working on your vocabulary, have you?"

"Oh, you think I'm stupid? I knew you were sleeping with him the moment I saw him. The way he looked at you. You don't care about me. You don't care about him. You only care about the size of his—"

"Enough!" We both jerked our heads toward Maria. She held Clyde up and shook him again. He squirmed in her grasp, his little eyes begging me to help. I couldn't. *I can't.* If I showed any emotion, any sign of caring about him, we'd all be dead. I turned back to Dalton so I wouldn't have to look at Clyde's pleading eyes. "Jerk," I said, acting as though I was too mad at him to even notice the monkey.

"Bitch," he muttered back.

"What'd you call me?" *Keep it up. Keep the attention from Clyde. Maybe we'll all get out of this alive.*

Dalton grew silent, solemn. He put his head down. "All I've ever wanted was for you to be happy, for you to have special things."

"Well, *honey bunny*, all you need to do then is shut up." I turned my attention back to Maria. "You dragged us up here in this god-awful heat." I pulled my wet blouse from my skin. "Look at me. I need a shower." I shot her a look of disgust. "Do you have an offer or what?"

She didn't miss a beat. "Right now, I'm offering you this monkey." Her eyes bore into me like a dentist's probe, poking into the dark crevices of my thoughts, scraping at my emotions. "What do you think? Do you have a buyer for him?"

"Don't waste my time," I said. "I told you. I'm only interested in big ticket pets. Exotics. I can get a monkey anywhere."

Her eyes narrowed. "You're right," she said. I breathed a little. "These are a dime a dozen. Besides"—she held up his right hand—"this one is damaged. Worthless." She rubbed the top of his head with one hand and tightened her grip on his neck. His tiny tongue stuck out from his mouth. Her eyes locked on me and she said, "Another mouth to feed." With a quick jerk of her wrist, she snapped his neck and tossed him to the floor at my feet. His little body landed with a thwack.

The breath left my body. I stared, way too long. Clyde lay still, a tiny pool of blood forming under his head. I tried to find my voice. All I could think about were soldiers, soldiers who give their lives for liberty, for freedom, for justice for all. Young boys who go off to war, for a promise of amber waves of grain, of purple mountain majesties, for a land of the free and the home of the brave, willing to give the ultimate sacrifice. For a cause. For something they believed in. For their brothers.

Poor Clyde. I could not let his death be in vain. I would not. *For your brothers, Clyde.*

I raised my chin and looked her in the eye. "What the hell woman? You almost got that on my shoe."

Dalton shook his head and muttered, "Heartless bitch."

I turned my gaze on him so I could think without her seeing my eyes. This was a test. Just a test. I drew in a deep breath. *Hold it together, McVie. Think!*

Okay. None of this changed the fact that she was desperate to sell. She'd brought us this far. She must've had a plan once we passed the test. If she had class I species, they couldn't be crated, ignored for days, then transported like snakes and frogs.

They'd need regular care. They had to be housed somewhere. I was betting it was nearby. And we're here now.

I huffed an annoyed huff. "You're wasting my time."

Maria studied me as though she still wasn't convinced. I rose from the chair. "C'mon, John. Let's go."

He got up and followed me toward the door.

Maria followed right behind us. "Now let's not be too hasty," she said.

I shrugged as though I really didn't care either way.

She passed between us and turned and motioned for us to return to the shed. "I'm sure you understand, in this business, I can't be too careful." I knew it. This was really happening. "I'll have my man bring some samples right away." She whistled again.

A guard came around the far corner of the shed and headed toward us with a two-way radio in his hand. He nodded to Maria, then looked right at me. It was the guy, the one who had chased Noah, the one I clobbered. *Crap!* I dropped my head, but it was too late. He recognized me. "Es ella. ¡Esa es la chica!" he shouted and raised his weapon.

Dalton looked at me. "What's—"

"Run!"

CHAPTER 19

Bullets zinged past me—pop, pop, pop—as I sprinted double-time across the concrete slabs. I plunged into the wall of green, branches and leaves whipping at my face.

Dalton was right behind me. I could barely hear Maria shouting commands to her guards, telling one to follow the ridge, another to follow the tree line and flank us.

I tore through a tangle of vines, dodged tree trunks, and ducked under broad-leafed palms, my lungs burning, my heartbeat banging in my ears.

At once, I realized Dalton wasn't with me anymore. I whipped around. He was limping toward me, his pant leg soaked with blood at his ankle. "You're hit," I said. As he neared, I noticed blood dripping at his elbow, too.

He didn't slow. "I'm fine."

"You're not fine. We can't run like this."

"You can. Go."

No women in combat burst into my head. Then our whole conversation. I looked into his eyes and realized he'd purposely run directly behind me, shielding me from the gunfire. *Oh, Dalton!*

Pop, pop, pop came the crackle of gunfire. I couldn't think about that now. I turned my head one way, then the other, listening. She'd sent them to flank us. That meant they'd separated, spread out. That was good. I looked around to get my bearings. To the right, about twenty paces should be a bell alarm. To the left, one at about fifty paces. "Can you make it about—"

"I'm fine."

"Okay." I nodded. "Okay, follow me," I whispered. "I have an idea."

We moved through the foliage like predators. My dad had taught me how to stalk prey, how to hide, how to become one with the forest and sneak up on a subject without making a noise. Dalton was a SEAL, so, needless to say, I had to keep checking to be sure he was behind me.

I came upon the bell wire and held out my hand to halt Dalton. I pointed down. He saw it and nodded. I stepped back to whisper, "We need to draw them in."

He frowned. "There are five of them, armed. We're outnumbered."

"They're not military. They're boys with guns."

He held his right hand at his left shoulder where a blood stain had formed and winced. "Yeah? How do you know?"

I heard movement behind us. "No time. Fall down and act hurt."

He glared at me with big eyes. "I'm not going to put myself in a prone position."

The sound of a weapon, scraping through foliage was near by. We both heard it.

"Trust me," I said. He hesitated. I stepped on the wire, enough that the bell made a light tinkle that only someone close by could hear.

Dalton gritted his teeth.

I gestured for him to go down.

He regarded me with a cold examination. No doubt, he was running through the tactical advantages, remembering my skill at hand-to-hand combat, sizing me up against the probable skill of the guard who was now twenty paces away and closing.

In an instant, he spun around, grabbed some branches and

stumbled, flailing at leaves as he went, then tumbled to the ground with a grunt.

The guard halted. He'd heard him. He launched into a run toward us.

I dropped to all fours. The guard barreled by. I lunged at him from behind, catching him right in the knees. He collapsed, face down in front of me. I crawled on top of him. He tried to roll, but he was encumbered by his weapon. I pinned his hands to the ground. Dalton crawled toward us and wrenched the weapon free. He flipped it around and trained it on the guy. The guard put his head down. "¡No disparen! Me rindo. Me rindo." *Don't shoot! I surrender. I surrender.*

I scanned the forest floor. A thin vine ran up the side of a nearby tree trunk. I grabbed hold of it, ripped a length from the tree, and wrapped it around his wrists. I pulled his legs up to his back and tied his ankles together and to his wrists.

Dalton smirked. "Been cattle ropin' much?"

"Hey, he's not going anywhere."

Dalton checked the magazine. "Five rounds."

I nodded, but I really didn't want to have to shoot anyone.

There was movement to my left. I looked at Dalton. He'd heard it, too. He scooted to get his back against a tree. I rolled under some ferns.

The guard came running, tromping through the jungle like a bull elephant in rut. I stuck out my foot and he tripped, performing some kind of sideways triple salchow maneuver. I got to my feet to pounce, but he swiped my ankle with a well-executed leg sweep. I fell into the ferns, tucked and rolled, and I was back on my feet. He was scampering along on his hands and knees, one arm out, groping around in front of him. He'd dropped his weapon.

I jumped onto his back, slamming him to the ground just as he'd found the gun. Pop, pop, pop. Bullets zipped through the leaves. I wrapped my arm around his neck and got him in a chokehold. He bucked and flipped me over on my back, the full weight of him on top of me.

A third guard appeared, his weapon pointed at us. He was the one who'd recognized me. The guy I was holding with his belly facing the gun grunted a terrified, "¡No disparen!" *Don't shoot!*

Dalton fired. The bullet grazed the guard's shoulder. Purposefully no doubt. These men weren't trying to kill us. The man threw down his weapon and his hands shot upward.

Dalton motioned with his rifle for him to get down on the ground. I rolled my opponent off of me. He put his hands behind his back, anxious for me to tie him up. I quickly wrapped their wrists with some vine like I had done with the first guy.

Dalton scanned the forest. "Something's not right. That was too easy."

I sat back on my haunches and pulled moss from my hair. "Seriously?"

"We need to move. Now." He picked up the other two weapons.

"Wait," I said. "There are two more. We don't know where they are."

"Exactly. But they know where we are. Now move."

"But we know they're headed this way, right?"

He glared at me. "Defensive tactical maneuver. We need to move."

I shook my head. "If we retreat, Maria will have time to get away, to alert others, to get rid of evidence, to—" I shook my head "—do other stuff. No way I'm giving her that chance."

Behind Dalton, a walking palm tree stood tall, its multitude of roots reaching out in many directions. I pushed past him, grabbed hold of a root, and shinnied upward, hand over hand, until I was about twenty feet off the ground.

"What the hell are you doing?" Dalton said in a whisper shout.

I surveyed the surroundings. The foliage was thick, but I thought I caught sight of movement about fifty yards out. I zeroed in. There it was again. A bird. Nothing. I slid back down the tree.

"I don't see anything," I said. "The other two must be with her."

"We don't know that," Dalton said. He quickly checked the other weapons for rounds. One was empty, the other had two left. He handed it to me and tossed the empty one into the green abyss.

"It makes sense." I looked at the three men tied up on the ground. They weren't trained guards. They probably didn't even know how to aim their weapons. I held the old, tape-covered rifle out in front of me. "You weren't shot with one of these," I said. "They sent these guys out to—" My eyes met Dalton's and simultaneously we said, "scare us off."

"What the hell's going on? Back at the shed, that guard recognized you." Dalton said. He put his hands on his hips and eyed me up and down.

I glanced over my shoulder, stalling.

"C'mon, Poppy. What's going on? You obviously know a lot more about this whole operation than you let on."

"Me? You're the one who was sleeping with her."

He glanced over his shoulder.

"Quit stalling," I said.

"Hey, she came on to me. I had to see where it would lead."

"And?"

He shrugged. "And I got nothing, okay?" He looked around again. "Other than she's kinky as all—"

"I got it," I said. I stared at him for a moment. What was I feeling? I mean, he could sleep with whomever he wanted. And the fact that he was joking right now, well—I shook my head. Despite the danger, or maybe because of it, he was enjoying this—the thrill of the chase, the undercover con, the adrenaline high. He was a junkie like me. And being hit on by a beautiful woman like Maria must have been—"Wait, why would she seduce you?"

He raised his eyebrows in an arrogant, macho, have-you-not-seen-my-pecs expression.

I slapped him on the arm.

"Ouch!" His hand jerked up to cover the wound.

"Oh, sorry," I said. "Maybe to see if you'd cheat on me? If so, maybe you'd be a crook, too. Then why use it to pit us against each other?"

"I'd been trying to figure that out." He squeezed his shoulder tighter. The wound was hurting. "Then yesterday, you were mad at me, so I went to see if George wanted to play a round of golf. He wasn't there but Maria invited me in." He wouldn't look me in the eye.

"Is that when you decided to take me to dinner?"

"Well, that's not—"

"Forget it," I said.

"Something was hinky about the whole thing. She was fishing for how I was feeling about you. I couldn't put my finger on it at the time. But just now, in the shed, I realized—"

"She saw us run into Noah at the fundraiser. She was trying to figure out if he and I—"

"Were having an affair."

So she did know about Noah being an activist. But does she know I was the one behind the whole Carlos takedown?

Dalton bore down on me. "What was that with the monkey?"

I clenched my teeth together. *Can't cry now. Focus.*

Dalton threw up his hands. "What am I saying? It doesn't matter. Our cover's blown."

"That's not...exactly true," I said.

He glared at me. "What does that mean?"

"She doesn't know we're cops. She thinks we're activists. Eco-terrorists." I gave him a please-don't-be-too-mad-at-me grin. "At least, she thinks I am."

"Dammit it. I knew it. Because of that Noah guy."

"Yeah, no. Maybe." I searched my brain for insight.

Something. "She was testing us, right? To see if we were activists or really potential buyers"—*that's it!*—"She still brought us *here*."

"That doesn't make sense."

It all made sense. She must have thought of the gang as a nuisance more than any serious threat. They'd been here before, several times. But Noah had only ever targeted the shed. She used the shed as a temporary shelter, one they could use to show animals, but was easily emptied. If she confirmed we were activists, no harm done. If we were buyers, she could have some class I species brought in for us to see. The guard had been about to hand her a two-way radio. That meant they were nearby. Perhaps she's always had them nearby. I looked at Dalton. "I can't explain right now but…I think I can still get what we came for." I looked over my shoulder. "You're gonna have to trust me."

He shook his head. "Do I have a choice?"

"Follow me."

He took a step and faltered.

"Let me look at that," I said.

He didn't want me to, but I pulled up his pant leg. The bullet had grazed his leg and left a gash in the side of his calf. When I looked up, he was looking down at it with an annoyed expression. He started to take off his shirt.

"I think it will take more than that," I said.

He rolled his shirt, then tied it around his leg above his knee. I snapped off a branch from the walking palm tree, broke it at the right height, then shoved it under his armpit—a make-shift crutch.

Now, with his shirt off, I could see the wound at his shoulder. A bullet had penetrated his chest just below his shoulder. Blood oozed from the wound. "That's not good," I said. "You need to sit down, sit still."

"I'll be fine," he said. "Now go."

"But—"

He had a look on his face like I was insulting him.

I shook my head. SEALs.

I darted through the jungle, heading toward the edge of the clearing. I came to a halt where I could see the horses.

"Still there," I said to Dalton as he came up behind me. "All three."

He nodded toward the shed. The two guards were at the doorway, eyes searching the forest. "So are they. I don't get it. She has two guns guarding an empty shed."

"Exactly." I turned to him. "Ever hear of the shell game?"

CHAPTER 20

We emerged from the foliage at the edge of the ravine where the cable stretched across to the other side. It was fastened to a tree above our heads. The basket hung on the far side. "She's over there," I whispered. "I think the class I species are too."

Usually there would be a rope to pull an empty car from one side to the other so a passenger could board from either direction. On this one, the rope was missing. Seemed Maria didn't want anyone sneaking up behind her.

I had to get across.

The rocky edges of the ravine were too steep or ragged to traverse. The cable was the only option. I craned my neck out to have a look. At the ravine's lowest point, the cable was about sixty feet above the ground.

"Give me your belt," I said.

"Are you doing what I think you're doing?"

"Give me the belt."

"She could be watching. She'll shoot you off that wire like a dove."

"Yeah," I held out my hand for the belt. "If she's watching."

He thought a moment, holding his shoulder. "I'm going with you."

"We only have one belt."

"I don't need a belt."

"You're injured. You could make it worse. I need you to

secure this side so I have a safe retreat. Besides—" I looked him up and down "—your pants might fall down."

I could tell, he was thinking of objections.

"You know I'm right."

He unclipped his belt and handed it to me, but before he let go of it, he looked me in the eyes. "Be careful." He raised the weapon. "And let me get into position to cover you."

I nodded, took the belt from him, and paused, eyeing him. A thought niggled at the back of my mind. "Stan said you could never connect George to a sale—no emails, no phone calls, whatever. But you were sure he was involved somehow because of intel you gleaned through a smuggler you'd nabbed, right?"

Dalton nodded. "Yeah, all the information he gave us panned out so far."

"Cell service is sketchy in the valley. I assume that's why George and Maria have a landline at the house. You've monitored that and George's cell phone, right?"

He nodded. "And we got nothing."

"Did you ever check for a mobile phone for Maria?"

"I think we checked. I mean, it would have been standard procedure. I don't remember there being one registered under her name." He shook his head, frustrated. "We never thought of her as a possibility."

I looked across the ravine. The hill sloped upward from where the cable car landed. There was probably good cell service up there.

I looked up at the cable and drew in a long, strengthening breath. *I have to get that phone.*

"Just confirm they're there, then get right back over here," he said.

I looked him in the eye. "Right. Intel. Not evidence."

He winced. For a moment, I thought it was from my comment, but he shifted and I could see he was in pain.

"You're going to hold the line, right? You'll stay awake,

right?"

He barely nodded.

"Dalton, don't you flake out on me. Keep hold of that weapon."

"I got it," he groaned. This time from annoyance. *Good.*

I climbed the tree to the cable, wrapped the belt around my waist and over the cable, and fastened the buckle. I tested my weight. It held. I pushed off from the tree, wrapped my legs around the cable, and pulled myself out into the open and paused. If she was watching and ready to shoot, she'd do it now.

Nothing.

I leaned back and, hand over hand, pulled myself out and over the ravine. The cable dipped with my weight. One hand, pull, other hand grab, pull, grab, pull, and I was across. I unhooked the buckle and dropped to the ground. I looked back. Dalton was watching me. I gave him a thumbs up and ducked into the cover of the trees.

A narrow path led upward toward the top of the ridge. Maria couldn't be far. Taking the path was too big of a risk and I had to be careful. I decided to parallel it through the thick jungle. I shoved my way through vines and branches, trying not to make any noise. It took me five minutes to get twenty-five feet. And I was soaking wet. Not to mention the threat of snakes. This wasn't going to work. Not without a machete. And a silent one at that. I had to take the trail after all.

I crept on hunter's feet. The trail meandered through the forest at a low uphill grade then turned and shot upward over rocky terrain, slick with the perpetual wet of the rainforest. There was no wind or rain to mask the sound of my footsteps. Just the buzz of insects and the occasional cackle of jungle birds. I took my time, cautious at every turn. She could be waiting for me, could be poised, ready with a gun.

The trail cut back, heading yet upward through a copse of bamboo. The forest was quiet here. I carefully placed each footstep, inching through to the other side. I stopped a moment. What if she hadn't come this way? What if this was all a diversion too, and I was missing something? Maria had proven to be sharp and devious. To bring Clyde was—no, I couldn't let my mind go there. *She's here. I know it.* I moved forward. I was getting closer; I could feel it.

The choking foliage of the jungle started to thin. I was reaching the top of the ridge.

The closer I got, the more it made sense. Maria could easily slip away under the guise of a leisurely horseback ride, hike up to this ridge, and without anyone listening, make calls, send emails. When I'd seen her a few days ago, at 11:30 at night, she could have been up here to call a contact in China or Indonesia. No one would know.

My heart started to pound faster. Everything would be on that phone.

I stepped around a banyan tree and saw movement. I ducked back to the cover of its thick trunk. About one hundred yards ahead, the path went under an enormous rock ledge, a natural overhang. On this end, a waterfall trickled from a tiny stream above. Beyond that, several cages had been built beneath the rock ceiling, protected from the blistering sun and rain. Explained why I hadn't seen it on Google Earth.

It looked like a trailside menagerie where one might stop and buy a handful of grain from an old gumball machine to feed the animals. The cage frames were crooked and hodgepodged together, built on makeshift risers. The sides were wrapped in chicken wire or chain link fencing or both. There were at least eight I could see. From this angle, it was difficult to discern what was in the cages, but in two I could easily see the bright red of scarlet macaws. The cage on the far end was built on the ground and large enough for a jaguar.

I took a step out from behind the tree to see further down the ledge. There was Maria. On the phone. She was pacing, chattering away. I couldn't make out the words over the trickle of the waterfall, but the tone of the conversation was not a happy one. She waved her hands in the air, making demanding gestures as she talked. Her little dogs lay in a patch of sun, snoozing. She yanked the phone from her ear and stood with her hands on her hips, fuming.

I pressed against the tree and clutched my shaking hands together, willing them to stop. I breathed in. Breathed out. My heartbeat started to return to normal. I took another long, soothing breath, letting the adrenaline dissipate through my bloodstream, then peeked from behind the tree again.

Maria had dropped her hands as though resigned to something. She stepped toward the cages and, I noticed now, a large cabinet tucked between them. She opened the hinged door and dragged out a bucket with a scoop. She surveyed the cages with an attitude of disgust. Must be Carlos usually fed the animals here. She set down the bucket and fiddled with the latch on a cage. This was my chance.

While her back was to me, I crept up behind her.

She shook some food into a bowl and slammed the door shut. "Animal sucio," she grumbled. *Filthy animal.*

"You're under arrest," I said.

She paused for a microsecond, then shrugged without turning around, as though she had known I was there. The dogs leaped from their naps, yipping and yapping their annoyance. "By whose authority?" she asked as matter-of-fact as if I'd asked her the time of day.

"U.S. Fish and Wildlife service, in coordination with Costa Rican authorities."

She turned to face me with an amused grin. "And what exactly am I being charged with?" Her eyes narrowed. "Because I'm certain I didn't make an offer to sell you anything."

"No," I said. "I'd have to have proof of that anyway, which I don't. But you know that."

She shrugged and turned her back on me.

"It is, however, illegal to have a class I species in your

possession."

She smirked at me over her shoulder. "A slap on the wrist. You'll get a bigger scolding for dragging me in." Her lip curled into a half grin. "That is, if you're really a cop."

I simply stared at her, giving her time to ponder.

She looked me up and down. "And you think you can take me in?"

"You could go willingly."

She huffed.

"Either way, with testimony from your brother Carlos, I think—"

She spun around. "Carlos has nothing to say." The dogs started yipping again.

"Oh, I don't know," I said. "He spent last night in jail facing charges for drug trafficking. He might be in a mood to deal."

Her eyes narrowed. I could see her mind racing. "¡Silencio!" she snapped at the dogs. *Hush!*

I grinned with satisfaction. "But even if he doesn't," I said, "if I arrest you on the minor charge, we have probable cause to check all items in your possession." My eyes dropped to her pocket where she had stuffed her phone.

She was smart enough to know she had all the evidence we needed right there to put her away for a very long time. Her nose twitched as if she'd smelled something rancid. Her eyes darted toward the trail behind me. I was right.

Then something in her demeanor changed. It was subtle. A confidence she didn't have a moment ago. She took a step toward me. "You think you're so clever. You have no phone, which means you haven't called for backup. Assuming you are a cop, like you say you are, you're undercover, so nobody knows you're here. Your partner was hit. Am I right? You're all alone. Young and desperate to make a bust." She paused. "You could just"—she waved her hands in the air—"disappear."

I steeled my gaze. "So could you." I shrugged and gave her a curt smile. "Then I could take over. After all, you've gone to a lot of trouble to hide your identity. No one knows who you are, right?"

She threw her head back and laughed, then she lunged at me with more force than I was expecting and knocked me to the ground. She took a step to run and I swiped her ankle with my hand. She stumbled and I was on my feet. I pounced on her back, slamming her against the cages. The birds fluttered and squawked. A howler monkey shook a door and bellowed at us. The dogs shrieked, scratching at my legs.

She spun around and grabbed me by the hair and yanked my head back. I brought my arm around and down hard on her elbow. As she let go, I rammed my forearm upward and slammed into her throat. She rammed her knee into my gut, knocking the wind out of me. That ticked me off.

I reared back and slapped her, open-handed right across the face. *Take that, bitch.* She tried to hit me back, but I deflected her arm and twisted, pinning it against her chest. She twisted somehow and we fell to the ground. I managed to get on top of her and she bucked beneath me. With the downward motion, I head-butted her right in the nose. I pulled back. Blood ran down her cheek. "That's for trying to steal my husband."

She tried to roll over on her side. I rammed my knee into her kidney. She groaned. I got to my feet. "Go ahead. Get up," I said.

She looked at me skeptically, assessing me, wondering, I'm sure, what I intended to do.

"C'mon, get up."

She rubbed blood from her nose.

"Get up!"

She got on her hands and knees, then slowly raised herself up to her feet.

"You're not a real cop," she said.

"Did I show you a badge?"

I saw a dawning awareness in her eyes, an awareness that she had completely misjudged me, followed by a gathering fear.

"Who the hell are you?"

"Doesn't matter. What's important is how much I know about you. I know you're a ruthless thug," I spat at her. "You torture and kill animals for money. With no remorse."

"Don't give me that righteous crap." Her lip quivered, ever so slightly.

"I'll give you my fist." I punched her in the face. She reared back. "And my foot," I said as I kicked her in the knee. She dropped to the ground. I grabbed hold of her by her hair and dragged her toward the big cage. As I shoved her inside, she grabbed hold of a poker stick that was propped against the side and swung it at me. Her arm couldn't extend enough to make any impact. I grabbed hold of her arm and reached for the door and slammed it shut, right on her wrist. She cried out in pain. "That's for Clyde." The stick dropped from her grip.

I snatched the phone from her hip pocket, slammed the door shut, and clicked the latch into place.

I leaned with my back against the cage and, after I caught my breath, fired up the phone. "What's the password?" I asked her.

"Go to hell," she growled.

The dogs whined at my feet. I reached down and picked one up. "You poor little orphan," I said, just to stir her up. I opened a cage and let out two scarlet macaws. Beautiful birds. Most people think of them as the iconic parrot. I watched them soar away in a flash of red, yellow, and blue. I put the dog in the cage, picked up her other dog, and put him in, too.

"Let them out!" she screamed.

I picked up the poker stick. The end had been whittled to a sharp point. "What's the password?" I shoved it between the bars and poked her in the shoulder. "You filthy animal."

She cried out. "Screw you!"

"I see," I said. "You want to play the guessing game." I plopped down, crossed my legs, and fiddled with the phone like a kid with a puzzle. "Your little pups have names. What did

George call them, Frick and Frack?"

She glared at me.

"Wouldn't be George. I mean, you don't really love him, right?"

She turned and wouldn't look at me.

"But Carlos. Tu hermano. Now there's definitely some love between you, no?" Her head swiveled around. "Ah, now we're getting somewhere. What was it that he called you? *Mariposa*?" I purposefully enunciated, emphasizing the proper pronunciation in Spanish. She winced. "M-a-r-i-p-o-s-a." I typed in the letters and the main screen came up. "For a big shot smuggler, you're not so bright," I said, shaking my head at her. I pulled up her email account and scanned through it—her contact list, her accounting files. "Tsk, tsk. Tú eras una niña muy traviesa." *You have been a very naughty girl.* I looked up from the phone. Her eyes were filled with rage. "You better get used to living in a cage."

CHAPTER 21

Sirens came roaring from the valley, first police, then the ambulance. The two remaining guards ditched their weapons and fled into the jungle. Dalton and I came out into the open to greet Nash.

I stood back and let Dalton do the talking while I chewed my thumbnail into a bloody mash. I hadn't exactly followed procedure. Or the line of command. Or the law. I switched to the other thumb.

Dalton was too stubborn to go in the ambulance until he'd told Nash everything. The shoulder wound needed immediate attention. He'd be taken directly to the hospital and into surgery right away, the paramedics told me. They paced. I paced with them.

Finally, he gave in and I watched the ambulance bump down the two-track driveway and disappear.

"We've got a lot to sort out here," Nash said to me. "But you two did a fine job."

"Thank you, sir." Hm. What exactly had Dalton told him?

"Do you have anything to add?"

I was tempted to tell him about Felix, to look for his body nearby. But the investigative team would search every inch of the grounds anyway. "No, sir." I hesitated. "If you don't mind, though, I do have a request."

Nash regarded me with curiosity. "Go ahead."

"The dogs, sir. I know a good home, someone who would love them. May I?"

He shrugged. "I supposed they'd end up at the local shelter anyway."

"Yes, sir."

"Get some rest." He eyed my tangled hair. " You look like hell."

"Yes, sir." I scooped up the dogs, put them in their saddle bags, mounted the horse, and headed back toward the house and the car.

As I rode, I thought of how I was going to tell Isabella about Clyde and the tears finally came. Poor Clyde. He had looked at me with those sad eyes, pleading for my help and there was nothing I could do. Maria might as well have ripped my heart from my chest for the hole that was left. I had filled it instantly with self-preservation, then rage. But now, there was nothing but an emptiness, an ache for the innocence of one little monkey. *What do I say? How do I explain?*

By the time I got to the horse barn, I had found my resolve. I didn't know quite how, what words I'd use, but I was going to tell Isabella he had been brave, that he died saving me.

I went straight to the tree house. The sun ducked below the horizon as I drove up. I let the dogs run free and they scampered along at my heels. A fire was crackling in the pit, four silhouettes encircling it. As I got closer, I could see it was Isabella, Noah, Claudia and Matt.

I stopped and drew in a deep, calming breath.

The dogs romped ahead.

Noah stood when he saw me, waving hello, a smile spread across his face, but I went straight to Isabella and wrapped my arms around her.

She knew. I didn't have to say anything. "Di' you get her?" was all she said.

I nodded. Her muscles relaxed as the tension left her body. I held her tight. Finally, she pulled away from my embrace. "I'm okay," she said. "I knew when her man show up at The Toucan and he want Clyde. I knew."

Claudia softly said, "Are these her dogs?"

"They need a good home now. I was hoping maybe…"

Isabella scooped one up and hugged it tightly. I smiled.

Claudia grinned and gave me a supportive nod. "Let's go get them some water," she said to Isabella. She grabbed Matt by the hand and tugged him along, leaving me alone with Noah.

He'd been watching without comment. Once they were out of earshot, he said, "That was really cool." He gave me a reassuring smile. "She'll give them lots of love."

"I know."

He turned his hazel eyes on me. The flickering firelight made them look like they were on fire. We both sat down in the sand.

"I'm sorry you got arrested," I said. "I couldn't risk my cover to—"

He held up a hand and shook his head. "I would do it again," he said. "But"—his eyes fell on my lips and I felt a surge of desire—"you do owe me one thing."

"Yes?" I managed, trying to keep the quiver from my voice.

He leaned toward me. "Your real name."

I grinned. "Poppy."

He smiled wide. "Seriously?"

"Special Agent Poppy McVie."

"It's nice to meet you, Special Agent Poppy McVie. Noah Kingston."

He kissed me, a long, passionate kiss. Then he sat back. "What now?"

I curled my lip. "I have to leave tomorrow. Back to Michigan."

His eyes got that then-we-have-all-night look. But I couldn't stay, not with Dalton at the hospital. "What about you?" I asked. "What will you do now?"

He eyed me with a thoughtful resignation. "I don't know.

Once the gang leaves for the season, and I no longer have to keep watch at the shed, I'll get pretty bored, I imagine. I was thinking maybe I'd join the Sea Shepherds," he said. "What do you think?"

I laughed. "Yeah, that's just your style."

We sat together by the fire for a while before the others began showing up. Once the whole gang was there, I told them about Maria and the take down, as much as I could reveal.

"Hear, hear!" someone said and the conversation turned to new adventures.

It didn't feel right to say goodbye. I'm like my father; he never accepted goodbyes. As we traveled, whenever we made new friends, he always wanted to believe we'd see them again. Instead of goodbye, he'd say happy trails and fade off into the sunset.

I gave Noah a kiss on the cheek, and when he went for more beer, I slipped away from the fire. Happy trails my smoking-hot-set-my-pants-on-fire friend, I thought. Perhaps our paths will cross again.

I fell asleep in a hard plastic chair in the waiting room. Sometime during the night, a nurse led me to the recovery room where I watched Dalton sleep for a while. His shoulder was bandaged with a mountain of gauze.

Finally, at 8:07 a.m., his eyelids fluttered and he looked around the room, taking in his surroundings. When his eyes found me, he relaxed and managed a smile. He muttered something.

"Don't try to talk," I said. I took his hand in mine and squeezed. "Go back to sleep."

His eyes drooped and gave in.

Two hours later, he awoke, bright eyed. A few hours and lots of paperwork after that, the doctor said I could take him home.

I drove toward the bungalow, but decided some fresh air and a nice view sounded much better. I picked up a take-out lunch, turned into the park, and took the short road to an overlook where I parked and we got out.

With the cool ocean breeze in our faces, we walked to the edge and peered out at the sea. A magnificent frigate bird soared overhead. Waves rolled in and lapped on the rocky beach below and the cry of the gulls echoed in the distance.

As soon as we sat down at a picnic table, I heard chittering. From the top of a palm, perched in the crook of a frond, a white-faced capuchin sat, eyeing our sandwiches.

"Look at him," I said.

Dalton smiled. "Right where he's meant to be."

His phone rang and he tried to answer it with his left hand. I clicked it on and held it to his ear until he could comfortably take it from me. He nodded, agreed, nodded some more.

I went back to the car, got my binoculars, and scanned the ocean while I waited. Far out from shore, I spotted dolphins playing in the waves.

Finally, Dalton disconnected. "That was Nash," he said. "Maria's phone was the mother lode. She had connections we had no idea about. Nash is downright giddy."

"That's great," I said.

"He says that because she ran her business so secretively and mostly via email, he's going to be able to step into her role, see who he can identify up the line. He's going to offer George a plea deal to keep him in place as the front man."

"What do you mean by step into her role?"

"He'll keep her business going exactly as she has been to draw out a bigger fish."

"So he'll actually keep selling and smuggling animals?"

He sighed. "Yes, sometimes that's what we have to do."

My hands tightened into fists. "But that's not right."

Dalton stared at me with a blank face. He was exhausted, too tired to argue.

I sat down at the picnic table across from him. "You're saying we did all this for nothing?"

"Of course not. As long as there is wildlife trafficking somewhere in the world, we need to infiltrate wherever we can. We've arrested Maria, she'll get her punishment, but it's all about supply and demand. As long as there's demand—"

"For the right price, someone will be happy to supply." I sighed.

"We took Maria out and we got Nash in. That's huge."

It had been our objective. But it didn't feel like a victory.

"You and I both know the problem is cultural," he said. "In the west, people want their own one-of-a-kind pet, something exotic that no one else has. It's all about status, elitism, whatever. And in the east, there are those who believe eating crushed rhino horn or shark fin soup will make them more virile. It's human nature. Only science and education will change it. It has to come from the top. Better laws. That takes time. Lots of time."

"And meanwhile?"

Dalton sighed. "Meanwhile, you and I keep the wolves at bay."

I frowned.

"Yeah, pardon the old saying. That's an insult to wolves."

At least we agreed on that.

We looked out at the ocean for a while.

"One more thing," Dalton said. "The nurse said the butterfly gardens received an anonymous donation for $200,000 on their web site. She said it was front page news. Know anything about that?"

I shook my head. "Not a clue."

"Uh-huh."

I tried to think of something else to say, but nothing seemed honest enough. My eyes dropped to the bandages taped across his chest and shoulder. "I should have told you earlier what was going on."

"It's okay."

"You weren't exactly straight with me either, you know. Sleeping with Maria. Is that even allowed?"

"I wasn't exactly going to spell it out in the report."

"But you already suspected her. No wonder you were so frustrated with me showing up."

He wouldn't acknowledge it.

"I'm sorry you were saddled with me, you know, a probie agent."

He flashed a smile. "I don't mind babysitting."

I kicked him under the table.

He laughed. "Actually, I think of you more as a little bundle of bad ass."

I laughed with him. It felt good. "Where will you be headed now?" I asked.

"Nash mentioned an op in Norway. Beautiful country." He seemed pensive. Maybe he wasn't allowed to share the details. "What about you?"

"I'm headed back to Michigan. I have a few weeks left of my field training." I still wasn't quite sure what Dalton thought of me. I sat up straight. "I busted a couple of rednecks taking a live bear the day I got called to Special Ops. My SAC got to catch the bastard they were selling to without me."

"Yeah, well, I'm sure he's anxious to have *you* back."

I shrugged. "He says I'm giving him an ulcer."

Dalton threw his head back and roared with laughter.

"Hey, it's not that funny," I said with a grin.

His eyes settled on mine and for a moment I saw the kind, loving eyes of the man who had held me while I cried, who had kissed me so tenderly. He held my gaze, then turned away.

"Well, hey, Norway. Wow." I reached for my sandwich. "I'm super jealous."

With his one good hand, he fidgeted with his sandwich wrapper.

I opened it and tucked the sides for him so he could hold it like a fast food burger. "Don't you want to go?" I asked.

"Oh yeah, I want to go. It's just, the cover needs to be just right, you know, to get approved."

Something in Dalton's expression made me feel uneasy.

He turned to face me and with a sigh of resignation, he said, "Nash says I have to take my wife."

Author's Note

Wildlife trafficking is estimated at over $20 billion annually and is rivaled only by illegal drugs and weapons in the money it earns criminals. The number of organized crime syndicates profiting from large scale trafficking is mind blowing. Millions of wild animals are captured and slaughtered each year for traditional medicine and aphrodisiacs, exotic pets, souvenirs and religious trinkets.

This cruel holocaust MUST STOP.

If you'd like to learn more and stay in touch, please sign up for my newsletter or follow my blog at www.PoppyMcVie.com

A POPPY McVIE NORWAY ADVENTURE

OPERATION
ORCA
RESCUE

KIMBERLI A. BINDSCHATEL

OPERATION
ORCA
RESCUE

a Poppy McVie adventure

CHAPTER 1

Norway. Land of the midnight sun. Cascading waterfalls, deep fjords, breathtaking views and abundant wildlife—the mother lode to a notorious wildlife criminal.

Sure enough, a few weeks ago, Headquarters received an anonymous tip that Ray Goldman, the U.S. Fish & Wildlife Service's most-wanted, was sailing these waters, on the prowl for killer whales. Rumor was, he was planning a live-capture for the mega-aquarium industry. And I was going to catch him.

Special Agent Poppy McVie, reporting for duty.

Since U.S. law prohibits an American citizen from hunting, capturing, killing or even harassing a killer whale anywhere in the world, and we wanted him—we wanted him bad—here we were.

"I feel like a damn circus bear jumping through hoops," said Dalton as he ended the call with the informant. "I'm starting to think he's just some crackpot getting his kicks."

My partner, Special Agent Dalton, up until now, had patiently dealt with him through every stage, even promised the man that his anonymity was a top priority, but the guy still wouldn't even give his first name. We'd started referring to him as Johnny, as in: *Here's Johnny*, the nutjob.

"At least he stays on the phone longer than thirty-eight seconds now," I said. "Maybe Hollywood called and told him that even they'd given up on that old drama ploy."

"Hollywood." Dalton rolled his eyes. "I'm sure that's why he believes agents are all 'gun-wielding, cowboy cops who shoot first and ask questions later'." He paused, looked at me. "Well, maybe he's got you pegged."

"Hey!" I frowned. "We're making progress with him. Now we have a time and location to meet, right?"

"He said he'd be at the Vikinghjelm pub down on Bryggen wharf after lunch. I'm supposed to wear my sleeves rolled up and sit at the bar with a beer and wait."

"That's it?"

"That's it."

"All right. I'll go in ahead of you and scope out the place," I said, "see if I can identify him, then I'll keep an eye on him for any suspicious behavior before you arrive."

Dalton started shaking his head before I'd finished my sentence.

"What? You don't think I can handle a little reconnaissance."

"No, that's not it." The edge of his lip curved upward into a half grin as his eyes traveled down to my waist, then back up. A slight tilt to the head. "You don't exactly blend in."

"What? I blend in." I winked and, in my best Irish brogue, said, "Me Ireland's jist a 'op, skip an' a jump dare, fella."

"I don't mean your American accent, my dear."

I thrust my hands onto my hips. "What then? I don't *look* Irish enough with this red hair and freckles?"

"This isn't a tourist pub. It's a local hangout for dockworkers and fishermen."

"So," I said. "I can blend in."

He frowned.

Geez. "Have some faith."

I wasn't going to give this informant a chance to change his mind and slip out the back door. Ray Goldman was a ghost. If there was any chance, any chance at all, that Johnny-boy actually had real intel, I wanted a piece of it.

In the 1970s, Ray Goldman had single-handedly decimated the Pacific Ocean killer whale population. He had permits to capture, but so many died in his careless capture attempts, scientists say that group of whales might never make it back to sustainable numbers and have declared them endangered. During his escapades, some drowned entangled in the capture nets, some died after being tranquilized with darts, and in at least one instance, he and his cohorts feared the terrified orcas would capsize their boat and opened fire with high-powered weapons.

His rogue methods started a political shitstorm and details only emerged later, when his help finally talked. By then, he'd fled to Iceland, where, at the time, whaling was not only acceptable, but welcomed. Fishermen wanted the competition gone, claiming the whales depleted their stocks. Which is absolute bullshit.

In 1982, the International Whaling Commission enacted a total ban on whaling, trying to protect whales from total annihilation, but Icelandic whalers used a loophole to continue to kill whales on a commercial scale under the guise of scientific research. Like Japan still does today. Iceland only quit whaling because of a public boycott of Icelandic fish in Europe and the U.S., plus the threat of U.S. Government-imposed trade sanctions.

Even with the public outcry for the whales, Ray Goldman never showed an iota of remorse. Then, he simply vanished into the ether.

Until now. Assuming it's really him. But it seems plausible. China and Russia are building new mega-aquariums and the demand for live orcas has resurged. One live killer whale carries a one million dollar price tag. That's a lot of dollars floating around in the sea. And nothing brings a trafficker back to work faster.

I turned to head for the pub when Dalton's phone rang.

He held up one finger, signaling me to wait. "It's Nash."

Joe Nash was our supervisor, a legend in Special Ops. He'd been the Special Agent in Charge on my first assignment with Agent Dalton in Costa Rica. Dalton and I were undercover as a married couple, buying illegal animals for the pet industry. Nash thought Dalton and I made a good team. He had no clue that, before we caught the kingpin, we'd damn near killed each other.

Dalton punched the speaker button. "Yep."

"Hey," said Nash. "How's it going over there?"

"We're heading to meet the informant right now," said Dalton.

"Good. Proceed with caution."

Dalton flashed me a like-I-said look.

"I don't have to remind you, we're out on a limb on this one. I did some fancy dancing to get you on this special joint effort with NOAA. Your directive is to confirm it is indeed Ray Goldman, gather the evidence we need to convict, then call in the Norwegian authorities to make the arrest. Got it? Just do that cute couple routine and you'll slide in under his radar."

I tried not to roll my eyes. From day one, our fake marriage felt like it was headed for a fake divorce.

"Got it," said Dalton, winking at me.

"A lot of people around here have been wanting to bust this guy for years. Keep it by the book. I don't want any loophole he can slither out of."

"Right, boss," said Dalton and disconnected.

Before he could say anything, I said, "I'm going to head in."

He shook his head.

"What?" My cheeks flushed pink. "I'm quite sure I can handle a little reconnaissance. You just make sure you've got those shirtsleeves rolled up."

I turned on my heel and left him standing alone in the middle of the sidewalk holding onto his phone.

Bergen is the second-largest city in Norway, as modern as any other in the world, but for some reason Johnny-boy wanted to meet at the Bryggen wharf in Old Town.

A series of buildings lined up in a row, all the same shape and size, distinguished only by their bright colors—red, yellow, orange, and white. I wished I had time to explore, learn about the history of this place. All I knew was that these buildings had been here since the late Middle Ages, part of the Hanseatic merchant guild that stretched along the north European trade routes. There was even a Hanseatic museum here to get the whole, sordid scoop. Alas, maybe next time.

Occasionally an alley separated two buildings where a wooden-plank boardwalk provided passage to the many shops and pubs tucked behind the storefronts. On this late fall afternoon, the shadows were already darkening the corners. I made my way down the main thoroughfare, through the crowd of tourists, then turned down one of the deserted alleys.

When I managed to find the pub, I had to admit, Dalton had been right about it. The place smelled of stale beer and fish guts and everything was coated with the brownish hue of tar from decades of cigarette smoke.

Five locals hunched over the dimly-lit bar—fisherman, or dockworkers maybe. Two other men ate at a table in the corner. At another sat three looking like they'd spent the last ten weeks on a boat and had dragged themselves down the dock to land here before hitting the showers. Otherwise, the place was empty.

With the exception of the computer cash register, it felt like I'd stepped back in time to circa 1650.

Yeah, I got the looks, the side-glances, the what-the-hell-is-she-doing-here expressions. But hey, a girl should be able to get a beer in peace, right? Wouldn't take long and they'd forget I was even here.

I climbed onto a stool at the end of the bar and waited for the portly barkeep to mosey my way.

He wiped his hands on his apron—also appeared to be circa 1650 by the amount of crusty grime glommed onto the front of it—and gave me a curt nod, his way of welcome.

"A Beamish, please," I said in my best Irish accent. Everyone knows the Irish drink Beamish. None of that Guiness sludge.

In good time, a frothy mug of my favorite, tasty malt beverage was slid my way. I took a sip and settled in to watch for unusual behavior.

The five men at the bar eased back into their conversation. Thankfully, nearly everyone in Norway speaks English and I could follow along.

The one who sat on the end, closest to me, seemed to have the attention of the others and I got the sense he wasn't from around here. He was about my dad's age, though this man's manners would never have been accepted at my mom's table. He had both elbows propped on the bar, his chin leaning on grubby hands. His features—large, bulbous eyes, pointy nose, protruding ears, pencil-thin lips—weren't all that odd, individually, but the combination somehow didn't quite go together, like he was a toddler's Mr. Potato Head creation, come to life. Even his weathered skin resembled an old spud.

"I tell you what," he said to the other four men. "Another go at it?"

They glanced around at each other, nodding, then dug some paper kroner from their pockets and slapped them on the bar.

"All right," the first man said. "I'm a slippery fish in a cloudy sea; Neither hook nor spear will capture me; With your hand you must hunt and seize this fish; To see that it ends up in the dish."

The four fishermen's eyes darted about, to the ceiling, to the floor. One scratched his beard in thought. A few glugs of beer, some barstool shifting, but no one spoke a word.

"Not even a guess?" the riddler asked. He waited. "Do you need a hint?"

One of the men eyed the pile of cash on the bar and grimaced, shaking his head in frustrated resignation.

The first man slapped his hand over the money and slowly dragged it in.

"A bar of soap," I said, then quickly drew in my breath. *Dammit.* I'd said it out loud.

The man flashed me a dirty look.

I flashed back an innocent, apologetic smile.

He turned back to the men. "One more? Just for fun?"

A young, rosy-cheeked man with a round, cheerful face piped up. "Sure, man."

The riddler glanced at the bartender and some unspoken signal passed between them.

"What has rivers but no water, forests but no trees, and cities but no buildings?"

More head scratching and lip chewing. "Dunno," said the one on the far end, a young, blond man of about my age, built like a barn. He tipped up his mug and chugged.

"Me neither," said the bearded man next to him, shaking his head. "What's the lady say?"

All eyes turned my way. *Crap.* I was supposed to blend in.

The riddler glowered at me.

"C'mon. Nothin's ridin' on it," one of them said.

The riddler raised his eyebrows and nodded his consent.

Rivers but no water, forests but no trees. "A map?"

The men snickered and grinned.

"Put the lady's beer on my tab," the riddler said to the bartender. "Okay, boys. Another bet?"

The bearded man shook his head right away, but the guy next to him dug into his wallet, then nudged the bearded guy, goading him until he finally dropped a bill on the bar. "My money's on her," he said, his gnarled finger pointed my way.

I shook my head and turned my attention to the contents of my mug. *Why didn't I find some hidey-hole in the corner with a view of the bar and keep my big mouth shut? Dammit, McVie. Blend in. Blend IN.*

The others nodded their agreement and coughed up the cash.

"Fine by me," the hustler said. He leaned forward on the bar as though ready to tell a ghost tale of old 'round the campfire. "I can't hear you, but I can touch you; You can feel me, but you can't see me; I can't see you, but I can kill you; You can't kill me, but you can hear me."

The blond barn on the far end dropped his face in his hands, then shook his head, tipped back his mug, and drained the contents in one gulp. The others seemed to try to solve the riddle, their eyes glassy and tired.

The bearded man raised his finger. "What about it, sweetheart?"

Crap. I couldn't win either way. If I didn't answer, the four men would be in an uproar. If I did, the hustler would get pissed off. I gritted my teeth. *I hate hustlers.* "The wind," I said.

The bearded man flung his head back and roared with laughter.

The hustler didn't flinch. He saw his opportunity. "Double or nothing," he said.

The men shelled out the cash without hesitation.

"No, no," I said, shaking my head. "I'm not—this isn't…"

"All on the girl," the hustler said, his potato-face puckered with amusement.

I kept shaking my head, no, but the men were back in the game now.

They pushed the cash into a tidy pile.

With a starchy grin, the hustler said, "With no wings, I fly. With no eyes, I see. With no arms, I climb. More frightening than any beast, stronger than any foe. I am cunning, ruthless, and tall. In the end, I rule all."

I stared. I had no idea. *I fly, I see, I climb.* How'd I get myself into this mess? *Cunning, ruthless, and tall?*

"C'mon, lass," someone said.

"I…" I shook my head. *In the end, I rule all?* "I don't

know."

"Give the lady a minute, now," said the round-faced man with the kind smile.

My mind was blank. "Really," I said, "I have no idea. I'm sorry."

Outsmarted by Mr. Potato Head. Could my day get any worse?

The hustler grinned wide and swept the cash off the bar and into his pocket. "Sorry, men."

"Now wait just a minute," said the bearded man, rising from his stool. His blue eyes flared with rage. "Why do I feel like we just been swindled by you two?"

"What? No." I shook my head.

His fury wasn't focused on the hustler, but me. The other three men fell in behind him.

"I didn't have anything to—"

The hustler started to slip from his stool.

I nudged him in the shoulder with my finger. "Where do you think you're going?"

The four men turned to him. His buggy eyes darted from one to the other as he assessed his foes.

I said to him, "I'm pretty sure what you just pulled isn't legal. So go on, give these men their money back and call it a day."

He smirked and stood taller. "I'll do no such thing." He looked to the barkeep as he adjusted his collar and smoothed his shirt sleeves. "It was a fair bet."

"Maybe we should let the police sort it out," I suggested to the bearded man.

The hustler grabbed me by the arm and shoved me against the bar. He probably stood about five-ten, two-hundred pounds of net-hauling muscle. "Maybe you should mind your own business, sweetheart."

This guy was really starting to piss me off. I looked down at his hand, then looked him in the eye, and, with a smile pasted on my face, my voice all dripping with syrup, said, "Take your hand off me or I'll break it."

This seemed to encourage him more. "That's not very ladylike," he grunted through gritted teeth.

I matched his stare. "I'm not sure you know how to treat a lady."

"What's this? Part of your act?" the bearded man bellowed.

The hustler glanced at the door, the quickest of glances, but I caught it. He was going to bolt.

He shoved me into the bar and I reacted. I jabbed my elbow upward at his throat, extended my arm, gave his head a twist, and knocked him off his feet. He stumbled to catch his balance, but I had my foot on top of his. He teetered forward and, with a little help from my hand, face-planted into the edge of the bar. *Take that.* I brushed off my hands and wiped my brow. *Mashed potato.*

From his pocket, I pulled out the wad of cash and handed it to the bearded man. He responded with a bewildered expression, staring open-mouthed at the money as though it had magically shimmered into existence right there in his hand.

The hustler crumpled to the floor.

I picked up my Beamish. "Thanks for the grog," I said and held it up in salute.

The four men exchanged glances, unsure whether this was still part of some elaborate con.

The barkeep tapped me on the shoulder. "Out."

"What? Me?" I glanced down at the hustler, now sitting upright on the floor holding his head. "He's the one who—"

The gruff old barkeep jabbed his finger at me. "I'm not going to ask you twice."

Dammit. I didn't even get to enjoy the beer.

I slinked out the front door.

As I walked down the wooden-plank sidewalk, I spotted Dalton coming my way.

"What's going on?" he asked, his face wrinkled with

concern.

"Nothing. I just—" I clenched my teeth together. "I just got kicked out of the pub is all."

A grin spread across his face and his eyes lit with amusement. "Seriously?"

I wanted to punch him in the stomach. "Enjoy the moment."

"What on earth happened—wait, I probably don't want to know." His eyes closed shut, then the grin took over again. He blinked them open. "Anything I should know?"

"No," I said with a frown.

He shook his head and snickered. "I'll meet you back at the lodge."

I watched him saunter away, grinning all the way to the pub, the pub where I was supposed to be hunkered down in a dark corner to keep watch.

I headed down the wharf to walk it off. A couple of tall ships were docked, their wooden masts bedangled with complicated rigging. I'd always wanted to sail aboard one of those old ships, flying the Jolly Roger and spitting into the wind. Maybe drink rum from a wooden cask. I couldn't go for the eye patch, but a pet parrot would be fun. I could teach him to swear with an Irish accent.

I sat down on the edge of the pier and let my legs dangle over the water. A couple of gulls skittered into the air, then circled back to perch on the pilings and the stench of backwater and diesel fumes wafted my way.

Of course I wouldn't have a pet parrot. And some kind of partner I was. Dalton was in there alone right now, with no backup. Sure, the risk was low, but still. It was my job. And he was my partner. All because I'd misjudged the scene. And then I opened my big mouth. I wouldn't blame Dalton if he sent me home tonight.

I grinned in spite of myself. That ass deserved to get clobbered. And by a girl, as he would say. That probably really pissed him off. Thought he was so clever with his riddles. *Cunning, ruthless, and tall.*

"Imagination!" I shouted to the gulls. *Dammit.* Head slap. *Now it comes to me.*

About four hours after Dalton went in, the warm light spilled out into the dark alley as he came out the front door of the pub and headed toward our lodge. I stepped from the shadows and followed him. Made it two blocks before he spotted me.

"I thought I said I'd meet you back at the pension," he said.

I shrugged him off. "I wanted to hang close. In case you needed me."

"Uh, huh," he said. "So how'd you get yourself banished anyway?"

"Some old man had grabby paws." It was only a half fib.

Dalton grinned. "You're something, you know that?"

"Whatever." I gave him the look. "Did our informant show?"

He shook his head. "Waited all this time. Then the bartender hands me this note."

He held it out for me to read. *Fish Market, 10 a.m. Two days. Come alone.*

"*Two days.* But Ray Goldman is out there, somewhere, right now. We need to get going. We need to know which direction."

Dalton sauntered along, unaffected.

I kicked a tiny chunk of concrete that had crumbled from the edge of the curb and watched it skitter down the sidewalk. "We don't have two days to wait."

Dalton stopped and turned to face me. "Patience, my dear."

"Don't patronize me. You know time's a factor here. We've got a tiny window to catch this guy. If he gets a whale before we catch up to him, he'll sail off into the sunset, to sell it in Russia or China or Timbuktu. He'll be beyond our reach. Don't you care?"

His hands went to his hips. "Of course I care."

"Well, how can you be so—"

"You're so cute when you're angry."

My bottom lip was sticking out. I sucked it back in. "Cute!" A rush of color heated my cheeks. *Errrrr!*

"I want to catch this guy as badly as you do," he said, calm as can be. "But some things are out of our control."

"So, what? You're saying we wait around and do nothing?"

"You don't like cold coffee and stale doughnuts?"

"Dalton!"

"Actually, I have an idea." He grinned. "I think you'll like it."

I didn't like the sound of this.

"When I was a SEAL, we used down time for training, trust building, that kind of thing. We could use a little of that."

"Like a little of what?"

A grin spread across his face. The hint of challenge in his eyes made me nervous.

CHAPTER 2

I leaned out over the granite ledge and gazed down at the fjord 3,208 feet below. A white sheen of glistening sunlight spread across the greenish-blue water. Two endangered Eurasian peregrine falcons swooped and soared on the wind below us. One caught a thermal and gently glided into a circular flight path, its wings outstretched. The fastest animal on Earth, a falcon can dive over 200 miles per hour. I don't know how Dalton knew, but I'd been wanting to see one for as long as I could remember.

At last, there were two in my sights. But today we weren't here just to see them. We were going to soar with them. If they'd have us.

"You ready?" I asked Dalton.

He nodded and smiled, the dimple in his right cheek appearing. "You're the one who's been lollygagging."

"I want to time it just right." I shaded my eyes with my hand and searched for the sliver of grassy shoreline onto which I was supposed to land. "See you on terra firma."

I ran back to where my paraglider wing lay in the grass, clipped it to my harness, then gave it a yank. It lifted from the ground, filling with air. I turned and ran and as I reached the edge, I was airborne, held aloft by the warm ridge-lift air current.

My breath left my body as the great expanse of the fjord

spread below me, the cliffs on either side narrowing downward. No matter how many times I did this, it still took my breath away.

As I glided outward, I felt a slight uplift and shifted to catch the thermal, which lifted me up and up as I circled.

I scanned below for the falcons. There was the one I'd seen, its wings spread wide, still riding on a thermal below. I leaned right, yanked on my brake, and went into a sharp, spiraling, tickle-belly descent, heading toward the bird on a corkscrew path. I dropped about a hundred meters in eight seconds.

I released the inner brake, shifted left, and planed out.

Curious, the falcon flapped its wings and cut right, circling to get a look at me. I spread my arms wide. "Come fly with me!"

I entered the core of the thermal and caught some serious lift. As I circled, Dalton appeared, riding on the wind beside me.

The two falcons darted between us, banked and soared upward, then circled back and streaked past like feathered bullets.

I grabbed my radio. "Oh my god! That was incredible!"

Dalton gave me a thumbs up.

Now I could relax and enjoy the view. Blue sky dotted with tiny, white puffy clouds contrasted with the jagged granite peaks. Below, strokes of green, white, brown and yellow covered the landscape—an abstract painting come alive. I settled into the peacefulness of no sound save for the breeze against my ears. It was perfection.

Between my feet, a tiny spec of a boat left a wake on the water's surface, a white line etched in blue. Amid the patches of green that spread across the mountain side, little dots of white randomly roamed. Billy goats.

I leaned back and breathed deeply the cool, clean air. To ride on the wind, to soar like a bird, to see the world from this perspective, in pure solitude, where I was the spec, the tiny dot, made me wonder, is this what it is to know God? Or the spiritual essence some call God, that something beyond, the unexplainable sensation of being more than flesh and bone?

Is this what was meant by transcendence? To defy the law of gravity? To be held aloft by an invisible force of nature like some great hand, lifted from below? What is the wind but an illusion, made manifest by the collision of hot and cold air?

However it could be explained, it felt like touching the divine.

I closed my eyes and when I opened them again the colors looked deeper, more vivid. So many varied shades of green. The blue of the water, rich and deep against the sky. Simplicity. The purest form of beauty.

Dalton's voice came over the radio. "Last one to the LZ buys dinner."

He pushed on his speed bar, leaned left, and shot away, circling downward toward the landing zone.

I grabbed my B-lines and went into a stall, chasing after him. Like two giant raptors, we rode the wind downward.

He dropped away from me, gaining speed. The wind was perfect, the sun shining. Why rush?

Okay, fine. I admit. It grinded my butt that he got the drop on me. There was no way I could catch him now. Another dinner on me. Maybe he'd go for some peanut butter and jelly.

I controlled my descent, taking my time to plan my approach. As I lined up into the wind, Dalton was already touching down.

The landing site was a grassy patch along the shoreline. I circled to head into the wind and as I approached the ground, I pulled a quick brake, flared, then my feet touched the ground and I had to run a few steps to stay upright as the wing settled behind me.

"Took you long enough," Dalton hollered.

He was wrapping his wing and stuffing it into the sack.

I had a mind to stuff his head in the sack. "We have enough

daylight to make one more run," I said. "Double or nothing?"

He shook his head. "We need to check in with Nash."

I nodded. Work. Of course. That's why we were here in Norway. But we had nothing new to report. We'd have called if Johnny the informant had changed the meet time again.

Dalton flipped on the flashing light that would alert the ferry of a pickup, then helped me gather my wing.

We hauled our packs to the shoreline and sat down to wait. My pulse was finally settling to normal after the glide. I'd stripped off my thick coat after landing, but now the chilly breeze coming off the water gave me goosebumps on my bare arms.

Dalton sat with his arms comfortably wrapped around his knees. His hair looked almost blond in the sun. A hint of stubble showed on his chin. Suddenly I was remembering watching him shave in Costa Rica, fresh from the shower, with nothing on but a towel. He hadn't liked me much then. I'd been sent to fortify his cover story in a floundering operation and he wasn't too happy about it. I'd barreled into the bathroom and demanded he talk to me.

"What are you thinking about?"

"What?" I snapped out of my reverie.

"You seemed a million miles away."

"Oh, sorry, I..." I looked up at the sky, searching for a subject. "When you're up there, do you, I don't know, do you feel like—" I looked around "— like with all this, there's something greater, you know—"

He raised an eyebrow, his dark eyes challenging me. "Are you getting soft on me, McVie?"

"Nah," I snorted. "I was just testing you."

He shook his head but his eyes lingered in the clouds. Then when they met mine, they revealed that he felt it too.

I held his gaze for a moment. *This guy, I swear.* I turned away.

"Here it comes now," he said. The ferry was chugging down

the fjord toward us.

We got to our feet and hauled our packs onto our backs.

The blue and white ferry pulled up and dropped its front loading ramp right on shore so we could walk on.

Once aboard, Dalton slumped to the floor, leaned on his pack, and closed his eyes. I stayed at the rail, counting waterfalls as we puttered back toward town. The landscape here was too much to behold. I turned to Dalton, "You're missing the—"

His eyes were open; he was staring at me.

"What?" I said.

He smiled. "Nothing."

"Don't you want to see the scenery?"

"I'm full. Too much beauty for one day."

I suddenly felt self-conscious of how I must've looked and ran my fingers through my tangled hair. "What are you talking about, cornball?"

"Nothing."

"Hey, what was this exercise all about? What was I supposed to learn today, anyway?"

"Did you have fun?"

I shrugged, unsure what that had to do with it. "Yeah."

"There you go." He closed his eyes again. "Now, leave me be. I'm dreaming of that dinner you owe me. I'm gonna order a big, juicy steak."

I milled around the fish market, keeping Dalton in view while checking out every man that looked like he might be our Johnny. Then the guy appeared out of nowhere, wearing a hoodie, his back to me. Dalton didn't look uncomfortable or alarmed, so I hung back, scanning for anything out of the ordinary.

The whole conversation lasted no more than two minutes and he was gone. I never saw his face.

Dalton moved toward me. "The description fits. It's Ray

Goldman all right. He's been busy getting a crew together and all the gear he'll need. No doubt about it. This guy's sure he's going after orcas."

My pulse pitter-pattered in my ears. "We gotta catch him, Dalton. This one's big. Imagine the impact it will have, the message it will send to all the poachers out there."

"Simmer down. We've got to find him first. The informant said he's in Tromsø right now, on the fishing vessel *Forseti*, but he's not sure which way he'll set sail. We need to get up there, find him, and rent a boat before we lose his trail."

"What then? We just follow him? That's your plan? Won't we be too obvious?"

"What else did you think we'd do?"

"Well." I pursed my lips, thinking. "I don't suppose Norway requires AIS on all commercial vessels? We could track him that way but keep our distance."

"I doubt it. That would be too easy. Besides, he'd likely turn it off anyway. It's a big ocean. Easy to hide if you don't want to be found."

"If only we could get away with planting a GPS tracker on his boat."

He stopped and turned to face me. "We'd have to be awfully creative and I'm not sure—"

My head jerked back. "Isn't that illegal? No matter how we did it?"

He gave me a half shrug.

An idea sizzled through my gray matter. "Maybe we don't have to. Follow the boat, I mean." *Why didn't I think of this before?*

Dalton clenched his teeth. "I recognize that look."

"What?"

"You're thinking. Scheming." He crossed his arms. "Let's get something straight. We're going to work together on this one. Do you understand? No secrets, no sneaking around."

"I wasn't—"

"And nothing off book. You got it?"

I lifted my hands in innocent surrender. I couldn't blame him for being irritated with me. In Costa Rica, our first time working together, I hadn't exactly been straight with him. Of course, he hadn't quite rolled out the red carpet for me either. But now we were officially partners. He had to listen to me.

"I was just thinking that the orca pods don't follow a predictable migration route like other whales."

Dalton waited, expectantly. "Yeah, so?"

"Well, I wonder how Ray plans to find them. Did your pal Johnny mention that?"

Dalton shook his head.

"I've got an idea," I said. "We need the Internet." I turned to make my way out of the crowded fish market and head toward the main street.

Dalton grabbed my arm. "First, you tell me what you're thinking."

"Maybe we don't need to follow Ray," I said and started walking again.

Dalton followed. "Slow down," he said. "It's not a race."

"Actually, it is," I said over my shoulder. I rounded a corner and saw a sign—Internettkafè—down one block. I picked up the pace, Dalton on my heels.

Inside the cafè, teenagers filled the booths and tables, plunking away at their laptops, sipping from cups of coffee as the expresso machine squealed, making its magical brew. The scent of fresh muffins lingered.

I went straight for an open computer along the wall and plopped down in the chair. Dalton hovered over my shoulder, so close I could smell his aftershave. For a moment, I forgot what I wanted to search. "Maybe you could get us some coffee," I said.

He stood up straight and glared at me.

I gave him a sweet smile. "And some of those mørkaker shortbread cookies?" My eyebrows went up, a gentle pleading.

"They are to die for."

He crossed his arms. "Not until you fill me in."

"It's like I said, if we find the orcas, we find Ray."

"Yeah?" He didn't budge.

"I figure *someone* knows where to find them. Must be scientists monitoring the pods, right? Identifying their members, documenting their behavior."

The corner of his mouth turned up with the hint of a smile. "Mørkaker shortbread cookies, huh?"

I nodded.

He slowly turned away from me and headed for the line.

When he got back, I'd already found what I was looking for. "Look," I said. "Right here."

I pointed to the page for the Center for Marine Research at the Havforskningsinstituttet.

"Now there's a Norwegian word if I've ever seen one. It's ten miles long," he said.

"I think you mean ten kilometers." I looked up at him. "They're hosting an American biologist, here to study the vocalizations of killer whales. April Parker, Ph.D. If anyone knows right where to find killer whales in the north Atlantic, it'll be her."

"Yeah, but will she tell us?"

CHAPTER 3

The cafeteria at the Havforskningsinstituttet bustled with students. Dalton and I meandered through the crowd looking for Dr. Parker. Her Internet picture was no help. She was all bundled up in a down jacket with a hood and sunglasses. We'd checked in her department where we were told she was at lunch.

"When we find her, I think I should approach her alone," I said. "She's likely to be more trusting of another woman."

"Actually," Dalton said. "I was thinking I'd approach her alone. I have more experience with this kind of thing."

"That might be," I said, holding back, "but the key is to build trust right away, right? I can do that, you know, woman to woman."

"This is going to take some finesse."

"Finesse?" I said, amused.

"Charm," he said.

I pressed my lips tight, trying to squelch a smile. "Dalton, I think you overestimate your—"

"We only have one shot at this," he said, his voice stern now. "I'm doing it."

I spun on him. "Dalton, you're not being reasonable. Just admit I'm right."

He got that look on his face. Man, this guy could be stubborn. Through a forced smile he said, "It's not about being right."

Then the condescending grin. "It's about the line of command. Or have you forgotten who's the senior agent?"

"So it's not about what's most effective? It's about who's in charge?"

He sighed. Thought about it a moment. "Yes."

"Fine," I said, holding back an eye roll. "Now, let's find her."

He nodded toward a table in the corner. "She's right over there."

Sitting with her head down, a fork in one hand, a book open in the other, was a woman not much older than me, her long blond hair tied back into a stylish Chinese bun, two hair sticks poking out from it, criss-crossed.

I spun on him. "How do you—"

He held his phone in my face. "Her DMV photo. Nash sent it."

"What? You knew she was there all along?" I frowned. "What is it with you today?"

He flashed his half-grin.

I asked, "So what are you going to say?"

"I've got it covered."

"She could be informing for Goldman, you know. I'm sure he'd pay big money for that kind of info. Maybe we should test the waters a little and—"

"I said, I've got it covered." He brushed past me and crossed the room to her table.

I circled around, eased into a chair at a table nearby so I could hear their conversation, and tried not to stare. Flawless skin, high cheekbones, curvy, voluptuous lips. I hadn't expected a whale biologist to be so…so stunning.

"Hello," he said. "Are you Dr. Parker, the whale researcher?"

She looked up at him, hesitating. "Yes," she finally said as she tucked a stray lock of blond hair behind her ear.

He flashed his tummy-tingling smile. "I was hoping you

might be able to help me."

Her brow creased and she examined him through squinted eyes. She had the look of a porcelain doll, but this woman was no naive little plaything.

He shifted his weight to one side, easing into a comfortable, disarming stance. "You're even prettier in person."

Real smooth, Dalton.

"What is it you need?" she said, blank-faced.

He smiled, trying to keep it light. "I hear you're the expert on the killer whale population here in Norway and I—"

She shook her head. "I can't help you."

"Oh," he said. "I was really hoping you—"

"Listen—" she gripped her lunch tray "—I don't know what you're up to, but no amount of money—"

"Oh no, ma'am, I think you misunderstand," he said, then shot a quick glance my way. "I'm a federal agent with the U.S. Fish and Wildlife service." He motioned for me to join him. "We've been alerted to a possible live capture attempt by an American here in Norwegian waters."

Her sharp blue eyes darted back and forth between us, then landed on me. "You don't look like federal agents. Show me your badges."

Dalton shifted on his feet. "We don't carry badges when we're undercover."

"Well, that's convenient." She grabbed her tray and started to rise to go.

Dalton stepped forward with open hands, a subtle gesture of peace. "We'll do whatever you ask to prove it to you."

She hesitated, her eyes back on me.

"Please." He held his hand out in an invitation to sit back down.

She set the tray down, but remained standing. To me she said, "You said *U.S.* Fish and Wildlife. Why would you be here, in Norway?"

"We're after a notorious criminal, top of our most wanted

list."

She stared, unsatisfied. This woman was not short on intelligence.

I went on. "The Marine Mammal Protection Act of 1972 prohibits hunting, capturing, killing or even harassing any marine mammal in U.S. Waters *or*—" I paused for effect "—or by U.S. citizens *anywhere* in the world."

"You're clever," she said crossing her arms. "But not clever enough."

I smiled. Held up my hands. Of course she would know this would normally be handled by NOAA agents. "You mean, of course, because the MMPA is the purview of NOAA. We're here as part of a joint effort with their enforcement agency. They're concerned that the suspect would recognize most of their agents, so here we are. This is a high profile case, you know, with the news lately—" I smiled at her "—and politics. Orcas are very popular and a protected species so—"

"Of course I know that." She let her hands fall to the table and, with one finger, slowly spun her plate a quarter turn. "This is my life's work."

I let out my breath. She was warming to us. "We need to find this guy before he finds the whales so we can catch him in the act. If we miss that tiny window of opportunity, he'll get away with it. Please help us stop him."

Dalton added, "We don't know who else to turn to for help."

She looked into Dalton's eyes and held his gaze for what seemed a bit longer than necessary before she said, "You don't have the eyes of a killer." She sank into the chair and pushed the tray out of her way. "I've been afraid of this."

"How do you mean?" Dalton asked as he eased into the chair across from her.

"You've been approached, haven't you?" I said.

She didn't respond, but I could tell I was right. "Oceanaria. It's a dirty word if you ask me. We should be destroying these—" she shuddered "—these prisons, not building more. Do you know what happens to them in captivity?" She didn't wait for a response. "They're crammed into chlorinated tanks with bare concrete walls, forced to perform circus tricks under neon lights with horrible music blasting over the loud speakers. No wonder they show signs of aggression. To claim that having killer whales in captivity is teaching us anything about them and their natural behavior is absurd. If anything, all we're learning is what happens when you enslave a sentient being."

I smiled and nodded, hoping to convey my sincerity. Listening to her describe the horrors of captivity stirred my anger and made me feel more desperate to gain her trust.

"We'd been hearing rumors of new demand for wild captures. I had hoped it was just that, rumors, until…" She looked down at her half-eaten sandwich and frowned. "The breeding loan program is a farce. That's the problem. Breeding in captivity has been mostly unsuccessful. They breed them too young, and they're matching whales that are too genetically-close, all causing an unnatural percentage of stillborn calves. With demand for more orcas in marine parks around the world—Russia, China, and Japan—they have to fill those tanks from somewhere."

"Exactly," I said. "And with Norway's political—"

"That's if the whales actually survive being captured. It's awful you know. Many die from the trauma. Not just physical, but emotional." Her lip quivered, ever so slightly. I got the sense she was holding back tears. I felt for her. A scientist would be criticized for being too emotional about her subjects. "Orcas have strong family bonds. When one is captured, it's agonizing for the entire pod. But imagine for the one captured, being lifted from the water, what that must feel like, while your family members are wailing in distress." She covered her mouth with her hand. "It's inhumane."

Dalton gave her his warmest smile. "We're going to do

everything we can."

She went on, her focus on Dalton. "If only they'd been called the pandas of the sea. The name, killer whale, comes from a time of ignorance and fear. They're not mindless, brutal killers, you know. They're highly intelligent beings. Clever and amazingly adaptive. What we've learned about them from their vocalizations alone is—"

She went silent and pursed her lips. I don't know how she didn't burst into tears. I was on the verge of blubbering myself.

Dalton and I exchanged a quick glance.

She sighed and forced a smile. "You said you received a tip on a live capture attempt?"

"Yes," Dalton said. "But we're not clear on how accurate it is or up-to-date. The informant said our man's sailing near Tromsø."

"Tromsø?" She took hold of the lunch tray, a determination in her posture. "We should go to my lab."

Sunshine streamed through a two-story wall of glass, bathing the Cetacean Research lab in warmth. No back-corner basement rooms dimly lit with sickly-green fluorescents here. The architecture was all glass and sleek lines—distinctly Scandinavian.

A long counter ran along the opposite wall, its surface cluttered with bones of assorted cetaceans, stacks of plastic trays, and boxes of tools. On one end of the room, several desks housed computers and on the wall, photos of whales, all grouped by pods, it seemed, were pinned to a giant map of Norway.

Dr. Parker strode to the wall, her willowy frame carrying her like a model down a Paris runway. She swept her hand across the map. "There are about 3,000 killer whales in Norwegian waters. Half live in the Barents Sea and up around Svalbard.

That covers a great area of open sea, very remote, so I doubt your—" she hesitated as though trying to find the right word "—*criminal* would target that area. Along the coast and out in the Norwegian Sea, however, offer him a lot of opportunity. Tromsø isn't the best staging port. Too far from the migration paths. If he's there now, he's probably getting crew and supplies and planning to move on."

Move on to where, I wanted to ask, but she seemed on a roll, so I didn't want to interrupt the flow of words.

"All killer whale migration, across every ocean in the world, is tied to their prey, which varies from pod to pod. A pod is a complex and cohesive family group. Here in the North Atlantic, there are two distinct types of killer whale pods, transients and residents. Resident pods tend to have a defined home range, which would make them most vulnerable. Transients travel over considerable distances hunting marine mammals, making them a little harder to find."

Dalton, hanging on her every word, asked, "So you can easily locate the resident pods? They follow a certain pattern?"

She paused as though seeing him for the first time. Her eyes traveled up and down his body. A flirty smile skipped across her lips. "Not exactly. The main prey of killer whales in Norwegian waters is spring-spawning herring. The herring don't follow any certain pattern."

I thought so. "But are they—"

"So find the herring, find the killer whales," Dalton interrupted, his eyes glued to her.

"Yes, you're right, very good," she said, smiling at Dalton like he was her star student, then turned her attention to the map once again. "The herring used to migrate every fall like clockwork into Vestfjord near Lofoten,"—she ran her hand along the map, her finger landing on, then tapping at the Lofoten islands—"but in recent years the herring stock changed its migration pattern and has been wintering in the open ocean, north and northwest of the Lofoten islands." Her hand swirled, motioning out to sea. "It's made our research more difficult, that's for sure. The whales, when we do see them, are traveling fast and in an unpredictable fashion. In the last three years, we've only spotted them in Andfjord."

Dalton stepped closer to her. "So you're saying their feeding habits have changed?"

"No, just the locations. Their feeding technique, which is a specialized technique seen only in these waters, is called carousel feeding. Their ingenuity is quite impressive, actually. In close cooperation with each other, the whales will chase the herring school into a tight ball formation close to the water's surface. They then slap the herring ball with their tails, stunning them, making it easy to pick off the fish one by one.

"A carousel feeding event can be exciting to watch and seems quite chaotic. The herring jump out of the water, huge numbers of birds descend on them, and the whales often make high, arched dives. Below water, though, it's apparent, it's a carefully choreographed maneuver. And the vocalizations during the event—" She paused, shaking her head in awe.

Her fascination with these creatures was contagious. I wanted to see this feeding event, to witness the excitement, to hear them communicating.

Her gaze became unfocused as though she'd fixed on some distant thought.

"That's amazing," Dalton said, bringing her back.

"Wait a minute," she said to no one, her eyes scanning the board. She rushed to a computer, plunked at the keys, her eyes darting about the monitor. "Oh no." She looked up from the screen. "I think I know which pod he's going after."

Dalton and I glanced at each other. My heart rate picked up. "Which one? Why?"

"The K-pod." She covered her eyes with her hands. "Dammit! I should have realized."

"What?" Dalton asked. "You should have realized what?"

"Last week. My assistant went on a date. It went badly.

She said the guy wouldn't shut up about the whales. It took her awhile to realize, that's all the creep wanted. When she told me about it"—she flung her head back and stared up at the ceiling—"I figured he was an environmental reporter or something."

Dalton said, "We need to talk to this assistant."

Dr. Parker nodded. "That's fine but, that's what made me realize. Trust me, they're going after the K-pod." She launched from the chair, back to the board, pointing at a photo. "K-12 has a nursing calf. That slows the whole pod down, making them an easier target. Plus this pod has several adolescents, the primary target for wild-caught captives. They're strong and healthy...exactly what..." She plopped back into the chair. Her shoulders sagged as though grief was already setting in. "He'll be able to easily herd them." She shook her head. "He'll have his pick."

"Not if we get to him first," Dalton said.

"The K-pod is..." Her eyes locked with Dalton's. "Very special."

"Why?" I asked, fighting to keep my own emotions in check.

"All killer whales form matrilineal groups, that is, all are offspring of one female. Even the male killer whales stay in their birth family for their entire life. Except to go mate, of course."

Did she just raise an eyebrow at Dalton?

"We know of no other creature where all children— daughters and sons—stay with their mother all her life." She looked at me as if she'd noticed me for the first time since we entered her lab. "Can you imagine that kind of family bond?"

I shook my head. I couldn't imagine wanting to stay with my mom. My dad maybe, but my mom, no way.

"Anyway," she went on, her attention back on Dalton, her smile returning. "A large pod might be made up of a couple of these groups. In the K-pod, K-4, we call her Granny K, is eighty years old. She saw too many of her loved ones ripped from her family back in the 1970s and 80s when this particular pod was targeted for capture. Over half of the family was taken. They've been struggling to regain a sustainable number ever since. The new calf, well,—" a pink blush came to her cheeks and she gave Dalton a conspiratorial wink "—I call her Baby Kimmy, she's the first we've seen in several years." She drew in a sharp breath. Her eyes lit with fear. "If he takes Kimmy's mom—"

"All right," Dalton said in a soothing voice. "Let's not get ahead of ourselves."

She shot up from the chair. "You can't let this happen. You can't."

"Okay, okay." He was nodding.

She eyed Dalton with the ferocious glare of a mother bear. "What are you going to do about it?"

"Well," he said. "First we have to locate the suspect. Then we'll take video of the capture. Once we have the evidence in hand, we'll call the Norwegian authorities. They'll make an arrest and we'll have him extradited to the U.S. for prosecution."

"Why don't you call the Norwegian authorities now?"

"Well," he gave her a placating smile. "We need to first confirm it is indeed Ray Goldman and that he is here with the intent to capture a killer whale. Whaling politics here in Norway have been—"

"Yeah, I know," she said. "But what he's doing is illegal here. Why do you need video? That means you have to actually stand by and let him capture one, right? Can't you just arrest him when it's clear that's what he's going to do?"

"We don't have the authority to arrest him here. Since we're not sure which way the Norwegian government would sway, we want our own evidence to convict him. The distinction is important."

"Not to the whale it's not."

I had the same thought. "Exactly," I said. I didn't want to lose her now that we were finally getting somewhere. "The whales are our first priority. That's why the timing is so important."

Her eyes flicked back and forth, from him to me.

"We'll get this guy," Dalton said. He paused, waited, looking at her with those eyes. "That is, with your help."

We waited while she chewed on her lip, her eyes fixed on some distant space.

"So," I said, easing back into the discussion. "The whales are likely to be in Andfjord then? That's where we should look?"

"Huh?" She looked up at me, her eyes shifting into focus. "What?"

"Andfjord? You said that's where they'd likely be?"

She shook her head and plopped back down in the chair. "Oh no. They're not there."

What the hell? "I thought you just said—"

Her fingers hammered at the keyboard. "If your whale hunter is in Tromsø, he's got miles to go. My guess, if he knows what he's doing, he'll arrive in the Lofoten Islands within a few days. You should go to Reine. The K-pod has been south of there and they're turning back north."

"How can you be sure?"

She said, matter-of-fact, "Granny K is satellite-tagged."

CHAPTER 4

We hopped on a train north, then a quick flight, then the ferry to the tiny, historic fishing village of Reine. Right out of a Scandinavian fairy tale, granite peaks jut straight up out of the blue-green sea. Bright red fishermen's cabins with grass roofs dot the rocky shoreline, suspended in time on their wooden stilts, the sea splashing below the floorboards. In the middle of it all, Stetind peak dominates the skyline. Norwegians call it *gudenes ambolt*, the "anvil of the gods," because its summit looks as though it had been lopped clean off, leaving a flat, level precipice.

First thing, we walked the docks, but saw no sign of the *Forseti*. I asked Dalton. "So how do you want to play this?"

"We rent a boat, a newly married couple on holiday"—he winked at me—"and make sure all the video equipment is charged and rigged. When we get a fix on him, we'll keep him in our sights as much as possible and stay in direct communication with April."

"April? You mean, Dr. Parker."

"Yeah, that's what I meant."

"I thought your approach was real smooth by the way. *You're even prettier in person,*" I said with a wink. "I don't know what her problem was. You'd have had me at hello."

Dalton crossed his arms. "So you're going to gloat?"

"Just for a while," I said with a victorious grin. We turned toward town. "Do you really think Goldman will be so bold as to try to take a whale with another boat close enough to witness it?"

He shrugged. "If not, we've come a long way for nothing."

I frowned. There had to be a better way. Right now, I couldn't think of one. Not one that stayed within the law anyway.

I shot off a text to Dr. Parker to let her know we'd arrived and there was no sign of Ray Goldman yet, hoping she'd keep her word and send us regular updates on the K-pod's movements.

Without knowing exactly what to expect, we weren't sure what would be the best vessel for our needs. Finally, we decided on a cruising sailboat, figuring worst-case-scenario, running out of gas wouldn't be life-threatening.

We managed to find a company that rented pleasure craft to tourists. Conveniently, nearly everyone in Norway speaks English, even in this tiny village, and we were able to get exactly what we wanted.

The *Sea Mist* she was called. A forty-foot sloop with two cabins, one head, and a nice galley with a deep-freeze. The salon was paneled in teak and smelled of the sea, as a boat should. The seat cushions had been updated with an aquamarine and imperial blue striped fabric. Every door and drawer bore a white sticker listing the contents and an *In Case of Emergency* poster had been stapled on the wall above the main radio controls.

The owner, a friendly local with an easy-going demeanor, gave us an hour-long orientation that included personal tales of his adventures on a sailboat. When his stories ran out, he wanted to see our ASA certification or some kind of documentation to be sure we were qualified to sail a vessel this size. Being a Navy SEAL, Dalton would be given the helm no problem, I'm sure, but this was a small community and we had to be careful what we revealed. To them, we were a married couple on holiday.

"Gee, I didn't think to bring anything," Dalton said,

stalling.

"Perhaps you could quiz us, to satisfy your requirements?" I suggested.

The man shrugged. "Um, okay. How much rode do you put out to anchor safely? I believe that is the English word, rode."

"Yes, you are correct," I said. "Rope or chain?"

"Rope."

"Seven to one scope."

I could feel Dalton's eyes on me.

"All right," the man said. "If two sailboats on the same tack are approaching one another, which is the give-way vessel?"

"The windward vessel," I said. "It should alter course to pass astern of the stand-on vessel."

He stared at me for a moment, then turned to Dalton. "It's late in the season to be out on the water."

"We came to see the whales," I said.

"You're going to pay the balance up front?"

We nodded.

"Have a good time," he said with a dismissive wave and went back into his shed.

Off to the grocery store we headed to fill our stocks. We had no idea how long we'd be on board, what amount of supplies we'd need, so I loaded the cart to the brim with canned vegetables and boxes of crackers while Dalton wandered around the store picking up packages of mystery foods.

"What was that back there? You've been on a sailboat?" Dalton asked as we crossed in front of the frozen food section.

Does he think I was born yesterday? "Nah, I learned all that from an episode of the Brady Bunch. Greg and Marsha wanted to sail to India and—"

He crinkled up his brow.

Fine. "I spent a summer on one once. With my dad." It was the best summer of my life. Just me and my dad and the sea. No one telling us what to do, how to live. If I could go back to one time in my life… "I was twelve. Four months we sailed the Pacific coast, from Vancouver to Alaska. My dad had made some deal with a Navy buddy and voilà, we were living on a boat."

"You remembered the anchor scope and right-of-way rules from when you were twelve?"

I shrugged. "That summer is etched in my memory."

He waited.

I looked up at him. "It was my last summer with my dad."

He nodded in understanding. "Before he was killed."

I nodded. "The irony is, when he was planning it, my mother never shut up about it, going on and on about how dangerous it would be." I paused. If only we'd stayed on that boat. He never would have—I couldn't go there. Not right now with Dalton. I laughed, keeping it light. "I admit, I wasn't sure it would float at first, but once my dad and I were on the water, it was like I'd gone home. The serenity of the sea, the simplicity of a single-minded focus, going where the wind took us. I learned so much that summer."

"I bet," he said.

"I didn't exactly have a typical childhood."

"No kidding?" He shrugged. "They're overrated anyway."

I grinned. "I sailed the high seas, swimming with dolphins and singing in the wind."

"Explains a lot."

I elbowed him in the gut. "What about you?" I asked. "You know how to handle a sailboat?"

He raised one eyebrow.

"Oh right, you were a SEAL. You've done everything."

"Not everything," he said with a sly grin. "On a sailboat, that is."

He held my gaze until I turned away with a huff. "Oh, you are incorrigible."

The next morning, still no sign of the *Forseti*. We were lounging in the cockpit with cups of coffee and, though I'd done my morning yoga, I was feeling restless. The surrounding peaks beckoned. I must have been gazing up at them, my ankles twitching, because Dalton asked, "You up for a hike?"

"We can't leave the marina. What if—"

"If the *Forseti* arrives, he's going to stay at least one night to resupply."

"I don't think we should risk missing him."

"You're probably right," he said. "Unless…" He gestured toward the mountain peaks. "I bet, from up there, we could see any boat coming or going for miles."

I grinned. "I like the way you think." I pointed to the highest peak. "How about we try that one?"

"Is there even a trail, do you think?" he asked.

"Why? Do you need one?"

With a curt shake of his head, he said, "Just to keep track of you, McVie." He tossed the magazine he'd been reading aside and rose from the seat. "Let's go."

He offered to pack our lunch while I walked the docks one more time to be sure we hadn't missed the arrival of the *Forseti* while we'd slept. Within fifteen minutes, we were on our way.

There was indeed a trail, we found out. At the end of a short road, an arrow had been painted on the concrete, pointing to the trailhead.

We ducked into the foliage, single-file, and started an easy ascent.

The air was crisp, the piney scent of the forest refreshing. The morning sun warmed my back. For the first five hundred yards or more we walked on a solid plate of rock, then the hillside sloped upward and the trail turned to a rich, dark soil cut through thick grasses and low bushes. The path switched back and forth through a forest of alders and birches, the ground covered in a blanket of ferns and dotted with the occasional purple of bluebells. The rich aroma of fresh moss infused the air even though it hadn't rained for a few days, luckily. Otherwise, the trail would be slick with mud.

I came to a halt. On the edge of the trail, two enormous toadstools sprouted from the moss. They looked like tiny Smurf houses. One even had a mark on the stem that looked like a door. "Look," I said. "Three apples high."

"What?"

"Three apples high."

Dalton's blank stare made it clear he had no idea what I was talking about.

"The Smurfs. You know, little blue elves that live in the forest in tiny mushroom houses." When I was a kid, my dad would send me in search of Smurfs in the forest. Kinda like a snipe hunt, I suppose.

"Smurfs?" he said as if checking to be sure I wasn't delusional.

"It was a cartoon," I said, suddenly feeling silly. "Forget it."

About twenty minutes later, we emerged from the birches and the trail took a sudden turn upwards. I heard a strange sound, so out of place it made me stop and look around, trying to get my bearings. Then I heard it again: a metallic jangle from the trail above us. Clank-clank-clank. A billy goat.

He stopped when he saw us, tilted his head to the side, then continued toward us in that silly hoppity bounce, all four hooves springing in unison, like a toddler who's found a mud puddle. Another followed, then another, bouncy-bouncy-bouncing down the hill, braying at us.

Within moments, we were surrounded by a whole gaggle of goats, swarming, nudging, maneuvering in their skittish way. I held out my hand and five pushed and shoved to check it out. I didn't have food, but that didn't stop them. One brave goat with nubbins for horns gummed my fingers. He pulled away with a look of disappointment. *Sorry, bub.*

Another chewed at my shoelaces. I shooed him away. Goats will eat anything.

"Let's get some pictures," I said to Dalton and leaned down and put my arm around a goat. It nuzzled my cheek.

Dalton started to laugh.

"Get the shot. Get the shot," I said.

He snapped a few and bent over, cracking up. "You're a nut, you know that?"

"Yep," I said. "Deal with it."

Once the goats realized we had no food, they lost interest and meandered away, munching on grasses.

Dalton swept his arm upward with a flourish, gesturing toward the trail. "Shall we continue?"

"We shall," I said and led the way.

I had to grab hold of rock edges and small tree trunks to crawl up the steep incline. I glanced back at Dalton. He kept pace with me without any sign of complaint, as though we were taking an easy stroll on the docks. He made it look effortless. I, on the other hand, tried not to huff and puff too loudly. He'd never let me live it down.

Then all trees and bushes were behind us and the hillside was a jumble of rocks, mud, and grass. Our hike turned into genuine rock-scrambling as we clambered over boulders using hands and feet. In some of the steeper spots, rope lay across the rocks, strung there by some local trail angel. I took hold of one to help keep me steady on all fours as I climbed upward.

"Don't load it with your entire weight," Dalton said.

I nodded. I knew. We couldn't be sure how securely fastened it was at the top.

Dalton stayed right behind me, giving me the sensation that he was patiently waiting, following at my pace like you would a toddler taking her first steps. It made me want to take out his left kneecap.

Finally, I crawled over the rounded edge of the summit and could finally walk upright once again. I spun around, a full three-sixty. I could see for miles. The landscape looked like a photograph, it was so perfectly stunning. Above, blue sky stretched into forever with wisps of fluffy clouds. Below, a dark blue sea shimmered in the sunlight. The two were separated by spikes of gray blanketed in lush green.

I found a boulder, plopped down, and leaned back to take in the warm sun on my face.

Dalton sat down beside me, tipped up his water bottle, chugged down a few swallows, then offered it to me.

"I admit," he said. "I never really gave Norway much thought, but it's stunning. Just look at that."

I wiped sweat from my forehead. "Yeah, takes your breath away, doesn't it? So pristine."

"It's nice to know they appreciate it here. So many places I've been, the citizens are too busy trying to survive to think about the environment." His expression turned gray, his mind off in one of those places.

"Afghanistan, you mean?" I guzzled down some water.

"In the mornings, a mist would linger in the mountains. It made everything look soft and peaceful." He turned away as though he didn't want me to see his eyes. He absently traced his shoelaces with his fingers. "But it was more like a shroud, hanging over all the death and despair."

I looked out over the ocean, giving him space and feeling like a heel for all the times I'd given him crap about being a SEAL. He'd served his country. Honorably. I respected that. Sometime I'd drum up the nerve to tell him. Not now, though. Now wasn't the right time.

I picked up a dry leaf from the ground and rolled it between my fingers, crackling it into dry bits that fluttered to the ground. Then, hoping it had been a respectful length of time, I raised the binoculars and scanned the surface of the ocean. "I don't see any boats. Do you think we could see whales from this far away?"

"I don't know," he said, slowly coming back to me. "But

we've got all afternoon."

We sat together, under the sun, taking in the magnificent view. It was easy. Comfortable. I felt a little closer to him. He'd let me in. A tiny opening, but he'd shared something of himself with me.

"Dalton, what if she was wrong? What if he doesn't show up here? What if we can't find him?"

He gave me a warm smile. The dimple appeared again. "We'll find him."

"Yeah, but the odds—"

"We'll find him."

"How do you figure?"

He flashed a lopsided grin. "With your brains and my stunning good looks? How can we lose?"

I smiled, a full, contented smile. His optimism was contagious. And the sun was shining. And the air was fresh and clean.

"You hungry?" he asked and slipped off his daypack.

I had no idea what he'd packed and it made me a little nervous. I'm not a fan of mystery food.

He unzipped the pack and took out a tiny tarp and laid it on the ground. Then he set out a plate of grapes and cheeses, then another plate with mini-sandwiches—some with peanut butter, some bologna—another with crackers, and olives. Then another plate with hummus and veggies.

"Wow," I said, genuinely impressed. "That's quite the spread. You found all that in that tiny grocery store? How'd you even know what it was?" And he'd remembered I'm a vegetarian. Nice.

"Ah, but that's not all." He pulled from the pack a water bottle filled with red wine and two plastic stemmed glasses. He handed them to me to hold while he poured. He set down the bottle, took his glass in hand, raised it, and said, "To our new partnership."

Warmth rushed to my cheeks. *Don't turn pink. Don't turn*

pink.

His eyes locked with mine, his expression serious. "I'm sorry I gave you such a hard time in Costa Rica. It wasn't fair of me."

I nodded. I didn't know what to say. He'd already apologized.

"Onward," he said. "You and I are going to make a great team."

His eyes held mine and I was speechless under his gaze. *Just don't blush. Please don't blush.*

"I'm a lucky man."

A tingling rippled at the back of my throat and I felt the heat in my cheeks, marring my face with splotchy patches. *Damn.*

He raised his glass to his lips.

"Yes, I…me too," I stuttered, then tipped back the glass and drank down a warming swallow.

He picked up the plate with the sandwiches and held it for me to take one.

"Thank you," I said and stuffed one into my mouth, thankful for the excuse to say nothing.

He watched as I chewed, making me feel all squirmy and self-conscious. "Good?" he asked.

I nodded, then swallowed. "Yum."

Then I reached for another and in minutes we'd devoured the meal.

Dalton popped the last mini-sandwich into his mouth and licked the tips of his fingers with a flourish, then wiped them dry on his pants. "Not too bad if I do say so myself," he said with a grin. He leaned back on his elbows to relax, then sat back up with a jerk. "I almost forgot. I brought dessert."

From the pack, he offered a chocolate bar. *Chocolate!*

"Oh," I drooled. "I could kiss you."

His eyebrows shot up. "Yeah?"

"Well, you know what I mean." I snatched the bar from his hand, ripped the paper wrapper open, snapped off a square with my teeth, and mashed it around in my mouth, all the chocolaty goodness caressing my taste buds and soothing my soul. "Nom, nom, nom," I said, grinning with pleasure.

"My, my," he said. "I'd always heard chocolate was an aphrodisiac, but wow, you look like you're about to..." He let the sentence hang unfinished.

I froze, my teeth clamped together. "What?"

"Nothing." He was staring at my lips. "You've got a little..." He raised his hand as if to wipe the side of my mouth, but paused, then wiped at the corner of his own mouth. "A little chocolate." His expression seemed almost embarrassment.

I stuck out my tongue and licked the corner of my mouth.

His eyes grew wide and I burst out laughing.

He shook his head and chuckled. "You're crazy, you know that?"

I couldn't stop laughing.

"You really are something."

"What does that even mean?" I asked.

"It means..." He turned away from me, looking out at the landscape. "It means I have no idea what to do with you."

"You should trust me, that's what. If you would have trusted me in Costa Rica—"

His head jerked back in my direction, his eyes gone dark. "I said I was sorry."

I was quiet a moment. "I didn't mean..." *Dammit! Why'd I go and say that?* The silence lengthened. Finally, I got up and stretched. "We should probably head back," I said.

"Yeah."

Chapter 5

After a quiet dinner where Dalton pushed food around on his plate and stared into space for long bouts, I retreated to the cockpit to watch the evening sun turn the gray peaks into shades of pink and try once again to get interested in the paperback I had brought, some dime-store mystery I'd picked up in the airport. After that hike, I should have felt relaxed, but a nagging restlessness persisted. I hadn't meant to insult Dalton. *He just...dammit. I swear, we're like oil and water.*

I stared at the open page of the book—page 46—for about an hour.

Around eight o'clock, in the pitch dark, a fishing vessel puttered into the marina. She turned to dock and under the halogen lights, I was able to clearly see the name painted on the transom—*Forseti.*

"It's him," I whispered down the companionway to Dalton. "Ray Goldman is here."

"I'll be damned. Dr. Parker came through," he said as he climbed out of the cabin and stood beside me.

"The boat's much smaller than I'd imagined. I thought we were looking for a whaling vessel."

Dalton frowned. "I'm sure that's what the informant said, the *Forseti.*"

"Could there be two?"

"Unlikely. Usually the name has to be registered."

"How will he bring an orca aboard such a small boat? Either he's an idiot or we're missing something."

Dalton combed his fingers through his hair. "Or we've been sent on a wild goose chase."

I didn't like this revelation. I didn't like it one bit. I tried to call Dr. Parker, but there was no answer. "We need to get a look at that boat."

Dalton shook his head.

"I'm going to go see what I can find out," I said and moved to step off the boat and onto the dock.

He blocked my way. "We shouldn't be so obvious."

"What? You can't trust me to take an evening stroll on the docks?"

"That's not—" Dalton said to the back of my head as I stepped off the boat.

I halted in my tracks. *Dammit.* I'd done it again. I turned around but Dalton had already turned his back and was headed down the companionway.

I meandered toward the fuel dock where the *Forseti* had tied up. As I approached, I snuck glances at the three men who stood near the bow, talking in low whispers. One nodded over his shoulder as I walked by and said, "Well, hello there."

He was about my age, maybe a bit older. Not bad looking. His hair separated at his forehead in a perfectly placed cowlick, giving him an irresistible look of boyish-sophistication. The kind of guy I'd give a chance if he hit on me in a bar. Maybe let him talk for a while, see if there was anything worthwhile going on upstairs. His jeans fit nicely, that was sure. Snug, but not too tight. His hands were tucked into the pockets of his fleece jacket. He smiled at me and I felt all tingly. Yep. I admit. He was damn yummy.

"Oh my gosh, you're an American, aren't you?" I sighed, that silly American-girl sigh. "What are you doing in Norway?"

He turned from the other men without a word, his eyes on me, and said, "Work."

"Fishing?" *Yep, stating the obvious.*

"For now," he said. Whatever that meant. His eyes said, *It's time to play.*

"Is this your boat?" I moved toward it. If I could get him talking, I'd have an excuse to hang around, see what I could see. "She's a beauty. I've always wondered how the fish are caught with those nets and such. How does that work anyway?" I shoved my hand at him. "I'm Poppy, by the way. Here on, well, vacation I guess, if you call being on a boat a vacation. And you are?"

His smile widened. I tingled some more. "Michael."

I glanced at the other two men, but neither even looked my way or acknowledged me. They turned their shoulders toward each other, blocking me out. *Grumps.*

I took another step toward the vessel. Maybe Michael would invite me on board. "I bet you're real familiar with the surrounding area, all the inlets and coves. I was wondering about good spots to anchor, you know. Maybe you could point out a few? If you don't mind."

An older man strode down the dock and stepped between me and Michael. With a crumpled, unlit cigarette clamped between his fingers, he gestured for me to move along. "My men have work to do."

I blinked twice. It was him. Ray Goldman. In the flesh. He didn't look too menacing, clad in Carhartt overalls tucked into floppy rubber boots. In fact, with his hulking shoulders and heavy brow, he looked more like a caveman than an internationally-wanted criminal. He'd certainly passed his prime, with worn, yellowed teeth, ruddy cheeks, a nose wrought with broken blood vessels, and greasy hair, what he had left of it anyway. His skin was rough, a weathered texture from too much time in the sun or too many cigarettes or both.

He flicked open a Zippo lighter and lit the cigarette, a purposeful message—I'm done talking to you—then turned his back on me. I wanted to scold him; he was standing on the gas dock, for god's sake. Arrogant ass. Men like him made me want to scream. No, not scream. Made me glad we'd invented handcuffs. I kept my feet firmly planted for fear I'd give him a swift kick in the ass, sending him into the drink.

"Right," I said. "Sorry." I smiled at Michael. "Maybe tomorrow then?"

Michael shook his head. "We'll be setting out again before dawn."

"Oh my." I winked. "All work and no play."

His eyes widened, ever so slightly, then traveled down to my waist and back up. I had his attention.

"Well, I wish you calm seas," I said with a little wave.

As I walked away, two men passed me by, tall, thin and blond, most definitely Norwegian, heading down the dock in the direction of the *Forseti*. I glanced back to see them slow as they approached Ray. Perhaps locals Ray was hiring? But for what exactly? I couldn't stroll back that direction to eavesdrop now. Oh well.

My trip down the dock wasn't a total waste of time. I'd learned that the *Forseti* was headed back out to sea in the morning. That meant I had little time to get that Michael talking. If I had any sense of human nature whatsoever, I knew exactly where he and the crew would be tonight.

I hustled back to the *Sea Mist* to let Dalton know I was headed to the pub to see what I could find out.

"Not a good idea," he said with a shake of his head.

"Why not?"

"They're going to be suspicious of anyone. Especially anyone asking questions."

I tipped my head down, batted my eyelashes, and flashed my doe eyes. "Anyone?"

He rolled his eyes and turned his back on me.

"C'mon, Dalton. We need to gather as much information

as we can before they set out in the morning. This is our only chance. Besides—" I winked at him "—you don't think I know how to flirt with a guy without being obvious?"

He paced, his arms crossed, thinking. Then he stopped, looked me in the eyes and said, "What is it with you? It's like you've got something to prove." His hands went to his hips. "I don't disagree with you just because it's fun to argue, you know."

I stared back at him. Was that true? Did I come off like that? I admit, I did feel that I had something to prove. I wanted a permanent position in Special Ops. I had to show I was up to it, that I was a top-notch agent, the best of the best. I wasn't a former SEAL. I wasn't former law enforcement. My resumé… well, I didn't look like much on paper. Sure, I'd done all the extras I could in school, but experience is what they wanted to see. All I had was my own gumption. So, yeah, I guess I did have something to prove.

I opened my mouth to respond and he said, "You know what? You're right. Go on, do your thing."

I hesitated. "Really?"

"Yep. No one would suspect us of being agents. Not with the crap you pull. Yep, darlin', go ahead—" He winked as he crossed his arms. Was he mocking me now? "You're right. Nobody's going to see *you* coming."

I had some time before the crew of the *Forseti* would be headed to the pub and I couldn't shake whatever it was that was going on between me and Dalton. I found a bench with a view of the water and called my friend Chris. He's been my BFF since high school. We were Navy brats and our parents had the same duty stations. Now he's a flight attendant for Delta Airlines and I see him every few months or so. He's got a good heart but he almost got me fired when he showed up uninvited at my first undercover gig. I've forgiven him, especially since he helped me nail the kingpin, but I'm not sure Dalton ever will.

"Hey, Poppy-girl," he said when he picked up. "Whatsup?"

"Hey."

"What kind of trouble have you gotten yourself into now?"

"Funny," I said.

"Seriously, that was some risky action in Costa Rica. You back in the States now, safe and sound?"

"No. Came straight here." I paused. Wouldn't hurt to tell him. "I'm in Norway."

"What the hell are you doing in Norway?"

"And don't come here."

"Girl, I learned my lesson on that one." He snorted. "Besides, you're in one of the safest countries in the world. Nothing for me to worry about. What are you doing there?"

"Dalton and I are here undercover and—"

"Dalton, huh? I thought that was a one time deal."

"It was supposed to be but—"

"Buuuut?"

"Nash wanted us here. Together. I can't tell you the details."

"Okay."

The breeze had picked up, pushing ripples across the surface of the water.

"So why'd you call?" he asked.

"I don't know." I shifted the phone to my other ear. "Just haven't talked to you in a while."

"You never call just to talk. You're not that kind of girl. What's going on?"

"Well, I just wondered, I mean, you're a man and—"

"Oh, here it comes."

"Chris, I'm serious. I really need your advice right now."

"Poppy-girl, there's only one thing you need to know: he's got it bad for you."

"What? No, he's been assigned—"

"Sweetheart, I could tell. He's got it bad."

"You met him once, for like, five seconds."

"Uh, huh. And that's all it took." He made that clicking noise with his lips. "I'm telling you."

"Whatever."

"Oh and you aren't hot for him? This is Chris you're talking to."

"Yeah, well. Your radar is way off. He's my partner. That would be unprofessional."

"Uh, huh."

Silence.

"You talk to your mom lately?"

"Chris, don't start with me." My mom and I weren't exactly on speaking terms. Well, she was. I wasn't.

"She called me, asking about you, said she hasn't heard from you in months."

"New subject."

"She's worried about you. Especially this week, you know. Because of the anniversary of your dad's—"

"New subject!"

"Okay, okay." He paused a beat. "How's the love life?"

"Chris!"

"Touchy buttons today. He's gotten you that riled?"

"I gotta go."

"That was like thirty seconds. Must be a record."

I huffed. "Fine. How are things with you?"

He paused. "Yeah, I've gotta go too. Say hi to Dalton for me."

Errrrgh! I shoved the phone back into my pocket.

The village was so small, it couldn't be that hard to find the pub. I strolled toward the main street and, sure enough, there it was on the corner.

The lights were low, the decor typical of a seaside pub—paintings of old ships on the walls, brass fixtures, wood plank flooring—the kinds of items that would be made of plastic and arranged in an attempt to create an authentic atmosphere in some themed restaurant in the U.S. Here, they were the real deal. So was the odor of sea salt, weathered wood, and mildew mixed with the bitter smell of stale beer.

Music played on some old speakers and there were enough patrons to create a low roar of conversation. In the back, some men played billiards.

I scanned, looking for any of the crew I'd seen.

Bingo. In the corner sat Michael, the American man I'd met on the dock. Next to him was a Norwegian who had the look of an old salt. No doubt, he'd spent his life on the deck of a fishing vessel—crusty beard, wrinkles at the edges of his blue eyes from squinting in the sun, cheeks a permanent rose color.

On the other side of the table sat a boy who couldn't be a day over twenty, with red hair and freckles and a pair of glasses that belonged on a professor of archeology. He was so tall and gangly, he looked like he had to neatly fold his legs and arms to fit into the booth. They looked bored and restless, tired of each other's company.

I waited at the bar until Michael looked my way, then flashed him a come-hither-smile. Without a second glance, he abandoned his beer and mates and crossed the pub to greet me.

"Hi there. Poppy, was it?" He had an easy smile and soft eyes.

I nodded.

"Hey, I'm sorry my father was so gruff with you. Let me buy you a drink?"

"Sure, a drink would sooth my sorrows," I said with a wink. His Father. Michael was Ray's son. *Interesting.* I needed to be extra careful.

"He can come off as a crotchety old man, but he's really not that bad," he said. "Times have been tough and he's not thrilled about being out fishing again. Hopefully, after this trip, he can retire."

I bet. With a cold million. "Who are your friends?" I asked.

"Oh, that's the crew. Bjørn is the helmsman. Dylan's cook and deckhand."

I eyed Bjørn. Was he the informant? Damn, I should have gotten a description from Dalton.

Michael had a look on his face. I'd stared too long.

"Be-yorn?" I said to cover. "He doesn't look like a Be-yorn. Wasn't that the name of the songwriter in ABBA?"

Michael shrugged, uninterested.

"My father was into ABBA," I said, feeling as though I needed an explanation.

"Oh," he said, nodding with the fake, that's-so-interesting smile.

The front door swung open and a man strolled in, looking around with the agitation of someone who'd been called away from an expensive hooker's bed.

I drew in a breath and quickly turned away. It was the man from Bergen, the hustler in the pub. He still had the mark I'd put on his potato face. *Crap!* Five hundred miles north and here he was. *He must be the informant.* Head slap.

"I've got to talk with this guy." Michael turned away from me. "I'll have to catch you later."

I put my hand on his shoulder. "Hey, we were just getting started."

He jerked from my grip. "I said I gotta go."

Okay, geez. You don't have to be an asshole. "I'll be around," I said to the back of his head.

The informant went straight to the table with Bjørn and Dylan. Michael followed him over there, but then the two of them moved to a different table to talk. The old Norwegian, Bjørn, followed them with his eyes, his expression unreadable.

I tried not to be conspicuous while I kept a close eye on them. They leaned forward, into the table and talked in low voices. Whatever they were talking about, Michael didn't want Bjørn or Dylan to know. Then the door opened and Ray pushed through to their table. Oh, to be a fly in his beer.

Potato Head glanced around the pub, annoyed. He thrust his chair back in a huff and headed for the bar. Right next to me. *Crap.* I needed to take control of this.

"Can I get something to drink," he said to the bartender.

"What'll you have?" The man responded without looking up from the counter he was wiping with a wet rag.

He ordered some beer I'd never heard of.

"Excuse me," I asked, "Have we met before?"

He smiled and looked right at me. His smile faded and his eyeballs rattled around in his skull, searching for an escape.

I clamped my hand down on his arm and gave him a sheepish grin. "Sorry about the misunderstanding in Bergen."

He glanced over at Ray, then made an overly exaggerated examination of the contents of his wallet.

"Put it on my tab," I said to the bartender, then whispered, "I had no idea you were, well, you. You wouldn't give my partner your description. How was I supposed to know?"

From his expression, I gathered he'd like to knock my head against the bar.

He turned so his back was to Ray.

"Do you have any new information to share?" I said as quietly as I could.

"Are you kidding?" he said, rubbing his temple.

"I said I was sorry?"

His face turned a lighter shade. "Don't you know how dangerous he is?"

Dalton had been right; this guy was squirrelly. I'd be lucky if he didn't tell Ray who I was right now.

He glanced over his shoulder, fidgeted with his sleeve, then took a cigarette from a box in his pocket and clamped his thin lips around it. "I ain't sayin' nothing more."

Informants always said that, but deep down, they wanted to

blab. "How long is your little powwow gonna be? I want to get a look at that boat."

He shook his head. "No, no, no. Not a good idea. Too risky."

"I only need a few minutes." I didn't want to push him, but this was my best chance. "C'mon. Keep 'em busy?"

He eyed me up and down, making a decision, then as the bartender set his beer on the bar, he said, "And another round for my friends." He pointed to the table with one hand, grabbed his beer with the other, and left me without another word.

I downed the rest of my beer, tossed some kroner on the bar, and headed straight for the docks, a smile on my face.

The *Forseti* was a typical seine fishing vessel with the addition of a crow's nest, which was common on whaling ships. Michael had made it sound like Bjørn, Dylan, his father, and he were the entire crew. That meant no one was aboard the ship right now. I wanted to see what I could find out.

The early nightfall this time of year was a great advantage. I slinked down the dock without seeing anyone and slipped aboard. The wheelhouse might, by some chance, have information, but poking around in there was pretty risky. What I really wanted to know was how they planned to capture and transport an orca. Everything they needed must've been on deck.

There were several lazarettes, large stowage containers built into the hull. Six I could see right away. Problem was, they had big, heavy lids. If I opened one, I risked making a lot of noise. I needed to lift the lid a few inches and peek inside. But to do it one-handed while I held my phone up for a flashlight was going to be tricky.

The first was pad-locked. Not a good sign. The second had a clip in the latch. I pulled it out and heaved up the lid. Nothing but netting inside.

The next one was full of extra floats.

I turned to cross to the other side and someone grabbed me, his hand over my mouth. I rammed my elbow into his gut and spun around.

"It's me," Dalton said, wincing. "Someone's coming down the dock."

Crap.

He grabbed my hand. "We've got to hide," he said and dragged me across the deck. He lifted a pile of nets and I crawled under. He rolled in next to me and flopped the nets down on top of us. They stunk of musty, salty sea, and fish. I tried to breathe through my mouth and stay still. There was no way I was getting caught on board and blowing this op before we even got started.

"What are you doing here?" I whispered in his ear. His body was pressed tight up against me like a spoon.

He shook his head, telling me to be quiet.

Someone stepped on board, then another someone. They walked across the deck, but didn't go inside. I heard mumbling, but couldn't make out the words. Then the scratchy click-click of a cigarette lighter.

"We're going to be here for a while," I whispered to Dalton.

He nodded.

I lay there listening for any recognizable word, wondering who it was. Probably Ray. He smoked. And maybe the informant.

Dalton was warm against me. He didn't move a muscle. Not a twitch. I couldn't even tell if he was breathing. What the hell was he doing on board, anyway? Always harping on me about doing things by the book.

Finally, footsteps again. The two men moved toward the wheelhouse, then the clunk-clunk of shoes on metal stairs. Dalton rolled over. "We've got to go," he said. "Slip off at the stern and swim at least two docks over."

"What? This is the North Atlantic. Do you know how cold that water is?" Jumping into water that temperature was too risky. I wasn't sure I could do it. The shock of the cold alone could cause an automatic gasp reflex, then uncontrollable hyperventilation. Everyone in town would hear me in freak-out mode. Then, within minutes, my legs and arms would seize up. I'd sink like a stone.

"It's our best choice," he whispered.

"It's official. SEALs are insane."

Footsteps again. Someone else boarded the ship. Dalton pulled me to him and held me tight. I lay still, pressed up against him, our faces smooshed together. My heart was thrumming, but not from fear.

Whoever it was followed the others into the wheelhouse.

"C'mon, an evening dip," Dalton whispered. "Think how romantic it will be."

I elbowed him. "What are you doing here, anyway?"

"What am I doing here? What are *you* doing here?"

"Isn't this considered an illegal search? Trespassing or something?"

"Do you mean whether you do it or me?"

Good point. "Now what are we going to do?"

"Wait until they're all asleep, then slip off the back like I said."

"But once they're down below, they might hear us walking on deck." I thought a moment. Lights were on inside the wheelhouse. That meant they couldn't see in the darkness outside. "I'm taking the dock." I rolled from under the nets and took off crab-crawling across the deck before he could grab me.

"Dammit, Poppy," he said in a whisper yell, but he was right behind me.

I poked my head over the rail. "Coast is clear," I said and leaped over the side and onto the dock.

Dalton appeared beside me. He took my hand in his and

we sauntered down the dock like any other tourists out for an evening stroll.

As we neared our boat, a couple sailors appeared out of the darkness, walking toward us. Dalton put his arm around me and whispered in my ear. "That was risky, McVie."

I leaned into him, my head on his shoulder. "You smell like fish."

CHAPTER 6

It was still pitch dark at six a.m. when Dalton fired up the engine. I shuffled around the deck, careful not to trip over any lines or a cleat.

Dalton helped untie the lines and we cast off.

The vessel came equipped with a hand-held spotlight. I stood on the bow, shining a path through the marina while Dalton steered past the fishing docks.

The *Forseti* was still docked, but we wanted to get out of the harbor first. That way, they wouldn't think we were following them.

Once we were past the break wall and out in open water, we could relax a bit. I gazed up at the night sky. Stars spread across the heavens, sparkling like sequins on a royal blue evening gown. The air was cool and crisp. The water calm. The *Sea Mist* gently pushed through the current leaving a tiny white line of froth on the black surface of the sea.

I joined Dalton in the cockpit. "How does she handle?" I asked.

"Like a dream."

"I'm glad you won the coin toss," I said with a grin. "I'd prefer to take the helm when we've hoisted the sails anyway."

"For now, we play cat and mouse. We keep the *Forseti* in our sights while looking like incompetent tourists."

"I don't know about you, but I could use some coffee."

"I won Captain for the day. That makes you the galley wench, right?"

"Don't push your luck," I said and slipped down the companionway.

I found a percolator pot in a bin, filled it with water and coffee, clamped it onto the stovetop, and fired up the burner. Within minutes the aroma of fresh coffee filled the cabin. Dalton poked his head down the hatch. "A fine galley wench you are, mate. My mouth is watering up here."

I found a couple thermal mugs and joined Dalton on deck with the fresh brew.

To the east, the horizon glowed orange. The clouds above looked rimmed with fire.

Dalton had chosen a location where we could safely drift, waiting for the *Forseti*.

I kicked back and sipped my coffee. "There are worse jobs," I said.

"Don't I know it," Dalton said with a grin. He let the engine idle.

"I hope this isn't a waste of time."

He shrugged. "Time on the ocean, fresh air, a sunrise, just the two of us. How could it be a waste of time?"

"You know what I mean."

"There's no wind. Perhaps we should hoist the sails until we determine which way he's headed. We'll look like amateurs caught in irons."

"No time. Look." A fishing vessel was rounding the breakwater. "I bet that's them." I raised the binoculars to check the number on her bow. "It's the *Forseti*."

Dalton took hold of the throttle and eased the boat into gear. "Any indication to which way they're heading?"

I shook my head. "Can't tell."

If the *Forseti* headed southwest, it meant Ray was headed around the peninsula into the open ocean. To the northeast was miles of fjords leading into smaller, narrower fjords. His choice would tell us if he had up-to-date information as to where the killer whales would be.

I raised the binoculars again. "South," I said. "He's turning south."

Dalton turned the wheel to match the heading of the *Forseti* and gave her a little more throttle.

"What do you think, my darling Brittany? Shall we go sightseeing? Maybe some whale watching?"

I nodded. "The cameras are ready." I paused. "But please don't call me Brittany. I left that moniker in Costa Rica." *That and having to play your ditsy wife.* That hadn't worked out so well. "From now on, I'm Poppy."

We followed the coastline for what seemed the entire length of Norway, but was more like twenty miles or so. Puttering along at six knots, the scenery goes by awfully slowly, as stunning as it is. But I'd never get bored.

That's what my mother didn't get, what she never gets. Not like my dad. When we set sail that summer when I was a kid, he knew I'd take to it like a true adventurer. That was my first taste of absolute freedom. We had the whole world to explore.

If only our trip hadn't been cut short.

The day had been like any other, though the wind had shifted from a constant, gentle, westerly wind, to a southerly, twenty-knot blow. We were running downwind, the breeze at our backs. My father, always the patient teacher, had explained the points of sail, the techniques and maneuvers, and I was anxious to learn. My job was to man the sheets. I'd let them out or pull them in using the winch, depending on my dad's commands.

What I didn't realize then, was that he had learned pretty much all he knew about sailing from reading *Chapman's*, the bible of sailors. He had no practical experience. But he'd warned me about the danger of an accidental jibe when sailing downwind like we were, how the wind could catch the outside of the mainsail and send the boom whipping across the boat and slamming against the lines on the other side.

"You're awfully quiet," Dalton said, interrupting my memories.

I nodded. "Thinking about that summer with my dad."

"Want to tell me about it?"

"There's not much to tell." I looked at Dalton. His expression was earnest. *What the hell. Why not?* "Except this one story."

"I could use a good story," he said, his smile kind.

"My dad and I, well, we weren't exactly seasoned sailors and then this one day—well, we'd practiced the jibe many times. My dad would handle the sheets, so he could control the boom as it crossed the deck. I loved it because I got to take the helm—"

"Well, that certainly hasn't changed," Dalton said, his eyes teasing.

"Do you want to hear the story or not?"

He made like he was zipping his lips.

"That day, I stood on the bow looking for wildlife. Not three days earlier, I'd spotted a pod of humpback whales, the first I'd ever seen, and all I could think about was spotting more of them."

I'd seen dolphins quite often, playing at the bow. Seals and sea lions, even a couple otters, had bid us hello.

"Something caught my eye. To this day, I couldn't say for sure what it was, but at the time I was convinced it was an injured otter."

Dalton was nodding, but now I wasn't sure I wanted to tell him about it.

Just thinking about my dad made my eyes get all misty.

The thing is, it all started with my need to help a hurt animal.

I had hollered to my father, pointing at the water. "It's hurt, Daddy, I'm sure!" I shouted. "Turn around."

He leaned from the helm, looking over his shoulder. "What is it?" he hollered back. He leaned a bit further. Then it happened. The boat shifted. Ever so slightly. The wind caught the back of the sail and the boom swept across the deck and slammed into my dad's head, knocking him down. He collapsed in the cockpit, slumped against the wheel.

Blood gushed from his forehead, his neck turned at an unnatural angle. I rushed across the deck. "Daddy! Daddy!" He was out cold. I felt the boat start to shift again and I ducked as the boom came whipping back across, shaking the boat as it slammed to the end of the lines.

I had to get control of the helm before I could take care of my dad.

I spun the wheel to tack through the wind, leaving the jibsheet secured on the cleat, and let the mainsail flutter, trying to get the boat to heave to. We hadn't practiced the maneuver and I had to do it twice to get the boat to settle, but when I was sure it had, I lashed the wheel to lock the rudder, and we floated with the waves, the boat steady.

"Wake up, Daddy! Wake up!" He didn't respond.

I rushed down below for the first aid kit. With a mound of gauze, I stopped the bleeding on his head, but I knew a concussion was much more serious. I got on the radio and called out the emergency code, "Pan-pan, Pan-pan, Pan-pan."

The U.S. Coast Guard replied, asking me to explain my emergency.

"My dad's knocked out cold by the boom," I said, my voice shaking.

"Okay," the man came back. "Is it just you two on board?"

"Yes."

"Okay. I'm going to help. What's your name and how old are you?"

"I'm Poppy. I'm twelve."

There was a long pause.

"I've got the boat hove to and I've bandaged his head, but…" I tried not to cry. "But he's not waking up."

"Okay, Poppy. I'm going to send someone right away to help you. But I need you to tell me where you are. I need your coordinates, if you can. Does your dad have any electronic—"

"No, we don't have GPS," I said.

"All right," he said. "Do you remember what port you left from and how long ago that was?"

"Well, yeah, but don't you want to know exactly where we are?"

"Yes, Poppy, that's what I'm trying—"

"Hold on." I flew down the ladder and grabbed the chart.

Whenever my dad and I traveled, I was in charge of navigating. I'd been plotting our course, keeping watch on the coastline, our speed and direction, marking our progress with a pencil every hour. I checked the clock, used the ruler, and quickly scribbled down our current longitude and latitude. I raced back up the ladder. Dad was still out cold. Into the radio, I rattled off the coordinates.

"Are you sure that's your location?"

"Yes, sir," I said. "I'm the navigator."

"Okay, okay," he said. "I'm sending help right now. A helicopter to take your dad to a doctor."

"Well, tell them to hurry," I said.

"I will," he said and I could tell he was suppressing that disparaging, isn't-she-cute-chuckle. "I want you to stay on the radio and talk to me, though, okay."

"Why? Don't you have work to do?"

Another long pause.

"Yes, Poppy. This is my job. To make sure you and your dad are all right, to be right here to talk you through everything while others come in the helicopter. Is your dad still asleep?"

I looked over at him and tears bubbled up in my eyeballs. "Yes."

"Okay, everything's going to be okay."

"He's getting sunburned."

"What? What do you mean?"

"The sun. I don't know if he put on sunscreen today. He's like me. We have to be careful in the sun. It's the red hair,"

"It's all right, Poppy. The helicopter will be there soon. Listen to me, Poppy. Do you know how to sail the boat?"

"Yes. Of course," I said.

"Okay, then." He asked me a bunch of questions about the boat, about my dad, where we were from. He even asked where was my mom. I told him she was in the Navy. After awhile, I realized he was trying to keep me talking.

My dad moved, shifting a little. He groaned and blinked open his eyes.

"Daddy, are you okay, Daddy?"

He squinted in the sun. "What the hell?"

Tears showered down my face, stinging my sunburned cheeks. "You got hit by the boom."

He rubbed his head and the mound of gauze I'd taped there. "Did you...?" His eyes traveled to the sails, then to the wheel. "What happened?"

"It's okay. The Coast Guard is coming."

"I don't need—"

"My dad's awake," I said into the radio.

"Good, Poppy. Now look south. Do you see the helicopter? It's almost there."

"I see it." The orange aircraft was flying low, headed right for us.

My dad looked up, then leaned over and threw up on the floor. Then he leaned back and passed out again.

"He's sick. My dad is sick."

"Did he vomit? That's okay. He's probably feeling a little dizzy and it's nothing to worry..."

The roar of the helicopter drowned out his voice. It slowed and hovered overhead, so loud I had to cover my ears. The blades whipped the water into a mist. Then the rescue swimmer jumped from the helicopter into the water beside the sailboat. I thought Superman had arrived, I swear.

Once he was in the water, the helicopter flew up and away. Not too far, just enough so I could hear the man talk. I helped him get on board. I'll never forget his name. Petty Officer Jon Ardan. He kept asking if I was okay. I nodded like crazy.

"Are you okay?" Dalton was saying, bringing me back to today. He stared at me with expectant eyes. "You were saying you saw an otter in the water, then your eyes glazed over."

"Yeah, I thought I saw an otter. My dad turned, the wind caught the sail, and he got hit by the boom. Knocked him out cold."

"Wow, that's serious. What'd you do?"

"I called the Coast Guard. They came."

"That's it? That's your whole story?"

"Pretty much. When they got there,—" I pressed my lips together, wincing at the memory "—'Help my dad,' was all I could say through my blubbering."

Dalton gave me a sympathetic smile. "Poppy, you were twelve."

"Yeah, well…"

The helicopter had circled back and a huge basket was lowered on the cable. Petty Officer Ardan strapped my dad onto a litter in the basket, then I watched, powerless to help, as my dad was brought up into the helicopter and it flew away, leaving the petty officer on board with me.

"It's funny," I said to Dalton. "I remember…"

"What?"

I turned away from Dalton and gazed out at the horizon. "Nothing."

I remember staring at the petty officer, in his jumpsuit, a real superhero, and it hit me that my dad was just a man. An ordinary man.

"So your dad, was he okay?" Dalton asked.

"Yeah."

They had kept my dad overnight and I got to sleep on a little pull-out-couch in his room.

In the morning, he opened his eyes and smiled at me. "My hero," he said.

I shook my head. He took my hand in his and I started to shake, then my eyes filled with tears and I buried my head in his chest. "Oh Daddy, I thought you were going to die."

"Now how could that be? With you there to take care of me?"

I shook my head, snuffling.

"Did you remember what I taught you? About breathing?"

I nodded. He'd shown me how to control my heart rate, to keep from panicking, by controlling my breath.

"It's important to always practice the pranayama. Your breath is your life force, the vital energy we share with all life."

I nodded again. I drew in a deep breath and felt better.

Then my mom arrived. "What were you thinking? I knew something like this would happen," she said to him before he could sit up in the bed. She was still in her uniform and her eyes were red. She must have flown through the night. I remember thinking, that must be why they call it the red eye.

My dad held his head in his hands. "Georgia, calm down. Everything turned out all right."

"But she was on her own. What if you'd have fallen off the boat? Where would she be, a twelve-year-old, trying to rescue you on her own?"

"She'd be further ahead than most twelve-year-olds, that's where, because she'd have done it."

My mother got that look on her face, the one that said, *don't you dare say another word*. She crossed her arms. "This trip is over."

"What!" I shot up from the chair.

She almost bowled me over with a bear hug. "Oh my dear. Are you okay?"

"Why does everyone keep asking me if I'm okay? It was Dad who got hurt, not me."

"You must have been terrified." She rocked me, rubbing my back.

I tried to pull away. "Well, I really didn't..." I'd learned not to confirm anything my mom said. She'd turn it around on me.

"We're going to get your things and you're coming back to the base with me."

"But Mom, I'm not—"

"No buts. Now get your things."

And that was that. Mom had brought down her fist and our sailing trip was over. She enrolled me in school and my dad decided to go off on a photography trip on his own.

Dalton took hold of my hand. "Your hand is shaking."

"I'm fine." I turned away. I couldn't look at him. "That was the last time I saw my dad, is all."

"Poppy, don't be too hard on yourself. You were just a kid."

I pulled my hand from his. "Yeah," I said and escaped to the cabin below.

When I got back topside, Dalton was at the helm, one arm draped over the top of the wheel, the other holding his cup of coffee, his hair ruffled in the wind. He seemed at ease, content. I couldn't help but stare a moment. If he wasn't so damn aggravating, I might have found him attractive. He was an adrenaline junkie like me. Bold and confident. And he had the looks—that strong jaw line, the way he held his shoulders, how every muscle formed to create a body that Michelangelo's *David* would envy.

Yeah, no. He was so damn aggravating.

I forced my eyes forward, to the edge of the sea, and my mind somewhere else.

Around lunch time, the *Forseti* overtook us.

"I hope this all happens and is done quickly," I said. "I don't think they'll tolerate us for long."

Dalton said nothing but I could tell by his expression that he had the same concern.

In the galley, I flipped some lunchmeat and mustard on a slice of bread for Dalton, some peanut butter for me and we kept moving.

When I handed him his sandwich, he asked, "So after that summer, sailing with your dad, that's when he was killed, by poachers, right?"

"Yeah," I said.

"What happened?"

I shrugged. I didn't want to talk about it. This time every year, the date of my dad's death, always refueled my anger and frustration. I didn't like the conclusions of the authorities. Never would. They'd dismissed it too easily. They didn't know my dad like I did. Someday. Someday I'd track down the culprits and justice would be done.

"I'm sorry," Dalton said. I wasn't sure if he meant for losing my dad or for bringing it up.

I shrugged again. "How's the sandwich?"

"Great, thank you," he said, taking the hint.

Sometime in the late afternoon, the *Forseti* slowed and turned into a small inlet. It looked like they meant to anchor.

"I figured they'd press on through the night," Dalton said. "Didn't you say Dr. Parker's last text said that the whales are still quite far out?"

"Maybe they know something we don't?"

Dalton continued another mile to a nice, secluded cove and we dropped anchor. We had to assume they'd continue in the morning. "I don't like this," I said. "Do you suppose they got word there are other killer whales close by? A pod Dr. Parker doesn't have tagged? And they're going after them instead?"

He scanned the ocean with the binoculars. "We should get some rest while we can. We'll take shifts."

"You've been at the helm all day. You go ahead," I said. "I'll wake you in four hours."

"You'll wake me if anything else comes up though, right?" he said. "You're not going to take off in the dingy on your own for some clandestine nighttime assault, right?"

I crossed my arms.

"Right," he said and grabbed the handrails and swung into the companionway.

I shook my head. *That man.*

The cockpit wasn't the most comfortable for lounging, but I managed to prop up a cushion and face the open sea. I once again opened my book, but I wasn't in the mood. It wasn't very often I got to watch the sunset on a sailboat anchored at sea. In fact, a glass of wine seemed appropriate. I slipped down below, found a plastic mug, and filled it with Cabernet from a box. (On a boat, it would do.) *Ah.*

I settled into the cushions and thought of calling Chris back, but I didn't want Dalton to hear my conversation. I'd been snippy with him and he was just trying to be my friend. It was the mention of my mom. Always put me on edge. I sighed. He'd understand.

The sea was calm as glass, the reflections of the surrounding peaks a perfect mirror image. The kak-kak of sea birds mingled with the babble of distant waterfalls. I sipped my wine. *Sure beats lying in the mud in a blind swatting mosquitoes and hoping the poachers don't have itchy trigger fingers.*

A faint soothing sound broke the quiet. I grabbed the binoculars and as I lifted them to see, I heard it again—the distinctive whoosh of a humpback whale exhaling as it broke the surface. I stood up. There were three, no four. Maybe five. About a half mile out. And they were headed toward us.

I stood in awe, watching as the group surfaced for air three more times, their warm breath held aloft in tiny clouds of mist. Then on the fifth exhalation, each arched its back and as it dove, showed its distinctive fluke.

I zinged down the ladder. "Dalton, wake up. Wake up."

He sat up with a jolt. "What is it? What's wrong?"

He rubbed his eyes and ran his fingers through his hair, sitting on the edge of the bunk, shirtless and wearing only his boxer shorts. For a moment, I forgot what I'd come down for. "Nothing," I said and forced my eyes to the floor. His shoes had been placed next to the bunk in perfect alignment atop his shirt and jeans, folded with perfect corners and stacked one atop the other. "Come see," I said, louder than I intended to as I backed out of his cabin.

We got top side as one of the whales surfaced again, this time within two hundred yards. It exhaled and water sprayed into the air with a resounding whoosh, the wistful whisper of a giant.

In moments, another surfaced, then another, their exhalations without hurry, a peaceful yogic breath, and I was reminded of the pranayama. I drew in a long breath and exhaled, concentrating on an easy, constant letting go. Just me and the water and the sky and the whales. Nothing else mattered. Then the first arched his back and as he dove, his fluke broke the surface and water poured off, separating into countless tiny streams as the tail flattened then tipped upward and slowly disappeared below the water.

As though choreographed by some ancient force, each followed in the same manner, showing us their wide tail flukes.

I turned to Dalton. "I thought you'd want to see."

He nodded, his smile wide. "Yes, thanks. And keep an eye out. Orcas often travel with humpbacks. Or the other way around. Both take advantage of the others' fishing techniques."

A whale surfaced right next to the boat, its exhalation so loud I fell back on my butt with a start. Dalton let out a whoop and I giggled. I couldn't help myself. I giggled with delight as I ran to the bow. The whale passed below in the crystal clear water, then came up on the other side and blew out a breath. The mist sprayed me in the face. "That's amazing!" My whole body tingled with joy. "Fish breath!" I said to Dalton and giggled some more.

Dalton's smile said it all.

The other humpbacks surfaced about fifty yards off the starboard bow, circling back.

"How could anyone want to harm such beautiful creatures?" I whispered.

He shook his head.

"They're just so beautiful," I said.

Dalton turned to face me. I could feel his eyes on me.

I met his gaze and his eyes held mine. Whoosh, came another watery breath. "We should take some pictures," I said and hurried down below for the camera, escaping from Dalton's gaze. I stopped and drew in a deep breath. *Don't go there, McVie. It's dangerous territory.* I got the camera and headed back topside.

I managed to snap a few frames but the whales were quickly getting further and further away. "It's amazing how much distance they cover and it feels like they're moving so slowly."

"Yeah," he muttered. "I should hit the sack again." I could tell his mind was elsewhere. "Wake me in four." He headed down below without looking at me.

Chapter 7

On Dalton's watch, sometime around three a.m., an easterly wind brought waves rolling into our cove. I awoke to the rhythmic rocking of our boat. Then the rain came. First a patter on the deck, then the angry pounding of a thousand tiny hammers.

I donned my boots and jacket and started to head up the companionway to ask Dalton if he was all right, but thought better of it. He'd just give me that I-was-a-SEAL frown.

Neither of us were going to get any sleep anyway, so I fired up the stove and set the coffee pot to brew. I filled it only half full as the boat bobbed and rocked in the sea. Otherwise, I'd have a black mess to clean up.

A decent breakfast wasn't going to happen. Yogurt and a banana would have to do.

As I managed to get steaming hot coffee into the mugs without splashing it all over the place, the boat rose upward on a swell and the anchor broke loose. Dalton fired up the engine immediately. I secured the coffee mugs, flipped on the navigation lights, and clipped on my life jacket before I ran up top.

"I've got the helm!" I shouted over the thunderous rain as I took the wheel.

Dalton didn't hesitate. He headed for the foredeck, hand over hand along the rail, trying to stay upright as the bow rose and fell on the waves. He started hauling in the anchor.

"You're not clipped onto the jackline!" I yelled but he couldn't hear me. If he fell overboard right now, in the pitch dark, I didn't know how I'd find him. But he had to get the anchor up as soon as possible. We'd be in serious danger if it wrapped around the prop. And he had to pull it up without letting it slam into the side of the hull.

I kept her steady as best I could, aiming into the growing swells.

Finally, he had the anchor on board and secured on the bow roller. He headed back to the mainsail, walking with the wide stance of a seasoned sailor to keep his balance while the deck moved below his feet. He pulled off the sail ties and tossed them in the cockpit, put a reef in the sail, then went right to the halyard to hoist the mainsail to stabilize the boat so we'd stop bobbing around like a lost cork. "Head to wind!" he shouted. "Head to wind!"

"I'm trying!" I needed to keep her bow into the wind, so the sail wouldn't fill as he was raising it, but the waves were too big for the 45-horsepower engine to keep her steady.

The bow swung to starboard. I forced the wheel around and pushed the throttle down, managing to get her headed into the wind. The bow pointed up on the crest of a wave, then slammed down into the trough. As she tilted upward again, water crashed over the bow and sprayed me smack in the face, the cold a shocking jolt.

My feet were braced and I held her steady into the wind as Dalton cranked the winch double-time, hoisting the sail. The moment he cleated the halyard, I turned the wheel, bearing away. The sail filled with wind, and the side-to-side bobbing subsided. The boat eased into the rhythm of her design, pitching fore and aft as she cut through the waves.

Dalton plopped down on the cockpit seat. He was soaking wet, his hair sticking to his forehead.

"That was hairy for a moment," I said.

He nodded, wiping the back of his hand across his brow.

"We should get into our harnesses before raising the headsail. This looks like it might pick up," I said.

"I'll get 'em," he said and headed down the ladder, shaking his head, mumbling, "There was nothing forecasted."

"There's coffee," I hollered after him. "I already poured it. Mugs are cinched in the sink."

He poked his head back up and grinned. "You make a great wife, you know that."

If I'd had something to throw at him, I would have.

I licked sea salt from my lips.

The halyard rattled against the mast, a metallic bang bang bang. I wanted to tighten it down, but it wasn't worth risking a walk on the deck.

Dalton appeared with coffee and our harnesses. I got into mine and clipped the tether to the jackline.

"I feel like a dog on a leash," I said.

"Maybe it will tame you," he said with a smirk.

A gust came up and the boat lifted, heeling to port. "Never!" I said to Dalton as I tightened my grip on the wheel, holding her steady.

He shook his head. "I say we use the stormsail up front. What do you think?"

I nodded. "It's really going to blow." The steel-wire stays that held the mast in place hummed, vibrating in the wind. "I'm setting a course for Reine. Back to the harbor." I adjusted the mainsail angle by easing out the mainsheet. "We're going to be rocking and rolling."

Dalton made no response as he went to work unfurling the headsail while I managed the helm. The boat picked up speed right away.

I took a quick sip of the coffee. Warmth filled my chest.

There was nothing ahead but an inky-black sea with only a hint of white lace at the tip of a wave as it curled and ran alongside the boat. Ideally, sailing at night, I'd have a lookout on the bow, but it was too dangerous in these waves.

Another gust slammed into the sails. I shifted my weight to keep my balance. The wind was picking up and we had miles to go to get back to safe harbor.

"Make sure the companionway's sealed tight," I said to Dalton. He grabbed hold of the sliding hatch and gave it a tug.

The boat rocked to starboard as a roller wave lifted, then we rocked to port as we slid into the trough. The next roller was even bigger and crashed over the starboard side sending a wave of water down the deck and splashing into the cockpit. My right boot filled with icy-cold water. Every muscle in my body tensed with the chill.

"With these gusts, I need you to mind the mainsheet," I said to Dalton.

"Yes, ma'am," he said and took hold of the line.

The wind blew so hard, the rain swept horizontally, whipping at my face under the bimini top.

The bow slammed into a wave and I lost my balance. I grabbed for the lifeline and managed to keep upright as the bow broke through and we rode up the wave.

Another wall of water rolled over the deck and poured into the cockpit, over the top of my boots.

Up then down, up and down, she rolled right, then left.

"I see light ahead," said Dalton. "Off the starboard bow, at two o'clock. Could be the *Forseti*."

"I see it." If we could keep up with him, at least he'd be close by if we needed to radio for help.

Lightning zig-zagged across the sky, an instant of illumination, a contrast to the black, ominous waves that churned the surface of the sea.

Take 'em one at a time, Poppy. One at a time.

The size and duration of the waves was getting dangerous. With each crest, the bow dipped and slammed into the trough. The mast rattled and shook. The stays flexed, then pulled taut with each wave. I was starting to wonder if the *Sea Mist* could take it.

"We might want to have our satellite beacon at the ready," I shouted to Dalton.

"Where is it?" he said.

"Take the helm." I knew where it was stashed.

Dalton and I managed to move past each other, sloshing through the cockpit, always one hand on a rail. He grabbed the wheel and I headed down the ladder, a puddle of water forming before I could get the companionway hatch closed.

The cabin looked as though a tornado had thundered through. Cabinets doors had flung open, boxes of cereal, bags of pasta and chips scattered all over the floor. I managed to hobble to the equipment locker, moving from one handhold to another as the floor lifted and dropped. With the lid clipped open and my hip wedged against the bulkhead, I rummaged through and found the beacon. I pinned it to my life vest.

I really had to pee, but I wasn't sure I could get into the head. The door had come unlatched and was slamming open and shut with every rocking back and forth of the boat. I tried to get it latched again and decided I might as well go while I was down here. Climbing up and down the ladder wasn't exactly a safe endeavor in a storm like this.

One might think a twenty-four-year old woman could handle a potty break without incident, but on a sailboat in the high seas, well, let's just say that accidentally peeing in your own boot isn't exactly something to be criticized. Once you let loose, there's no turning back.

I braced myself against the bulkhead to get my pants buttoned back up, then tackled the ladder.

When I got back top side, the eastern sky had patches of pink light amid dark clouds. The sea looked as dark as ever. I glanced forward. The lights of the *Forseti* appeared, then disappeared behind the crest of a wave, then appeared again.

"They're gaining distance from us," Dalton said. "We can't

keep up with them."

"We need a bigger boat."

For the first time, I saw an expression of worry cross Dalton's face. There and gone. A ghost passing through, then banished.

"I don't suppose you brewed some more coffee while you were down there?" Before I could answer, he grinned and said, "I'm kidding. I think this blow is just getting started."

I nodded as I took the helm. I was afraid of the same thing.

Each wave seemed larger than the last. The swells were increasing and the *Sea Mist* rolled and rocked, tossed on the sea like a bath toy of the gods. Dalton and I held on in a constant deluge. The cockpit drain could barely keep up and soon we stood in knee deep water.

With a jolt, an exceptionally large roller crashed over the bow, surged across the deck and slammed into the cockpit, drenching us. "Whew!" shouted Dalton. "Makes you feel alive, don't it!"

"Absolutely!" I shouted back, gripping the wheel.

I glanced at the chart plotter. We'd been steadily blowing in toward shore. We needed to turn and head out, away from shore. "We need to tack," I said.

Dalton immediately got on the jib sheet.

"Ready about?" I shouted. "Helms-a-lee." I turned into the wind and released the port jibsheet. The headsail flapped and fluttered, then bent against the forestay. Dalton cranked on the winch in a frenzied hurry, tightening down the sheet as we bobbed to and fro. The mainsail boom came around, both sails filled with wind, and the boat heeled over to starboard. "We'll stay close-hauled to get away from the shore," I told him. "So hang on!"

The boat leaned so far over I had to grab hold of the rail.

With the force of the waves and the angle of heel, our forward momentum stalled.

"We need to reef the sail again," he said.

I shook my head. Not a good idea.

"We need to reef. We've got too much sail."

"I know what reef means. It's too risky to walk up on the deck right now to do it."

"I can do it," said Dalton. "Keep her steady."

"No. I'll bear away. We'll take the longer course."

"No, I can do it!"

He took three steps and slipped and fell down the side deck into the life lines. As if it were a mere stumble, he got back to his feet and continued. A monster wave crested in front of us and tumbled over the bow, thundered down the deck, and swiped his feet out from under him. He slammed into the lifelines and fell over the side.

The jackline pulled taut as he came to the end of the tether. "Dalton!" I screamed.

I turned into the wind, let the mainsheet loose, and ran to the railing. Dalton was hanging over the side, both hands on his tether, trying to haul himself back on board as waves battered him, crashing over his head.

Think! Quick! The boom slammed back and forth over my head. I grabbed the spare halyard line, wrapped it on the winch, and tossed the bitter end to Dalton. "Grab the line!" I shouted.

He tried to catch it with one hand as it flapped in the wind and water. As soon as he had a grip on it, I cranked the winch in double-time, hauling him back to the rail. He heaved himself over the lifelines and flopped into the cockpit. Dalton bent over, his head in his hands, trying to catch his breath. "Holy crap! That was quick thinking, McVie." He nodded, his way of praise.

"Just what we needed, a little excitement. It was getting boring," I said as set the mainsail and adjusted our heading.

He smiled wide, threw his head back, and let loose a hearty laugh.

Inside, my heart hammered away at my ribs. I checked the instruments and reassessed our course. "We drifted quite a bit, lost some ground. We'll have to stay on this tack for a while."

He nodded, then turned and stared at the sunrise for a long moment. "I thought I was going to have to cut loose. I was reaching for my KA-BAR." He turned back to face me. "Then there you were, with a lifeline."

"You'd do the same for me."

"Yeah, but…"

"If you'd have had to cut loose, I would've found you."

He looked me in the eyes. "No doubt you would have."

"It wouldn't look good on my resume, losing a new partner so soon."

He laughed again. "I'm sure you're right." He shook his head and turned away.

The gale blew all day, waves growing larger by the hour in the gray, dreary sea. By mid-day, we were exhausted, but we still had miles to go. We'd long since lost sight of the *Forseti*. Dalton and I took turns at the helm while the other manned the sheets, a steady mind-numbing routine punctured occasionally by moments of panic.

The cockpit never quite cleared of water and my feet were raw from cold, wet boots. My stomach growled but food didn't sound good. Besides, heading down below to get anything would be an adventure all its own.

The radio squawked to life—*Sea Mist, Sea Mist, Sea Mist.* The charter company trying to hail us. Dalton answered, told them we were en route to the harbor and our coordinates. By the time we got back to port, she'd need some repairs, he told them.

"Glad you are headed back," the man said. "The gale's supposed to blow for another couple days."

Dalton signed off and looked at me. "I hope the *Forseti* is back in port, too. Or we might never find him again."

The afternoon dragged on as the *Sea Mist* got pummeled by

wind and waves. Dalton and I held on.

By dusk, the harbor was in sight.

Once we had her back in the berth and tied up, Dalton wrapped his arms around me in a big bear hug. "We made it," he said.

"Yes, but what if the *Forseti* isn't here? What will we do then?"

Dalton combed his fingers through his hair. "My god, Girl. Take a breath."

CHAPTER 8

After a quick stroll, and finding the *Forseti* in the marina, I collapsed in my bunk.

Even in the protected harbor, the boat rocked and jerked against the lines all night. I tossed in my bed, too exhausted to sleep.

When daylight finally streamed in through the port light, I roused and set a pot of coffee to brew, then went up on deck to see if there was any movement on the *Forseti*. No sign of anyone.

Waves crashed into the breakwall and splashed twenty feet into the air, then poured over the back side. Flags fluttered at the tops of their poles. Halyards and stays rattled and hummed in the wind as boats rocked and shifted in their berths.

Back down below, I checked the weather forecast. Marine warnings darted across the screen. As we'd been told, the storm was expected to blow for another day at least, maybe more, before settling down. Thirty-foot seas and sustained forty-knot winds with gusts as high as fifty-five. No one was going anywhere.

I found a frying pan and cracked some eggs into it.

This plan wasn't going to work. We couldn't keep up with the *Forseti*, even in calm seas. There had to be another way. A better way.

I had to get on that boat.

Dalton stuck his head out of his cabin, one eye open. "Is that coffee I smell?"

"Nectar of the gods," I said. "Coming right up."

He slumped into a seat at the table. I set a mug down in front of him, trying to keep my eyes from his muscled arms and rock-hard pecs. The eggs were done, so I slid them onto a couple of plates and plopped them on the table. "Eat up," I said.

"Wow," he said. "She saves me from Neptune's mighty grip and cooks me breakfast."

"Yeah, well, don't get used to it."

I slid a fork across the table to him.

He wolfed down his eggs and chased them with two gulps of coffee.

"The *Forseti* is at the dock. I haven't seen any movement over there this morning."

"Morning? It's nearly eleven-thirty."

I glanced at the clock. He was right. I must have been more exhausted than I'd thought. I never slept this late.

"I suppose we should check in," he said and reached for his phone.

I shoved the plates in the sink. "I cooked. You clean up."

He grumbled some kind of confirmation as he scrolled through emails on his phone. "I got a note from Nash," he said. "Listen to this. He called Norwegian officials to give them a heads up and discuss arrangements, assuming we'd be successful in our mission, and it sounds like they weren't too keen on us being here. Some political crap about jurisdiction and the U.S. overstepping." He looked up at me. "The Op's been nixed. He wants us to head home right away."

"What?" I couldn't believe what I was hearing. "But what about Ray? What about the whales he'll capture?"

Dalton shrugged. "Nothing we can do if they won't have us here."

"Nothing we can do?" I plopped down on the bench across

from him. "But we can't just—"

"Poppy, I know you're—"

"You're damn right. I'm not going anywhere. Not while that man is here capturing whales. What about April? What about that pod? What about Granny K?"

"We knew this was a long shot at best coming in. Joe was going out on a limb sending us here in the first place. We don't have—"

"You write back and you tell him I'm already on the boat."

"What?" He shook his head, his jaw muscles taut. "No way. I'm not going to do that. You're not—"

"You tell him I found a way on the boat and you can't leave me without backup. Tell him there's no way to get word to me or to get me off the boat without risking my life. You tell him." I nodded emphatically. "I'm already on that boat."

"Poppy, no. No way. It's too dangerous. Besides, that is not even remotely an option. There's no way Ray is going to let a stranger on that boat. What you're thinking is impossible."

I crossed my arms. "Nothing's impossible."

Dalton stared at me, then sighed, closed his eyes. "And what exactly is your plan?"

"Well, I'll…I'm going to…I'll find a way."

He shook his head. "Poppy, you're not—"

"I'll get a job with him. I'll stowaway. I don't know." *Breathe. Breathe.* "But I am not walking away from this. I'm not. Not if I can stop it."

His eyes grew large. "Who said anything about stopping it?"

I gritted my teeth. Sure a video might be the evidence we needed to convict Ray, assuming we could convince the Norwegian authorities to take him into custody, but what good was it to the killer whale who, by then, would've already been sold into slavery and living in a bathtub in Russia or China? Of course I had to stop it.

I mustered calm. "I'm doing this. Are you with me or not?"

He stared at me, his eyes filled with apprehension, then he examined the inside of his coffee mug for a while, then finally looked back at me, shaking his head. "This is a bad idea." He frowned and set the phone down. "You realize, we're gonna have one shot at this guy. Once we're blown, it's over. And Nash is going to have our asses either way."

A smile spread across my face.

"But remember, if you're planning to get video from on board that boat, you can't stowaway. For it to be admissible in court, you have to be invited aboard."

I nodded. "Invited. Right." How the hell was I going to do that?

I shot up from the bench, headed for the sink, and went to work washing the dishes. I needed something to do with my hands while I organized my thoughts into some semblance of a plan. Dalton could do them twice later.

I scrubbed and scrubbed, my mind in overdrive. Perhaps they needed another hand on board. Not likely though, as they were already heading out. Maybe pose as a second captain? Probably all set there too. The cook? Maybe we could persuade that Dylan boy to quit. Put flour in his stew?

I stacked the dishes and paced while Dalton got dressed. There had to be a way to get on that boat. Something that man needed. What little I knew of him, which was from our one, short encounter, and as much as I hate to admit Dalton was right about him, he seemed like the kind of man who would be suspicious of my grandma. And if he suspected the agency was on to him at all, there was no way he'd let a stranger on board.

But the son, Michael, might. Yes. He was my ticket. He was my best chance. If I could get his attention, then get him talking, I could figure out what Ray needed. Then I would persuade Michael into thinking I was a valuable asset and get him to convince Ray to invite me aboard.

I slipped into the head and rummaged through my toiletry

bag. A little mascara, some eyeshadow. I swiped some lipstick on my lips.

Dalton was standing in the galley with his arms crossed when I got out.

"How do I look?" I asked.

"Is that lipstick?"

"There's a storm. Where do sailors hang out during a storm? The pub, of course."

"And what are you planning to do?"

"Well, Michael and I had a conversation going and—"

"The son? Are you telling me your plan is to—"

"The oldest trick in the book," I said with a grin.

Chapter 9

I fled up the ladder and down the dock before Dalton could say anything more.

The crew of the *Forseti* was at the same table they'd been at two nights before, each with a basket of fish and chips.

I found two empty stools at the bar, leaned on my elbows between them, and ordered a beer. After a moment, I spun around and looked right at Michael and smiled. He noticed. *Good. Now to reel him in.*

The bartender nudged me with my mug of beer. I tipped it back and chugged down a few gulps, then wiped my mouth with the back of my hand, my eyes on Michael.

He said something to the other two of his crew, then rose and walked toward me.

"You're back," he said.

"So are you," I said, letting my eyes travel down to his waist, then back up.

His eyes on my beer, he said, "Kinda early to start, isn't it?"

I shrugged, tilted my head down a little and looked up at him with my best glamour eyes. "What else is there to do?"

He grinned. "Well, you've got me there."

"So you'll join me?"

"Can't think of anything I'd like better."

I waved to the bartender and motioned for him to bring

another beer.

"So, tell me, what's a lady like you doing in a place like this?" Michael said.

"That's a terrible line," I said with a giggle. "Really."

"Yeah, well," he said, all matter-of-fact. "You're not here to fish." He tipped up his beer and looked at me over the bottle.

"True." I took another swig of my beer, stalling. If I was going to get anywhere with this guy, I had to ditch the married couple act. Make it known I was available. But not too easy. "My boyfriend thought it would be great fun to go sailing on vacation." I added a big eye roll.

He raised one eyebrow.

"My *ex* boyfriend, I mean," I added with emphasis. "He turned out to be a real jerk."

He nodded and sipped his beer, taking some time to formulate a response, it seemed. "Are you afraid of him?" he finally said, genuinely concerned.

I hesitated, trying to give him the impression I was, but wouldn't say. It could only help my cause, right? This guy might have been Ray's son, but he didn't seem so bad. Maybe his mom was a good person, one of those Ivy-bred women who took off with a rogue badass like Ray Goldman to piss off her parents. Maybe she'd raised him right, with good manners and a respect for women. He seemed to have a bit of chivalry in him. I could work it. "I've a mind to catch the next ferry out of here," I said. "But I'm stuck. This storm is quite something, isn't it?"

"Yeah, something." His eyes never left mine. He had that intensity of a guy who knows exactly what he wants and doesn't let up until he gets it. And right now, he was focused. On me. *Excellent.*

"I don't know about you," I said, "But I'm feeling a little restless, holed up like this, for days on end."

That broke the spell. He looked away, sipped his beer. "My dad says the storm's clearing already. We're heading back out in the morning."

"Oh?" I said. *Crap.* "Are you sure it will be safe to head out?"

He shrugged, as though he hadn't given it any thought. Either because his father had decided and that was that or he was too manly to let a storm keep him in port. I wasn't sure which.

I hadn't seen any report that the storm was letting up. Was Ray desperate enough to head out in this weather? To take that kind of risk to find the whales? Either way, this was my only chance then. I turned to Michael and gave him my best sexy eyes. "Meanwhile, what's there to do around here that's fun?"

One eyebrow went up. "What about your boyfriend?"

"My *ex* boyfriend."

"Oh, that's right," he said, his eyes all flirty now.

"So…any ideas?"

"Actually, yes." He took my hand in his and said, "There's something I want to show you."

He led me past the pool table, down the narrow hallway, and out the back door to a tiny, grass-roofed shed. The door had been left ajar a few inches. The wind whipped down the alley between the pub and the shed. I hesitated. Why in the world would Michael take me back here? My pulse picked up a bit. Was this a trap?

"Um, I'm sorry if I gave you the impression that I'm that kind of girl." If he expected me to knock one out in the back shed, I'd kick him in the nuts and come up with another plan.

"My, you have an imagination," he said with a warm, disarming smile. "C'mon." He pushed the door open, and with the grin of a boy showing off his older brother's secret clubhouse, he motioned for me to follow him in.

You're being paranoid now. Go with it. I took one step inside behind him and—was that…the mewing of kittens?

A bare light bulb hung over a crate, inside which a heap of little fur balls, maybe four weeks old, snuggled. Someone had rigged the light bulb for warmth. Their little blue eyes were open and they were squirming and crawling over each other. One rolled over, showing its little pot-belly. A gray tabby.

Michael had a conspiratorial grin. "Aren't they cute?"

I picked up the roly-poly one and cuddled it to my cheek. "Oh my, are they ever."

He picked one up and held it to his chest, petting it softly. "You're going to be just fine, little one," he said, then added, "The bartender has been trying to find good homes for them."

I picked up a second one. "Too bad people aren't responsible enough to get their pets spayed and neutered. It really makes me—" I stopped short "—want to take them all." *Crap.* I had to be careful.

"I wish." He grinned and nodded, showing no reaction to my semi-rant.

"You could take one on the boat," I said. "People do it all the time." I set the first one down and picked up another. "Just think, an unlimited supply of fish. A kitty-cat's dream."

He shook his head, but didn't say anything more. He leaned against the wall, stroking the kitten, making little soothing noises.

I leaned on the wall next to him. "They're so sweet," I said, but Michael seemed lost in the simple joy of petting the kitten. I tried to sort out in my mind how he could be on the hunt for an orca, that he could be here in Norway for the sole purpose of capturing one from the wild, yanking it from its ocean home, kidnapping it from its family, yet here he was, all sentimental, cooing at a tiny kitten. How could that be? Certainly it wouldn't be fair to judge someone by his father's behavior. But he was an adult, and there was no way he didn't know what his father was up to. He couldn't possibly be ignorant of the whole plan. But how could the same man do both?

"You surprise me," I said. "I wouldn't have thought you were an animal lover."

"Yeah?" he said. A question.

"You know, being a fisherman and all."

He shrugged, as though one didn't have anything to do with the other. Did he think of the whales as just big fish? Did he have no understanding of them at all? Their intelligence, their capacity to feel, to hurt, to love?

The little kitten purred as he scratched behind its ears.

Maybe he really thought there was nothing wrong with it. Maybe he thought whales were like cats and dogs, easily domesticated. Or maybe he was one of those who think all animals are better off being cared for by humans. Maybe he actually believed what he was doing was a good thing. Back in the 80s, his father had made the claim that what he did was for the greater good, that his work was changing public perception of the killer whale, that they were not to be feared, but admired. He'd claimed that showing them to the world in their special amphitheater-style aquariums did more to further the interest of killer whales than any scientist ever could.

I admit, times were different then. Some of his claims might even have been true. My grandma had taken me to an aquarium when I was a child and no doubt that experience contributed to my life-long love for animals. But that doesn't justify putting the whales through that hell. Not then and not now.

Sure, an argument could be made that back then, Ray, like everyone else, didn't know any better, but the difference was, he'd made a fortune in the process. And now, all these years later, there was no excuse. Pure greed brought him out of retirement—greed for that one-million-dollar price tag.

But what was it for Michael?

Maybe his father had some hold over him, some deep-seated psychological pull. What do they call it? The father complex? Always seeking his father's approval? Had his dad done a number on his confidence? I suppose I was lucky. My dad had always told me I could do anything I wanted, I could accomplish anything I set my mind to. But what had Ray told Michael? To shut up and follow orders? What a different experience of life.

Was that why he was here with him, following like a faithful servant, instead of somewhere living his own life, building his own career?

I'd always been a little baffled by my friends from high school who'd bounced around in different sales clerk jobs or fast food places with no apparent direction. Not me. There'd been no question in my mind where I was headed. At eighteen, I'd enrolled in college, got my bachelor's degree in three and a half years, all the while doing every extracurricular activity I could to make my application to Fish & Wildlife shine. I was on a mission. Every detail planned out and scheduled right down to the minute.

I looked at the man standing beside me. He didn't seem like the kind of guy who'd blindly follow in his father's footsteps. He had a confidence about him that didn't fit that persona. And I couldn't believe he really wanted to be a whale hunter, either. He had a gentle side, a chivalrous side.

Unless this was all an act to get me to sleep with him.

It didn't matter. Maybe I'd never be sure. Right now, I needed him to get me on that boat.

I looked into his eyes. "You're sweet, you know that?"

He put the kitten back in the box. "Another drink?"

"Yeah, sure," I said, handing him one of my kittens and setting the other one down with its mewling fur-ball siblings.

He held the kitten I'd given him, cuddling it to his neck. Then, as he pulled away, he said to me, "You're beautiful, you know that."

"I…" My cheeks flushed pink. "Thank you."

He leaned forward and I leaned forward. And we kissed.

Maybe I'm just a sucker for a man with a kitten, but— wow—was that a kiss. I staggered backward, my insides all squishy.

His eyes held mine and—dammit—I wanted him to kiss me again. *Crap.* I needed to be extra careful with this one.

"Shall we?" he said.

My mouth parted ever so slightly. "Shall we…?"

"Get another drink?"

"Um, yeah, sure," I said.

He set down the kitten, took me by the hand, and led me back into the crowded pub. We took our stools back at the bar and he ordered a couple of drinks. Then he turned to me and said, "The night is still young. What shall we do now?"

I blushed. "Well, I thought maybe—"

The front door swung open and Michael's head swiveled toward the man who walked in. It was Ray, lumbering in like he owned the place. Ray saw Michael right away and scowled.

Michael tensed up, as if fighting an impulse, battling some decision. He seemed more annoyed than intimidated. He chugged down his beer and set the empty bottle on the bar. "I'll catch you later."

Ray certainly had something over him. "I'll be here," I muttered, feeling like a fool. I had been so sure I'd had him on the hook.

Michael sauntered over to the table and eased into a chair with his father and the crew. Ray signaled to the bartender and moments later a round of drinks arrived. Ray held up his mug. "Boys, let's catch us a big fish!"

I wanted to march over there and shove the glass mug down his throat, but I quickly put a smile on my face when I caught Michael looking at me. Then Ray said something to him and he was drawn away.

That boy's got a short leash. This was going to be harder than I thought.

I tried to act bored, like I had all the time in the world. But the clock was ticking.

I sipped my beer.

The men chuckled, slapped each other on the back, the usual men-in-a-pub stuff.

Maybe I needed a different tactic to get Michael's attention back. The man on the bar stool next to me wasn't too old, wasn't too bad looking. In the dark pub. And in desperate times. I turned to him. "What brings you in?"

He looked at me like I'd gone mad, his bushy eyebrows crinkled together into one. "Beer."

"I mean, you know, how was your day?"

The unibrow shot up. "Why? Are you a prostitute?"

My jaw dropped open. *That conversation's not going anywhere.*

Behind me, someone rubbed against my back as he eased onto the bar stool. I swung around. It was Dalton.

"How's it going?" he whispered into my ear.

"Actually, it was going well until Ray arrived. That man is a—"

"Careful," Dalton warned.

"I'm glad you're here. I was just resorting to the make-him-jealous-by-flirting-with-someone-else tactic and, well—" I nodded toward the grump next to me "—this guy wasn't cutting it." I put my hand on Dalton's chest and giggled, a flirtatious gesture. "But you, my dear, might bring him running."

Dalton curled up his lip. "Women and their games." He glanced around the bar. "I'm not so sure this is a good idea."

"Of course it is. What else have we got?"

"I mean, I'm not sure it's worth it. C'mon back to the boat. We'll figure out something else."

"Let's just see how this plays out. I've got a good shot here. I think he's got a chivalrous side. I told him you were my ex-boyfriend, that you'd turned out to be a jerk." I gave him a confident nod and leaned in and whispered, "He took me out back to see some abandoned kittens. You should have seen him."

"Kittens? Really?" He leaned back with an eye roll. "I knew a guy once who borrowed puppies from the pound and walked them in the park to attract single women. He said they were chick magnets."

"Exactly. He's—"

"He's heading back out on a fishing boat for weeks. Trust me. He's just trying to get in your pants."

I shrugged. "Exactly."

"Don't tell me," Dalton said, going on as if he hadn't heard a word I'd said. "He told you you're beautiful."

"What is wrong with—" I drew in a breath. "You're jealous."

"Jealous? Pff." He shook his head. "Be serious."

"I'm dead serious. You don't like that he's really into me."

"What I don't like is this whole approach. You're not thinking of the full picture here. Of course he's into you. Maybe you're blinded a little by this guy's attention."

I sat back. "I beg your pardon."

"This guy could be—" He paused, realizing he'd been raising his voice. He glanced around, then leaned in close. "If you go down this road—"

"I can handle it." I was getting irritated now. Why couldn't Dalton support me? I knew this would work. "Just go with it."

Dalton shook his head. "I've got a bad feeling about this. Something's not right." He patted me on the arm and rose to go. "C'mon, let's just go."

"No. You go if you want. I'm not giving up on this," I said in a loud whisper. "You need to trust me for once."

"Is there a problem here?"

Our heads snapped to the speaker. Michael stood there, his hands on his hips.

I glared at Dalton. *Ha! Told you it would work.*

Dalton looked from Michael to me, then back to Michael. A shadow passed over his eyes. A surrender. A decision. "No problem," he said to Michael and put his arm around me, pulling me snug up against him.

"I'd like to hear it from the lady," Michael said.

"Well, I—"

"Buzz off," Dalton said. "Mind your own business."

Michael didn't budge. "I'm making this my business. Now get your hands off the lady."

Dalton huffed and turned on the bar stool to face Michael. "What's your problem?"

Michael looked at me, then back to Dalton and I swear he thrust his chest forward. "You're my problem."

"Oh yeah?" said Dalton. He swung high and punched Michael square in the jaw.

Chapter 10

Michael staggered backward, his eyes wide. Then, in a flash, his expression changed to rage. He charged forward, fists in front of him, jabbing at Dalton.

Dalton swung wide, missing Michael's jaw.

Michael grabbed hold of Dalton's shirt and pulled him from the stool and slammed him into a table. Dalton caught his balance and managed to stay on his feet.

Michael stepped back and shoved up his sleeves. Dalton lunged at him, all bluff and no force. This wasn't the Dalton I knew. He was faking. But why? Why had he thrown that punch to begin with? *What the hell is going on?*

The other men in the bar were on their feet, roaring amid the ruckus, shouting, "Hit 'em again! Knock 'em down!"

Michael managed to land a punch, then another, in the jaw, then in the stomach. He was beating the crap out of him. Dalton doubled over but didn't fight back.

I stepped between them. "Stop! Stop it!"

Dalton snarled at me, his lip puffy and bleeding. "Stay out of it."

"That's no way to treat a lady," Michael spat and slammed Dalton with a right hook. Dalton fell back into the table.

"Knock it off, boys!" hollered the bartender.

Michael ignored him and grabbed Dalton by the collar, dragging him to his feet. Dalton yanked free and head-butted him in the stomach and the two slammed to the floor.

The men in the bar roared.

They rolled, one on top of the other, fists flying. Michael got up on one knee, then to his feet and landed a kick in Dalton's side.

Why wasn't Ray breaking it up? I glanced around the bar, but he was nowhere to be seen. Maybe Michael had waited for Ray to leave and that's when he saw Dalton with me?

I grabbed Michael by the arm. "Stop! Please stop!" I wanted to beat him to a bloody pulp myself, right then and there. Michael stepped back, huffing, his eyes on Dalton.

Dalton got to his feet, grabbed me by the wrist, spun me around, and planted a big kiss on my lips. "Now step back, sweetheart." In his eyes I could see he meant it.

He went after Michael again, arms flailing with no measured target. It must have been hard for Dalton, a Navy SEAL, to pull his punches and take the fall. Why it was necessary was beyond me. What the hell was this going to prove? *Men!*

Michael on the other hand wasn't holding back. He'd obviously been in a few bar brawls in his time and he was a heavyweight. He went after Dalton with a hook, then a jab to the kidney. Dalton doubled over and Michael caught him in the jaw.

The bartender had finally had enough. He shouted to a couple of the regulars, "Get 'em outta here."

"Let 'em fight it out," one said.

Dalton hadn't had enough. He charged Michael again and they slammed into another table.

Bjørn, the old man on the boat, the helmsman Michael had said, grabbed Michael by the arm. "That's enough, now. A broken arm won't do on a fishing boat." He gave him a stern look. "You've made your point. Now leave him be."

Michael shoved the man away.

Someone grabbed hold of my arm. I spun around. It was the bartender. "You're leaving," he said.

"What?"

"You're the cause of it." He dragged me toward the door. "Now get out and don't come back."

I looked back toward Dalton. A hefty man, a six-foot-something-mountain-of-muscle was hauling him to his feet.

"You, too," the bartender told him, waving his wet rag at him. "Out!"

Dalton stumbled out the front door after me, holding his side.

Right behind him was Michael, Bjørn ushering him along. Michael brushed Bjørn off. "Hey, babe," he said when he saw me. "You all right?"

I nodded.

Bjørn whispered something in his ear and urged him toward the docks. Michael nodded to Bjørn and went with him.

I stood there like a dope, watching him go, not knowing what to do. Follow? Tell him thanks for saving me? Then what? I had no reference for dealing with this neanderthal behavior. If he'd have been a real-life date, I'd have already been out of there without looking back.

Dalton was limping toward our boat. I caught up to him. "What the hell was all that for?" I asked him. "You couldn't let it go. Now you've ruined my only chance to get on that boat. What the hell is your problem? Why can't you trust me?"

He shook his head and didn't answer.

"Men!" I planted my feet and watched him hobble toward the *Sea Mist*.

I spun on my heel and marched to the same bench and called back my friend Chris.

He answered right away. "Dr. Chris."

"Very funny."

"What's happened now?"

"What? I don't just call when I have problems."

Silence.

"Okay. You're not going to believe this." As I paced in front of the bench, I told him about my plan, how, for some reason, Dalton didn't like it and wouldn't support me. "And now this. He goes and picks a fight with the guy. In a bar. Ruining my only chance for a shot at him. I mean, what the hell?"

"Well, Poppy, I'm not sure—"

"What's his problem anyway? I bet he's pissed because I came up with an idea, a brilliant idea I might add, and he didn't think of it. Men, I swear. He couldn't stand having to play second fiddle, on the sidelines, backing me up for once."

"Poppy, maybe he's —"

"This guy's got it in for me. He doesn't want me for a partner, so this is his way of getting rid of me. Making me look bad. Sure, he wants to act like Mr. Nice Guy, all apologetic about Costa Rica, then this. You should have seen him, Chris. I had that guy eating out of the palm of my hand. He was frothing at the mouth. He was going to tell me everything I wanted to know and then some." I took a breath. "Dammit!" I plopped down on the bench.

"Are you done yet?"

"No!" I got back up.

Silence.

"You know what, I'm going to march over there and tell him what a jerk he is."

"Poppy?"

"What!"

"Did you call me to rant all night or for my advice? Because I've got a long flight in the morning and—"

"Your advice."

He waited.

"Okay, to rant, and I thank you, my very best friend, master listener, knower-of-all-the-right-things-to-say." I huffed. "All right, go ahead with the advice."

"Ask *him* why he did it."

"That's your advice? He's not going to tell me—"

"Poppy. Ask him."

I slumped down on the bench. "Fine."

When I got back to the boat, I found he had managed to get down the ladder on his own. I got some ice and held it to his cheek. His left eye was swollen shut, his cheek bloody.

"What were you thinking? Why in the world did you throw that first punch? I had him. Dammit, Dalton. I had him. I had him on the hook."

He took hold of the bag of ice and winced as he held it to his eye. "You wanted to do it your way."

"What?" He must have gotten his brain scrambled in the melee.

He looked at me with innocent eyes. "So we did it your way."

"What the hell are you talking about?" He did get his brain scrambled.

"Seriously?" He grinned and started to snicker, then held his stomach. "Where'd you grow up, anyway?"

I sat back and looked at him. "Why does that sound like an insult?"

"Guys like that—" He wiped blood from his lip and looked at it on his finger. "It's all about conquering, about possession. You were dangling the hook. I set it."

I stared at him. What could I say?

"Don't you watch National Geographic? Those big horn rams bucking their heads together. Polar bears wrestling. Even the whales ram each other for a female. The narrator always says they are fighting to continue their bloodline." He smirked. "They just want to get laid."

I clamped my teeth together. "So you...this whole thing was...all about testosterone?"

"Listen to me. You be careful. You're playing with fire."

I turned away from him. He was right. But I could handle it.

I opened the equipment locker, found the first aid kit, and sorted through the bandages and ointment. "Look at you," I said. "You're bleeding and you're—"

"I'm fine. I got it," Dalton said, waving me off. "What are you still doing here? You going to let me get the crap beat out of me for nothing? You wanted on that boat. Now go get on it."

I stared at him. "And you'll tell Nash…?"

He grinned. "Well, probably wouldn't sound so good if I told him you'd been kicked out of two bars already."

I started up the ladder, but stopped and climbed back down. Sure, I might be able to reel Michael in, get him to talk, but would he really get me on the boat with him? My luck, he really did just expect a sleazy romp in the lifeboat with the plan to disappear in the night. I needed an edge. I needed a slam dunk.

"Toss me the phone."

"Sure," said Dalton. "What are you thinking?"

"Michael said they're leaving in the morning. I've got one shot at this." I punched in Dr. Parker's number. "I need some advice."

Finally, on the seventh ring she picked up.

"Uh, hi, this is Poppy. Listen, I need to know as much as you can tell me about these fishing boats, how it works, what I could do that would be irresistibly useful."

"How would that help?"

"I'm trying to get on the boat."

"But they aren't actually fishing, right?"

"Well, right, but I need to have a reason to be invited on board, something that I know about fishing that would be useful capturing an orca. Maybe something they haven't thought of or I don't know." I turned so Dalton couldn't hear me. "I know it's a long shot, but…"

"What kind of boat is he on?"

"An old fishing trawler. Purse seine nets, I think."

"That's hard work. He'd never hire you. He wouldn't believe you could do it. You can cook, right?"

"Yeah, but he has a cook."

"Can't you put something in his stew? Get him fired or something."

"It had crossed my mind," I said with a chuckle. She and I were kindred spirits. "But they're heading out to sea in the morning. I've been working an angle, batting my eyelashes. Got a crewman's attention, the son actually, but I need something more."

"Okay, okay. I'm thinking." I could hear her tapping a pencil on something. "Is the boat big enough for an on-board tank? One large enough to keep the orca submersed?"

"No. That's the thing. It's a really small boat."

She was thinking. "So he plans to use a drag net for transport?"

"The thing is, Dr. Parker, I have no idea. I suppose he could use a drag net. I didn't realize that was an option." I looked at Dalton and shrugged. He shrugged. He hadn't been aware of that technique either. "Unless he'd put the whales right on deck."

"God, I hope not. They'd never survive it." She was quiet for some time. "This doesn't make sense. I can't imagine he has a holding facility nearby in Norway. I figured he planned to transport on board. This guy must be a complete amateur."

"He's no amateur. He's been doing this since the 60s."

"Maybe that's the biggest boat he could afford? Or he's planning to meet up with another boat?"

"The transport boat?" I said.

"Maybe, but that would mean extra work. Extra stress on the animals," she said with a sigh. "Well, whatever he's planning, at some point he'll be yanking one from the water. Their bodies aren't designed for it. Even if he has a proper harness, if he gets one on board, he'll have to keep its body temperature down with sea water, or even ice. Did you see anything on board for that?"

"I didn't get a good look—"

"This is tragic," she huffed, exasperated. "He's just going to kill them. No matter how he plans to transport, the odds of survival are slim. The risk is so high." She paused. "At least back in the days when it was legal to capture they usually had a veterinarian on board who knew about the—"

"A veterinarian?"

"I don't know how any reputable—"

My feet were already in motion. I handed Dalton the phone. "Get all the info you can on how to care for a killer whale during transport. I'll be back."

He raised his eyebrows. "You want me to—" he gestured toward the phone.

"What? You're tired of flirting?" I shoved the phone at him.

CHAPTER 11

I went straight back to the pub and flung the front door open. No one much cared that I was there save for the bartender. He threw down his wet towel and lumbered over to me. "I told you not to come back."

Michael wasn't anywhere I could see, so I frowned at the grumpy old man and backed out of the door. I'd learned what I wanted to know. Ray was back, and Dylan and Bjørn were there. That meant Michael was likely back on the *Forseti*. Alone.

I raced down the docks to the boat. Should I just step aboard? Etiquette says no. But how else would I get to him?

I crossed the deck and banged on the door to the galley. I could see there was no one inside, but if he was down below, he should hear me. After what seemed like forever, I went up the stairs to the wheelhouse and peeked in the window. He wasn't in there either. *Now what?*

Where else would he be? I went back toward the pub and slumped down on my now favorite street bench. The wind howled down the street. A plastic bag whipped in circles at the corner of the building. I held onto my hair with one hand to keep it out of my face and watched a raven hippety-hoppin' on the sidewalk, plucking at some tidbit of a snack floating in a giant mud puddle.

"Yer lookin' for Michael, ain't yer."

I looked up. It was Dylan, the gangly young man, the one Michael had said was the cook and deckhand.

"You know where he is?" I asked.

He had the expression of a child expecting to be punished for spilling his milk. He looked down at his hands, fiddled with his fingers. "If yer don't mind me askin', why's a bonny lady loike yer loike 'im anyway. It don't make naw sense."

I shrugged. "You're right. Sometimes the heart doesn't make any sense."

"Ain't dat de truth," he said and plopped down next to me, then unfurled his long legs out in front of him.

He seemed like a genuine, kind soul. Made me wonder if he had the slightest inkling what Ray was really up to. And what he would do when he found out. He might make a good ally, but I couldn't risk testing those waters now.

"So do you know where I can find him?"

He examined his boot laces, then scratched behind his ear. He pointed down the road. "Proobably de church," he said. "Sometimes yer man goes darc."

"Is he a religious man?" That'd be good to know.

"Oi don't tink so." He scrunched up his face in thought. "Proobably figures it's de last place 'is auld paddy wud luk."

I nodded. "Thanks. Dylan, right?"

His eyes brightened. "Yeah, Dylan."

An old stave church, one of the few remaining that had been completely constructed of wood during the Middle Ages, stood at the end of the road, its shingled steeple pointing upward, toward the heavens.

As I approached, I admired the intricately-carved timbers that criss-crossed over the entry. The large wooden door was adorned with swirling etchings that looked like angel's wings and reindeer with ornately-curved antlers.

If I hadn't been here for work, I could've spent hours learning the history of this place. The architecture alone was fascinating. I was tempted to take a quick walk around the outside, check it out, but I didn't want to risk missing Michael.

The iron hinges creaked as I pushed the heavy wooden door open and stepped inside.

A gust of wind followed me in, past the rows of pews, all the way to the altar, where a single candle burned below a simple wooden cross. The flame flickered and danced before it settled again to a peaceful glow, long after the door had closed behind me and my eyes had adjusted to the dim light inside.

As far as I could tell, I had the place to myself. Michael was nowhere in sight.

I silently stepped from the entry area into the empty sanctuary, my eyes drawn to the vaulted ceiling, suspended by ancient wooden timbers, and the painted cherubs and fluffy clouds that seemed to hover between earth and the celestial realm. The scent of incense lingered in the air. The place had a peaceful, dreamlike quality. Timeless. I could picture the Vikings, crowded into the long pews, horned helmets in their laps, tamed by the angelic choir and the gentle words of the priest. I almost envied the serenity they must have felt here, in this place of respite from their lives of constant conflict.

I sat down in the fourth pew from the back. Now what? Was I to pray to find Michael?

I wasn't much for church or religion. Nature was my sanctuary, the natural order, my code. But I had to admit, the solace some found in "giving it all up to God" was appealing. Comforting even. For those who believed. And this building made me feel it.

I don't claim to have any answers. I suppose that makes me agnostic. I just don't know. Maybe there is some invisible, guiding force in the universe. The sense of awe when I entered this old church was enough to give me pause, cause me to reflect, recognize that I was but a tiny speck in a vast universe, that my tiny, insignificant problems were just that—insignificant.

The only thing that truly mattered was love and goodness and living a good life. Wasn't that the point of religion?

What baffles me most is how, for so many, the call to be compassionate, caring, doesn't extend to animals. I know there is a debate over the very words of the Bible, as written in the book of Genesis, as to whether God intended the animals of the world to be here for the use of humankind or that humankind was to be the steward of all the animals and the environment. For me, the answer is clear. We are part of the animal world as sure as we live and breathe. Only arrogance keeps humans separate from it, that assumption that somehow humans alone have an elite birthright.

Interesting, how here, in this church, the walls are adorned with magnificent murals that prominently portray the animals of this region, obviously with great reverence. The antler motif repeats throughout. When did we give up this respect for the other living creatures among us? Seems it somehow coincided with our gaze being drawn ever skyward.

A door to the side of the altar squeaked open and the Reverend appeared.

Suddenly I realized that I didn't know what denomination this church was. Catholic, probably, right? Anglican? One of those that had taken over during the Protestant Reformation? I glanced around. No obvious confessionals. Is that what Michael had been doing? Confessing? Was he feeling guilt over his quest to capture a whale? Or was it the fight with Dalton that concerned him?

The Reverend approached me, his arms hanging comfortably in front of him, one hand holding the other. He wore street clothes, but I could tell by his manner, he was the reverend. And the kind smile, rosy cheeks. In fact, he looked a lot like Reverend Alden from *Little House on the Prairie,* the only Reverend I've ever known.

"May I help you, young lady?"

I shook my head. "No, thank you. I'm actually just here

looking for a friend."

"Ah," he said with a knowing nod. He glanced toward the door from whence he had come, then patted me on the shoulder. "Perhaps you need only to be patient."

I pointed to the door. "So he's...?"

A warm smile lit up his face. His eyes even seemed to sparkle. He nodded again, reassuring me, but gave no explanation. "I've someone to visit," he said. "But stay as long as you'd like." I watched him walk down the aisle and stop briefly in the vestibule for his raincoat, then push through the heavy door.

I turned around and leaned back in the pew. Patience, huh?

About thirty seconds later, Michael shuffled through the door. To look at him now, I could barely tell he'd been in a fight, save for the cut on his cheek and red knuckles. Dalton had taken most of the hits.

Michael saw me, but his expression didn't change. He ambled down the aisle and eased into the pew next to me.

"What's a lady like you doing in a place like this?" he whispered.

I couldn't resist a tiny smirk. *Adorable.* "I got kicked out of the pub and didn't want to go back to the boat so I—" I fiddled with the hymnal. Why play coy? "I was looking for you, actually."

He turned to me and smiled like a hyena on the prowl. "Yeah? How'd you know where to find me?"

"A little Irish bird."

He grinned and nodded.

"I wouldn't have guessed you were a religious man." Or a cat lover, actually.

"I'm not," he said with a slight shake of his head. "I just like it here, you know. The solitude. I can think."

I glanced around the sanctuary. "I know what you mean." My eyes found his again. "It keeps me humble."

He let go a laugh.

"I get it though, living on a boat. Close quarters and all."

I blew out my breath. "Especially with someone you don't like."

He smirked. "My dad can be trying."

"I lived on a boat with my dad for an entire summer when I was a kid." *Why'd I just share that?*

"Really?" He turned to face me.

"A sailboat." I started to chew my thumbnail, then yanked it back out of my mouth. "My dad died right after that."

His eyes turned soft. "I'm sorry."

"Yeah, well, it was..." I shrugged.

He turned back toward the altar. "Life's funny sometimes, isn't it? Here you are, back on a sailboat. What do you suppose that means?"

"That I'm crazy?"

"I was thinking it might mean"—his eyebrow shot up— "you've got a thing for sailors."

My turn to smirk. "Maybe you're right." I looked away. "My dad was the captain of my world. I swore one day I'd marry a man like him." Why was I being so honest with this guy?

"Is that why you agreed to go sailing with"—he jerked his thumb toward the marina—"*him*? You thought you'd marry him some day?"

"I could ask you the same question. Why are you on a boat with your dad, thousands of miles from home, when it sounds like you two don't get along."

He looked at me for a long time, his stare laced with suspicion. Or maybe he was contemplating an answer. Finally, he said, "You don't want to talk about him. I get it. So you turn the tables."

"Or maybe that's what you're doing right now?" I held his gaze. "It's okay. I didn't mean to pry. Your relationship with your father is your business."

"There's nothing to tell." He flashed me a disarming grin. "A man's gotta make a living, right?"

We both turned back toward the altar and sat in silence for a while. When he started to fidget, I whispered, "I'm sorry about my boyfriend."

His one eyebrow shot upward. "I thought he was your *ex* boyfriend."

"Yeah," I said. "Definitely."

I smiled. He smiled.

The wind whistled through the rafters and the timbers creaked.

I placed my hand on his. "I suppose I shouldn't have followed you here. It's just that, I know you're leaving in the morning and I didn't want you to go without saying goodbye."

"Where will you go now?" he asked. "And don't tell me you're staying with *him*."

"I don't know. I don't really have anywhere to go." I turned away, drew in a breath like I was fighting back tears. "I don't even know where I'm sleeping tonight." *Okay, here goes nothing.* I turned back and let my gaze linger on his lips. "I thought maybe…"

His breathing changed, more shallow. His eyes lowered to my breasts.

I turned away. "I'm sorry. You must think I'm a…" I covered my eyes with my hands. "I'm just, I don't know, frustrated." I turned back, tears in my eyes. "I had dreams, you know. When I got out of college, I thought I'd have a position right away. Maybe even open my own practice." I lowered my head and fiddled with my thumbnail. "I was so naive."

He shifted in the seat. "You went to college? What for?"

Atta boy. "Veterinary school." A hint of interest flashed in his eyes. Good. "I love horses, you know. But the business. You gotta know somebody." I shrugged. "The only internship I could get was at the Detroit Zoo." I hesitated. I had to be careful not to lay it on too thick. Thankfully, my verbal blunder about spaying and neutering the kittens could turn to my favor. "For three months I took care of the hedgehogs. Can you believe it? *Hedgehogs.*" I raised my eyebrows. "Do you know how to take the body temperature of a hedgehog?"

He shook his head. "Not sure I want to know." Something in his demeanor had changed. Subtle. He hid it well. But I could see he was thinking, pondering. Was he trying to figure out how to get me to come with him now without seeming too forward?

"Trust me. You don't." I sighed, let my shoulders slump. "I'll be lucky if I can get a job in some big city neutering feral cats."

Michael didn't say anything in response. His eyes fixed on his hands in his lap and I wasn't sure where to take the conversation from here. If I drove it home, I risked being too obvious.

I sat silently next to him for a while.

Finally, he said, "Well, we still have tonight."

Crap. He was either testing me or I'd misjudged him. I was going to have to take it up a notch. "I'm sorry. I was mistaken." I rose to leave.

He took hold of my hand. "What do you mean?"

I spun on him. "I thought you were my knight in shining armor. But I see now, you're just like all the rest." I pursed my lips. "I need to get out of here. Do something exciting." I looked him in the eyes. "Something bold. Like the Vikings, you know." I let my eyes travel to the ceiling, around the sanctuary, like I was being inspired. "Sail into the sunset, destined for new horizons. Conquer the world." *Geez. I should audition for a soap opera.* "You know what I mean?"

"Yeah, sure, I guess," he said.

Now we were in a careful cat and mouse game. I had one chance at this. *Here goes...* I plopped down and leaned back in the pew. "Maybe I'll just stowaway on your boat," I muttered. "Now that'd be a story to tell my kids someday."

He took my hand in his and said, "Maybe we could work something out. You know, just so you don't have to go back to him."

I laid my head on his shoulder. "You're kind. But don't worry. I can take care of myself. Besides, I'm sure your father would never—"

"You let me worry about my father."

I tilted my head back and he gave me a passionate kiss.

This better be worth it.

CHAPTER 12

As we walked down the dirt road, the wind still whipping in my hair, I snuggled against him, stroking his ego, when doubt creeped back unbidden. Maybe he wasn't what he seemed. Could it be that he and his father were already suspicious? And they were setting a trap for me? Get me on board, then once we were out to sea they'd—I shook the thought from my mind. If I was going to go for it, I was going for it. If something happened once I was on board, I'd deal with it when it happened. I could take care of myself.

When we got to the docks, the sun had already set, even though it was late afternoon. This close to the Arctic Circle the days were getting shorter fast. The sun seemed in a hurry to hide for good. The snow and cold, I could take. But nearly twenty-four hours of darkness. How do they do it?

Ray was in the wheelhouse when Michael brought me on board. Michael gestured for me to wait on deck. "Give me a minute," he muttered, his eyes on the wheelhouse as though it were a castle turret guarded by a fire-breathing dragon.

"Sure," I said. *Now we'll see what you're made of. Are you my knight or not?*

He drew in a breath, as if to gather some courage, climbed the stairs to the wheelhouse, and shut the door behind him. He was making a good show of it, anyway.

I could see Ray through the windows, shaking his head, his

frown making his caveman brow even more pronounced. As Michael continued to talk, Ray strutted to and fro. I bet his knuckles were dragging on the floor.

C'mon Michael. You've got all the pieces to the puzzle. You can convince him.

Ray leaned against the window to look out at me. Something in his eyes—the calculating stare of a stalking tiger, as menacing and fixed with threat—made me want to bolt. His pacing suddenly seemed more like that of a predator trapped in a cage.

I smiled wide, all innocent, my feet planted firmly where I stood.

Ray shook his head again.

Finally, Michael slinked from the wheelhouse and I could tell by his body language that it was over. He wouldn't make eye contact with me. I wasn't getting on the boat. Michael had been my best option and he turned out to be a waste of time. I wanted to slap him for being so spineless. I'd misjudged him all along. I thought we'd been playing a delicate dance, a careful maneuvering, a duet of deception.

"So?" I asked.

"My father says no."

Maybe he needed a good-old surge of testosterone. I wrapped my arms around his shoulders and practically stuck my tongue in his ear. "Did you tell him I don't eat much? I swear I'll stay out of the way."

He shook his head as he put his hands on my waist. "It's not that. It's—"

"What? I can work. I need a job anyway. There must be something I could do on board." I smiled, hopeful. "I can cook."

"We got Dylan." He frowned, but his eyes were trained on me, steady, calculating. He was thinking. Or making a show that he was thinking. The wheels were turning. Was he testing me now? "Anything else you can do?"

Was he serious?

"I'm sorry," he said, shaking his head. "Hey, the storm's going to pass. I'm sure the ferry will be running again tomorrow." The edge of his lip slowly curved upward. "I wish you well."

Dammit! "Thanks. Maybe if things were different, huh?"

"Yeah," he said, his eyes revealing nothing.

I scrambled down the ladder on the *Sea Mist*.

Dalton was at the table amid a tangle of power cords.

"Everything charged and ready?" I asked.

"Yep. Double checked each camera." He scribbled in a notebook. "All's ready."

I nodded and slumped onto the seat. "Great."

His eyes refocused on me. "What happened?"

"No go."

"Are you sure?"

"I really worked the vet angle with Michael," I said. "And he played coy about it. I was sure I had him. Then he went to talk to Ray." I ran my finger across my throat.

Dalton nodded, thinking.

"Maybe I could stowaway. Then, once we are out to sea, I get them to agree to let me stay aboard. Technically, that'd do it, right? Then I could plant the camera."

"I"m not sure that—"

"But, I don't know, Michael's too…"

"Too what?"

I let my head flop back, examined the ceiling for inspiration. "He's too clever." I sat back up and looked Dalton in the eye. "But there's got to be a way. I'm telling you. I have him on the hook."

"No doubt. I mean,"—he flashed me that grin of his—"you had me at hello."

I grabbed a pillow and smacked him with it.

Footsteps clomped onto the deck. "'ey! Poppy, ye down dare? 'ey!"

I leapt from my chair and climbed the ladder.

Dylan was in the cockpit. "Dare yer are. I've been lookin' everywhere," he said, out of breath.

"What? Why?"

"'tis Ray. Our Captain. 'e's 'urt."

"What do you mean? What's happened?"

"Dunno," he said with a shrug. "Michael sent me ter git yer."

"Sure, sure. Let's go," I said with a sideways glance to Dalton.

We raced down the dock to the *Forseti*. I followed Dylan up the stairs and into the wheelhouse. Ray lay on his belly on the bench, his face contorted with ornery discomfort.

Michael greeted me. "Thanks for coming."

"What's happened?"

"He had an accident."

Ray had his hand shoved down his pants, clamped onto his left butt cheek.

"What kind of accident?"

"Dylan, thanks. You can go," said Michael. When the door clicked shut, he turned to me. "You said you're a vet. That's a doctor, right?"

"Well, I…" *Crap.* "What kind of injury is it, exactly?"

Ray grimaced.

"Right. Why don't I just take a look." *Yeah, that's it. Show me your bare ass.*

I peeled back his waistband and tugged his pants down, trying to keep a straight face. Ray reluctantly let me pull his hand away. Blood gushed from a gouge down the side of his butt cheek. *Eeeew!* My throat constricted and I turned my head to hide a gag. I grabbed his hand and placed it back over the wound. "Hold it tight," I said, swallowed hard, and turned to Michael. "What happened?"

Ray scowled. "It doesn't matter. Just fix it."

Sure. Right. Was this a test? No way. He wouldn't actually injure himself to see if I was lying, would he? "We need to get you to a hospital. You need stitches."

"No hospital," Ray said.

"Sir, I don't think you're—"

Michael stepped between us, his arms crossed. "You do it."

"Me?" *Crap. Double crap.*

"You're a doctor ain't ya?"

"Well, yes, but"—*Oh. My. God.*—"I don't have any instruments, any supplies." I gestured around the room. "Nothing's sterile. Besides, it's Norway. No worries on the cost. Let's just take him to the hospital."

Michael shook his head. "He stays on the boat." His eyes turned cold. "And you're going to fix him up." It wasn't a request.

"All right. All right," I said, stalling, trying to act like that was a perfectly normal demand. "Well, do you have a first-aid kit on board?"

Michael reached for a box and shoved it at me. "Here."

My mom's the doctor. Not me. This was a serious wound. And, well, I hate blood and guts and bodily fluids. Sure, I had field triage training. But that was ketchup. This was real... *blood.*

Why me? I could get a desk job. Shuffle papers. Yeah, that'd be good. I could be happy.

I set the box down and rummaged through the kit. Ray needed stitches, that was clear. But I probably needed to stop the bleeding to be able to stitch him up. And what about infection? Wait a minute. Did I care if Ray got an infection? I suppose if I was a real doctor and not a quack. Ha, ha. *Oh my god, I'm losing it.*

No, you can do this. Straight face.

One thing about doctors: in a crisis, they take charge. My mom always did. To Michael I said, "Get something to prop up his legs. I want the wound higher than his heart." That's what my mom would say.

Michael didn't question. He just did as I said, grabbing a blanket and pillow from Bjørn's cubby.

"I'm also going to need water to flush the wound. Preferably pressurized. Squirt bottle, hose. Something."

He nodded and pushed through the door.

"You might have a risk of infection," I said to Ray. "Depends on what you were cut with. Do you want to tell me how this happened?"

"Just stitch it up," he grumbled.

Stitches. I had no idea how to do medical stitches. *Bitches!* When I was young, and my mom was going through one of her phases, she tried to teach me how to needlepoint, but I didn't have the patience, nor the desire. All my stitches were misaligned and sloppy. *Rip it out and do it right*, she'd harp. I could hear her voice now, *nice, tight stitches, pay attention. Take pride in your work.* Egads. It was a damn pillow for the cat. I knew he couldn't care less about perfect stitches.

I pushed her out of my head. Triage—that's what this was. Backcountry first-aid. "Good old duct tape will do the trick," I said. "Got any?"

He shook his head. "How do I know?"

Michael came through the door with more pillows and a water bottle. "This do?"

"Yep. Got any duct tape?"

He stopped short. "What?"

"You know, duct tape? Gray, comes on a roll."

"I know what duct tape is. What do you want that for?"

"Well, he needs stitches, and like I said, I don't have the proper supplies. Duct tape is actually a strong, secure option." *Man, I'm blowing some serious smoke.*

"Okay. I'll find some," he said and pushed back out the door again.

I propped Ray's ass up with the pillows, then piled a handful of gauze pads on the wound and had him hold them. I was tempted to snap a quick picture with my cell phone to text to the guys back at Headquarters. They were never going to believe this.

Michael returned with a roll of duct tape in hand.

"Start ripping it off in lengths, about five or six inches. Then I want you to cut them into tiny strips."

"Yes, ma'am," he said.

Yes, *ma'am*? Pshaw!

"Here's what's going to happen. I'm going to wash out the wound, then dry it and contain the bleeding. I want those strips ready so I can get them applied quickly." *If I don't throw up.*

Michael went to work. I put the hand to Ray's forehead, faking like I was taking his temperature. Then everything was ready. I drew in a breath.

Here goes nothing.

I removed the bloodied gauze. Bloody gunk stuck to his ass and oozed. I coughed and a little throw-up lodged in the back of my throat. I squeezed the water bottle, flushing the wound, trying not to actually look at it, then tamped it dry with another gob of clean gauze. I pushed a splurt of triple-biotic ointment onto it, then holding his skin tight with one hand—*oh, for the love of God!*—I placed strips of duct tape crosswise, all along the gash. Then I ripped off a big piece of tape, and laid it down across the strips. "There, that ought to do the trick," I said, my doctor face on. "Keep it clean, try not to rip it open again, and"—I handed the tube of ointment to Michael—"put this on it every day."

His eyes traveled from me to his father's bloody, duct-taped ass cheek. "I don't think so."

"He can do it then," I said, holding back a smirk.

Michael nodded. "That it?"

"Unless you've changed your mind and would like to go to the hospital."

He shook his head. "Thanks."

"No problem." I stood there for a moment, wondering what I could do to convince him to let me go with them. "Okay, then. Take care." I headed for the door.

Michael called after me. "Maybe you should come with us, you know, in case he needs you again."

"You mean, on the boat? Out to sea?"

Ray shook his head as if reluctant. "Yeah, on the boat," he grumbled.

You bet your bloody ass! "Are you sure? I don't want to be in the way and—"

"Go get your bag," Ray said, as though resigned to it. "We leave before daybreak."

Michael winked at me.

"Yes, sir."

Dalton was nodding but he didn't look happy. He was tense, his jaw tight.

"What?" I said. "It's going to work. I told you. Michael likes me."

"I know. That's what I'm afraid of." His voice sounded like he'd just swallowed a dry piece of meat.

"What are you saying?"

"Just that this guy is going to have—" he clenched and unclenched his jaw "—expectations."

"Actually, he's pretty sweet," I said. "Besides, I can handle myself." I was getting irritated and I wasn't sure why. I headed for my bunk to grab my bag.

Dalton followed me. "Like you did with that Noah guy in Costa Rica?"

I spun around to face him. "That was different and you know it."

"Yeah, well, fine, but with this guy, what are you gonna do?"

"What am I gonna do about what?"

He stared at me, stone-faced.

"I'll handle it." *Somehow*.

He was blocking the door. "Yeah, but what if—"

"Dalton!" I shoved him in the stomach. "You're really starting to piss me off."

"All I'm sayin' is you don't have to do this. We're not even supposed to be here. We could head home right now. Get a new assignment."

"What happened to *I got all beat up for you, don't blow it?*"

He blinked one eye. The swollen one. "Something's not right. It was too easy. We should take a step back. There'll be another shot at him. We should go back to Headquarters and—"

"Like hell. I'm not leaving. Not while that man is out capturing killer whales. Not if there's anything I can do about it."

"But these aren't cub scouts we're talking about, Poppy," he said, failing to contain his mounting frustration. "What are you going to do once you're on board anyway? How will you possibly get the video we need without putting your life at risk? Have you really thought this through?"

"Have I thought—" I looked Dalton up and down, my molars clenched together so hard I thought they might crack. He was looking back at me with those eyes. Neither of us moved, stuck in this emotional standoff.

Finally, into the silence, his voice shaky, he said, "You could get hurt. Or worse. You can't just expect me to—" He released the pent up air from his lungs and closed his eyes.

All my anger fluttered out of me like air from a balloon. "You're worried about me."

"Poppy, you are so—" He looked away.

"Admit it. It's because you don't trust me."

He crossed his arms, which made his biceps look huge. "You're a trained agent. Like you said, you can take care of yourself. But you're my partner and partners are supposed to work together, not—" He covered his face with both hands, then ran his fingers through his hair, and looked right at me with exasperation. "Do you have any idea what it's like to be your partner?"

"Well, I…"

His anger was gone. He seemed defeated, exhausted.

"Poppy. You're smart, you're clever, you're…more than capable of handling yourself. But…" He looked away, thinking, then his eyes came back to mine. "My god, you're this red-headed whirlwind. It's like you're on this mission to save the world. By tomorrow. And nothing better get in your way. Nothing and no one. Including me." He shook his head. "It's like you think I'm the enemy here, the one who's blocking your way. You want to do everything on your terms, your way. But there's a reason we have procedures, a reason we plan, and strategize, and, and," he threw his hands up, "and not fly by the seat of our pants. It puts everyone in danger."

Suddenly, the extent of my own myopia astonished me. He was right. I hadn't stopped to think. I hadn't considered for a moment what position I'd put him in, whether he was willing to risk what I was.

"You might be willing to die for these animals, but I'm not. Not like this. I care about them, sure. I care a lot. But what you're doing, it's reckless."

"I'm—"

"Now, listen to me." He paused, as though gathering courage before going on. "I know there's nothing I could say to change your mind. You can't say I haven't tried." He gave me a half grin. "I'm your partner and I'm going to back you up, but—"

"Oh, Dalton." I wrapped my arms around him, pinning his arms against his chest, and smacked him with a kiss on the cheek. He tried to untangle his arms and hug me back, but I quickly pulled away. What had I been thinking? I suddenly felt the need to press the wrinkles from my shirt.

"But," he said, "you need to listen to me right now. Once you're on that boat, you keep your head down. Just stick to your story. Only take the chance to place the camera if you're absolutely sure you won't get caught." He made sure I was looking at him. "Do you hear me? Absolutely sure. Then you keep your cover until you're off that boat. Do you understand? Don't do anything, and I mean anything, that will make him suspicious. Promise me."

"Helll-oooooo!" came a voice from the dock.

Dalton sighed, then turned and strode up the ladder. After a moment, he poked his head back down. "It's April." He said her name in a tone of familiarity.

"April? As in Dr. Parker, April?" She was on board and heading down the ladder before it sunk in. "What are you doing here?"

She smiled with genuine surprise. "Didn't Dalton tell you?"

He was lugging her bag in with a sheepish grin on his face. "Poppy just got back," he said to her. "Didn't have a chance yet."

Was that her suitcase?

"Oh? Well," she said, tucking her hair behind her ear and straightening to her full height. Her pants were pressed to a crisp perfection, her blouse tucked in at her tiny waist. *How does she look like she just stepped from her dressing room?* "After you left Bergen, I decided to come to our research station up here. When you called, well, Dalton and I had a nice chat." She smiled at him and he grinned back like a schoolboy. *Oh geez.* "You said you were getting on the *Forseti*, soooo, I thought maybe he could use my help."

"Well, I'm sure Special Agent Dalton is—"

"I told her that'd be great," said Dalton and set down her bag. He leaned on the ladder, his hand on his hip, looking so damn handsome, even with a swollen lip and black eye. "I could use an extra hand on board."

She nodded as if that settled it. "So it's worked out perfectly."

Yeah. Perfectly. Except Dalton could damn well manage this boat on his own. Hadn't he lectured me about involving civilians? And the way he was staring at her I thought he might need a bib.

"I'm not sure—"

"We'll be right behind you," he said. "The moment he makes contact with a killer whale, we'll have the video rolling, then I'll call the authorities and coordinate the bust."

"This is all very exciting," April said, practically in a giggle. "To be part of a Special Operation and help bring this man to justice."

Dalton blushed, all humble-like, as if she were some kind of Special Ops groupie.

"Well," she said, clasping her hands together. "I suppose I should get moved in. But if you don't mind, I'm quite thirsty."

"Oh, my gosh. Where are my manners?" said Dalton, heading for the icebox.

Oh my gosh? Seriously?

"What can I get you? Tea, coffee? We have wine."

"Water's fine, thank you." She stiffened slightly, her eyes flicking back and forth from him to me.

She must have thought I'd be gone already and they could play house.

He poured her a glass from a gallon jug, then handed it to her, gazing at her all google-eyed.

Geez. I half expected some violin music to start playing. *I gotta get out of here.* I grabbed my bag and headed for the ladder. "Okay, then. Gotta go."

"You be careful," he said to me.

I nodded. *Yeah, yeah, you're the one who*—"Wait. I still need the information about how to care for the whale. I don't want one hurt while they are trying to get it on board."

"Right," said Dr. Parker. She set down her purse, took from it a pamphlet on killer whales, and spread it open on the table. "Here," she said, pointing to a drawing of an orca, her finger on the underbelly. "Just like us, the belly is soft and vulnerable. You'll want to make sure the entire belly is supported by a sling if you try to lift one out of the water." She turned to me, her eyes on fire. "Whatever you do, don't let him raise one by the fluke."

"Okay, but I assume he knows that much. What about keeping the whale cool enough? And how do we keep it from flailing around on deck?"

She winced. "He's likely to bring them up already wrapped in a full body net. Once out of the water, you'll want to keep a close eye to make sure the body temperature doesn't go up. It averages the same as ours, about ninety-eight degrees."

"I doubt they'll have a thermometer."

"Just…make sure to constantly bathe the whale in sea water, particularly the flippers, dorsal fin, and fluke, the areas that are thin and highly vascularized."

"Vascularized? What does that mean?"

"Where the blood vessels are—"

"You know, forget it," I said. "It won't come to that." I had the tiny Go-pro mini remote camera stashed in my bag. The moment I had the footage we needed, I'd give Ray an ultimatum, tell him that if he put the whale back into the water, I'd put in a good word with the judge. There was no way I was going to let him keep a whale.

Dalton's eyebrows twitched with skepticism.

I grabbed my bag. "I need to get going." I could tell Dalton was about to pepper me with questions.

"Good luck," April said.

"Hold on," Dalton said.

Dammit.

"What did you mean, it won't come to that?"

I had to throw him a bone. "I mean, it won't come to, you

know, he's not going to quiz me on big words that he doesn't even know. I got the concept. That's what's important."

His eyebrows kept twitching.

"What?" I said, all innocent.

He spun around, a full three-sixty, his hands on the top of his head. "Poppy!"

"I'm outta here," I said and shot up the ladder.

Dalton followed me. He grabbed ahold of my arm, holding me back, controlling his breathing, trying not to explode. "Tell me you heard everything I said."

"I promised, didn't I?"

"Knowing you, you had your fingers crossed behind your back."

We stood in the cockpit in the dark for too long, staring at each other.

Finally, he muttered, "I know you're not going to—" He puffed out a lung full of air. "Just remember what I said. You know, about Michael. Be careful."

"Me? What about you?"

"What about me?"

I leaned forward and lowered my voice. "You were laying it on a bit thick down there, don't you think?"

He gave me a look of confusion.

"Don't act all innocent. You didn't have to flirt with her. She's already helping us."

"Just doing my job. Just like you."

"Aren't you the one who lectured me about involving civilians? What happened to that?"

"She's not a civilian. She's an expert informant." He grinned with satisfaction. "Do I need to remind you: we need her for *your* whole plan to work."

I averted my eyes, suddenly uncomfortable. "It's just not nice. To lead her on."

"You're the one who called her."

"Yeah, but—" I clamped my mouth shut. "Forget it."

"Poppy," he whispered, his gaze intense. "Promise me."
He looked so serious.
"Oh crap," he said, his eyes drawn over my shoulder.
I spun around. The *Forseti* was backing out of its berth.

CHAPTER 13

I sprinted down the dock, waving my arms like a damn fool, my pack slung over one shoulder. If the boat came close enough to the dock, I was prepared to launch like some crazy Hollywood stuntman.

The *Forseti* turned, the engine puttering along, and eased up to the fuel dock. I slowed to catch my breath. They were just fueling up tonight, before the dock staff left for the evening.

As the lines were tossed to the dockhands, I waved. Michael waved back. "I thought you were leaving without me," I said, trying to look amused rather than distraught. "Request permission to come aboard, sir."

He stepped to the side and held out his hand to help me.

Ray came pounding down the stairs from the wheelhouse, shouting orders, pointing with a cigarette clamped between two fingers. When he got to the deck, he came to a halt and eyed me up and down.

"Hello, Captain," I said. "You really should be careful walking around with—"

"Never mind that," he grumbled in my face. His breath smelled like an ashtray. He ran a hand through his greasy hair and snorked in a nose full of snot.

I suppressed a gag. Disgusting. I straightened up. "Ship's doctor, reporting for duty, sir."

"Just stay the hell out of the way."

I nodded, trying to look sheepish.

"On deck, you do what you're told."

"Yessir." *A-hole.* What I really wanted to do was wrap a fishline around his neck.

His head slowly bobbed, then he took a long drag on his cigarette, his Neanderthal eyes on me. Then when he exhaled a stream of white smoke, I had the sense he wouldn't give me another thought. *Good.*

Michael watched him walk away, waiting for him to get out of earshot, then said, "Don't mind him. He'll come around." He kissed me. "I'm glad you're here."

"Me too," I said.

I glanced around. I wanted to determine as quickly as possible where the best place to stash the remote cam might be so I could plan a midnight walk. "Do I get the grand tour of the boat?"

"Sure," he said with a shrug, as though the thought of a tour of the fishing vessel was amusing. "Drop your bag. We'll start up here." He pointed toward the bow. "Fore—" then pointed toward the back "—and aft. That's the direction on a boat,"— he winked—" in case you're told to move or something. Starboard is the right side, that is, if you're facing forward. Port is left." He gestured up the stairs. "That's the pilothouse. You won't be allowed up there." He pointed to the tall pole jutting from the top of the pilothouse like a mast with a bucket-like thing near the top. "That's the crow's nest. They climb up in there to watch for whales."

"Whales?" I said.

"Yeah," he hesitated. "They show us where the fish are."

"Oh." I nodded. That made sense, if he was really fishing anyway.

He walked aft. I followed. Behind the crow's nest, a large crane-like arm overhung the deck. The end of the fishing nets were attached to a cable that ran to it. "That's the derrick," he said. "We use it to haul in the nets."

And to haul an orca out of the sea, I bet. I looked around for a harness like Dr. Parker had described, but saw nothing.

He gestured toward a large rectangular tub. "That's the holding tank for fish." It was a tank, all right, but certainly not large enough to hold a killer whale.

He glanced around. "That's pretty much it. Ha, ha. The grand tour."

I smiled. "How do you get up in that crow's nest? It looks like fun."

He glanced up at it like it had never occurred to him to wonder. "There are rungs on the pole, I think."

If I could sneak up there, it would be an ideal place to rig the remote camera for a full, wide-angle view of the entire deck.

"Let's head in," he said and flung open the door.

I picked up my bag. He didn't notice. So much for being a gentleman.

Inside to the right was the galley, about six feet by three feet with a tiny oven and an even tinier refrigerator. To the left, a cracked laminate table sat about eight, I'd say, if they crammed in along the bench. It could have been any fishing boat on the seas for the lack of personal touches, save for an old plastic parrot that hung on a ring in the corner and an ashtray overflowing with crumpled cigarette butts wedged behind the bench and the windowsill.

To the right of the galley was a head, the door labeled with a brass plaque. Beside that, a ladder led down into the hull of the ship. "Bunks are down here." He spun around and slipped down the ladder.

I handed my bag down to him, then followed.

The berth smelled like dirty socks and wet, rubber boots. Bunks lined the hull, two on either side. The ones on top had a porthole looking out. "Bjørn sleeps in the pilothouse," Michael said. "So there's an extra bunk."

Thank goodness for cramped spaces. It'd be a lot easier to fend him off with Dylan and his father two feet away. I plopped my bag onto the empty bunk.

"Are we headed out yet this evening then?"

"No, we'll stay tied off here for the night and leave early."

"Shall we head back to the pub? Get a beer?"

"Can't." He shook his head. "My dad wants us all on board for a meeting in the galley in thirty minutes."

I tried to look disappointed but my mind went into overdrive. What would Ray tell the crew? What would he tell me now that I was on board? What did the others know?

Michael stared at me, expectant.

Then it hit me. We had thirty minutes. Alone in the bunk room. *Great.* I eased into his arms and let him kiss me. Then I pulled away. "Have I thanked you yet? I mean, this really means a lot to me." I snickered. "He won't have any idea where I've gone."

"Yeah, sure," he said, pulling me against him, his hands sliding down my back to my butt.

"I'm just saying." I grinned. I had to appeal to his gentlemanly side. And fast. "You did turn out to be my white knight."

"Uh-huh," he muttered, his lips on me again.

I pulled away again. "I just—"

He shoved me down on the bunk and ran his hand up my thigh. "Enough talk."

Crap. "My, you're in a hurry," I said, trying to sound flattered. "What's the rush?"

The door to the galley above us slammed and someone was clomping down the ladder toward us.

"Dammit. It's Dylan," Michael muttered.

Dylan came to a halt at the bottom rung, his lips pursed into a little O. His eyes flitted from me to Michael then back. "Sorry," he managed and pushed his glasses up his nose with his index finger.

Thank you, Dylan. "Maybe we should make some coffee," I suggested.

Michael glared at me. "Coffee? Right now?"

I gave him a shy, now-I'm-all-uncomfortable shrug.

His face went blank and I couldn't tell what he was thinking.

I gestured toward the galley above. "For the meeting."

He looked at Dylan with suspicion, as though debating whether he'd purposefully interrupted us. Finally, Michael shrugged and headed for the ladder without looking back.

The old helmsman, Bjørn, stared into his coffee cup, about as interested in Ray's talk as I imagined he would be in the detailed description of a colonoscopy. Dylan sat at attention. Nice young chap.

Ray sat cock-eyed on the bench, keeping his weight off his wounded ass cheek. He rolled an unlit cigarette between his yellowed fingers as he spoke. "We'll set out at oh-four-hundred on a south-southeast course, get a good distance covered before daybreak." He lit the cigarette, then said through the smoke as he shook out the match, "I've gotten word the fishing should be good around here"—he ran his fingers along a chart, laying out the path we'd be traveling—"maybe day after tomorrow. I want to get as far south as we can."

Yep, right where Dr. Parker said the K-pod would be.

Michael added, "Fuel is topped off. Supplies on board. We're good to go."

Ray nodded in acknowledgment. "Bjørn, you can sleep in. Dylan and I will take the first shift."

Dylan's eyebrows shot up with surprise. Obviously, this was an uncommon occurrence. "But I'm—"

Ray glared at Dylan, who snapped his mouth shut. "Once we're out of the harbor and have a course set, you can get to work on breakfast."

"Roi, sir," Dylan said, forcing his cheer.

"Bjørn and Michael will take the evening shift. We're not stopping until we find what we're looking for."

"And what about me, sir?" I asked.

"What about you?" he said as he ground out the stub of his cigarette without even a glance my way.

"How can I help?"

He reached for another cigarette. "Stay out of the way."

I looked to Michael, who averted his eyes.

Ray said. "When we launch the nets, I don't want you out on deck. You stay inside. Got it?"

"Oh?" I said. *Crap.* "I'm sure I can lend a hand. I'm stronger than I look."

"It's for your own safety," Michael said with a dismissive shrug. "Deep water fishing is dangerous work."

I swear I saw Bjørn hide a harrumph. I wasn't sure if it was on account of the danger of fishing or because he knew there'd be no fishing. He was hard to read.

Ray sat back, a smug grin on his face. "All goes as planned, and Christmas'll come early this year, boys."

I smiled—a big, fat naive smile. *We'll see about that.*

Chapter 14

If Bjørn slept in the wheelhouse, it would be difficult to get up and into the crow's nest without him hearing me. I needed an excuse. Preferably for a time when no one would be watching and see me mount the camera. But what excuse and when?

I lay in the bunk listening to Ray snore. Every exhalation gave me visions of the roof peeling back like the lid of a sardine can, then rolling back up when he inhaled. How can a man breathe like that, anyway?

Michael was asleep in the bunk opposite his, oblivious.

Dylan, in the bunk next to me, slept with his legs pulled up to his chest, curled up into a ball, blankets swirled into a nest. Like a baby hedgehog. I grinned. I had no clue how to take the temperature of a hedgehog. Good thing Michael hadn't asked.

I had no idea how to take the temperature of an orca either. Not that it mattered. I wasn't going to let it get that far. I needed to allow Ray to do what he was going to do, to get one in the sling if I had to, but there was no way he was getting one on board and keeping it. Not if I could help it.

Sure, Dalton might get close enough in the *Sea Mist* to get the video evidence we needed for a court trial months from now, assuming the Norwegian authorities would do their part and arrest him, at some point, but what if they didn't? What would happen to the whale? I had to stop him myself. I had to find a way to get the video *and* sabotage the whole damn operation.

I had to find it fast.

There was no reason I could think of to be in the crow's nest tonight. It was too risky. Sleep was what I needed. Then tomorrow, I'd figure out what to do.

The engines rumbled to life and I sat up in my bunk. I hadn't heard Ray leave the cabin. *Damn.* What the hell kind of agent was I?

My watch read four a.m. At least Ray was punctual.

There wasn't a thing I could do right now but go back to sleep, get it while I could. I lay back down and stared at the bunk above me. *One sugar plum fairy. Two sugar plum fairies.* Nope. Wasn't going to work. And I'd really rather not be alone with Michael in the bunk room. Might as well get up.

I crept into the head, washed my face, and pulled my hair into a ponytail. I patted the remote cam that was stuffed in my jacket pocket to be sure it was there before I went topside.

Dylan was on deck, manning the lines while we pulled away from the dock.

Dalton had anticipated our departure. The *Sea Mist* was gone from her slip.

With April on board. I crossed my arms, Dalton's voice in my head, *I told her that'd be great. I could use an extra hand.* Geez.

I wasn't sure where to go. Michael had said I wouldn't be allowed in the wheelhouse. Perhaps I needed to ingratiate myself to old Ray.

I slipped into the galley and rifled through the cupboards. I found the coffee pot and coffee. That ought to do the trick.

Ten minutes later I knocked on the door to the wheelhouse, cups in hand. "Coffee?" I said with a sweet, innocent smile.

Dylan smiled back. Ray grumbled something indiscernible.

I took it as a welcome and strode in and handed each of them a cup.

Ray didn't make any noise like I should get out, so I eased onto the bench, watched out the windows as we left the harbor, and kept my mouth shut, hoping he'd forget I was there.

I liked being in the pilothouse. All four walls were windows so I could see in any direction. It was too dark to see the *Sea Mist*, though. But sure as the sun, Dalton was out here somewhere.

By the time we'd cleared the harbor and turned south, Ray'd smoked his third cigarette and I was starting to feel green. I needed out of here. I needed fresh air.

I held up Ray's empty coffee mug. "More coffee?"

"Dylan'll get it," he said, a command, not a suggestion.

"O…K," I said.

Ray kept his eyes forward as Dylan took his cue and slipped out, mugs in hand.

The door clicked shut and the air in the roomed seemed even more oppressive—sharp and metallic smelling. The darkness felt like a blanket over the windshield, the eerie glow of the instruments the only light. The low rumble of the engine seemed to mask every other sound.

Ray didn't turn or even look at me as, in a low tone, he said, "Why are you on my boat?"

The hairs on the back of my neck stood up. "I don't understand," I said with a shrug. "I thought you wanted me to keep an eye on your—"

"And here you are," he said. He eased back in the chair, a deliberate move, and tilted his head to look at me. The greenish reflection on the surface of his eyes made him look ghoulish.

I drew in a quick breath and my eyes dropped to his hands. He drew his fingers into tight fists, then flexed them and picked up a length of rope that Dylan had been using to practice knot tying.

"I meant, what are you really doing here?" He turned and

looked at me with a blank expression, his entire body held taut save for his rough, tar-stained fingers, testing the strength of the rope.

"Well, I…" *Stick to the story.* "My boyfriend, well, he turned out to be a real ass."

His eyes narrowed. "And why's that my problem?"

The hands clenched the rope, slowly twisting the end around one hand, working it like he was working out my story, turning it over in his mind. He switched hands, wrapping the end around his left hand.

"I planned to leave on the ferry, but Michael seemed…well, I liked him—"

"That so?" he said. His right hand gripped the rope and snapped it tight.

"Well, I admit, when we met, I'd kinda hoped—"

"You know what we do on this boat?"

"You fish?" I said with a shrug as if I had no idea what he was getting at.

"We work." He held up the rope, examining it as if it were some kind of clairvoyance-inducing object, then his eyes settled on me. "We work hard. Ain't no room for girly drama."

"Yessir," I said. "I can work hard. You wait and see. I won't disappoint."

His expression turned to one of amused contemplation, as if he thought what I'd said was funny.

The door creaked open and Dylan strolled in, mugs in hand, his cheerful presence like a gust of fresh air.

Ray tossed the bit of rope onto the console and rose to take a cup.

"I think I'll watch the sun rise from the deck," I said, escaping the room.

Ray grunted and turned his back on me. Dylan watched me go with a look of confusion.

On the bow, the crisp morning air whipped my hair against my face and chilled my ears. I worked to get my breathing back to normal.

Michael came up behind me. "You were up early," he said. A statement that felt like an accusation.

"I couldn't sleep. New bed. New noises."

"Well, you shouldn't wander around the boat by yourself." He wrapped his arms around me, pinning my arms at my sides, and it took all my will power not to break from his embrace. "It's not safe," he said. "A fishing boat has so many hazards. You could easily trip and fall overboard." He squeezed me tighter and added, "No one would even know you were missing."

A shiver ran through me, but it wasn't from the cold. I tried to shake it off. I was just a girl who left her boyfriend and ran off with a fisherman. Nothing to worry about.

As we stood at the rail, his arms around me, the light blue sky in the east turned to pink, then orange rimmed the edges of the peaks on the horizon. A muted reflection of it all shimmered on the ocean's surface. Ray had been right. The storm had passed earlier than predicted. Wispy clouds stretched across the sky.

"Looks like cotton candy," I said, trying to keep it light.

"You're right," Michael said. "I don't usually pay much attention to the sights."

It was an opening. I had a job to do. "Ooooh, I hope we see whales," I said. "What do you think?"

His arms tensed. "Possible," he said.

I swiveled within his embrace, facing him now, and pointed to the crow's nest. "From up there, right?"

He craned his neck to see. "Yeah, I guess."

"Didn't you say you watch for whales from up there?"

"Yeah, well, I meant in the old days." He hugged me tighter. "Aren't you cold?"

"Yeah, kinda." I sighed. "I think it's romantic. How the ancient mariners would set out on the ocean, sometimes for months at a time, on a whale hunt. What an adventure. Wouldn't that be exciting?"

He didn't flinch. He leaned forward and nuzzled my neck.

"Uh-huh."

I spun around. "You're right. I'm cold. Let's go back inside."

I gave him a quick peck on the lips. *Now, get your hands off me.*

I needed to get this job done fast and get the hell off this boat.

The best time to get up in the crow's nest would be when Ray and Michael were both down below. After dark would be ideal. Ray might turn in early since he'd been up before dawn. That is, if we didn't get to the killer whales first. But Michael had the late shift. I'd keep my fingers crossed.

After lunch, during which Ray had said a total of seven words, especially nothing about the proximity of the whales, I went back out on deck. The fine mist in the air clung to my face, soft and cool. I glanced back and caught sight of the *Sea Mist,* tucked in a cove. *Good.* Dalton was lying low.

The *Forseti* puttered along the coast of jagged granite mountains, the slopes covered in a velvety-green carpet, their peaks dusted with a fresh layer of white snow. I breathed in deeply, the crisp sea air filling me with calm. Such beauty, all around us. And men like Ray, all they can see is money. The mountains, the trees, the waterfalls, the sea, the whales. All for the taking. The plunder to those who would be bold enough, strong enough. With no regard for anyone else, any other being.

It seemed a sad state of living. With no reverence. No appreciation.

The Buddha would have me pity Ray. But truly, I wanted to wrap my hands around his neck and squeeze. He reminded me of a troll like those who lived in these mountains—curmudgeonly creatures, short and stout with bulbous noses and bushy eyebrows. Under the cover of darkness, they spirit away beautiful maidens, tucking them in their mountain lairs, forcing them to spin by day and scratch the trolls' heads by night. Gift shops in Bergen were stuffed full of all renditions of them, from the cutesy to the obscene.

Fantastical trolls fueled my imagination as a child, but I was more interested now in the real creatures that inhabited this land. I was content to watch, waiting for a glimpse of one, then sure enough, off the starboard bow I caught sight of something in the water. Then it was gone. I kept my eyes where I had seen it and a gray head popped up again. Big round eyes set in a bulbous head, whiskers like a dog's. A harbor seal.

He disappeared below the surface again. But for a moment, I'd seen him and he'd seen me.

"That your boyfriend back there?" I spun around. Ray stood behind me, his Cro-Magnon stare fixed on me. Michael hovered behind him.

The *Sea Mist* puttered along now, following not far behind. *Damn.*

"What? Boyfriend? I don't have a boyfriend."

Ray handed me a pair of binoculars and gestured aft with his cigarette. "That him following us or not?"

I raised the binoculars. Dalton was at the helm, April standing next to him. Did he have his arm around her? "Yeah, maybe, I don't know."

Ray took a long drag from his cigarette, looking at me with suspicious eyes.

"He can chase me if he wants. I'm not going back to him." I smiled at Michael, all flirty. "Not now." I felt like I should be chewing on a mouth full of gum, maybe tug a strand out and wrap it around my finger for the full effect.

Ray grumbled something to Michael and climbed the stairs to the wheelhouse.

"What are you doing out here?" Michael asked. "I thought I told you to stay inside." His stare said it all. The bottom dropped out of my stomach.

"Yeah," I said. "Sorry. I just needed a quick breath of fresh air."

His expression didn't change.

"It's cold out here anyway. I was thinking of making some coffee," I said, trying to act as though I was used to being talked to like that. "Should be ready in ten minutes or so if you want some." I headed for the galley, hoping he wouldn't follow.

Dylan was at the sink, earbuds in his ears, his hands plunged into a tiny mountain of soap suds. He was humming along to the tune, oblivious to my entrance.

"Can I help you with those?" I asked, moving into his peripheral vision.

"Huh?" he said, startled. He yanked the earbuds from his ears, splattering suds down the front of his sweatshirt.

"The dishes," I said. "Can I help?"

"Uh, sure." He handed me a dish towel. "Yer can dry."

I took care of the plates, then the cups, listening to the Irish band blasting from the tiny speakers now dangling from Dylan's neck. How could he abuse his eardrums like that?

"So what made you want to be a fisherman?" I asked.

"Does anyone *want* ter be a fisherman?" he said with a grin, then shrugged. "De pay is gran'." He handed me a freshly scrubbed and rinsed saucepan.

"You grew up in Ireland, right? By the sea? Was your dad a fisherman?"

Dylan's light complexion turned pink. "Naw, naw. Oi jist wanted ter git away, 'av an adventure, oi guess."

"And has it been? An adventure?"

"It's been lashings av derdy dishes, I'll tell yer dat."

He pulled the drain plug and rinsed the sink clean while I tucked the dish rack into a cupboard.

"Wanna play Cribbage?" he asked without much enthusiasm, as though he assumed I'd say no.

"Sure," I said.

A brief flicker of surprise crossed his face before he composed himself. He flung open a drawer and tossed a deck of cards on the table.

"You don't have other work to do?" I asked.

"Not 'til dinner." He shuffled the cards. "Unless they fend a school av cod. But they won't," he said, matter-of-fact.

"What do you mean?"

He glanced toward the door, then leaned forward and whispered, "They're not pure gran' at it."

"Fishing, you mean?"

He nodded. "I've been wi' dem nigh for foive weeks. 'aven't dropped a net."

"Maybe the herring are late this year," I said.

He shook his head. "Oi asked in town." A grin spread across his face. His eyebrows raised, he said, "At laest 'e's payin' me."

"What are you saying, Dylan? You think something is fishy?" I snickered at my own joke. Trying to keep it light.

He stared at me for a long, drawn-out moment. I wasn't sure if he was going to respond. Then he made the slightest nod.

I whispered, "What do you think's going on?"

The door swung open and Michael came in with a gust of cold air. *Damn.*

"Coffee ready?" His eyes searched the stove, then the countertop, as if the coffee pot might be lurking in some mysterious corner.

"No, I ended up helping with the dishes." I gave him an innocent smile. "Warmed me up."

"Uh-huh," he said, his eyes shifting from me to Dylan. He was trying to catch me in a lie. I wondered what he'd do when he did. Dalton following in the *Sea Mist* wasn't helping. It had put Michael even more on edge with me. "Well, make some, will ya?"

"Sure," I said and got up from the table.

Michael left, slamming the door behind him.

Dylan raised his eyebrows but said nothing.

After I set the pot to percolate, I sat back down with Dylan. "He's probably annoyed because my boyfriend, I mean, my ex-boyfriend is following us. Like he won't let me go and he's chasing after me or something. Can you believe that?"

"Yeah," he said without looking at me. "If yer were me lassy, oi nu oi wud."

I paused. *How sweet.* "He's already got another girl." *April.* April with the pretty blond hair and the Ph.D. "She's on board with him."

He looked me in the eyes and grinned. "Well, dat seems ter 'av put a bee in yisser bonnet."

I crossed my arms. "Not at all. He and I are through."

"Gran'." He shuffled the cards some more and dealt.

I kept a crappy hand and tossed a ten and a five in his crib. Dylan might end up being an ally, but it would serve me that he and everyone else on board think I was an airhead.

"De coffee's ready," he said.

"I'll take it," I said and went to play waitress to a wildlife thief and his son while I tried to figure out how the hell I was going to plant my video camera.

CHAPTER 15

After dinner, the darkness had already returned. The slow forward momentum of the boat moving through the water was making me drowsy. Nothing had been spotted. Thankfully. Because I still hadn't found a way to get up to the crow's nest and plant the camera.

Ray and Michael pored over charts at the dining table in the galley. Bjørn was in the wheelhouse alone.

"I'm going to see if Bjørn needs anything," I said and got up and left.

I circled the deck once, debating if I could get up the ladder without Bjørn hearing me. Probably not. Maybe I could give him a reason. I circled once more, then climbed the stairs and poked my head in through the door to the pilothouse. "May I join you?"

"Don't see why not," Bjørn said, a hint of wariness in his posture.

I took my perch on the bench. "Thanks."

A greenish-blue glow from the monitors lit the old man's face as he looked out at the sea, his eyes moving in a slow, steady scanning pace along the horizon, then to the chart plotter, then to the radar screen, then back out the front window. In his hand he held a dirty coffee mug, the rim chipped in three places, the logo long since rubbed off.

"How long have you been a captain?" I asked.

"Helmsman," he said, as though the distinction were quite important.

"Helmsman then."

He hesitated before he answered. "I could steer a boat as soon as I was tall enough to reach the wheel, if that's what yer asking."

"And fishing?"

He turned to look at me with tired eyes. "I'm Norwegian. It's in my blood."

I sensed I'd irritate him if I talked too much, so I held back, listened to the silence for a while.

Bjørn set his cup down on the console and leaned back in the chair. Something about him seemed perfectly at home, as if he were part of the boat itself. Suddenly I realized why. This *was* his boat. Ray hadn't hired him to come on as helmsman; he'd hired the whole kit and caboodle. I wondered if Bjørn knew what he'd signed up for. Maybe he was desperate for cash. Or maybe he was as ruthless a criminal as Ray.

Watching him closely for any kind of reaction, I asked, "You see whales often?"

He slowly turned and looked at me, his lips pursed, crinkles at the edges of his sharp, blue eyes, all so subtle, if I hadn't been looking for it, I might not have noticed. He raised the mug of coffee. Took a sip. "Yeah."

"I'd love to see a whale," I said, easily conjuring the excited anticipation of my twelve-year-old self. "I hear there are humpbacks and killer whales in these seas."

He nodded, his eyes shifting back to his monitors. "Yep."

"Do you think we'll see any?"

His eyes came back to me, measuring. "Could."

"I'm going to keep watch," I said.

The coffee cup was raised to his lips again as he scanned the horizon, then the monitors. Bjørn didn't strike me as the kind of man who got rattled easily. They say deep sea fishing is one of the most dangerous jobs on the planet. I suppose if you spend a lifetime doing something like that, staring death in the face every time you go out, everything else seems trivial.

If he didn't want to, he wasn't going to give up any hints as to what he knew, how much he'd been told, what he'd agree to, or what he'd surmised on his own. This man was a closed book.

"Michael says that's what the crow's nest is for. To watch for whales. You ever been up there?"

Bjørn grinned. The first I'd seen. "When I was a boy. It was my job."

"Really?" Maybe I could get him talking after all. "Was your father a whaler then?"

"My father. My grandfather. My great-grandfather before him."

"And you were the spotter? How young were you?"

"Oh, I started at six or seven. When I was old enough to see over the rail."

"I bet it was exciting." *Not to mention horrific.*

"It was work. Not much else." He looked at me. His eyes soft. "Why you asking so many questions?"

I shrugged. "Bored, I guess." I chewed on my fingernail. Time for some pointless questions. "How do you live out here, anyway, day after day? Nothing but blue on blue."

He chuckled. "I suppose you'd see it that way."

"What do you mean?"

"It's a way of life. It's part of who I am." He looked out at the dark sea and I sensed a weariness in his manner. "It's what it means to live in the north."

"Fishing and whaling, you mean?"

"Blue on blue, as you say."

I waited a few minutes, to not seem too eager, before I asked, "Do you have any children?"

"A son," he said, the thought taking him far away.

"Is he a whaler, too?"

He retreated into his cup of coffee for a time, then said, "No money in it." He sighed. "My boy works on an oil rig in the south."

"That because the whales are going extinct?"

He smirked. "It's the whalers that are going extinct."

"Oh?" I had to tread carefully. "What do you mean?"

"Politics." He adjusted something on the plotter, then turned to me. "Easy for some rich kid from the continent, sitting in a Starbucks, sipping on a chocolate latte, or whatever dey call dose over-priced coffee drinks, plunking at keys on a computer all day, buying and selling electronics or oil or vatever he can make money at, vearing some fancy suit." He picked up his coffee mug again but kept talking, his accent really pronounced. "His vife buys 'is dinner some time between nine and five at a store with fluorescent lights, a slab of someting shrink-wrapped to a sheet of styrofoam." He gave me a sharp look. "Don't look at me like dat, like I'm some raving lunatic. I ain't saying it's right. I'm saying that fool ain't got de right to judge me is all." He shook his finger. "Dat ain't tofu he's eating. Ask a man who lives hand to mouth, trying to feed a hungry family, living in a land like dis. Ask him what he thinks of killing a whale."

I wasn't sure if I was in more awe of the content of his rant or the fact that he'd said so many words at once. But I was sure that, somewhere in there, he'd said it wasn't right.

He drained the last of his coffee. "I don't know what I'm going on about. It don't matter no how."

"What do you mean, it doesn't matter?"

"I mean, the cost of hunting whales is high, returns are low. Supply and demand. Nobody eats whale meat anymore." He smirked. "They're living on chocolate lattes."

"Well, I know one thing."

"What's that, little lady?"

"Now I'm craving chocolate."

He grinned.

We sat together for a while. It was comfortable. I liked

Bjørn. He seemed kind and gentle. Not the evil whaler of the tabloids. This man knew what it meant to live by one's means, to work hard. He had convictions. They might not match mine, but they were there just the same. I suspected he wasn't fond of Ray Goldman.

Ray came into the wheelhouse and told Bjørn he wanted him to anchor for the night. And I saw it. Subtle. Bjørn's eyes gave him away. I was right. He didn't like Ray much. He didn't like him much at all.

Michael stepped into the room, took me by the hand, and led me out. "We're anchoring so we might as well turn in," he said. "Big day tomorrow."

"Oh?" I said.

"We think we've found fish."

On the other side of the door, Bjørn and Ray were hashing something out. Their tone revealed an argument, but I couldn't make out the words.

"I think I'll stay up for a bit longer," I said.

"Aren't you tired?"

"Nah," I said. "Besides, Bjørn and I were having an interesting conversation." *And I have a camera to stash.*

Michael looked through the window toward Bjørn with an expression of confused suspicion. "That old man?"

I shrugged. "What can I say? I like his fish tales."

Ray flung open the door and pushed past us without a word.

Michael lingered for a moment as though pondering what might come of me staying with Bjørn before he shrugged and followed.

"I won't be long," I said. I breathed in deeply. This was my chance.

Bjørn gave no hint of his disagreement with Ray and a half hour later, I'd been lulled into a sleepy daze by the chug-chug-chug of the engine and the warmth of too many electronics, when Bjørn brought the boat to a halt, the hook was dropped, and the engine went quiet.

"Look at that," Bjørn said and pointed at the sky through the window.

I ducked to see. "Is that—"

"Go out on deck."

I raced to the bow. The night sky shimmered with strands of green. The aurora borealis. Light pulsed in vertical ribbons, like a giant drape of chiffon moving in a gentle breeze. Green shafts with tips of red against a black velvety sky pocked with millions of sparkling stars. No wonder primitive peoples stood in awe of the mystery. Like dancing spirits, moving through the heavens, casting a green glow across the snow-capped mountain peaks. I'd never seen anything like it.

Bjørn, standing beside me, his voice low, said, "Some say it is the spirits of old maids, dancing in the sky. Others say it is the Valkyries, the immortal, female warriors of legend. Ravens by the light of day; by night, they carry spears and armor that glow in the dark sky." His voice changed to a low, reverent tone. "In battle, they are the ones who decide who lives and who dies."

"Are you saying it's some kind of omen?"

"I'm saying some things are better left to the gods."

I stared at the awe-inspiring light show before me. Is that how life should be? Leave everything to the gods? Should I let them decide the fate of the whales? Nope. I would decide. "They didn't make capricious decisions, though, right?" I said. "I always thought they were the goddesses of vengeance and retribution."

He smirked. "You're all right, you know that?"

I nodded. This was my chance. My chance to get up to the crow's nest and mount the camera. But how could I do it without him watching? Would he tell Ray I'd been up there?

I let my eyes travel to the top. It wasn't going to be a quick and easy climb. The danger lay in the time it would take to get up there and back down again. If Ray or Michael happened back on deck and caught me, their suspicions would launch into the stratosphere.

If I got caught up there, and they found the camera, it'd be the end.

"I bet the view is spectacular from up in that crow's nest. Mind if I give it a try?"

His tired eyes rose about halfway up the post. "That is where a raven would go," he mumbled and went back into the wheelhouse.

Hand over hand, I climbed the pole toward the crow's nest. The steel rungs were ice cold, but I moved quickly, afraid my clammy hands might stick. I flipped myself up and over the edge of the bucket and inside. I popped up and scanned the deck for Ray or Michael. It was too dark to see a damn thing. One of them could be standing there watching me right now and I wouldn't know it. Well. This was my only chance. It was now or never.

The bucket had a rim all around, but nothing onto which I could attach the camera. It would have to go under the bucket, on the bracket there.

As fast as I could, I climbed back out of the perch, scrambled down a few rungs, and, as I held on with one hand, took the camera from my pocket with the other. I scanned the deck again, from one side to the other for movement. Still couldn't see anything. If anyone was watching, there would be no doubt what I was up to. What I wouldn't give for a pair of night-vision goggles right now. I took a deep breath and tried to stop my hand from shaking.

I clipped the remote cam to the bracket, checked again to make sure I wasn't being watched, pointless as it was, then reached back up and angled it toward the aft deck. I couldn't check the view without my laptop, so I had to get it right the first time. There was no way I was going to get a chance to climb up here again. My best guess on the angle would have to do.

I backed down the pole, then went down the stairs and circled the deck to be sure no one had seen me. With a sigh of relief, I said a silent prayer to the Valkyries that no one would look up and see it, then climbed the stairs and slipped back into the wheelhouse. "Whew, too cold for that," I said. "I don't know what I was thinking."

He gave me an amused nod.

CHAPTER 16

Bjørn turned in for bed. I went into the galley and rifled through the cupboards for chocolate. You'd think they'd at least have an Oreo cookie or something on board.

I sat down at the table empty-handed and confessed to myself. I was scared. Scared shitless, actually. All they had to do was look up and they'd see it and then...

If I got lucky, and they kept their eyes from the pole, I'd get what I came for. But video footage was one thing. I had to do more. Scared or not, I needed to figure out a way to keep Ray from getting a killer whale on board at all. If he got one in a net, that was enough to convict, but if he got one on board, it would be life threatening for the whale. Dr. Parker had said its chances weren't good, especially if Ray didn't know what he was doing.

A harness would be attached to the winch arm to haul the orca on board. That was the key. That's what I had to take out of the equation. The harness. But where was it?

Dalton had said to do nothing else, to keep my head down. But how could I stand by and do nothing?

I checked my phone. There was actually one bar of service out here. I shot off a text to Dalton.

Poppy: You there?

I waited. Nothing. Maybe he didn't have service where he was anchored. I leaned back and tried to picture the layout of the deck. The harness must be made of canvas, or plastic maybe.

My phone buzzed.

Dalton: Yep. You ok?

Poppy: Fine. Camera's in place.

Dalton: Good. Sit tight.

Poppy: You're pushing my cover. You need to stay back.

But not too far.

Dalton: What happened?

Poppy: Just don't push it.

Dalton: Poppy, what's going on?

Poppy: Nothing. Everything is fine.

I can handle it.

Dalton: Just stick to your cover story and hold tight.

I can't. I've got to stop him.

Poppy: Yep.

Dalton: Everything ok with Michael?

Poppy: Fine.

Dalton: Are you sure? I can still get you off that boat. Say the word.

Poppy: Just trust me already.

Nothing.

Poppy: Gotta go.

I clicked off and deleted all the texts in case Ray checked my phone. I took a deep breath. I had work to do.

The boat gently rose and fell on the waves, the fishing gear creaking and clanking with the rocking. Hopefully, any noise I might make would blend in with the ruckus and no one would notice.

My guess was that the lazarettes with the padlocks were the ones with the harness and other whale-hauling gear, but I had to check anyway. I started on the side of the boat opposite where I'd already checked back in the harbor.

Again, on this side as well, the first one was padlocked. I stepped lightly, moving to the next one. No padlock. I lifted the lid a few inches and peeked inside. This was it. The harness. I was sure of it. What luck! I eased the lid back and clipped it to the rail to keep it open.

Clank-clank-clank came footsteps down the stairs. *Crap.* A dose of adrenaline shot into my bloodstream. I clicked off my flashlight and ducked beside the bin. Bjørn must have been going to the head. The door to the galley swung open and the light clicked on. I waited, unable to hear anything over the lapping of the waves against the hull and my heart thumping in my chest.

A few minutes passed and he didn't come back out. If he woke anyone down below and they noticed I wasn't in my bunk, I'd be screwed. I needed to come up with a good reason for being on deck, and quick.

More time passed and he still didn't emerge. What was he doing in there? I crept from my hiding spot to peek in the window. Bjørn was at the stove setting a teakettle to boil. *Damn.* My crappy luck. He was probably a world-record-setting insomniac. What if he sat at the table doing crosswords or writing letters to his wife back home for half the night? All I could do was wait him out. I couldn't head to bed now, having to pass through to below decks without an explanation.

Back to my hiding spot I went to wait. I had no coat and the night was freezing cold. *Bad planning, McVie.* I considered crawling under the nets to get warm, but that made me think of Dalton and his body snuggled up against me. And how I'd smell like rotten fish.

Finally, my lips blue and my hands too cold to work properly, I heard the clank-clank-clank of footsteps on the iron stairs as Bjørn headed back up to the pilothouse.

As soon as the door banged shut, I slipped from behind the

lazarrette and shined my flashlight inside. The harness had two poles with a canvas sling attached, a basic home-made contraption. If I could cut the sling where it attached to the poles, I could weaken it. When the orca was being lifted from the water, the canvas would rip.

I started to unroll it when I realized that wouldn't work. What if they had the whale high in the air, or worse yet, over the deck, and it came slamming down? I needed to render it completely unusable.

With my pocket knife, I could saw at the roping, cut the canvas to bits. That would do it. But then, when Ray saw it, he'd know it had been purposefully sabotaged. Too risky.

The best option was to tangle its cords, rip the canvas in a way that looked like it had happened when it was put in the bin. I lifted one end of the harness and started to rewrap the cords when the hinge of the galley door creaked. I froze. Someone was out on deck. I shoved the harness back in the lazarette.

"Poppy?" It was Michael.

I threw down the flashlight, sending it rolling across the deck to distract him and eased the lid down. "You startled me," I said, my heart going zippity-zap.

He picked up the flashlight. "What are you doing out here?" he said, his tone accusatory.

"I couldn't sleep." *Crap.* "I was feeling kinda cooped up, you know. Needed to walk." *Did he see me close the lid?*

"What did I tell you about being out on the deck alone?" I couldn't read his expression in the dark, but his arms were crossed and his stance was threatening.

"Well, I figured since we were anchored—"

"Oh, you figured, did you?" He put his arm around me, pulling me toward him with a powerful grip. "Well, darlin', it's going to be a long journey if you can't get a handle on this cabin fever."

"I'll be all right," I said, hoping he couldn't feel my pulse racing into oblivion. "I'm sorry. I didn't mean to worry you."

"C'mon back to bed and try it again," he said, his tone softened. "After this cold air, you'll get toasty warm and fall right to sleep. I promise."

I nodded. I was plenty warm now, what with my nerves set on fire. Maybe I should have had Dalton pick me up. *No. The job isn't finished.* I could handle this. But I couldn't think of any excuse Michael'd accept for me to stay out here alone now. And if he caught me sneaking up here again, that'd be the end. *Dammit!*

Reluctantly, I followed Michael back down to the bunks. I'd have to think of something else. Before they found the whales.

CHAPTER 17

The engines roared to life and I sat up so fast I knocked my head on the bunk above me. My watch read 7:30. Ray's bunk was empty.

Then the clank-clank-clank of the anchor being raised echoed through the hull. Had Ray got word that whales were nearby?

I got dressed, clipped the camera remote inside my jacket pocket, and went topside.

Ray and Michael were in the pilothouse. Making coffee had gotten me in there yesterday. *Let's see if it will work again.*

I brewed a pot, poured mugs, and knocked at the door.

Ray's scowl burned through the window. I smiled wide, acting like I didn't notice. "Coffee?"

Michael ambled over to the door and took the mugs from me. "Thanks."

Ray gripped the edge of the door. "We're busy," he grumbled and pushed it shut in my face.

Damn. Must be I was right. Orcas are close.

I shot off a quick text to Dalton.

`Poppy: You up? We're on the move.`

I waited. No answer. I checked again. The one reception bar flickered and went out.

I paced around in the galley dining room, glancing out the window every eight seconds. The sky to the east was a light blue. We were moving through the water at what I assumed was full throttle for this vessel. Pans and plates rattled in the cupboards. The plastic parrot swung back and forth on the ring. I pressed against the window, searching the dark sea for a glimpse of an orca, the other direction for Dalton. Nothing either way.

Might as well make something to eat. I found eggs, milk, and flour, whipped them together, poured the batter into a high-sided pan, slid it into the oven, then paced some more.

About twenty minutes later, Dylan stumbled in, one eye open. "Dat coffee oi peggy dell?"

"There's probably a cup left in the pot."

"Mercy," he said.

"I've got a German pancake in the oven."

He looked my way and opened the other eye. "Tryin' ter take my job?"

"No, sir," I said with a grin.

He poured the mug of coffee and slumped down at the table. "Must be 'e's finally foun' sum cod."

"Why do you say that?"

Dylan shrugged. "We're actually movin'."

"Does that mean we'll have fish for dinner?" I asked.

"Oi wouldn't play dohs odds," he said.

I wondered again if he really didn't know what was going on. He seemed so genuine, it was hard to believe he did. "Do you think maybe we're not out here for fish but something else?"

"Loike waaat?" he asked, his expression pure ignorance. "Mermaids?"

The door opened and Ray poked his head in. "I need to talk to you. Outside."

I looked to Dylan, then back to Ray. He was staring at me. My stomach lurched. If he'd seen the camera, I was done for. "Me?"

"You," he said and shut the door.

Dylan and I exchanged a what-the-hell-is-that-about look before I got up and followed Ray out the door.

When I stepped on deck, Ray pointed aft. "He's still following us."

Dalton. A surge of relief flooded me. "What? Who? No way."

Ray fished a battered pack of Marlboros from his coat pocket, whacked it until a cigarette emerged from the opening, then shoved the stick of chemically-soaked tobacco into his mouth. He cupped a lit match in his hands to block the wind and took a long drag before he said, "I want him gone." When I didn't react, he leaned forward, smoke oozing from his nose and mouth. "Now."

"Well, I'm sure he's just out—"

"I'm not going to tell you twice."

I believe you. I opened my hands and gave him an innocent shrug. "What do you want me to do about it?"

"You'll think of something." He flashed a condescending frown. "Or I'll throw you overboard to give him something to do."

His expression didn't change. He wasn't kidding.

I swallowed hard. "Can I use the radio?"

He held out his hand, mocking a cordial, be-my-guest gesture.

In the wheelhouse, I took the transmitter in hand and held down the button. "*Sea Mist, Sea Mist, Sea Mist*, this is the *Forseti* hailing. Over."

"*Forseti*, this is *Sea Mist*, switch to channel 68. Over."

I turned the tuning dial to 68 and heard Dalton's voice. "*Forseti*, this is *Sea Mist*."

"Yeah, *Sea Mist*, uh, you need to divert your course."

"Come again?"

"Stop following us." Dalton was smart enough to know I wouldn't be calling on the radio if I wasn't being watched. He'd know to play along.

"What is it they say, hell hath no fury like a woman scorned? Ha ha. Get over yourself, sweetheart. We aren't following you. You happen to be on our course."

I shook my head. *Good Dalton, keep it up.* "Whatever. Just choose another course."

"What? I will not. You don't get to tell me where to go."

Ray was hovering like a vulture over a kill, his beady eyes fixed on me. Michael stood behind him, arms crossed.

"It's over. There's no point in chasing me," I said. "I'm not coming back."

"Chasing you? Very funny." There was a click and a second of static. "Our days are over, babe."

"Good, then just turn around. Go another way."

"No can do. Over and out."

I turned to Ray and shrugged.

He curled up his lip as though he'd just got a whiff of rotting carcass. "Come with me," he said and grabbed me by the wrist.

"All right, I'm coming," I said. *What the hell?*

He stomped down the stairs and headed toward the stern, to one of the lazarettes on the port side. The one with the harness inside. My pulse started thrumming, my brain whirring with excuses, denials. He opened the lid, looked inside, and slammed it shut. He moved back to the one with a padlock on it and fished a key from his back pocket, opened the lock, and flipped open the lid. "Take a look," he said.

I leaned over the side, making it clear I was obeying. There was an army green case with Russian writing on the side—the case for a rocket-propelled grenade launcher. *Oh crap.* My knees went numb. "What is it?" I asked as innocently as I could muster.

Ray reached down and flipped open the lid to reveal the weapon. "It's proof that I'm not talking out my ass. You don't get your boyfriend to back off, I will." He slammed the lid shut and the latch rattled, echoing in my brain.

"Right," I said, my eyes wide. "I'll convince him."

Apparently Ray wasn't concerned at this point about what I knew. *Not good.* I went straight back to the wheelhouse. Ray didn't follow me, but I had the feeling he would be listening. I hailed Dalton again. "Listen, my captain won't take no for an answer. He wants you out of our fishing area."

"What does he care? I'm not fishing."

"Well, he's a little hot-headed. Just leave, okay. Don't make me thump you on the head."

Bjørn gave me a curious look. There was no response from Dalton for a moment. I hoped he would pick up on my hint. In the Navy, grenade launchers were nicknamed thumpers and hot meant firepower.

"Fine. Whatever," he finally responded. "Have a great life."

"I'm set on the course I want to be. You need to find yours."

There was no answer.

I replaced the transmitter to its hook. "Breakups," I said to Bjørn with a shrug.

He glanced my way but didn't acknowledge my comment.

I chewed my thumbnail, trying to figure out what to do next. With Dalton backing off, I was on my own. The remote cam had better work. My best strategy now was to lie low, give Ray no reason to even think of me again. I'd wait until I was sure I had incriminating video before I made my move. That's when I'd...I wasn't sure yet. I'd figure something out.

"Did you love him?"

"What?" I turned in surprise. Bjørn initiating conversation was so unexpected.

He gestured aft with his head, referring to the following boat. "I saw you two in the pub. I don't know what happened between you—" he turned to face me "—but that boy loves you."

My mouth opened, but I didn't know what to say.

He grinned. "I might be an old codger, but I recognize love when I see it. He had that look in his eyes."

"He and I, we…" I shook my head.

Bjørn smirked. "Young 'uns. Can't tell 'em nothing."

The door swept open. Michael came barreling in, his finger pointing forward. "Orca! Off the starboard bow!"

Bjørn calmly swung forward, raised a pair of binoculars, and nodded. His shoulders sagged with resignation.

Michael, on the other hand, was fired up like a kid waiting to rip his Christmas stocking down from the hearth. I followed him out to the rail. Five hundred yards or more in the distance, a pod of killer whales moved through the waves, their distinctive triangular dorsal fins breaking the surface. Unlike the slow, steady movement of the humpback whales, these predators cut through the water with menacing speed.

There were at least twenty of them.

Bjørn throttled up the engine and changed course. Right for the whales.

"You stay inside, in the galley or down below," Michael said and turned to join his father.

"What? I want to see the whales."

He spun around and grabbed me by the arm. "You do as I say. Do you understand?"

Every fiber of my being wanted to smack that stern, I'm-in-charge look off his face. "Fine," I managed in a wimpy voice.

He stormed off. This was it. They were going to try to capture one.

I had to let Dalton know. My phone read no service. *Damn. Damn. Dammit!*

The radio. But Bjørn was in there at the helm. What could I say? What excuse could I give?

I'd think of something. I went back into the pilothouse and straight to the radio.

"Don't touch that," Bjørn said, his voice calm.

"I forgot to mention—"

"Doesn't matter. Ray's using it now with the handheld."

The radio had been switched to a working channel. Ray's voice came over the line. "Flank from the east."

"Yes, sir," a voice crackled back.

I had to come up with a reason to stay in the wheelhouse so I'd know what was going on. I looked at Bjørn and he looked at me and frowned. He wasn't happy about something.

"Coffee?" I suggested with a casual smile.

He studied my face for a long moment before responding with a nod.

"I'll get some brewing," I said and slipped out the door.

Dylan wasn't in the galley. Probably on deck, helping get ready for the capture. I filled the pot with water and ground coffee and set it on the stove to percolate.

Then I paced, my stomach churning up a sour bile that fumed at the back of my throat. How was I supposed to stand by and wait while they were about to do…what they were about to do?

I checked my phone again. Still no service. *Dalton, please turn back.* If my remote camera didn't work, all this was for nothing. And even if it did, I had no way of uploading the footage right away. If I was made, the digital files would be here on the boat with me. Ray could easily destroy them—and me—and get away with it.

I paced some more, twirling the bracelet my dad had given me, round and round my wrist. How was I going to hide my feelings and pretend this was no big deal? Then how long would I be stuck on this boat with them before I had a chance to escape?

Maybe I could mutiny. Dylan would most likely be an ally. And Bjørn, well, I was sure he wasn't too keen on this. Maybe he wouldn't help, but wouldn't interfere either? That left me against Ray and Michael.

The boat slowed. The engine quieted. I crawled across the bench and looked out the window. The pod of orcas was directly alongside. This was happening.

My dad always told me, where there's a will, there's a way. When your heart's in the right place.

I gave my bracelet another twist. *Oh Daddy, you died with your heart in the right place.*

But I can't stand by and do nothing.

CHAPTER 18

I dumped the entire pot of coffee into a Thermos and hustled back up the stairs to the wheelhouse. Bjørn was standing at the door, looking out the window, his arms crossed.

"Hot coffee," I said, pushing past him and reaching for his cup.

He nodded without comment.

"Bjørn, what's going on?" I said as I poured.

He accepted the cup from me and took a sip. He acted like he was savoring it before he answered, but then his eyes turned misty. "Best if you don't know."

"Why? What do you mean?"

"Little lady, you should've stayed with that other boy. This one's up to no good."

"What are you talking about? What's going on?"

He took another sip of the coffee. "Like I said—"

"It's better I don't know. Yeah, I got it." I was disappointed. I hoped he'd tell me now. I needed to know for sure if he was an ally. "Mind if I stay in here with you?"

Ray came busting through the door. His eyes settled on me and his lip curved into a snarl. "What did I tell you?" he said as he went straight for the deck controls. "Out!"

"I was just—"

"Leave her be. She brought me coffee," Bjørn said.

Ray flicked a switch, fiddled with a joystick, and the whirring of the winch rattled the floorboards. They were deploying the seine nets. Michael and Dylan were on deck, hauling the nets and making sure they went into the water without getting tangled.

I made like a chameleon and blended in with the paneling.

Bjørn eased the engine throttle forward, turned the wheel, and steered the boat in a circle as the nets unfurled into the ocean.

Bjørn gestured out the front windows. "Svein and Jænis are here."

Two small speedboats zig-zagged through the waves beyond the whales, criss-crossing each other in an irregular pattern, heading toward us. They zoomed back and forth, herding the whales, making them disoriented and scaring them into changing direction, driving them toward the nets.

I watched with my fingernails dug into my palms, an expression of innocent curiosity pasted on my face.

Bjørn had steered more than a half circle and was closing the loop. The pod was now a few hundred yards off the starboard bow, the whales crowded into a confused bunch.

"Gotcha," said Ray. He pulled back the winch control stick, locked it into place and pushed through the door, heading back out on deck.

Out of nowhere, a small prop plane dropped from above and buzzed along the surface of the water, right toward the whales.

I stepped out on the deck as it roared over my head.

The whales dove and surfaced in frantic patterns, running into each other, their formation getting tighter as they called out with their distinctive chitters and squeaks. I shook with anger. I had to stop this right now before—*no, it'll be okay. Get the video you came for first.*

A few whales slipped from the main pod, but the boats let them go now, staying on the core group, forcing them forward, toward the nets. Ray was taking advantage of the killer whales' strong family instinct. The pod would remain tightly bunched together for support, making them easy to corral into the net.

The orcas dove and changed direction as though they recognized the nets and were looking for an open gap to escape.

I clenched and unclenched my fists. *Damn you, Ray Goldman. You're going to rot in prison for this.*

Then the whales dove, as though synchronized, and disappeared. Ray came charging back up the stairs. "Which way did they go?"

Bjørn shrugged with indifference.

About five males surfaced with a loud whoosh. "There!" Ray shouted into the radio. "Flank 'em. Flank 'em."

Both speedboats zoomed toward the whales and cut them off, making them turn back toward the nets.

Then came another whoosh. The other whales—the females and younger ones—surfaced past the nets. They'd slipped around.

"Dammit!" Ray slammed his fist down on the console. He glared at Bjørn as if it were all his fault. "Michael, get those nets back in," he spat into the handheld radio, then slammed the joystick forward and the winch squealed into motion. "I'm too old for this," he grumbled.

I suppressed a grin. They'd worked together and outsmarted him. *Ha! Way to go whales!*

Bringing in the nets took several minutes and the orcas were getting away.

Ray shouted some indiscernible command on the radio and the speedboats chased them down. The plane circled back, flying low over the water, and the whales dove in fear.

"Damn lines are jammin' it." Ray slammed the winch joystick back. "Don't you dare let them get away, boys. Force them back," he barked into the radio as he pushed through the door, then bounded down the stairs, shouting at Michael.

I held the door open behind him, watching through the

opening.

One of the speedboats turned and zoomed along the far side of the pod. The driver raised a gun and fired something into the water. Two seconds later, an explosion reverberated across the water. The whales surfaced in a panic, blowing with frightful force, squealing and screeching.

I rushed back into the wheelhouse, slamming the door behind me. I stared down Bjørn. "What are they doing?" I knew. They were using seal bombs, explosive devices similar to M-80 firecrackers, to scare and disorient the whales. But I wanted him to say it.

Another bomb was fired into the water. Kaboom! Then another. Kaboom! The whales became frantic, churning up the water in their terror. The boats circled around them, forcing them into a bunch.

"Get this old tug in gear," Ray ordered Bjørn over the radio.

"Yessir," Bjørn said, but he took his time getting to the throttle.

Dylan pushed through the door and came to a halt, his eyes on Bjørn. "Yer man towl me ter run de winch." His hands shook and he looked as if he expected to be drawn and quartered if he didn't get to it right now.

Bjørn shrugged, so Dylan lunged toward the console and fired it up, his hands fumbling at the controls. The nets once again unfurled into the sea.

More seal bombs went off. Kaboom! Kaboom!

Ray's voice thundered over the radio, shouting orders as Bjørn pulled back on the throttle. The nets were fully deployed. The speedboats closed in, pushing the frantic whales inside.

My guts churned, building an unbearable pressure in my belly. I took hold of the edge of the console, trying to steady myself for fear I'd burst like a water balloon.

Ray would adjust the nets now, cinching up the bottom, then the top, forcing the whales closer and closer together, making it easy to get one lassoed. I kept my vigil. Once he had the nets cinched and the whales next to the boat, that was my cue to start the camera recording. My blood pumped double-time in my veins.

Bjørn set the boat to idle, took a sip of his coffee, then leaned back on the console and crossed his arms. "I've got it now," he said to Dylan, dismissing him. As soon as Dylan was out the door, he turned to me. "I'd go down below, I were you," he said, barely above a whisper. "Before he comes back."

I nodded to Bjørn. Staying clear of Ray was a good idea. I couldn't risk him seeing me start the camera with the remote. Or that I'd lose it and beat him to a bloody pulp before I had my evidence.

Having the whales in the nets definitely constituted harassment. Hell, the seal bombs alone were enough to arrest him, but once he had a whale in the sling, there was no denying his intent. That was what I needed on video to nail him to the wall. That was the moment I'd confront him. Stop this terror. I'd bluff, tell him I'd instantly uploaded a video via satellite link. It was plausible enough. A good plan.

You're going down, Ray Goldman.

I slipped out the door and headed for the galley where I'd be able to see the progress as they pulled in the nets.

The orcas swam round and round inside the net, checking out the boundaries, their exhalations faster and more rapid, sending spurts of misty-spray into the air with loud, forceful breaths. It sounded like they were hyperventilating. Some spy-hopped, vertically pushing themselves out of the water like a human treading water, trying to see. Others slapped their flukes and flippers on the surface of the water, a rapid-fire thwack-thwack-thwack while vocalizing with their high-pitched calls.

The few whales that had not been forced into the nets were now circling outside it, frantically calling out to those trapped inside. Their shrill cries turned my insides out.

The winch fired up again, clankety-clanking as it slowly

pulled in the net, drawing the circle in tighter and tighter. Inside the circle, there were twelve whales in all—eight adults, three juveniles, and staying next to her mother, an infant. Baby Kimmy.

My lip began to quiver. *Don't think about it, McVie.*

I checked my phone again. Still no service. *C'mon, Dalton. I need you.* I pushed the button on the remote, starting my video recording, and sent a silent prayer to the Valkyries for support. Vengeance and retribution were in order. *Vengeance and retribution.*

The winch shuddered and stopped. The whales were now confined inside a net that had been cinched down around them to an area the size of a small swimming pool. The whales became docile, lying at the surface along the line of floats, facing out to sea, their voices now reduced to a low moaning-like hum. It was as though they were already giving up.

Ray reached into one of the lazarettes, extracting an aluminum pole with a noose on the end, then extended it to its full length, and headed for the aft deck. I slipped out the galley door and moved to where I could see.

Michael was there, pointing. Ray came alongside him, pole in hand. He lowered it into the water, adjusting the noose, and as Michael pointed, Ray worked the lasso.

Soon, they'd be raising one in the harness. The act I was waiting for. Not long now. I couldn't watch, but I had to watch. I glanced up at the crow's nest. Too far away to see the camera, to confirm that the little red light was on.

Ray had already made a choice from the group and was trying to get it lassoed. They'd pick the healthiest, most robust one, a teenager, young enough to train, old enough to be strong and healthy for the long journey and the time it took for training, not to mention the transition to living in captivity.

I kept my distance, waiting for my moment.

Then Ray dropped to his knees. He had one lassoed around the neck. He let out a whoop. I stepped forward, trying to get a look. He had ahold of the lasso, towing a whale to the side of the boat. I took another step to see and stopped cold.

The baby. He had captured the baby.

Noooooo! Not baby Kimmy! The tiny whale twisted and twirled against the noose while her mother thrashed in the water next to her. I spun around, my eyes stinging, my throat contracting. *Don't let them see you.* I pressed my fingers underneath my cheekbones trying to hold back the tears.

What in the world was Ray thinking? He had to know she was still nursing. How on earth did he plan to keep her alive? Why take the risk? This didn't make sense. None of it. Dr. Parker had said they would take an older whale, an adolescent that was more likely to survive and—

Then it hit me. Ocean World of Miami. They'd been advertising for months, anticipating a captive-born baby whale. News outlets had been picking up the story, splashing headlines across the nation's papers.

All zoos and aquariums rely on signature species—cute and cuddly panda bears, big cats, gorillas—as their main attractions. The only attraction that brought more attention was a new baby, of any species. And with a baby orca, they had the best of both. A marketer's dream. Ocean World was planning special celebration days at the park, with parades and fireworks. They'd already sold out tickets. Baby orca dolls were flying off the shelves.

Had something happened to the infant? Dr. Parker had said an unnatural percentage of captive-bred babies are stillborn. Had it already happened? If the press got wind of it, they'd have a heyday. Ocean World would lose millions. Were they planning to slip a wild-caught baby into its place, hoping the mother would adopt it as her own and no one would be the wiser?

No wonder Ray hadn't bothered with a larger boat. Baby Kimmy had been the golden prize all along.

It took everything in my power to keep my feet planted

where they were. Even my hair hurt from containing my fury.

Ray and Michael yanked and pulled, dragging the infant to the side of the boat while the mother thrashed beside her, flipping her tail, churning up the water around them, all the while calling with agonizing squeals of anguish.

How they were immune to her torment was beyond my comprehension. My heart was damn near ripped from my chest.

You've got a mouth full of teeth. Now's the time to use them!

Michael lowered the sling into the water and got it under the baby, slid her tiny pectoral fins into the slits made for that purpose, then gave a thumbs up to Bjørn in the wheelhouse.

My fury threatened to consume my soul. *Ten more seconds, McVie.* The winch creaked into action and as the baby was lifted from the water, the entire pod of whales became silent. As if being taken from the water meant certain death, they gave up.

CHAPTER 19

It was now or never. I'd either gotten the video or not. I charged down the deck, shouting, "Put her back in the water! She's just a baby! Put her back in the water!"

Michael looked up at me. His eyes narrowed. "I told you to stay inside."

The baby whale's little snout was the only part I could see, poking out from the canvas sling. The mother now floated motionless in the sea.

I swallowed hard. "Put her back into the water right now and—"

"Dammit!" Ray was on his feet and charging toward me. "What the hell did I tell you about him?" he bellowed as he brushed past me.

What? I spun around. Behind us, the *Sea Mist* bobbed in the sea. *Dalton!* I'd been too distracted to notice. *Yes!*

Ray flung open the lid of a lazarette, grabbed the rocket-propelled grenade launcher, raised it to his shoulder, and aimed.

No! I pounced on his back just as he pulled the trigger. He slammed into the lazarette, doubling over the edge. The grenade rocketed toward its target and hit the *Sea Mist* in her bow, shattering it to pieces in a fiery explosion.

My heart stopped. I couldn't breathe. *No, no, no, no! Dalton! No!* A ball of fire hovered over the water.

Ray regained his balance and tossed the grenade launcher into its case. He spun on me. "You bitch!"

I dropped my head and lunged, pinning him against the side of the lazarette.

"Knock it off!"

Ray smirked.

I pulled back and spun around.

Michael held a revolver pointed at me. "You're not going to make any more trouble, now, are you?" he spat, his eyes ablaze.

My eyes traveled from Michael's face to the weapon in his hand, where I fixated. A Smith & Wesson J-Frame, the most popular revolver on the market. Accurate. Deadly. His hand held it steady.

What the hell had I been thinking? *Dalton. Dead. And*—I shook my head, my lip quivering, tears stinging at the back of my eyes. *I'm way over my head.*

"You wanted a job," Michael sneered. "Keep that fish alive. Or when I toss its rotting carcass overboard, you'll go with it. Got it?"

I stared back at him and managed to nod. Beyond him, a pillar of black smoke billowed skyward from the *Sea Mist*, but she was still afloat. Flames engulfed the bow. I conjured a silent prayer for Dalton. There was a chance. Maybe he'd seen it coming. He could be okay. And Dr. Parker…

I had to keep calm, do my job.

Breathe in. Breathe out.

"I suggest you forget your boyfriend and get to work," Ray growled.

"Yes, sir," I said. I turned to Dylan, who stood stone still, gripping the end of a net line, white-faced, his mouth hinged open. "Will you please help me get her into the hold. We need to keep her wet and her temperature down."

Dylan snapped out of his daze and immediately started following my commands.

Ray shouted up to Bjørn in the wheelhouse and the winch creaked into service. As the baby whale was lowered into the shallow water in the bottom of the holding tank and started to float, Dylan and I tried to unhook the sling from the cable.

"'Tis stuck," Dylan said.

I got up on the rim of the tank and tried to work the hook from the harness. It was wedged in too tightly.

"What's the problem?" said Michael.

"It's stuck," I said.

He shoved me to the side. "I'll get it." He halted, glared at me. "You must think I'm stupid."

"What?" I had no idea what he meant.

He turned to Ray and handed him the gun. "Keep it pointed at her," he said.

Michael took the hook from me and, with sheer might, worked it free. At least he could see I wasn't lying.

With a grunt, he stepped down from the edge of the tank, wiped his hands on the front of his pants, and without a word, he and Ray went to work pulling in the net. They were letting the other whales go.

I stared at the baby, my hands interlaced over the top of my head. I was supposed to keep her alive. My insides burned with rage. *I'm not a real vet!* What had Dr. Parker said, to keep it cool, the areas that are vascularized? What had I been thinking? I looked at Dylan for help. He was staring at me, wide-eyed, waiting for me to tell him what to do.

I turned around and stared at the *Sea Mist*, worry threatening to shut me down. *No. Dalton can take care of himself.* He'd been trained by the best in the world. He knew exactly what to do.

If he wasn't dead.

The flames had died down, but black smoke still wafted from the *Sea Mist*. Debris floated in the water around the main hull, which was still partially afloat. It was too far for me to see anyone on board. *Dammit, Dalton. I told you to stay back.*

Dylan touched me on the shoulder. "What's wrong wi' it?"

I spun back around. The baby orca was listing to the side, her eyes closed. She floated, but made no movement, no attempt to stay upright.

"Tighten the sling back up a little," I said taking hold of the roping on my side and tying it off. "Just enough to keep her upright and her blowhole out of the water."

"It doesn't luk loike she's breathin'." Dylan's face was pasty white. He'd stared down the barrel of Michael's revolver, too.

Baby Kimmy's tongue lolled out of the side of her mouth.

"She's in shock," I said, trying my damnedest to sound like I knew what I was talking about. Not that I knew what the hell to do about it.

"The water in the tank is too warm. Buckets of sea water," I said to Dylan. "Pour them over her."

He stared, nodding like a bobble-head.

"You got a bucket?" I said.

"Oh yeah," he said and turned a full circle before finding direction.

I held my hand a few inches over her blowhole. Nothing. I couldn't feel the slightest bit of air.

I closed my eyes. *Please breathe. Breathe! C'mon. You can do it.*

Dylan was back, slowly dumping water over her back.

"On her fins," I said. "Her flippers and her tail."

The winch stopped. The net was back on board. The engines fired up again and the boat lurched into gear.

Ray came up behind me. "What's going on?"

"She's uh…nothing. Everything's fine."

He turned to poor Dylan who looked like he'd wet his pants. "She's not breathin'," he blurted out.

Ray spun on me. "Well, get it breathing."

I stared at him, wishing for a fillet knife. I'd have happily demonstrated the workings of the mammalian lungs as I eviscerated him.

Michael came up behind him. "You're a vet, ain't ya?"

"Yeah, but—"

"It's simple, chicky," said Ray, pulling the revolver from his pocket and shoving it at me. "It lives, you live. It dies…" He held up his free hand and shrugged.

This amazing calm came over me. All my anger and fury simply disappeared. I was going to die either way. Once they sold baby Kimmy, passed her into someone else's care, I'd be a liability. A witness to the crime. No matter whether they ever knew I was an agent or not.

My fate was in my own hands.

I sized Ray up. With a quick lunge, I could take him down. But what would Michael do? I wasn't sure I could handle them both. But now Ray had the weapon. An advantage to me. He was the easier of the two to take down.

Dylan wouldn't fight me. But would he help? I wasn't sure. I had to wait for the chance to take them by surprise, one at a time.

Right now, my priority was to get this baby breathing. There was nothing I could do to help Dalton. My stomach clenched. He was on his own too. *Oh Dalton.*

The baby whale floated in the sling. No sign of life. It was a mammal. I could try CPR. Dogs have been saved by CPR. But how would I do it? How do I blow into that mouth? Could I blow into the hole?

I rested my hand on the baby's back, trying to feel a breath. Nothing.

"I'm not sure—" I started to shake, all the feelings returning in a rush. The sharp prickle of tears threatened behind my eyelids. I blinked them back. My chest tightened and I struggled for air. I stepped back, closed my eyes, and drew in a long breath. "I'm not sure I can."

Ray took the radio from his belt. "Bjørn," he said. "Call the men back. I'm not going home empty-handed."

CHAPTER 20

The boat changed direction. The high-pitched hum of the speedboats echoed in the distance. They'd drop more bombs in the water. They'd push the whales back into the nets. This was happening. Again.

Something inside me snapped. I'd be damned if he was going to kill another whale. I needed to stop this insanity and get to Dalton. But how? *Think!*

Ray headed for the bridge to run the winch. Michael turned to work the nets.

I looked up and down the length of the winch. It was the key. If I could disable it, he'd have nothing. "Stay with her," I said to Dylan. "Keep her wet."

"But oi tart yer said—"

"Just do it, okay." I didn't need Dylan giving me away.

I sneaked around the backside of the winch, hiding from Michael's view. As the net was drawn in, the winch turned, wrapping a cable around the drum. To let out the net, the drums turned in the opposite direction, unfurling the cable. If I could shove something in there as the nets were being deployed again, maybe I'd foul it. But what? I looked around the deck. What was strong enough, but couldn't be easily yanked back out? Something that would bind it up for good?

I crossed the deck as we bounced through the waves. There must be something in one of the lazarettes. The extra floats maybe. If one got crushed in the drum, would it cause enough damage to make it inoperable? I sorted through the pile, trying to find anything.

The engine idled down. The winch started to turn. Michael had his back to me, guiding the nets into the water.

The wheelhouse door slammed and Ray came down the stairs toward me, his eyes on Michael and the nets. This was my chance. As he rushed by, I swiped his ankle with my foot. He stumbled forward, trying to catch his balance, and I pounced on his back, slamming him to the deck.

He rolled, wrenching his arm free, and grabbed me by the hair. Nothing pisses me off more than being grabbed by the hair. I brought up my knee and rammed him right in the crotch. He bent inward with a groan. "Bitch!" he managed.

I got to my knees, reached around and grabbed his ass, right on his duct-taped wound.

He howled in pain.

"This *bitch* is a trained federal agent," I said and brought my elbow down on his neck, knocking him out cold. I reached into his pocket and spun around, the revolver sighted on Michael. He still had his back to me, concentrating on his job.

I let out my breath.

Dylan peeked around the winch, his eyes wide.

"Help me tie him up," I said to Dylan, making sure I didn't take my eyes off Michael. "Grab that old piece of net. And that line."

Dylan obeyed, scurrying about like a puppy bringing me toys.

Once Dylan had Ray's hands tied, I moved to the back of the boat, to Michael. "Drop what you're doing and put your hands up where I can see them."

He looked over his shoulder at me and froze with his mouth open. So he hadn't suspected me of being an agent. His eyes flicked to Ray, then back to me, his expression turning from surprise to anger.

"I'm a federal officer," I said. "He's under arrest. And so are you. Put your hands where I can see them."

Michael looked to his father, then back to me. "Do you seriously think—"

"Your hands!"

He slowly raised his hands, but I got the sense it was to placate me, not a gesture of surrender. His lip curled up into a plastic smile. "It was only this one. Just one. To get back on our feet."

"And you have the right to remain silent," I said. "So do it." I didn't care what he had to say, the arrogant, lying son of a bitch. "Get over there and sit down," I told him, gesturing toward Ray. I gave Dylan an encouraging nod. "Tie him up, too."

With his narrowed eyes glued on me and the gun, Michael edged toward his father, but there was something about the way he moved, the way he carefully placed each footstep.

"Get down on the deck. Now," I said.

He stopped, eyeing me with disdain. "You gonna make me?" His voice had lowered an octave, the boyish charm vanished. "You think I'm an idiot? You got no authority to arrest me or my dad. This is a foreign country." Without taking his eyes from me, he said, "Dylan, untie him."

Poor Dylan. The boy bit down hard on his lip, his eyes flicking back and forth from me to Michael.

"She's not going to hurt you, Dylan," Michael said, his words dripping with hostility.

Dylan remained where he stood, frozen in place while I debated what the hell to do.

"Dammit, Dylan!" Michael shouted

Dylan lurched back with a start.

"What the hell?" It was Ray, coming to. He blinked a couple times, his eyes working to focus.

"Fine, I'll do it," Michael said to Dylan and turned toward his father.

I fired. The gunshot echoed across the water.

Michael jerked upright, surprise and uncertainty in his expression.

"Are you resisting arrest?" I said, aiming the weapon at his chest. "Because if you are, I've got just cause to shoot."

"Michael, sit down," said Ray. "She's all fluff. She's got nothing. It don't matter if she's an agent. It's still her word against ours."

Michael stared at his father, unsure.

"That fish was dead when we pulled it out of the water. We was just curious, was all. Ain't nobody gonna tell the difference." He was nodding, urging Michael to understand. "So just sit down and don't go making it worse."

Atta boy. Good old Ray.

Michael stared at me as if trying to decide whether to charge me, see if I'd follow through on my threat to shoot. Finally, he slumped to the floor beside his father, a scowl on his face. Dylan hurried to tie him up.

I checked both their wrists and told Dylan to also tie their ankles before I bounded up the stairs to the pilothouse.

Dalton and April were probably in the water by now, hypothermic—if they were still alive. I crashed through the doorway, the weapon held in front of me. "Turn this boat around," I demanded. "We need to go get them. Turn this boat around."

The two speedboats were circling the orcas. The airplane was back, flying low toward us. "Do it now!"

Bjørn held up one hand in surrender as he reached for the microphone for the radio with the other and shouted orders in Norwegian. The only word I recognized was Svein. One of the speedboats changed its course and headed for the *Sea Mist*. Bjørn turned to me. "He can get there much faster."

I motioned with the gun. "Still, turn this boat around, too."

"I can't. The nets are in the water."

I pointed at the winch controls. "Then get 'em back on

board."

Bjørn shook his head. "We can't without a man on deck. If the nets get tangled, we'd have to cut them loose."

"Fine," I said. "Dylan will do it."

"Svein'll have them in the boat before we could move. Don't worry."

My training would have me subdue Bjørn right now too, to be sure to neutralize any threat, but he was a Norwegian citizen. And he was cooperating. And my gut told me I could trust him. Right now, I needed him to stop this nightmare.

"Just the same," I said. "Get 'em in."

I hollered down the stairs for Dylan to bring in the nets. Bjørn worked the controls while the winch tick-tick-ticked. I swear I could've hauled them in faster by hand.

I found the binoculars. All I could do was watch out the back window, powerless to help Dalton. The speedboat slowed alongside a floating piece, what remained of the hull. Then something was hauled into the boat, but on the far side. I couldn't see anything. Then a figure stood up. It was April.

The boat was put into gear again, circling. *Dalton's there, too. He's got to be there. Somewhere.* My hands shook.

Then the boat slowed again and they were reaching for something. *Please let it be Dalton. Please.*

The crew of two hauled something up over the side. A man? Was it Dalton?

A seal bomb exploded in the water in front of the *Forseti*. I spun around. The whales flipped and turned in a panicked frenzy. *Dammit!* "Stop that right now!"

Bjørn held up his hand. "All right." He went to the radio.

I went back out on deck, tucked the weapon in the back of my jeans, and headed for the stern. The speedboat was pulling up alongside our vessel. I raced to the side. Besides the driver, two figures were on board, wool blankets wrapped around their shoulders. Dalton threw off the blanket and rose to toss a line to Dylan. My legs went weak. He was alive. *Alive!* I gripped the side of the boat, my whole body shaking with relief.

"Are you all right?" I shouted over the engine.

Dalton nodded. April looked shaken, but she was alive. Wet strands of hair stuck to the side of her face, her lips drained of color. Dylan helped her onto the *Forseti*.

"He saved my life," she said, shivering. "I've never seen anything like it. He was calm as could be."

Dalton stepped aboard behind her. I barreled into him, my arms wrapped around his shoulders. "You're all right," I cried. "You're all right." I squeezed until I was sure he was real.

"I don't know what I would have done," April said, gazing at him as if he wore a cape and tights. "Suddenly, out of nowhere, kaboom, and the whole boat was on fire. It was…" She shook. "Dalton got it contained with the extinguishers, but then"—she squeezed her eyes shut—"the cabin starting filling with water."

"She's in shock, but I kept her out of the water until our rescue boat came," Dalton said, all business. "We got splashed then, but briefly. What happened here?"

Svein, the driver, was right behind Dalton. The informant. "Yeah, what's going on?" he asked.

I shook the man's hand. "Thank you for saving them, Svein."

He hesitated and I got the idea he didn't like that I knew his name. His buggy eyes darted about, looking for Ray, I assumed.

"It's all right." I gestured toward the men who were leaning against the bulkhead, their hands tied behind their backs. "They're in custody now. We owe you our thanks." *And I'm sorry I called you Potato Head.*

"Are you all right?" Dalton asked me.

"Yeah," I said with a reassuring smile. "After Ray fired on you, Michael pulled a weapon on me. But I subdued them."

He raised one eyebrow. "Subdued?"

I gave him a what-can-I-say shrug.

"Don't say nothing," Ray shouted to Svein.

Svein looked to me, then back toward Ray. "You're arresting them, then?" He moved toward Ray.

I followed, talking to his backside. "Yes, we have the evidence we need."

He stood with his arms crossed, looking down at Ray. "So he won't be coming back here? He's going to prison?"

"Yep."

"She's lying," Ray spat. "She's got nothing."

"Not true." I pointed to the crow's nest. "I've got video of the whole thing."

His eyes traveled to the crow's nest and back.

"It don't matter. You came under false pretenses."

"Bong. Wrong again," I said. "You invited me on board. And I am not required to identify myself as an agent thanks to Hoffa v. United States, 1966. Oh, and the videotape, that's admissible thanks to U.S. v. Wahchumwah, 2012."

Ray had his lips clamped together so tight I thought his head might blow off.

"You lying bitch!" Michael said and leapt to his feet and charged me. Somehow, he'd gotten his hands untied. He plowed into to me, knocking me off my feet. We slammed to the deck. Blew the wind right out of me. Then Dalton was there, lifting Michael off of me, Michael's arms flailing at him. It all happened so fast.

"I took you once, I'll do it again," Michael threatened him, his face red.

Dalton smirked. He looked to me as I got to my feet. "He needs a serious attitude adjustment."

"Well," I said, brushing myself off. "I think you deserve the honors."

Dalton shook his head. "Wouldn't be a fair contest."

"No, really," I said. "You took the fall and all."

"Both of you can shut up," said Michael, raising the gun and pointing it at me.

My hand went to my waistband. *Crap!*

Dalton lunged, knocking the gun from Michael's hand and slamming him to the floor. In an instant, Dalton had him pinned, bent over and moaning, his elbow twisted into an arm lock.

Svein picked up the gun.

"Nice move," I said to Dalton, shaking.

"Now apologize to the lady," Dalton said.

"Screw you," Michael spat.

Dalton twisted harder. "Nobody talks to Poppy like that."

Michael's face flushed red.

"Apologize"—he twisted harder—"or I'll demonstrate my—"

"I'm sorry. I'm sorry," he groaned.

Dalton let up and Dylan scurried forward, the rope in his hand.

Dalton tied Michael back up and shoved him to the floor. "Now stay," he said.

I took a quick glance around. April's eyes were wide, her mouth hanging open.

Svein looked annoyed more than anything. He stepped toward the fish hold. "What about the whale?"

"I..." My eyes met Dalton's. "I couldn't save her."

Dalton gazed back at me, his eyes filled with sympathy. I wanted to fall into his arms and cry my eyes out.

"What are you saying?" Svein said, holding me back from making a fool of myself.

"The capture was too traumatic. She didn't make it."

April pushed past me, rushing to the tank where the baby whale floated, motionless.

Dalton followed.

"There was nothing I could do," I said, my tongue stuck in my throat.

The airplane buzzed low overhead, blowing my hair around and into my face. "I told him to call them off!"

"I'm on it," Dylan volunteered and took the stairs two at a time.

The pod of whales appeared off the starboard side, emitting squeaky calls in their panic. We all rushed to the side of the boat. One of the killer whales surfaced and let out a wail like I'd never heard.

"That's K-12," April said. "The mother. That's the calf's mother."

From behind us came a tiny squeal in response. The baby. My eyes met Dalton's. "She's alive!"

CHAPTER 21

I spun around and raced back to the tank. "She's alive! She's alive!" Dylan, flying back down the stairs, grinned ear to ear and wrapped his arms around me.

"We need to get her back in the water," I said. "Get the winch cable. Get the winch cable!"

Dylan leaped into action.

I grabbed hold of the edge of the sling to hook it to the cable. "Dalton, help me with this."

April was there, taking hold of the other side.

I couldn't believe it. *She's alive!*

"Not so fast."

I whipped around.

Svein held the gun pointed at me. "Back off."

"What?" I shook my head in disbelief. "No. We need to get her back in the water."

"She's not going anywhere." He pointed the gun at Dalton, then back to me. "That's a million dollar whale, right there. Now step back."

I slowly lifted my hands into the air. "I don't understand. You're the one who called us here. You're the informant." *How did I not see that coming? I let him pick up the gun. He should just take my badge, too.*

"What's going on?" Bjørn hollered. He was coming down the stairs from the wheelhouse.

"Mind your business, old man," Svein called to him over his shoulder, his eyes on me and Dalton.

Dalton took a step away from me. Then another step. He was trying to cause Svein to split his attention, put him at a greater disadvantage.

"Americans. The world's policemen. Always sticking your noses where they don't belong. There was no doubt you'd come." He smirked and his cheeks puffed out like a baked potato. I wanted to poke him right in the eye with a fork. "Now do your job. Take those two thieves back to America." He gestured toward the speedboat. "Take them and go."

Dalton took another step. He was weighing the odds. If we were far enough apart and Svein fired the weapon, one or the other of us had a chance to take him down before he could turn and fire a second round.

"We're not going anywhere," I said, trying to keep his attention on me and away from Dalton.

Baby Kimmy wiggled and squealed for her mother.

"And you're not taking this whale."

Dalton shook his head. Subtle, but I saw it. He didn't want me to provoke Svein. Just keep his attention. But I meant it, dammit. I wasn't going anywhere until she was back in the water with her mother.

"You have no authority here," Svein said. "In fact, I'm quite sure you were told to go home, that you aren't welcome by the Norwegian government."

"How'd you know about that?"

He took a step forward, an amused grin on his spud face. "This is my land. My sea."

"That was your plan all along," I said. "Let Ray do the dirty work, then take the fall, while you took off with the whale and cashed in."

"I knew you were sharp." He winked his buggy, potato eye. "You go on home and throw them in jail and smile pretty when you get your award. The rest is none of your business." He turned toward Dalton and raised the gun in warning. "Don't make the mistake of underestimating me. Now step back."

Dalton did as he commanded, his hands in the air.

Thwack! Svein slumped to the floor. Bjørn stood behind him, a fire extinguisher in his hands, his eyes on the baby whale. "This isn't right," he said, shaking his head. "This isn't right."

Dalton and I pounced on Svein. Dylan was there with some rope to tie his hands.

Bjørn set down the extinguisher. "No respect. Men like him…" His eyes traveled to Ray. "And men like him. No respect."

Dalton took the rope from Dylan with a quick thanks and wrapped it around Svein's wrists.

I took Dylan by the arm. "Get that winch going."

"Roi on," he said.

April, Dalton, and I held up the sides of the sling while Bjørn clamped on the hook.

"Lift her up," he hollered up to Dylan in the wheelhouse.

The winch clanked into gear, the cable pulled taut, and it started to lift, then—snap! One of the ropes broke. Then—snap!—another.

"Down! Bring her back down!" Bjørn shouted.

The winch creaked to a halt.

"Dammit!" I looked at Dalton, anger burning in my belly. "I cut the ropes. I tried to ruin the harness, but Michael caught me. I didn't get it finished."

"Well, let's see what we can do to fix it," he said, his voice calm.

The baby squealed. The whales in the water squeaked and called back.

"That's a support call," said April. "I think they know we're trying to help."

"We need to hurry," I said.

Bjørn pointed to a bin. "The tool chest is there. Extra lines and net over here." He rushed to a lazarette.

While we went to work, April poured buckets of sea water on the orca baby, trying to keep her cool.

"This isn't going to work," Bjørn said, tangles of net in his hands.

"It has to," I said.

"There's plenty of net," said Dalton. "We can get something rigged pretty easily to hold her. But how do we make sure she can get out once we've lowered her into the water? What if she gets tangled in it?"

"Get it rigged. I'll worry about that," I said.

Bjørn and Dalton cut lengths of rope and net and we shoved it under the baby whale and secured it to the harness while she chirped to her mother.

"That should hold," Bjørn said. "But—"

"I got it," I said.

Dylan put the winch into motion and I crawled up the side of the holding tank, placed my feet on either side of the harness, and grabbed on tightly to the cable. I held out my hand to Dalton. "Give me your KA-BAR."

"Are you serious? That's your plan?"

"Gimme the knife!"

He shook his head, a frown on his face. "You don't know what those adult whales out there will do."

"You're right. I don't know."

"I'm telling you," said April. "They know we're trying to help."

"Yeah," Dalton turned on her. "What if you're wrong? We can't risk it."

"I'm not wrong." She held his gaze.

"Dalton, gimme the knife!"

His eyes flicked from her to me. "This is insane," he said as he pulled the knife from its sheath on his belt and handed it to me.

The winch arm turned and the whale and I swung sideways.

Bjørn hollered. "You should have a life jacket on."

"No time!"

Dalton watched, shaking his head, his hands on his hips.

We hung there, suspended over the water. The baby chittered away, her voice getting higher in pitch. The adult whales circled, popping up to get a look at us, slapping fins and calling with a haunting fervor.

The winch shuttered and clanked and the cable started to lower us.

As soon as we were a few feet from the surface, I began to saw at the net with the knife.

Killer whales circled, closer and closer. Heads popped up and submerged again, circling. Five, six, maybe more. I sawed and sawed.

One surfaced right next to us and splashed. The frigid water hit me in the face and soaked my hair. It took my breath away. I shuddered, trying to breathe again.

"Lift her up. Get her out of there!" Dalton yelled.

"No, I've almost got it!"

The net cut free and the baby started to roll out, but her pectoral fin got caught. I reached down into the water and shook it. She tugged against it, trying to get free, making it worse.

I yanked the net, slipping it around her fin. She arched her back, flipped her tail, and she was free. With her weight gone, the harness shifted. I couldn't stop it. I plunged into the sea.

My muscles seized. I gasped, my body jerking with the reflex. Frigid water entered my lungs. Which way was up? *Ice. Cold. Darkness.* Something rammed me, bubbles everywhere. I burst to the surface, gasping for air, water coming out of my nose, my lungs on fire.

I reached for the harness, but grasped nothing but air. All

was a blur, a blue blur, my eyes smacked with icy pain. There was nowhere, nothing. I sucked in, coughed. My breath gone. My lungs frozen still.

The water churned around me and I was under again, immersed in searing numbness, pressing in on me from all directions. *Blackness*. My arms wouldn't move, my legs felt gone. Air? Where? I had to break from this icy grip.

My body wouldn't respond. Too...cold. Sinking. Sinking. No! I wriggled, moved. Dalton!

Waves pushing me away, away from the boat. Too late. Too far. Gone.

Then something pushed, raising me from the depths. Whoosh. I burst into the air. Free.

Hands, grabbing, pulling me from the sea.

Dalton's hands.

CHAPTER 22

I couldn't stop shivering. My hands were numb and I couldn't feel my feet. Dalton wrapped his wool blanket around both of us and pressed me against him, trying to get me warm. "Good thing Dylan was quick on the crane. The whales were going after you."

"No, no," I said, my teeth chattering. "They were pushing me up." *Weren't they? Yes.* "They were trying to save me."

He put his hand on my forehead. "No, I got you out before they really realized—"

"No, I…I know," I said. *I felt it. They knew I meant no harm. They knew.*

"Well, you're all right now," he said, hugging me tighter.

"Good thing you weren't in there any longer. You're in danger of hypothermia as it is," Bjørn said. "Let's get you inside." He shooed us toward the door like sheep. "All of you."

April, Dalton, and I were ushered into the galley.

"No hot coffee. Warm some milk," he said to Dylan who rushed around the tiny galley, opening and closing cupboard doors. "Just lukewarm. And maybe some oatmeal."

Dylan found a saucepan, but Bjørn snatched it from his hand. "I'll get it. Run down below and get her some dry clothes."

Dylan shook his head, his face turning pink, as though poking around in my suitcase was a trespass he wouldn't commit.

"It's all right," I said. "Grab anything. I don't mind."

His eyes fluttered about before he disappeared down the ladder.

Dalton and I settled onto the bench next to the heater.

"Not long now," Bjørn said. "I called Kystvakt. They're on the way."

"What?" I asked, my mind in a fog.

"The Norwegian Coast Guard," Dalton said. He had his arm around me, rubbing my other arm, trying to get me warm. "To take those three into custody."

I tried to massage my throbbing temples, but my hands were still cramped up and numb. "The cold water must have froze my brain."

Bjørn plopped a cup of warm milk on the table in front of me. "There. That'll help you thaw."

I looked to Dalton. "But I know. They were trying to save me."

"All right," he said, smiling.

Dylan appeared with an armful of clothes. He dropped them into a pile on the bench, then stood staring, his hands shoved in his pockets, not knowing what to do next.

Dalton rose from the bench and handed him a corner of the blanket. "Hold this up," he said. "Give her some privacy while she gets changed."

I reached for a sweatshirt but my hand still wouldn't grip. "I don't know if I can."

Dalton handed me the sweatshirt, worry etched on his face. "You have to get out of those wet clothes."

"I'll help her," April said and she started yanking at my pant legs, then pulled my shirt up over my head. I felt like an oversized toddler. She gave me a sympathetic frown. "Undies, too, don't you think? You want to be all cozy and dry."

Dylan cleared his throat and shuffled his feet. The blanket billowed with the movement.

I nodded and shifted on the bench, hooked my thumb into the waistband of my panties and slid them off. She unhooked my bra for me. I'd never been overly modest, but somehow being undressed by Dalton's new girlfriend was too much.

"I've got it. I've got it," I heard myself saying.

"Sorry," she said, barely a whisper.

"I didn't mean…" I frowned. "Thank you."

She nodded in understanding, then bunched up the sweatshirt and pulled it down over my head. I poked my arms through and she snugged it down. She did the same with my sweatpants, yanking them up my damp legs, then stepped back. "All right guys, she's dressed," she said.

Dalton ripped the blanket from Dylan's hand and wrapped it around me so snugly it felt like a baby's swaddle.

He leaned me against his chest and rubbed my arms. "How's that?" he said. "Feeling better? Is the feeling coming back to your hands? Let me see them."

"You've got me wrapped up too tight."

He flushed, embarrassed, and loosened the blanket.

I held out my left hand and he took it between his and held it, gently rubbing.

April watched with a curious expression. "I guess I owe you an apology," she said.

Dalton and I glanced at each other. We weren't sure which one of us she was talking to.

"Whatever for?" I asked.

She blushed. "I didn't realize you were a couple."

I sat back, yanking my hand from Dalton's grasp. "Oh, we're not," I said, shaking my head.

"Yeah…right," said Dalton, his hands finding the tops of his thighs and clamping on. "We're partners, that's all."

April looked from me to Dalton and back, then turned to Bjørn who was setting a bowl of oatmeal on the table. He grinned and gave her a wink.

"No, really," I said.

She gave us a mollifying smile. "Well, you make a good team."

I shook my head. Not me. I'd been stubborn and impulsive and put her and Dalton in danger. I got lucky I didn't end up fish food. I'd underestimated Ray. I had every intention of bluffing him, but he'd have shot me on the spot and dumped my body overboard.

I looked down at my bracelet and gave it a twist.

"Your dad would be proud of you," said Dalton.

My eyes clamped onto his. "Why would you say that?"

He shrugged. "You've been thinking about him all week. And today is…"

Something in his expression gave him away, a fleeting sign of guilt, then it was gone.

"You pulled his file," I said. An accusation.

"I was curious, is all," he said, all innocent. "I didn't think it would bother you."

I glared at him. What business was it of his what had happened to my dad? "Well, it does."

Dalton turned away, saying nothing. The silence lingered. I glanced around the galley. Dylan wiped at the counter with no particular purpose. Bjørn examined his thumbnail and April suddenly found her shirtsleeve interesting.

My stomach clenched. I hated making people feel uncomfortable.

"I'll go make our calls," said Dalton and rose from the bench.

"I'll 'elp wi' de radio," said Dylan, scurrying after him.

April's eyes flicked to the window, then the door as it shut. "I need the ladies' room," she said with an uncomfortable smile, then escaped to the head.

Bjørn stared at me with a fatherly expression. "Touchy subject, eh?"

I frowned and stared into my bowl of oatmeal.

He set his mug of coffee on the table and eased onto the bench across from me. "He cares about you, that boy. Good heart."

"He's my boss. I mean, my partner." I pushed a spoonful of oatmeal around in the bowl. "Whatever."

"Don't matter," he said. "The heart wants what the heart wants."

I said nothing. What could I say? And what the hell did he know about it anyway?

"I did know," he said. "What Ray was up to."

I raised my eyes to meet his.

"At first, I thought it was a fool's errand. And…" He stared into his coffee, then glanced around the galley, his eyes misty. "Well, I needed the money. This old boat…" He shook his head. "I had no idea he actually knew what he was doing. The other boats, the plane." He shook his head again. "I underestimated him."

Me too, I wanted to say. "Did you know about Svein?"

He rubbed his eyes and shook his head

"You helped me stop him. That's what I'm going to tell the authorities."

He examined me for a long moment with those sharp blue eyes, then gave me the slightest nod. "The Valkyrie," he said, almost a whisper. "She decides who lives and who dies."

"No," I said. "I believe, in the end, people get what they deserve."

The door to the head popped open and April came out. She hesitated. I smiled and she moved toward us and sat down. Dalton and Dylan tromped down the stairs and came back in.

"I've confirmed, the authorities are en route. Ten minutes out. And I called Joe. You're not going to believe what he said." He paused. "He wants us in Alaska."

"Are you serious?"

"You up for it?"

"Of course I'm up for it." I crossed my arms, suddenly feeling unsure. "But do you want me?"

The edge of his lip curved upward, ever so slightly. "Do you promise to stay out of the bars?"

"Funny," I said. "What's our directive in—oh, my video—"
I pushed from the bench "—we'd better make sure—"

"Hold on," said Dalton, his hand on my arm. "You're still recovering."

I brushed past him. "I want to be sure we've got 'em," I said, heading for the crow's nest.

"Poppy!" He was right behind me.

I took the stairs two at a time, then started up the pole.

"You could get dizzy. Let me get it." He was right behind me.

"I'm fine."

"Both hands. Hang on with both hands," he was saying as he followed me up the pole, ready to catch me if I fell.

I climbed right up, unclipped the camera with one hand, and crawled into the bucket.

"Are you crazy? Do you know how high up we are?" Dalton said as he flipped a leg over and squeezed into the bucket with me.

"There's not exactly room for two," I said.

"Just check the video," he grumbled.

I clicked through the menu and hit play. The tiny monitor showed a perfect angle on the deck. I hit fast forward and there it was, like a Hollywood box office hit, in full Technicolor, Ray and Michael hauling baby Kimmy out of the water and onto the deck.

I grinned at Dalton. "We got 'em."

"We got 'em," he said with a nod, holding my gaze.

For the longest moment, I stared into his eyes. "Listen, I'm…" I had to look away.

"We got 'em," he said again.

"Yeah, but…" I swallowed and turned back to face him. "I underestimated them. I put you and April in danger and—" I sucked in my breath. "I never should have asked you to—"

"I don't do anything I don't want to do."

"Yeah, but I need to be more—"

"Poppy, there are bad guys in the world. There always will be." He smiled at me. His tummy-tingling smile. "Don't ever let it change who you are."

Yep. My tummy tingled.

"And look at that," he said, pointing over my shoulder. I spun around. A killer whale breached with a big splash.

"I thought they'd be long gone."

"Look!" April shouted from the deck below.

The mother whale was splashing and twirling in the water. The baby frolicked on the crest of her wake.

April held her hands over her mouth. "You did it. You saved her. You saved baby Kimmy!"

Dalton put his arm around my shoulders and whispered in my ear, "We do make a good team."

This guy, I swear.

Author's Note

According to WDC, Whale and Dolphin Conservation, as of June 2015, in 14 marine parks in 8 different countries, there are:

- 56 orcas currently held in captivity (21 wild-captured plus 35 captive-born).
- 148 orcas have been taken into captivity from the wild since 1961.
- 161 orcas have died in captivity, not including 30 miscarried or still-born calves.

All for entertainment.

In 2013, seven wild orcas were captured by Russian fishermen in the Sea of Okhotsk for the mega-aquarium industry, the first caught in more than a decade. This is not a thing of the past.

Don't let the ads fool you. For every $1,000,000 SeaWorld makes, about $600 goes to conservation. That's 5 cents per ticket.

Please do NOT support them or any other marine park.

If you'd like to learn more and stay in touch, please sign up for my newsletter or follow my blog at www.PoppyMcVie.com

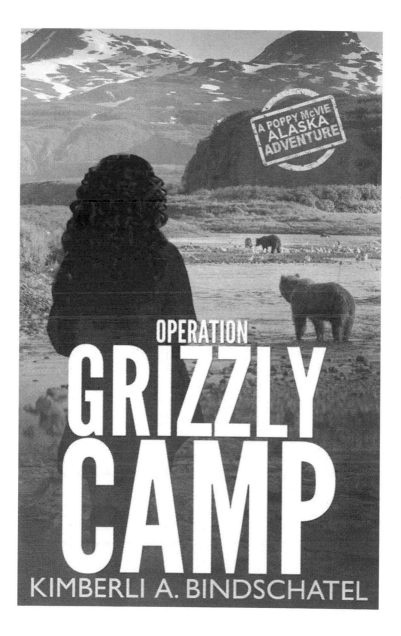

A POPPY McVIE
ALASKA
ADVENTURE

OPERATION
GRIZZLY
CAMP

KIMBERLI A. BINDSCHATEL

OPERATION
GRIZZLY
CAMP

KIMBERLI A. BINDSCHATEL

CHAPTER 1

Across the airport terminal, through the blur of hurried travelers between us, I caught sight of Dalton, facing the other way. There was no mistaking him, the way he fit in a pair of jeans. *Ooooh my*. He turned and saw me, waved me over with a smile, but as I approached I could tell by the way his eyes held mine that something was up.

Special Agent Dalton had been my partner now for nearly six months, but not without some fireworks between us. I'd learned that when he was in this mood, the best strategy was to take a deep breath and find my inner calm. I'd yet to be successful, but hey, a girl can try.

Our relationship had come a long way in a short time. I trusted him with my life. As an agent, he was top-notch. He was sharp, experienced, everything you'd want in a partner. The trouble was, he set me on fire—in more ways than one. I was still trying to figure out how I felt about him. I was pretty sure he had feelings for me. The problem was, with Dalton, well, it was complicated.

Despite our...I don't even know what to call it, we'd just had two successful ops and now, without so much as a two-day breather, we were heading to Alaska on a mission to catch a bear poacher who'd been eluding authorities for years. That's how things work out sometimes. Get 'em when the gettin's good.

I set down my duffel bag between us. "What is it?"

"Hey Poppy." He paused for a beat. "Alaska, here we come," he said with a forced grin.

"Seriously?" I planted my feet. "I know that look."

He hooked his thumb in his belt, looked down at his shoes.

"Oh my god, Dalton. Spit it out."

His eyes made their way back to meet mine. "Stan Martin called me yesterday."

"Stan Martin? As in the head of Special Ops, Stan Martin? Our boss?" *Crap. This can't be good.* "And?"

"He wants me to come in for an official interview—" his tongue stuck in the corner of his mouth for a moment "—an investigative hearing actually, on—" he stared at me "—on what happened during our op in Norway."

My brain started to swirl around inside my skull. "I don't understand. It was a clean bust."

"I know. I know." Dalton nodded, too much. "I'm sure it's all a formality. Politics, you know. Apparently Norway officials have been making a stink about it."

"Well, when does he want us to come in?"

Dalton managed a half-shrug.

My brain rattled. *Investigative hearing.* The roar of the airline passengers hustling past rose in my ears and suddenly made me feel dizzy. I sucked in some air. *Oh crap.* "It's about me."

Dalton held up a hand, a caution to stay calm. "I don't know that for sure."

"Of course you do." I blew out my breath. "What'd he say exactly?"

He looked away.

"C'mon."

"He might have mentioned that he's not sure you understand procedures, protocol, that kind of thing."

I held myself erect, forced calm. "I know I pushed the

envelope a little. Maybe taken it right to the edge." *Dammit.* "Okay, maybe a little over. But who doesn't? It was all legal. In the end. We nailed Ray Goldman, his most-wanted. We caught the bad guy and I'm proud of it."

"I know." He nodded some more. "It's just that, I think the thing is, you're still, technically, in probationary training and it's standard procedure to—"

I shook my head. "There's nothing standard about it. You said it's an investigative hearing. So stop sugar-coating it."

Dalton sighed, his shoulders slumped. "He used the words brazen, greenhorn, half-cocked, and—" he hesitated "—lone wolf."

I looked down at my hands and drew in a long breath to keep myself from exploding. My left hand turned white where my right one wrung the life out of it. "I don't understand. I nailed the guy and—" My jaw tensed when I realized what I'd said. "*We* nailed him." *Crap. This can't be happening.* "You were on board the whole time. You approved everything. We were in it together and—"

"Yes, I did." He gave me an encouraging smile. "Don't worry. I'm you're partner. I've got your back."

I let myself relax a little. In spite of all the things I was still unsure of with Dalton, I trusted him. He wouldn't lie to me.

"Well, what's going to happen? Will I be suspended?" I couldn't lose my job. It was everything. Everything I'd ever wanted. I'd worked hard to get where I was. And now it was at risk. Everything on the line. Because I was unorthodox, different, creative. Because I'd done it my way. Same old story.

Now I'd be summoned to the office of Stan Martin, head of Special Ops. My heart raced like a little rabbit being led into the cave of the fierce and almighty king-of-the-jungle.

"I don't know. But I told Martin I couldn't come in until after this op in Alaska is done. It's too important. That will give us some time to go over the details, make sure our report was solid, our stories match."

"All right." Now I was the one nodding like a bobble-head.

I picked up the duffle bag, ready to get out of here. I had things to think about, to sort out.

I looked to Dalton and pasted a smile on my face.

He eyed me, still tense. There was something else. I dropped the duffle. "There's more?"

His tongue went back to the same corner of his mouth. Then I realized: he only had one gun case. He was supposed to pick up firearms for both of us.

"Where's my gun?" I took a step back. "Don't tell me—" *No. No, no, no!* "I'm already suspended?"

"Huh?" He glanced down at the gun case he'd set on the floor. "No, I put them in one case. For weight. On the small plane later."

"Oh." I let out my breath. "Then what is it? You're killing me here."

He stared at me for a long moment, then seemed to come to a decision. "Are you ready for this op?"

"Ready? Of course I'm ready. I mean, I'm a little worried now, about the Martin thing but—why are you asking me that?"

"I just need to know, you know, if you're ready. I want to make sure, I mean, with everything going on, that you're up for it. That it's what you really want to do. You know, this kind of op, with all the ins and outs of it. I mean, it's a different kind of situation and—"

"Now you're babbling." *What the hell?*

"What?" He drew back, defensive. "I don't babble."

"You do. And you are. What's your point?"

He frowned, hands on his hips. Then he ran his fingers through his hair, the way he does when he's thinking, leaving it a little ruffled.

I melted a little. That hair. *Not the time. Focus.*

"It's a hunting trip. We're going hunting."

"I know that."

"But you've got to be able to play the part." His expression turned stern. "I know you're against hunting."

"I am not." *Well, not exactly.* "I think hunting is…well, most hunters. I mean…"

"Yeah?" Those eyes stared at me, waiting. Those ever-so-tempting, knock-me-flat eyes. The way he'd look at me sometimes—just a glance made my insides flutter. Downright embarrassing. *Focus!*

"I understand hunting for food. I get it. I don't like it, but I don't condemn it either. I—" *be honest* "—accept it. Honestly, if you're going to eat meat, hunting is more humane than factory farming and—"

"I know. I've heard you say it. Many times. But I'm not convinced. And it doesn't matter anyway, this op isn't about sustenance hunting. We're talking about *bear* hunting."

I pursed my lips together.

"Well?"

"Oh all right. It's abhorrent. To hunt a predator, just for the sake of killing, to brag about the conquest, make the hide into a fur rug to show off your prowess, or whatever reason people do it, it's barbaric. It's just plain murder."

"You see." He rocked back on his heels, crossed his arms. "That's exactly my point."

"But that's why we're going."

"That's *not* why we're going." He stepped closer, lowered his voice. "We're not going to bust bear hunters, Poppy. We're not activists with Greenpeace. We're federal agents and bear hunting is legal, whether you like it or not." He paused. "Our directive is to catch them poaching. There's a difference."

"I know there's a difference." *Under the law.* "And yes,

I have my issues with hunting. What's your point? Are you questioning my ability to do my job?"

He stared, blinked, then blinked again as if he were carefully choosing his next words. "I'm just thinking that maybe this is too personal."

I drew back, anger bubbling up. "Because of my dad?"

"I know this must—"

"Yes, he was killed by poachers. Yes, I'm angry about it. But that doesn't mean I can't do my job." I crossed my arms. "If you think I'm not qualified, fine. Or Joe thinks our cover is weak, fine. But my dad's file is confidential. You had no right to read it."

His eyes turned soft from…what? Guilt? Compassion?

He looked away, then back. "I was told to."

"By whom?"

He gave me the you-know-who frown.

I turned away. Of course my boss would know about it. I'm a federal agent. They'd done a full background check when I applied. But that didn't mean he had a right to show it to Dalton.

The file didn't give the full story. At best, it was a few, scant reports from the investigators, low-level government employees who'd arrived on the scene days after his murder. It was Africa. The politics of an American killed by poachers could get out of control, so justice didn't matter as much as keeping the peace.

My dad's murder was declared inconclusive, lacking evidence, likely an accident, though anyone who knew anything about the situation knew exactly who had killed him and why. The whole thing made my dad look like an idiot. It was a load of crap.

"That report was bullshit. My dad was murdered."

"No doubt," he said and meant it.

My resolve softened. I looked him in the eye. "I don't hate

poachers because a few killed my dad. I hate poachers because they poach."

He nodded in understanding.

"It's not going to affect my job. I swear it."

He held my gaze. "You say that but—" He shook his head.

"But what?" God, he was exasperating!

He leaned toward me. "What's rule number one when undercover?"

Eye roll. "Never break your cover."

"Right." His eyes narrowed. His tone turned dead serious. "Your cover is a trophy hunter and an unethical one at that. Not only do you need to cozy up to these men, you need to act like you actually like them. No doubt you can. But that's just the half of it. Much more important is when you're in the field, gun in your hand, with a bear in your sights, will you pull the trigger?" His eyes bored into me. "Because that's what we're doing. That's where we're going. That's the job. Are you ready for that?"

My teeth clenched together. "You don't need to tell me my job."

His eyes flared with frustration.

I stared right back at him. "You assume—" I paused, thinking for a beat. I needed to find the right words.

"I know that mind of yours. You're thinking of ways around it. You think you can outsmart them. And maybe you can. But right now, you're under the microscope. The head of Special Ops is watching. You. Me. And I'm only willing to go so far. I'm not going to lie to him. This is it, Poppy."

I set my jaw, reached down and picked up my duffel bag. "Well, you don't have to worry, *partner*. I'll do my job."

CHAPTER 2

I turned my back on Dalton as I slid into my large, cushy, first-class seat then gave him a little wave as he passed toward the back of the plane. "See you in Anchorage."

Having a best friend who's a flight attendant for the airlines comes in handy. He'd upgraded me. Actually, Chris was more like family. With my life changing so dramatically lately, being called to Special Ops, off to Costa Rica, then right away to Norway, I admit, I'd neglected him. I owed him a phone call, some time together. Yep, as soon as I got back from this op, I was going to schedule a couple days to see him. A big thank you dinner was in order. Maybe a bottle of his favorite Malbec.

I exhaled. *Dalton.* What was I going to do about Dalton?

And this thing at headquarters. Investigative hearing. What did that even mean anyway?

I leaned my head back and took a deep breath. Right now I needed to set all that aside and focus on the mission at hand: Operation Grizzly Camp.

We were heading to Alaska to rendevous with Joe Nash, our supervisor and Special Agent in Charge, on an op to catch a bear poacher he'd been courting for years, practically his entire career. The elusive Mark Townsend. The State boys had given up. This guy knew all of them by name and knew every loophole. He'd become untouchable. Part of the reason was he never took new clients. Well, almost never. Joe had found a way in: me. The guy liked the lady hunters, especially daughters. It ensured, in his mind, that the men weren't law enforcement. Having me on board was Joe's ticket. Of course I was thrilled to play along.

My cover was the daughter of a wealthy trophy-hunter (Joe, of course) from Oklahoma, land of tornadoes, rodeos, and bubblin' crude. Oil that is, black gold, the stuff that lines our pockets and funds our adventures. And adventures we shall have. We're out to collect every big game trophy on every continent. Daddy's building a wing on the house to display every one of them, so any time I want, I can relive the moment, the moment when that animal breathed its last breath, when I conquered it and could call it mine.

Egads. How do these people stand themselves? That was enough prepping. I didn't want to drive my head into a black hole of depression. I'd wing it when I got there.

I glanced around the first-class cabin, quickly assessing the other passengers. Some of the other hunters staying at the lodge we were headed to might be on this plane.

Directly behind me sat a man and woman with graying hair, wearing those oversized, square-lensed sunglasses on their heads, the kind that fit over regular glasses. The woman fondled a homemade, quilted handbag stuffed to the gills that rested in her lap. Definitely not hunters. Tourists, most likely, going to catch the train south to Seward to board one of the many monster-sized cruise ships that sailed the Inside Passage.

A flight attendant, whom I assumed was the purser since she'd already served a few drinks to other first-class passengers, came down the aisle, checking on passengers. She was a slim woman, her uniform perfectly pressed. Yep, she was in charge. "Your bag needs to fit down at your feet or go in an overhead compartment," she chirped as she passed by.

The woman shifted and moaned, trying to shove it below the seat.

"I told you not to bring all that crap," the man grumbled.

"Oh George, don't start with me."

"There's room in the overhead," I said, getting to my feet. "I'd be happy to put it up there for you."

"Oh, aren't you sweet," she said, trying to lift it over George to hand it to me.

George crossed his arms with a harumph as I took the bag and lifted it into the storage compartment. I gave him a big smile. See if a little sugar could melt that heart.

I made a quick scan of the other passengers before I sat back down in my seat. On the other side of the aisle, two men, also in the row behind me, looked like possibilities — morning stubble, camo baseball caps, flannel shirts. Once we were in the air, I would be able to hear them talking. I could even strike up a conversation with them. They couldn't have been five years older than me. A little flirting might do the trick.

The woman seated next to me, by the window, sat upright with the posture of a 1950s debutante and had the hairdo to match, all pinned and coiffed.

With my Oklahoma accent, which I'd been practicing for a couple weeks, I asked, "What takes you to Alaska today?"

A warm smile spread across her face. "Visiting my grandchildren. My son is in the service, stationed in Anchorage. And where are you going, my dear?"

"Oh, I'm heading out to the backcountry."

"Well, you be careful. There are bears everywhere, you know." She patted the back of my hand. "Make sure you wear bells on your shoes."

I stifled a grin. Someone, somewhere had come up with the notion that wearing little bells would scare bears away. No doubt some ambitious souvenir vendor. Sure, you wanted to make your presence known, avoid startling a wild animal, but little jingly bells tied to your shoelaces were more likely to arouse curiosity than to actually scare away a bear. Bells aren't terribly loud and the jingling is easily lost on the wind or amid the sounds of the forest. It's much more effective to use your own voice.

"I won't need any bells," I said with a grin. Then, loud enough for the men behind me to hear, "I'll have my Ruger 375 H&H Mag rifle. I'm taking me home a trophy."

Her face turned stone-like and her lips made a tiny pucker. *Yeah, I'm with you, Grandma.*

She slowly reached into the seat pocket, pulled out the in-flight magazine, and with a curt smile, turned her attention to it.

Well played, Grandma. Well played.

I turned in my seat, caught the eye of one of the hunters, and gave him a little you-get-it shrug.

He nodded and asked, "Where are you headed?"

The man seated next to him leaned in to hear my reply.

Gotcha. "A lodge near Katmai. Hunting bear." They both nodded, as if they knew where that was. "You?"

"North of Fairbanks," the one said. "We've got two more flights after this one."

I could see now, by their eyes, they were brothers. The one chattered on. "Bears are fun, but a bull moose in rut, whew-weee, now there's a beast to reckon with."

The other one chimed in. "What my brother means is, statistically, you're more likely to get attacked by a moose than a bear. Here in Alaska about ten people are wounded or killed by moose annually."

The woman behind me leaned over her husband to join the conversation. "Are you sayin' them moose is dangerous? I thought them were big deer. They's just grazers, ain't they?"

"They are," the first brother replied. "Deer that weigh fifteen-hundred pounds with spiked antlers that span six feet." He held his hands up in the air, spreading them wide. "A moose gets fired up in the rut, he'll plow down half the forest to get to you. If one comes after you, run like hell."

"A moose can outrun you though," the other brother added, his face full of life. They were all fired up.

"Yeah, you'll want to zigzag between big trees."

"Zigzag?" she said, incredulous.

He nodded. "Zig zag. They don't corner well. Kinda top heavy."

"So you're on a moose hunting trip, I take it?" I asked.

Their heads bobbed, grins taking over their faces. They were downright giddy.

The first brother's eyes lit up. "We've been planning this trip our whole lives. We can't wait to take one down."

I hid my dismay behind a cordial smile. These men's lifelong dream was to kill a living being. A beautiful, magnificent creature. To chop it down. Rather than be thoughtful, introspective, they were bouncing in their seats. I really wanted to slap some compassion into them. Instead, I did my job and stayed in character. "Boy, that sounds exciting. You been hunting your whole lives?"

"Yep," the first brother answered. "We own a family ranch in Texas." The other brother dug around in his pockets for his wallet while the first kept talking. "A game farm. Two hundred fifty acres."

The brother handed me a business card that read: Wilson's Hunting Ranch. Giraffes, Kangaroos, Deer & More! Native & Exotic. 40+ Species for Hunt. 100% Success Rate. Book a hunt today!

My mind stuck on the size of the ranch. Two hundred fifty acres. Hunting there, if you could call it that, would be like shooting fish in a barrel. These brothers sold canned hunts. Whatever animal the *hunter* wanted they'd release from a cage into a small fenced area, so it could be shot on the spot.

I looked up at them, lost for words. Their whole lives

revolved around killing. I could hardly stomach any more. "Well, good luck," I said and started to turn around in my seat when I saw Chris, zipping down the aisle toward me from the back of the plane. I didn't know he'd actually be on the flight. A smile spread across my face.

He gave me a wink. *Crap*. My eyes went right to the hunters. I had to be careful. "I need your seat belts buckled," Chris said as he blew through. I couldn't believe it. He'd rearranged his schedule to be on my flight.

The man behind me gave his wife a look of disgust. "Of all the stewardesses in the world, we get this candyass," he said aloud while he took his sweet time fastening his seatbelt.

His wife's cheeks turned pink and her eyes dropped to her hands.

Asshole. I swung around and faced forward. Chris dealt with bigotry all the time, and always with class, it was one of the things I admired about him, but it got my cockles up. I tried to push it out of my mind. And the hunters and their lust for killing. What was it with this world?

I pulled out the in-flight magazine and stared at the pages, not reading a word. *Focus on the op*. Mark Townsend was his name. And we were going to nail him.

So sit back and enjoy the flight.

The aircraft pushed back from the gate. We were headed north.

No matter how many times I fly, I still love that sensation when the plane goes racing down the runway, the landing gear rattling and shaking, as the sheer power of the jet engines thrusts me back into my seat. Then there's that moment, that tiny, precious moment, when the wheels leave the ground and I'm airborne. Defying gravity. Freedom.

As we climbed and climbed, I leaned over to see out the window. All I saw, for miles and miles, was a landscape sectioned off in green and brown squares, with lines and lines of concrete roads, crisscrossing in intricate patterns. Amazing how we've carved and shaped and formed the earth to fit our needs. No part of this world has gone untouched, unaltered. I fear we'll regret it someday when all the animals are gone, and the ecosystems are damaged beyond repair, ecosystems we rely on more than we can possibly comprehend.

Over billions of years, the earth has come to a beautiful ecological balance, one where humans have thrived. Mess with it too much and we won't. Simple as that. Why doesn't everyone see what we're doing to this world?

Once the captain turned off the seatbelt sign, Chris came to my seat. "The purser would like to speak with you. Would you follow me?"

"Sure," I said with a shrug.

He led me to the galley area up front, just behind the cockpit and hidden from the view of most of the passengers.

"This is a full flight," he whispered. "I had to do some serious negotiating to get you in first-class."

I wrapped my arms around him in a big hug. I didn't realize until now how much I'd missed him. "Thanks, you know I appreciate it, but why didn't you tell me you were going to be on the flight?"

"I wanted to surprise you. I've never been to Anchorage and we haven't seen each other in forever and you've been so distracted and—"

"Oh Chris." I hugged him again then lowered my voice, "Just remember, I'm undercover and I—"

"I know. I know. I just—we haven't talked in a long time." He paused, drew in a breath. "You know, talked."

"What? We talk all the time on the phone."

"Yeah, but, well, you talk, but I just really, you know." He sighed. "It's just that I have something I've been wanting to tell you. In person."

"What? What's happened? Are you okay?"

He chewed on his bottom lip. "I guess I didn't think this through."

"Now you have me worried. What is it?"

He frowned. "Everything is great. I promise. It's good news." He stared at me for a moment with an intensity I hadn't seen for a long time, then shook his head. "I shouldn't have come. You're undercover right now. It can wait until after you get back."

"Are you sure? Because I can—"

"No, really. How long will you be gone?"

"Two weeks."

"Perfect." He smiled, satisfied. "We'll plan to get together then. You'll take a few days off, right? Promise me."

"Absolutely."

"Not some quick layover lunch. Mexico. For a real, honest-to-goodness va-cay. You need to take a deep breath and I need a long-deserved break. Beach, cocktails, sunshine. You got me?"

I nodded. "I can't wait." I gave him a kiss on the cheek, then started back toward my seat, but turned around. I had to know. "One little hint?"

"It's all right. Honestly. It can wait." A grin creeped across his face. "But I almost forgot. I got you something." He pulled a bag from a galley cabinet and handed it to me.

Inside was a jacket. Pink camouflage. "You didn't!" I grinned.

"I did." He snickered. "I couldn't resist."

"This is god-awful tacky."

He tried to contain a full-out giggle. "It's perfect."

A smirk came to my lips. "You're bad."

"I know."

I put it on. Snuggly fleece.

"I got you something else," he said. From his pocket, he handed me a tiny box.

"What is this?"

"Open it," he said. "And hurry up. I've actually got to work on this flight."

"I mean, what's it for? It's not my birthday or anything."

"I just"—he shrugged—"wanted you to have it."

Inside the box was a silver chain with a pendant—a tiny compass.

"To help you find your way," he said, his eyes all moist, which got my eyes all moist. *Oh Chris.* "I mean, I know it doesn't actually work—"

"I love it."

"It's just that you've been, well..."

Suddenly my throat stuck shut. "Oh god, Chris, what am I going to do if I get fired?"

"What?" He jerked backward. "What are you talking about?" His eyes softened. "Oh my god, you're serious. What's happened?"

I shook my head. "I can't talk about it right now."

"Whoa, whoa, whoa. Wait a minute. Dalton's probably just gotten a little hot under the collar. I'm sure if you talk to him—"

"Not Dalton." I puckered. "Stan Martin. Head of Special Ops."

"Head of—what the hell? Poppy! What did you do?"

"Nothing!"

He gave me that look.

"Dalton got called for an investigative hearing on our op in Norway. They're investigating me."

His hand went to cover his mouth. "Oh shit, girl. That ain't good."

"Dalton says not to worry, it's all politics, but—" I clamped my lips together. "If I make one mistake, one bad move, one slip on this op with Joe, it's all over."

"Okay, now I'm confused. I thought you said the *head* of

Special Ops. Joe's your boss. But isn't he Joe's boss?"

"Well, yeah, but that's not the point. I mean, it's Joe's op, so—I just need to—"

"You need to take a deep breath." He pulled me to him, wrapped his arms around me. "It'll be okay. Trust Dalton. I'm sure he's right. If this Martin guy is the head of the department, he's getting his ass chewed about something and he's got to pass it down the line. It'll probably blow over."

"I don't know. He's summoned Dalton for an interview and I don't know if he'll—"

Chris pulled away to look me in the eye. "Dalton's a lot of things, but he's no snitch. He'll stand up for you."

I nodded. "I know. You're right. You're always right. But it's just that…"

"Just what?"

"He knows about my dad. He's questioning whether I can do my job because of it."

Chris took hold of me by the shoulders. "You're the strongest woman I know. And the smartest. What happened to your dad has no bearing on that."

I managed a smile.

He took the necklace from the box, held it around my neck, and hooked the clasp.

I fingered the tiny compass, trying to find words. I looked into his eyes and was sure that he knew that I would lose it if I stood there any longer. "I should get back to my seat."

He nodded. "I need to get to the back and set up the cart service."

He shoved the empty shopping bag into the cabinet. As he turned, I thrust my arms around him again. "I love you."

"Me too," he said as he nudged my chin with his, just like my dad used to do. It made me smile and relax a little. "Everything's going to be okay. So don't go getting all sappy on me now. You're a big, bad hunter. Let's go."

I grinned and headed back to my seat, Chris right behind me. The old lady saw me coming and looked away. As I turned to slide into the seat, I noticed the man behind my seat's eyes fixed on Chris. I lingered, standing in front of my seat, as Chris passed me.

The man put out his arm to block his way. "I want another Jack and Coke."

Chris smiled his hospitality smile and said, "I'll let the purser know, sir," then tried to continue down the aisle, but the man grabbed him by the arm.

"You can get it for me. You're a stewardess, ain't ya?"

My pulse rate shot into the stratosphere.

Chris calmly responded over his shoulder. "The purser takes care of first-class. She'd be happy to get your drink. I'll let her know right away."

The man yanked Chris's arm, pulling him backward. "You'll do it now, fag."

I brain caught on fire. "Hey, hands off, mister!"

The man scowled and started to rise from the seat but got caught by the seatbelt. His face flushed red. He flicked the buckle open. "How dare you, girl," he growled, rising from his seat with surprising strength. He still had a grip on Chris's arm, tugging him.

I pushed into the aisle, chopped at the asshole's wrist with my forearm, breaking his grip on Chris. I latched on and twisted his arm back into an arm bar. "I said hands off." His face turned beet red.

Chris had his hands in the air. "It's all right. No harm done. Let him go."

I twisted harder. The man clenched his teeth and glared at me.

"Now say you're sorry," I hissed.

He lifted his free hand as though to slap me across the face, but the two hunters were on their feet behind me.

"The lady's right," the one brother said. "You were out of line there, Mister."

The man hesitated before easing back into his seat, his eyes on the brothers.

The brother nodded toward my hands where I still had the man's arm pinned back. "I think you've made your point."

I released my grip.

The purser appeared behind me, all perky smiles. "Everything all right here?"

The other brother piped up. "This man was choking on a pretzel, but he's fine now."

With a suspicious nod, the purser slowly turned before heading back to the front of the plane.

"Thank you," I whispered to the brother, filled with shame for how I'd judged him before.

Dalton came up behind Chris. "What the hell's going on, Sis?"

Shit.

"I'll get your drink right away, sir," Chris said. He turned to me, glaring. "Would you kindly get back in your seat?"

I glanced around the cabin. Everyone was silent, staring.

Dalton pushed past Chris and hustled me toward the front of the plane to the galley. "What the hell is wrong with you?"

"I...I just—"

He shook his head. "You just what? Dammit, Poppy."

I held up my hands. "I know. I know."

"What the hell were you thinking?"

"Nothing. I wasn't. I just, he was harassing Chris." I leaned closer and said through clenched teeth, "He called him a fag."

He spun around, hands on his hips. "Is that all? Do you not understand what it means to be undercover?"

"Yes, and I don't need a lecture."

"Apparently you do."

Chris poked his head around the corner. "What the hell, Poppy? Are you trying to get me fired?"

"What? No. Why would—"

"I got you in first-class. Under my company ID! You know the rules, the code of conduct."

Shit.

Chris flung open a drawer, mixed the Jack and Coke, then stomped off.

Dalton looked me up and down, shaking his head. "You'd better get your shit together."

Four and a half hours later, my nose dry and tongue like sandpaper, the plane banked right and started to descend. Chris hadn't said another word to me the entire flight. I owed him an apology, big time. Dalton was right. I did need to get my shit together, like he said, as clichéd as that might be. It was one thing to have my own job on the line for my impulsive behavior, but I'd put Chris's at risk too—oh, what was I thinking?

And Dalton. He'd just warned me about this very thing. I'd probably ruined any chance of us being able to work together again. That is, if I still had a job after this op. Maybe it wouldn't matter anyway.

I was tempted to start belting down some Jack and Cokes myself.

The plane banked again and we leveled off for the approach to the Ted Stevens Anchorage International Airport, the third-busiest cargo traffic airport in the world. Snow-capped mountains spread out forever in several directions. Cook Inlet provided a dazzling reflection of the Anchorage skyline, a metropolis the size of Delaware with a population exceeding 400,000, right smack in the middle of pristine, unending wilderness.

One of the many advantages of flying first-class is not having to wait for everyone else to deplane. Once on the ground and the door opened, I grabbed my duffle and bolted.

At the end of the jetbridge, I spotted a Cinnabon and figured standing in line there was the perfect place to watch for the man and his wife, see if he made a complaint to the airline agent greeting passengers as they filed past. Besides, I was in the mood for some sugar therapy.

I watched the couple as they stopped to catch their breath after huffing up the jetway then passed by the agent and headed toward the bathroom. Maybe I'd get lucky and that was the end of it.

Dalton sauntered up to me looking like he'd just woke from a refreshing nap. *SEALs*.

"Well, look at you. As fresh as a daisy," I said.

"Am I?" he said, looking down at his shirt. "And I wasn't the one in first class."

"Yeah, well." I frowned.

His eyes fixed on the Cinnabon case. "Seriously?"

"I thought it was a good place to keep a lookout." I made a subtle nod toward the jetway. "See if he files a complaint."

"Yeah? And what will you do if he does?"

I shrugged. I had no answer.

"You don't have to make an excuse if you want a cinnamon bun."

"Look what I'm wearing." I tugged at the pink camouflage.

He grinned. "It suits you."

"Funny." I smirked. "Anyone who'd seriously wear this would beeline for a Cinnabon."

"Uh huh."

"Really. It fits my cover."

"Yep." His lip curved up at the edge. His half-grin, I called it. Irresistible.

"You're so aggravating."

"If you say so."

I gritted my teeth. He was. Aggravating, that is. At least he was talking to me now.

Once I had downed half that bun of oozy, gooey sweetness, my stomach did a barrel roll in objection. I puffed out my cheeks, feeling stuffed.

Dalton shook his head. "Shall we get our baggage now?"

"You still here?"

I spun around. It was Chris. His eyes dropped to the remains of the Cinnabun in my hand.

"I'm sorry, Chris. I don't know what I was thinking." I held out the bun to him. An offering.

"Do you think a Cinnabun is going to fix it?" He glared at me, hands on his hips.

"No." I hung my head. "Do you think he'll—"

"I doubt it," he said as he snatched the bun from my hand and tore off a bite. "I kept serving him Double Jack and Cokes. I don't think he's in the mood to make a complaint. Besides, I don't think his wife was very happy with him either."

I nodded and stood there in the uncomfortable silence.

Chris held out his hand to Dalton. "I'm Chris, by the way. We haven't been formally introduced."

"Oh, I'm sorry," I said with a quick look around to make sure no one was within earshot. "This is my partner, Special Agent—" I paused for emphasis "—G. Dalton. Yep, you heard me. I don't actually know his first name."

Dalton gave me the tiniest smirk. "Just Dalton," he said to Chris.

Somehow, without my noticing during the introductions, the three of us had started walking. Chris chattered on about air travel or something. My head was lost in a sugar haze.

Near baggage claim, Chris stopped in front of a giant glass-encased grizzly bear. The animals stood on its hind legs, its mouth forced into a permanent roar. "Holy shit! Are they really that big? That thing's ferocious."

"It's a world record take," Dalton said. "Bigger than most."

"Yeah, but still." Chris shuddered. "You're going to be out there in the wilderness with those? What if one decides you'd be a tasty lunch?"

Dalton eyed Chris, shaking his head. "Don't worry, I'll be with her the whole time."

What was it with these two? "I can take care of myself."

Dalton went on as if I hadn't said anything. "The thing about bears is, if they do charge, it's often a bluff. Eight times out of ten. The key is to never run."

"A bear comes after me, my skinny ass is outta there."

"Not if you want to survive," Dalton told him. "If you run, you'll incite the bear to chase. They can sprint thirty-five miles per hour." He grinned. "I don't think you can hit forty."

I added. "Dalton's right. But generally you don't have to worry. They're the ultimate predator, yes, but their diet mostly consists of roots and grasses, berries and nuts, and salmon in the fall."

"Define *mostly*," Chris said, deadpan.

"I'm just saying. They're not the ferocious killers people make them out to be. They're really fascinating, actually. Did you know that a bear's sense of smell is seven times more powerful than a bloodhound's?"

Dalton tapped on the glass case, pointing to a plaque inside. "Look here." It read: World record Kodiak Brown bear (*ursus arctos middendorffi*) Skull score - 30 10/16 inches, harvested on April 20, 1997.

"Harvested?" Chris said, eyebrows raised.

I rolled my eyes. "Like a field of wheat." I leaned toward Chris. "The poor bear was probably snoozing when he shot it. Then it gets mounted in that heinous pose."

Dalton gave me a look.

I frowned. *I know.*

I stared up at the bear, into his glass eyes, and imagined meeting his real gaze in the wild. This beautiful creature once lived, breathed, walked the woods in all his majesty. Digging for clams with those six inch claws. And those teeth. Ripping a spawning salmon apart for the roe.

"I don't understand it," Chris said.

"Don't understand what?" Dalton asked.

"Bear hunting. I mean, I get wanting to feed your family, all that. But to go after a bear like that? Look at the size of that monster. His teeth. Those claws."

"It's a testosterone thing," Dalton said.

Chris turned to me, eyebrows raised in his playful way. "Is that supposed to be an insult?"

"No, nope, uh uh," Dalton stuttered. "Not at all."

"He means it makes them feel manly," I said. "Killing something. Something powerful."

"Yeah? Then why would a twenty-four year old girl want to hunt one?"

"Yeah, Poppy," Dalton said, glancing around. "You got that one figured out yet?"

I did. Those hours on the plane had given me time to think, to sort some things out. I winked. "It's an adrenaline rush, the thrill of the hunt."

"Now that sounds like you," Chris said and turned to go. "Remember, you owe me. A real vacation in Mexico."

I nodded. Did that mean he'd forgiven me? "I promise. The moment I get back."

His smile turned serious. "Be careful out there. With a beast that powerful," he said, gesturing toward the bear, "you can't be sure who's the hunter and who's the hunted."

CHAPTER 3

Dalton and I got our luggage and walked from the airport terminal, across the road, to the Lake Hood Seaplane Base, where we were to meet our pilot for our floatplane trip to the lodge. Snow-covered mountains and a crisp, blue sky filled with white, puffy clouds made a backdrop for the series of water channels that served as tarmac and runways for this, the busiest seaplane airport in the world. Orange, red, and yellow planes—hundreds of them—lined the side channels, some pulled right up on shore, a few tethered to moorings, all ready to go at a moment's notice. I'd never seen so many small aircraft in one place.

There was no terminal. Just a tiny wood shack next to the dock where the plane was moored. Joe had flown on a different commercial flight and planned to meet up with us there. As we waited, we watched other planes take off every few minutes, their pontoons slapping over the water and throwing spray into the wind.

On my first assignment with Agent Dalton in Costa Rica, Joe had played a rich exotic pet collector, complete with a penchant for expensive cigars and twenty-year-old scotch. Now he was my rich daddy, an oil tycoon intent on taking home a trophy. No doubt, scotch and cigars would play a role this time too.

With his seniority, when he got an op approved, he had a

decent budget to go with it. And boy, did he know how to do it up. When he strolled up to us, he looked the epitome of the part, like he was modeling for the Kuiu huntsmen catalog, with a Tilley waxed-canvas outback hat topping off the ensemble.

"Hi Daddy!" I shouted and gave him a big hug.

"How was your flight, sweetheart?" he asked.

"Long," I said. "I'm so excited to get out there."

I wasn't lying. I was excited.

"Son," he said to Dalton with a fatherly nod.

A man appeared from behind us on the path. "Mr. Pratt, are we ready to head out?"

Joe spun around. "Well, you must be Mr. Townsend. Pleasure to meet you."

The man nodded, shook Joe's hand.

He wasn't at all what I'd expected. Mark Townsend, big-time poacher, the target of our investigation, was a gangly, thin man with a scruffy beard, kind eyes and a wad of chewing tobacco tucked in the side of his bottom lip. "Ma'am," he said to me as he opened the door to the tiny shed. Inside was a large cargo scale. "Put all your bags on there," he said to Dalton.

Once he jotted down the weight, he looked to me with a sheepish expression. "Now I need yours."

"My what?" I asked. I knew what he meant, but I wasn't sure a spoiled college student from Oklahoma would.

"Your weight." He looked to Joe, then Dalton. "All of you."

"Well, I'll be," I said and stepped onto the scale with a frown.

Mark gave me a tolerant grin.

After everyone and all our stuff was weighed and Mark was satisfied, we followed him onto the dock and loaded the plane—a de Havilland Beaver, the workhorse of the Alaskan bush. Bright yellow, her big floats level on top to walk on, she looked like an oversized bathtub toy.

"I want to ride up front, Daddy. Can I ride up front?"

"As long as it's all right with the pilot, sweetheart."

Mark shrugged.

Joe and Dalton squeezed into the tiny backseat and I got into the front passenger seat, opposite Mark, and pulled the door shut, ready to go.

Fascinating how a hunk of metal like this, probably five-thousand pounds, with what I guessed to be a fifty-foot wingspan, could lift off and fly. A commercial jet airliner had enough power to force it into the air. But these little planes were all about aerodynamics, weight versus lift, rudder trim, flaps, all that coming together. I'd always wanted to learn how to fly one.

The dash was a hodgepodge of levers and switches, gauges and buttons, each controlling some small, but no doubt vital part of the equation. On my side, as well as Mark's, there was a yoke and foot pedals. I grabbed the steering apparatus and said, "Hey, I guess I'm the co-pilot, huh?"

Mark's eyes locked on mine. He paused, shifted the lump of chew from one side of his mouth to the other with his tongue before saying, "Don't touch anything."

Here's the thing. What if Mark had a heart attack or choked on his Beech-nut? My life was literally in his hands. At a minimum, I wanted to know how to put this bird back down on the ground. Or at least how to use the radio to call for help. Did that make me a control freak? Or a take-charge kind of person? How about brazen? Half-cocked?

I didn't know what Mr. Martin expected of me. Shouldn't an undercover agent have those qualities? Be a take-charge, grab-the-bull-by-the-horns kind of person?

Trust your team, Dalton would say. Rely on your partner. In this case, trust the expert. But was Townsend the kind of person who'd crumple under stress? What if we hit a flock of birds? What if the engines stalled? Was I supposed to sit back and do nothing? Go down with the plane shouting "See, I'm a good follower!"

Screw that. Mark might not want a co-pilot, but he was getting one.

I glanced around the dash, getting acquainted with what was where. Anything I recognized that is. A GPS locator was mounted in the left corner. The map pocket in my door had an operation manual. That was good.

Mark strapped on his seatbelt. I found mine and clicked it into place. He didn't check to make sure I had my door shut tight, nor did he mention the location of the life vests. Cowboy-type. Good to know.

He flipped a red switch on the dash.

"What's that?" I asked.

He paused, raised one eyebrow, but gave no answer. So that's how it was going to be.

One thing I did know about bush planes: everything is manually operated. With many parts, many things can break or go wrong. In the bush, you want solid components, easy to repair in remote areas with tools that are typically available. No fancy, complicated electronics here.

He handed me a headset, then turned to the guys in the back and motioned for them to put theirs on as well.

Next to his seat, on the left, he pumped a lever or something that made a whoosh, whoosh noise as he pumped, while he simultaneously worked a lever, up and down, on the center console down by his right foot. None of the controls had labels.

"What's that?" I tried again.

He gave me a half grin. "Wobble pump."

"Wobble?" *Very funny.*

More knobs were pushed and levers moved, one labeled throttle, at least that made sense, and the engine turned over and the propeller started spinning.

"Woohoo!" I said. "Let's get going."

Without looking at me, Mark said, "It takes about ten minutes to warm up." He tapped a gauge. "Need forty degrees oil pressure temp, one hundred degrees cylinder head temp."

The plane rattled and shook.

Mark clicked a button on the yoke and started talking on the radio to the control tower. The only part I understood was "requesting departure." He eased the throttle lever forward and as the plane started to move, he pumped a lever on the floor, then some other lever on the dash. He fiddled with some tiny wheels on the ceiling. I was starting to think none of them did anything. Maybe he just had a nervous twitch. Then his eyes met mine. "You ready?" he said with an amused grin.

I nodded.

He reached over and stroked a ragged old rabbit's foot that hung on a tarnished chain from the throttle lever.

Really? Part of a dead animal? *Figures.* "For good luck?" I said.

He grinned. "Out here, you're at the mercy of the wilderness. Sometimes, all you've got is luck."

He pushed the throttle lever all the way forward, the engine roared, and we moved across the water, the floats gliding beneath us. In moments, we were airborne, leaving me wondering how it was possible. We weren't going fast enough to lift a plane into the air. I could have been waterskiing back there. But we were in the air nonetheless.

As soon as we cleared the treetops, Mark turned and winked at me. "You're good luck." He gestured toward the north. "The mountain. She's showing her face today."

I turned. Denali's powerful peaks dominated the horizon, towering over the Alaska Range, dwarfing the surrounding mountains, most of which were as tall as the highest in the Rockies of the lower forty-eight. No wonder its Athabaskan name meant "the Great One."

"Up here, we call it Denali. Crazy bastards come from around the globe to try to climb to the top," Mark said, his voice crackling through the old headset. "It's the fourth highest peak in the world, but I'm told it has the appeal of the highest base-to-summit elevation of any mountain on Earth, rising 18,000 feet from its base. Everest is only a 12,000-foot-climb from its base."

"Really?" I said. "I had no idea."

Mark nodded. "She makes her own weather. The mountain has such mass, she sucks moisture from the Bering Sea and the Gulf of Alaska, stirring up storms year round. Winds average eighty miles per hour on the slope. Add the extreme weather conditions of this arctic climate, which makes for thinner air and a summit temperature commonly at forty degrees below zero." He shook his head. "Not the way I want to meet my maker."

I agreed.

He banked the plane south, along the edge of the Cook Inlet. We were heading for the Alaska peninsula, to a lodge tucked in somewhere near the edge of the Katmai National Park and Preserve.

Below, for miles and miles, vast swaths of nothing but green and white and blue stretched across the landscape. No man-made squares here.

Glacier-covered peaks along the shoreline, dotted with alpine lakes, offered streams that meandered downward, through the patchwork of green, toward the satiny blue sea. Beautiful, untouched, the way it was meant to be. Alaska was truly the last frontier. I held my breath, taking it in.

I glanced at Dalton. He had his head back, sound asleep. I suppose it's the SEAL training. Get sleep when you can. I eased into my seat and closed my eyes. Nope. I sat upright. Too much to see. I leaned on the glass window, so I could see as straight down below us as possible. The sun shimmered off the water, reminding me of a dazzling dinner gown.

After a while, I turned my attention back to Mark. Getting him talking about the hunt might give me some useful information.

"So, we're doing a fly-in hunt, but we'll have a guide, right?" I asked.

"For sure. We'll see how the groups sort out. I've got more than one hunting party at the lodge this week. Full house."

Excellent. We wanted to be put with other hunters, to witness the poaching act. The issue was that most wealthy trophy hunters wanted to hunt one-on-one with a guide. We had to walk the line. Act like we wanted a one-on-one, but then compromise to be put with others.

"But I was promised the best trophy opportunity there is. My daddy said—"

"Don't you worry about that. You'll get the hunt you want. I guarantee it."

Good start.

His guide service was absolutely legit, on the surface. Joe had booked a legal hunt, applied for licenses, et cetera, but he had long suspected Townsend of taking hunters inside the boundaries of the refuge or luring the record-sized bears out, which is illegal.

Townsend had proved to be sly over the years. No doubt, he'd have done his homework before taking us on as clients. Joe had painstakingly created backgrounds for us, complete with references from other shady trophy hunters, but we assumed Townsend would still need to feel us out. He'd dance around the subject at first, gauge our intent, in person, where nothing could be recorded or copied, before discussing an illegal hunt.

Once he did, that was only the first step. To be sure we could get a decent conviction, we had to witness the kill, then, if possible, mark the location. I had a camera with built-in

GPS, but DNA was an even stronger piece of evidence. If possible, we'd stash a piece of the carcass without the guide knowing. When the trophy got shipped to the lower forty-eight, crossing state lines, making it a clear violation of the Lacey Act (a federal law that prohibits trade in wildlife, fish, and plants that have been illegally taken, possessed, transported, or sold), then we'd have a solid case. We'd intercept at the change of hands and nail them both—guide and hunter.

"So we'll be camping backcountry, right, in a tent?" I gave him a whimpery smile, giving the impression I was uncomfortable with being alone in the wilderness.

He fiddled with the little wheel thing on the ceiling, looked over the gauges before he answered. "Depends."

"That's where the big bears are though, right? Deep in the woods."

"Honey," Joe piped up from the back seat. "Stop pestering Mark. Let the man do his job. I know you're excited, but we'll be there soon enough."

Joe'd been around long enough and had the confidence to know he didn't have to play it to the hilt. It was the little things that made a cover believable. He was a pro. I took his lead and crossed my arms and pursed my lips into a pout.

"See Mount Douglas?" Townsend pointed out the windshield, to the left. "We head that way, then to the right a bit. Not long. Sit back and relax. Enjoy the flight."

Right. I'd enjoy it a lot more if I knew how to fly this bird.

As we approached, I could see waves rippling across Iliamna Lake on the right, Mount Douglas up ahead, to the left. Townsend banked the plane and we started our descent. The lodge was somewhere to the southeast of Iliamna Lake, but north of the Katmai National Park and Preserve boundary, a swath of land larger than four million square acres.

Mark piped up again in his tour guide voice. "Katmai National Park was originally established because of the volcanic activity in the area known as The Valley of Ten Thousand Smokes."

He didn't mention that the protection of its brown bears has become equally vital. Most of the park is a designated wilderness area where hunting is banned. All wildlife is protected. Unfortunately, the bears don't live by the rule of boundaries. Nor do poachers, if they can cross over without getting caught.

"Over that way," he continued, gesturing out the window, "is the McNeil River. That's where the big boys hang out."

Famous among bear lovers, McNeil River Falls attracts the bruins in large numbers, the largest concentration of brown bears in the world, in fact. They gorge on the salmon that wiggle their way up from the sea, through the boulders and rocks, and try to jump the falls to continue upstream to their spawning grounds. Many of the bears have perfected catching the salmon in the air as they shoot out of the rapids. I've seen many pictures that were taken there. I'm told it's something to witness. I wished it was part of the tour.

Mark took us lower and flew along the coast before turning inland. The trees below showed the colors of autumn. Dark green spires of spruce popped up amid patches of yellow and gold with an occasional blot of reddish-orange. Trails cut through the alders and thicket, bear paths leading to and from the streams.

"Bears," came Joe's voice in my headset. "Off to the right."

I spun in my chair to see. A sow and her cub lumbered along a path, heading into the hills from the sea. I smiled. Wild and free. Beautiful.

"We're at the edge of the McNeil area. The lodge is just to the north. We'll be landing soon," Mark said and pushed the throttle forward. He'd just been showing us the goods.

Yep. We *so* had to bust this guy.

"Well, look at that," Mark said, leaning over to look out the side window.

I craned my neck on my side, trying to see what he saw.

He banked the plane to circle back. "The herd is moving."

Below, on the edge of a rocky slope, hundreds of caribou moved in unison, a river of shaggy coats. Their enormous antlers rocked to and fro as they ran. Caribou have the largest antlers relative to their body size among all deer species, and both male and female grow them. Running across the landscape, they looked like Santa's reindeer set free.

I watched them disappear over the hill as we flew onward.

Not ten minutes later, Mark turned the plane and lined up to touch down on a river. It felt like we were approaching at a pretty steep angle, but I didn't feel a deep descent.

"What's the trick to landing one of these?" I asked.

"No trick," he said. "They pretty much land themselves."

"How do you mean?"

He turned to me with a smirk. "What goes up must come down."

Right.

With Mark's experienced hand on the throttle, easing it back, the engine whir slowed and we simply glided right down to the water, smooth as can be.

I inhaled a deep breath. I love to fly, but there's always a sense of relief when I'm back on the ground. In this case, on the water.

We skidded along on the river's surface, then taxied to shore in front of the lodge, and pulled up next to another float plane. The propeller coughed and sputtered to a stop. We were here.

CHAPTER 4

After miles of pristine wilderness, the lodge stuck out like a festering scar on the face of the landscape. Tucked amid the pines, with the white mountains behind, its log walls and stone foundation matched the wilderness style, but its sheer size and modern shine seemed to spit at the idea of roughing it. I suppose it would appeal to an oil man from Oklahoma who was more interested in taking home a story than an actual wilderness experience.

A tall woman in a red flannel shirt waved from the porch, then came down to greet us, two Alaskan dogs at her heels. Close cousins to wolves, usually a mixed breed combining the best traits for sledding, with blue eyes, sharp noses, and thick coats, they looked like they had no problem keeping the bears at bay before curling up into a ball in front of the fireplace.

Townsend was out of the plane and securing it to a line before the woman got there. I climbed out onto the pontoon and leaped to the rocky shore where the two dogs greeted me with wet noses. Mark started shoving our bags out of the plane and the men lined up like in a bucket brigade, tossing the bags along, from one to the other to a pile on dry ground where a raven hopped about, his eye on the new arrivals.

The sky was such a vibrant shade of blue, it seemed to glow. Tall spruce lined the river. I drew in a deep breath. The air was so clean and fresh, as though one inhalation could cleanse my soul.

Feeling revitalized already, I knew I could handle anything that came my way on this op. And Stan Martin was thousands of miles away. Once we brought Townsend in, with everything by the book, he'd have to give me some credit. Dalton was right. I wasn't going to worry about it now. I'd focus on the op and deal with that later.

After the luggage was unloaded, Mark gestured toward the woman. "My wife, Irene." She stood at least a head taller than me, with a tiny frame, yet had the stature of someone who could haul half a moose cross-country, keeping up with Mark without breaking a sweat.

She acknowledged us with a warm smile. "Welcome to Moosepine Lodge. C'mon in. You're the last to arrive, so we'll get you settled, then make introductions." She glanced down at the pile of luggage, then me. "Which bag is yours, dear?"

I pointed to mine.

She hefted it over her shoulder and headed for the front door.

I let Dalton and Joe get the other bags. There were perks to playing the spoiled daughter.

Joe lumbered after Mark, but Dalton lingered, his eyes scanning the perimeter.

"Stop it," I whispered.

"What?"

"Stop acting like a SEAL. You're a farm boy from Oklahoma. Remember, the dopey older brother?"

"I know, Sis." He pointed at the treetops. "Look there. A bald eagle." The white-headed raptor circled in the sky. "Don't see them very often at home." He flashed his half-grin. My insides tingled. Damn. I had to figure out what to do about him. Yep. After this op, I needed some space to clear my head.

"Right," I said and spun around and followed Joe up the path, the crunch-crunch of stones beneath my feet.

Inside, Mark welcomed us with a grand gesture like we'd walked into Buckingham Palace.

Egads. Gaudy was an understatement. Cathedral ceilings rose high and spread wide to accommodate all the dead heads—moose, caribou, bear, dall sheep. Furs hung on the walls between the heads, draped on the back of the chairs, as rugs on the floor. The chandeliers were piles of antlers with tiny lights attached. The furniture was all brown leather and wood, lamps made of deer hooves and sheep horns.

The wood-plank floors stretched the length of the great room, to the fireplace on the other end, all stone to the ceiling, a giant moose head over the mantle. It was some kind of trophy hunter's live-in museum.

"Wow," I said, all bright eyed and impressed. *You like to kill things and show them off.*

Mark met my gaze. "You'll be leaving with your own, young lady," he said. "I guarantee it."

Irene still had my bag slung over her shoulder. "Show them to their room," she told Mark, then turned to me. "I'll take you to yours." To Joe and Dalton, she said, "And then if you will join us in the dining room, I'm just about to serve up some dinner."

"That sounds mighty fine," Joe said, rubbing his belly.

My room was small but quaint, in a hunter kind of way— deer hoof lamp, braided wool rug, red flannel bedspread. On the wall hung the head of a jackalope. Silly thing. A jackrabbit head mounted with antelope horns. Some kind of hunter's joke, a remnant of some hoax of the early 1800s. I wondered if I'd be able to sleep with its glass eyes staring at me.

Irene plopped my bag down on the bed. "It's nice to have another woman here to visit," she said. "Don't get that very often."

"I can imagine."

"Not many women from the lower forty-eights ever touch a

gun, let alone hunt. It's nice to see."

"Well, I guess you could say it's in my blood."

"Good," she said as she yanked the chain to turn on the deer-hoof lamp, then turned to me with a sadness in her expression. "Not many understand our way of life up here. Sometimes it's hand to mouth. We got to eat, ya know." There was an undertone to her voice that I couldn't quite figure out.

I nodded, not sure where this was coming from. Did she suspect me of being an agent and was she trying to play on my sympathy? Afraid for her way of life? Or was she simply a lonely woman looking for someone to talk to?

She managed a smile. "Though I suppose you're in it for the sport."

"I always liked guns as a girl. I suppose hunting was the natural thing to do next. But I admit," I said, returning a smile. "I've never had to hunt for my dinner."

"Yeah, I didn't think you did." She paused. "But that ain't the worst thing in the world." She sat down on the bed and let her shoulders slump as though this was the only break she'd have all day. "Take my advice, dear. Marry a nice young man with a degree in accounting. Or a doctor or dentist or something. Living off the land, well, it ain't all it's cracked up to be."

With the clients her husband had taken poaching, I couldn't imagine they were hurting for cash. Something didn't add up. Was it possible she didn't know? For a moment, I felt uncomfortable. My job was to go after the criminals, undercover, make friends, laugh with them, sometimes cry with them, then, when the moment presented itself, drag them off in handcuffs. They deserved justice, but still, with Irene, I felt a twinge of guilt. How would we know for sure if she was complicit?

She rose from the bed and moved toward the door, then turned and lingered in the doorway. "Well, like I said, it's nice to have you. And" — she jerked her head toward the window — "be careful out there."

"Thanks. I will," I said to her backside as she disappeared down the hall.

I sighed. *Damn.*

I quickly used the bathroom and headed to the dining room, anxious to meet the other hunters and guides.

Joe must have been thinking the same thing. He was already there, a glass of scotch in his hand.

Dalton stood beside him holding a bottle of Alaskan Ale. He looked so relaxed, at home, and so fricking sexy. I kept my eyes off of him, off that Navy-SEAL body ripped and hard in all the right places, and purposefully moved to meet the others.

There was no question who were the lodge staff and who were the hunters. Not just the clothes or physique, but there was something distinct about a true woodsman. "This is Jack," Mark said. "One of my best guides."

Jack nodded. Blue-eyed with a gentle smile, he must have been in his late twenties. He took my hand and gave it a squeeze. Nice guy.

"And that's Rocky," Mark said.

Rocky leaned against the dining table, his hands gripping the edge. I couldn't see his eyes. It was as though he purposefully hid them under the shadow of his ball cap. Lanky and awkward, he reminded me of a boy I'd gone to high school with. On graduation day, he'd told me he'd tried a hundred times to ask me out. I felt like a real snob because I didn't even know his name. Billy, maybe?

Rocky touched his greasy hat and muttered, " 'lo."

"He's also the mechanic around here," Mark added.

Something about him struck me as one of those people who were drawn to the wilderness of Alaska to get away from life in the lower forty-eight. Most times, they were running from something.

"You're practically neighbors," Mark said.

Alarms went off in my brain, bringing me fully alert. "Neighbors?"

"You're from Mississippi, ain't ya?" he said to Rocky.

Rocky gave a hint of a nod, staring at me with flat, unblinking eyes.

"You ride rodeo?" I asked, hoping he didn't.

"Nope," he muttered without moving a muscle. His eyes dropped to the floor.

Irene came through the door from the kitchen, saving me from the awkward conversation. She wore a starched white apron wrapped around her waist and carried a tray in her hand loaded with mystery meat chunks stabbed with toothpicks. She plopped it down on the table.

"What can I get you to drink, dear?" she asked me.

"Wine?"

She hesitated, eyebrows raised.

Oops. What is the drinking age in Oklahoma? Or Alaska for that matter? "My daddy lets me drink one glass when we're on vacation."

She nodded and disappeared without asking white or red. *Yep. I was getting White Zinfandel.* My penchant for wine wasn't going to be relevant here anyway.

Mark gestured toward us, addressing everyone else in the room. "This is Joe. His son, Dalton. And his daughter, Penelope."

"Everyone calls me Poppy," I said. We'd agreed that Poppy was such an uncommon name that it made the most sense to use it like a nickname when undercover. The last thing I needed was someone outing me by Googling my name.

Mark continued the introductions, turning to two men who appeared as though they'd just stepped from the check-out lane at Cabela's. Obviously brothers. They had the same rounded jaws, same pencil-thin necks, same pompous posture. East coast, Ivy League bred. In their late forties or early fifties. Eyes zeroing in on me like a couple of jackals. "And these are long time friends of mine, John and Patrick."

We all shook hands. True to form, Mark purposefully didn't share last names. No matter. We'd find them all later. Right now, our job was to make friends, get invited to hunt with them so we could witness the poaching act.

Dalton struck up a conversation easily with Patrick whose eyes lingered on me.

John made the move toward me with a grin, showing his perfect teeth. He'd obviously already had a few drinks. "Mark tells me you're here on your own hunt." His eyes lingered on my chest before slowly making their way back up. *Eyes up here, buddy.* "I wasn't expecting to meet Annie Oakley on the trip."

Was that supposed to be a compliment? Excuse me, there's still a price tag hanging on your jacket. Dope. "Oh, yeah," I said. "I've been Crawford County's Little Miss Sharpshooter champ since I was, like, three."

"No kidding," he said, his eyes alight as if I'd just told him I was a champion pole dancer.

"Daddy's been, like, promising to take me on a big hunt for since, like, as long as I can remember." I grinned with delight. "I can't wait."

"Oh honey, it's a rush like nothing else you could imagine."

His eyes dropped to my chest again. *Lech.*

"At least with your clothes on," he added.

Okay, that was enough. "You know, in Oklahoma, we have a saying—"

"Poppy," said Dalton, moving between John and me, "be a good sis and get me another beer." He shoved his empty bottle in my hand.

I shoved it back. "Get your own."

"Ooh, red hot and sassy," John tittered.

But Dalton had accomplished what he wanted and kept his place between us, establishing himself as the protective older brother. It was all about roles, playing off your partner's improv. You could always work it to your advantage. At least that's what Joe had taught me.

I grinned at John like I'd like to meet him out back later. That ought to keep him interested.

Already enjoying the hors d'oeuvres were a group of five men, foreigners I was sure. Russian. Maybe German. All in their fifties or older with the bellies of serious beer drinkers.

They were nodding and smiling, but I could tell they weren't sure of the content of our conversation. One of the five made eye contact with me and, with a respectful nod, said, "'Tis nice to meet you."

"You too," I said. "Where are you from?"

"East Germany," he said. "I speak little of the English. My friends, not so much."

"I see," I said. I speak some German, learned it when my mom was briefly stationed in Germany, and maybe it would get me invited to hunt with them, but my gut told me that right now, it would be best to keep that a secret, see what I could pick up.

Irene appeared and gave me a wink as she handed me a glass filled to the rim with pink wine. I thanked her and turned back to my German friend.

John hovered at my shoulder, whispered in my ear, "Ask him if he's a communist."

"So are you here to fish and hunt?" I asked.

"Here, in America?" John added.

The four other men wore the expressions of those lost in a maze, curiously trying to find their way.

"Fish, some, yes," he said. "Hunt, some."

"Of course," John muttered.

"Bear?" I asked.

"Bear. Yes. Big bear." He raised his arms like a bear standing on his hind legs. The other men grinned and nodded.

"Yes, big bear," I said.

"Oh Jesus," John said and turned away.

"Well, good luck." I held up my glass and produced the only phrase a red-blooded, American girl from Oklahoma would be likely to know, "Nasdrovia."

Instantly, all five men came alive, raising their glasses and simultaneously cheering, "Nasdrovia!" followed by chuckles and happy chatter.

Joe eased next to me. "It seems you're making friends, my dear."

"It seems so."

"Joe tells me this is your very first big game hunt," Townsend said. "I didn't realize."

"And nothing but the best will do for my little angel," Joe said. "I hope you've got something real special planned for her."

I nodded and grinned like an idiot. "I'm so excited." I took Joe's hand and leaned into him, a daughter affectionately snuggling up to her dad. "I can't believe I'll be hunting tomorrow already."

"Not so fast, young lady. You'll have to wait one more day," Joe said.

I frowned at Joe and looked back to Townsend. "I don't understand."

"Tomorrow, we sight in the rifles," he answered. "I'll be assessing your skills and discussing with each of you what you want from the hunt. Then I'll determine where we'll go. Some of our spike camps are quite remote." He winked. "I want to make sure you're up to it."

"You mean you want to make sure I'm not some frou-frou

girl who doesn't know which end of the rifle to aim at the target."

He grinned. "Something like that."

"Well," I said. "We'll see you tomorrow then."

Everyone retired to their rooms, anxious for the next day to begin. Being the only female guest, I had my own room, but we still shared bathrooms. After brushing my teeth, heading back down the hall to my room, I heard voices, a conversation in German. I paused outside the door, listening, ready to bolt at any moment.

„Er hat mir einen Bären als Trophäe versprochen versprochen. Ich komme seit drei Jahren hierher. Ich habe dafür bezahlt und dann bekomme ich das auch." *He's promised me a trophy bear. For three years I've been coming here. That's what I paid for, that's what I'm going to get.*

„Und er soll verdammt nochmal auch mit uns rauskommen und nicht einmal daran denken, uns mit irgend so einem Typen, den er angeheuert hat, loszuschicken. Oder wird sind hier fertig." *And he damn well better take us out himself, not send us with some hired man. Or we're done.* Something like that. My German was rusty.

„Da bin ich ganz deiner Meinung." *I agree.* I recognized the voice of the one I'd spoken to at dinner. „Ich werde ihm sagen, was ihr wollt." *I will tell him our demands.*

„Und ich gehe auch nicht mit diesem verwöhnten kleinen Mädchen auf die Jagd." *I'm not going out with that spoiled little rich girl either.* A new voice.

I frowned. Maybe I'd overdone it. If they got their way, and Mark took them out hunting himself, without at least one of the three of us, we'd be here for nothing.

„Ich hatte schon mit Frauen wie ihr zu tun. Pfff. Amerikanerinnen." *Pfff. Americans. I've had to deal with women like her before.*

„Alles klar" said the leader. *I understand.* „Ich spreche gleich morgen früh mit ihm." *I'll tell him first thing in the morning.*

The door flew open. I jumped back with a start, dropping my toothbrush. It skittered across the hardwood floor.

The German hesitated, suspicion in his eyes.

"Omigosh, you startled me," I said, gripping the front of my robe to hold it closed. "I thought everyone had gone to bed already."

The one who spoke English poked his head through the door. "So sorry, my lady."

"It's all right," I said. "No harm done." I flashed him a grin. "Got my heart going though." I added a giggle.

"Yah, yah. Good thing not a bear in da woods, no?"

I nodded and giggled some more.

The first man picked up my toothbrush and handed it to me.

"You will need to keep better grip on your gun, I am thinking."

"Yes, yes, I will," I said, all girly embarrassment. *Jerk.*

I slinked back to my room. *Damn.* My chances of hunting with them were nil. Joe would have to make that connection. I was left with the chest-ogling Lech Brothers if I was going to be successful.

CHAPTER 5

Sourdough pancakes dripping with boysenberry syrup, reindeer sausage the size of my arm and a heap of scrambled eggs covered my breakfast plate. My eyes must have revealed my overwhelmed appetite.

"Everything's big in Alaska," Mark said. "Eat up. We've got a busy day planned."

Dalton, playing up the annoying big brother, stabbed my sausage with his fork and dragged it over to his plate.

"Hey!" I said, secretly thanking him.

"Eat your eggs, then maybe you can have some more," he said with a smirk.

After the plates were cleared, Mark instructed us to bring our rifles from our rooms and we headed to a clearing behind the lodge, the two dogs following us as if they were our guards, keeping the wild things at bay. The shooting range had been set up with sighting benches on one end, targets on the other.

The Germans went to work right away, loading rounds into guns the size of shoulder-fired rocket launchers and pacing the distance to their targets. All business.

The Lech brothers hung back, more interested in watching me than getting their own weapons ready. I smiled and nodded, acting like I enjoyed the attention.

They were my target, our best shot at catching Townsend. The tricky part would be proving a monetary transaction occurred between them and Townsend. But we could make a case with the assumption. The odds were good that once we threatened them with jail time, they'd flip on Townsend. Fine by us. It was Townsend we were after.

Today was my chance to form the relationship.

Rocky came up to me. "You need any help?" he asked without making eye contact.

"Nope, all set," I said. "Old hat."

He nodded but with a hesitation, as though he were disappointed, then moved on to check with the Germans.

Dalton set the gun case on the bench and I removed my rifle, a brand new Ruger 375 H&H Mag, single-shot. Story was, Daddy Pratt had bought it for me, special for this trip. I dropped a single round into the chamber, then snapped it shut.

"Now for the show," I whispered to Dalton.

"Easy, Sis," he muttered.

I got myself situated on the sight bench and took a couple deep breaths. I hadn't done this in a while, but I wasn't worried. I'd won the firearm medal back in training. I knew how to obliterate a target.

When Mark hollered all clear, I lined up the crosshairs, inhaled, then on my exhale, gently eased my finger back on the trigger and fired a round. The butt kicked against my shoulder. I looked down the sights to confirm. Right smack in the bullseye, dead center. *Shazam! I rock.*

I cracked the barrel to spring the empty shell, then loaded another round and did it again. Then again. Three right in the eye.

"Hold your fire," Mark yelled.

Joe held the binoculars up to his eyes. "That's my girl!"

"Impressive," said John the lech, his eyes all heavy. *What is it with these men?* "What you got there? Some kind of canon?"

I held it up for him to examine, all proud. "This here's the finest in bear-huntin' weaponry." With a wink, I added, "Don't you go droolin' on it, now."

He ran his hand down the barrel. "That she is. Single-shot, eh?"

Single-shot weapons were an ego thing with big hunters. "When you only have one shot, make it count," I said, rattling off the company slogan.

"Well, aren't you something."

Part of me thought I should drive it home, ask to see his gun, play up the sexual innuendo. But like Joe had taught me, sometimes less is more. I took the rifle from his hands, passed it to Dalton with a two-handed toss, John Wayne-style, then jerked my thumb toward the bullseye. "Beat that score, Brother," I said and strutted downrange to put up a new target, knowing John watched my backside as I went.

Mark sauntered up to me, Rocky behind him like a shadow. "Nice shootin' Tex."

"Well, yeah, except I'm from Oklahoma."

"Right," he said, giving me a nod of respect. "I forgot." He stuck his finger in the hole my bullets had left in the paper bullseye. "You put all three in the center. But can you do it to a bear?" His eyes locked onto me. "When you got yourself all in a froth of excitement?"

Froth of excitement? Seriously? "I didn't start shooting yesterday."

"Shooting, yeah. But when a bear is charging, bearing down on you, and adrenaline is pumping through your veins, your heart hammerin' away in your chest, will Little Miss Sharpshooter hold that gun steady then?"

I eyed him, trying to get a read on him. Rocky hovered at his shoulder, standing at attention like a soldier, ready to serve.

"You make it sound like in the movies," I said.

"That's what you're here for, ain't ya?" Mark said with a sly grin. "The thrill? Like in the movies."

I looked from Rocky to Mark and held his stare. *Was that his pitch?* "Well, yeah," I said with a little too much smartass.

"Bear hunting isn't for light-weights with soft hearts," Mark said, taking a step closer to me. "You gotta be fierce."

"I'm fierce."

Rocky closed in on Mark's flank.

"Sometimes, shit happens," Mark said. "You've gotta be able to roll with it."

"I can roll."

Mark looked me up and down as though assessing my level of fortitude. I stared right back at him. "There are some mean, crafty beasts out there."

Rocky added, his tone matter-of-fact, "Rip yer pretty little head off with a single swipe of the paw."

I put my hands on my hips. "Are you trying to scare me? Cuz it ain't working. I'm not some little girl afraid of breaking a nail. I'm taking home a bear. The bigger the better." I glanced back toward Joe, who was watching every move without giving up that he was watching. "And I want a story to go with it."

Mark's lip curled up into a grin. "All right, little lady. I just might have the right one for you. One I've had my eye on. He's a mean old bear. He won't be taken easily. It will be extra work and the added danger—"

"No problem." I gave him my high-and-mighty-princess face. "My daddy will pay."

After cleaning our weapons and packing our gear for the backcountry, we were served a lunch, the portions sized for lumberjacks, during which I managed the art of keeping John and his brother Patrick interested with hunting tales laced with eyelash batting and winks. Then Mark took us all for a pontoon boat ride down the river.

I tuned out the hum of the engine and took in the scenery around me, the vast, awe-inspiring Alaskan landscape—a shoreline strewn with round rocks, tumbled smooth over eons of ice movement, granite hills at the river's edge clad with dark green forest, evergreens overhanging a dense understory of alder and devil's club, that thorny weed with giant leaves that's the bane of any hiker. A gentle mist hung amid the trees, a white swath, like cotton stretched across the treetops.

Eagles perched at regular intervals on the river, each claiming a territory. As we motored by, one lifted on his haunches and tipped forward, swooping from his branch, his great wings outstretched into a gentle glide toward the river's surface. Then in an instant, he changed the angle of his wings, thrust his talons forward, and snatched a fish from the water. With three powerful flaps of his wings, he headed skyward again, back to his perch, his meal pierced by his talons.

The men didn't say much as we motored down the river for several miles then finally came to a sandy spit. Mark drove the pontoons right up on shore and killed the engine.

"A short walk, my friends," he said as he got up from the driver's seat. He clipped a large can of pepper spray onto his belt, said, "Let's stay together," and led the way.

Seagulls scattered and took flight as the group walked down the shoreline, then up and over a ridge. Before us, a wide stream narrowed to a spot where the water tumbled over rocks into a natural pool, a place for salmon to gather before launching themselves into the air, hoping to clear the rocky barrier.

Three bears waded belly deep, their heads down, searching for fish. One saw something and pounced, the splash causing a wave to ripple across the pool. His entire head went underwater, but he came up empty, droplets of water clinging to his fur.

"Let's keep our distance," Mark said, holding up a hand, gesturing for us to stay put. "This is a good spot to watch."

"Looks like a good spot to hunt," said Patrick, crossing his arms.

"Nah. The big boys have moved on. These are the stragglers, picking off the last of the salmon. Just thought you might enjoy a little viewing. A preview, if you will."

There was a rustle in the bushes above the falls. A bear with fur the color of amber poked her head out, then ambled toward the stream. Two spring cubs followed.

I fought to contain a smile as my insides tingled with delight.

The sow scanned the area, alert for trouble. Her eyes sparkled with intelligence. She was a big bear, bigger than the three in the pool, which were likely adolescents. I'd guess six hundred pounds. If she had raised up on her hind legs, I'd guess she stood eight feet tall.

She lumbered down the edge of the stream, taking her time, and as she entered the water, just above the falls, the three young bears hightailed it for the woods. There was no confrontation, no growling, no threat. Just the hierarchy of the animal kingdom. She was a bigger bear. It was her turn at the table.

Her cubs stayed at the edge of the water, watching their mother, their innocent brown eyes taking it all in.

"That's a nice size one," John said to Mark, as if to prove him wrong.

His brother elbowed him. "She's got cubs, man."

It's illegal to take a sow with cubs, not to mention downright immoral. I harbored hope that even poachers wouldn't cross that line. Roy, the weathered old agent I was assigned to during my probationary training always said, "You can hope in one hand and shit in the other. What have you got?" Pretty much sums it up.

The sow's movements were slow and deliberate. No energy wasted. She had a long winter ahead and needed every pound of stored fat. So did her cubs. And feeding them was a big chore; they weren't worried about conserving energy. The two wrestled and tumbled, romping around in circles, their awkward little legs moving them about. Round a tree stump they chased, one, then the other, changing direction. Mom glanced in their direction, a tolerant expression on her face.

I wanted to pick one up and cuddle it. They were so cute, all fluffy fur and pink bellies. Those little round ears must be so soft. But if I even got close, it'd be the last thing I ever did. Mother bears were notoriously protective of their cubs. If she wanted to, she'd be on me within seconds. One swipe of her massive paw could rip my guts open. Rocky was right about that.

"Still," John muttered. "That rug would look damn good in front of my fireplace."

Patrick gave him a conspiratorial grin.

"And some little rugs in my den," John muttered.

My throat burned with acid. His arrogance was astounding, not to mention his lack of ethics. All he could think about was killing, yet the bear was the one with the reputation of being a vicious killer. The bear stood not forty yards away, a distance she could cover in seconds, yet hadn't given him a second look. She had no cause. We weren't overtly threatening her or her cubs. For her, like all wild animals, fighting is a dangerous business. One doesn't pick a fight without good reason.

The mama bear swatted her paw in the water, trying to stun a fish. She reared back and plunged in, coming up with a wriggling salmon in her mouth.

She plodded to the shore and plopped down, the salmon fighting a hopeless battle in her powerful jaws. She clamped her mighty paws around the fish and with her teeth, gripped it in the middle and ripped its skin off, all the way to the tail, revealing its pink flesh. The cubs circled round, whimpering for a bite.

Three gulls swooped in and danced about, squawking, trying to get a tidbit for themselves. The bear ripped off a mouthful, chewed sloppily as she kept a wary eye on her surroundings, always alert, then swallowed the precious protein and tore off another bite.

When the fish was gone, she waded into the pool again, milled around for some time, but found nothing. It was late in the year. Most of the salmon were gone. She gave up and hauled out, water pouring off of her, then shook, water spraying every which way.

At the river's edge, she lay down in the grass, rolled over on her back, and let her cubs crawl atop her to nurse.

I couldn't keep the smile from tugging at the corners of my mouth. I wanted to giggle with joy in seeing these bears, right in front of me, in their natural habitat, doing what bears do. I felt such wonder. I wanted to share it with Dalton, tell him about the awe I felt. But right now, my goal was to be someone else. Someone who didn't care. Someone who only wanted to kill, to own, to conquer.

"We should have brought our guns," I said and crossed my arms, like a bored, rich, gun-toting cowgirl.

Back at the dock, Rocky helped catch the pontoon boat and tie it up. Mark pulled Joe, Dalton and me aside while the other guests filed into the lodge. Rocky lingered behind him.

Mark addressed me. "We've talked and made a plan. Rocky has had his eye on a bear he thinks is just right for you. He's set up a spike camp in the area. He'll fly you out there." He looked to Dalton, then back to me. "Your brother here can go, too. Back you up with that fancy single-shot rifle." He cuffed me on the chin as if I were thirteen. "Just in case you're all bark and no bite."

I pushed out my lower lip. "Rocky? I thought you were the legend, the man to hunt with." I couldn't let him send me out with his sidekick. If that happened, the op would be over for me.

"Well, I wish I could take every client on every hunt, but I can't be everywhere at once, now can I? Trust me. Rocky here will take real good care of you."

This was my last chance. I had to be on the hunt with Mark. This was the moment. All or nothing. I needed to throw a class-A fit.

I glared at him, forcing my lips into a frown. "Seriously? This guy?" I said, jerking my thumb toward Rocky. "You said fierce. He doesn't look that fierce." I rammed my fists into my hips. "Give me a rope, I'll drop him on his ass." I turned to Joe. "Daddy, you told me I was gonna get the best. I don't wanna go out with this—" I flicked a dismissive hand in the air "—this clown. He doesn't even look like he's smart enough to come in outta the rain."

"It's all right, Poppy," Joe soothed. He turned to Mark, playing along. "Can't we work something out? If it's the cost—"

Mark held up a conciliatory hand. "Now, I understand your reservations. But trust me when I say, Rocky's my best guide." Rocky's eyes never left the ground. "He's got the highest kill rate of any I've ever worked with. You want to take home a trophy, he's your man." He slapped Joe on the back at the shoulder. "I know how it is. Everyone wants to go out with the owner. But believe me when I say, I only hire the best. That's how I built my reputation. When you come to Moosepine Lodge, you go home with a trophy." He rocked back on his heels, a smug smile on his face, satisfied that he'd been convincing. "Rocky's been scouting all summer. He's got his sights on the one for her. I'm telling you. Guaranteed. Your little lady won't be disappointed."

"But Daddy, you said—"

The look on Joe's face silenced me. Better to back off than blow it. You can always come around for a second shot at 'em if you keep the cover intact.

Maybe we'd been overly optimistic to think that the first time around Mark would take us out hunting himself. We'd have to play the game, bide our time, and book another trip next year. It made me want to scream bloody murder to let it ride for that long, but it was how the game was played.

I crossed my arms, filled with disappointment. "Fine."

After dinner and the obligatory cocktails and all the pomp of huntsmen's well wishes, we retired to our rooms. The plan was to meet in Joe and Dalton's room for a strategic discussion and update.

I took my time washing my face and doing some stretching before sneaking across the hall. Dalton was leaning against the dresser in his casual way, his hair ruffled. *Damn. Why does he have to be so good looking?*

Joe sat down on the leather chair, always professional and serious. "So. This is how it is. He's sending the two of you out with Rocky. The brothers are going together with someone named Bob." He threw his hands up with a shrug. We hadn't met anyone named Bob. "Maybe someone flying in? Anyway, Townsend's taking the Germans out himself. I'll be hunting with Jack. I tried to get him to combine the two groups, insisting I didn't need one guide to myself, since he'll have all five of the Germans, but he said he'd take his wife. He's smart. He's giving us the VIP treatment while simultaneously creating a situation with no witnesses for corroboration. Makes it awfully hard to nail him for poaching."

"Okay, but what if Rocky or Jack takes one of us inside the park boundary?" I asked, grabbing for anything. "Can't we cite Mark for knowingly promoting illegal hunting? I mean, he's the boss here."

"Doesn't matter," Joe said. "If an undercover agent acts as the hunter and makes the kill, they could claim entrapment. It wouldn't be worth it. It'd be a slap on the wrist anyway. When we nail this guy, I want rock-hard evidence."

"So we're stuck here in an our-word-against-his scenario?"

Joe nodded. "We'll have to play along, keep the cover, see if an opportunity arises."

"And if it doesn't?"

"Try again next year," he said with the matter-of-fact tone of many years of experience.

"But we've come all this way."

"I'm glad he's sending me with you," Dalton said to me. "There's something about Rocky. I don't like him."

"This sucks," I said, unable to contain my frustration. "Maybe I could talk to John and Patrick—"

"We don't want to push too hard and blow it," Joe said. "Stay the course."

I nodded. He was the boss. I'd go with Rocky and play along. *But that means—*My heart started to race and my stomach turned sour.

Dalton moved to within my gaze. "Poppy, if you're not sure—"

"I understand."

A look passed between him and Joe.

"I understand my job." I turned toward the door. "I'll be ready. See you in the morning." I needed some air, some space. I went straight down the stairs and out the front door into the dark night.

I pulled my jacket up around my neck and crossed my arms, snugging it tight. I wasn't to the dock yet when I heard footsteps behind me. Dalton.

"You okay?"

"Fine. I just needed some fresh air."

"Let's walk," he said and took me by the arm.

About forty yards down the shoreline, he turned to me and whispered, "Are you ready for this?"

"I said I was." *This again.* "I understand the situation. For now, we play the game. And someday we'll nail these guys. Somehow. Some way."

He nodded and stood in silence for a time, his eyes on me. I couldn't meet his gaze. He'd been trying to warn me. It was going to be just like he'd said.

We walked a little further.

"Could you believe John and Patrick today?" I said. "I wanted to smack their heads together and drop them on their asses." I turned to face him. "You know what I'm going to do? When we do finally bust Townsend, I hope those two go down with him. I hope they make a plea deal. I'll petition the judge to require community service from them.

"I want to see John standing in front of a school group, his ranger hat in his hand, telling the kids, 'Bears aren't vicious, savage beasts that stalk and kill humans like you might think. They're highly intelligent beings. Surely smarter than I am.'

"Yeah, I'm going to ask the judge to let me write their whole script. His brother will stand beside him. 'Humans aren't on the menu,' he'll say. 'But if a bear feels threatened, he'll defend himself, and then make a meal out of the kill. That's nature at work. The circle of life. The balance of prey and predator. The way it's supposed to be.' I'll make sure the judge requires that last line. Every time. 'The way it's supposed to be.'"

"Poppy?"

"I know." I plopped down on the rocks and pulled my knees up to my chest. "I know." I swallowed and drew in a breath. "You're assuming Rocky will even bring in a bear. The odds are—"

"The odds are good. He's a poacher. He'll do anything it takes. There's big money at stake."

I nodded, resigned. He wasn't telling me anything I didn't know. "God it's beautiful here. Look how the stars fill the sky like glitter sprinkled across black velvet." He stared at me. "I love how the air smells. Like fall, all earthy and wet. And listen to the river gurgle at the edges where it laps on the gravel. It's like music—"

"I know how you feel about this. And if we need to—"

"No, you don't," I said, too sharply. "You don't know how I feel about it."

He set his jaw, holding back. "Fine. But I do know that one mistake could get us killed." He paused and I could tell he was carefully planning his words. "And I don't like going in with a partner I'm not sure I can trust to do what needs to be done."

My heart rate shot up. "I told you. I'll do my job."

"I don't question your dedication. Or your abilities," he said through clenched teeth. "I need to know that you're gonna pull the goddamn trigger."

He stared at me. I bit my lip, staring back.

"I'm your partner. I've got your back. But—" He pressed his lips together.

I opened my mouth to answer, but I couldn't. I didn't have one.

"Poppy, listen to me. It's not going to be like you said about the trophy mount in the airport, you looking through the sights at some cuddly, sleeping bear. He'll probably provoke it. And the question is, when that bear is charging right at you, are you set in your mind to pull the trigger?" He moved so I was looking him in the eye. "I know you. You tell yourself that you wouldn't. You might even believe you wouldn't. But when it happens, when you are facing the reality, when it comes down to that life or death moment, I think you will."

What? I jerked back. "Are you saying I'm really a killer at heart?"

"I'm saying you've never stared death in the face. And," he paused, "you don't know how devastating it can be."

"Now you're confusing me. Are you worried I won't do my job, or worried that when I do, it will break my heart?"

"Both." He sighed. "I'm trying to tell you that you need to decide right now. You need to be ready. You need to have that set in your mind. Because in that moment, when that animal's bearing down on you, if you even hesitate—"

"I get it!"

He shook his head, exhaling with a huff. "I don't think you do."

"Oh, I do. You don't have to say it for the twenty-seventh time. You don't like working with me. Fine. When we get back, I'll probably be demoted or fired or whatever anyway and you'll get your wish."

"What?" He pulled back. "That's not true."

"You don't like my approach. You don't like my views. You're afraid that—"

"Yes, Poppy, I'm afraid. I'm afraid your idealism is going to get you killed."

I drew back. That stung. I closed my eyes and calmly said, "Please leave me alone. Go back to the lodge. And leave me alone."

"Not a good idea." A voice behind us. We both spun around. It was Rocky. *Crap.* How long had he been there? He stood ten paces away. A shadow in the night. "You shouldn't be out here at night. You never know what might be lurking in them woods."

Or who?

"Right," Dalton said. "We were just heading back in."

Chapter 6

The air had turned moist overnight and a hint of fog hung in the shadows. Like a scene from a postcard, the sun rose over the hills and bathed the forest in a misty crimson and ochre. Tiny specks of sunlight sparkled on the river.

Without a word, Rocky loaded our gear into the back of the plane, the same plane we'd flown in on with Mark. We were headed out to the spike camp for seven to ten days to find a trophy-sized bruin, a bear for the record books. No other details were given, of course. We were to smile and nod and put all our faith into the guide. That's how it works. There's no actual hunting involved. They serve up a trophy on a silver platter. All we needed to do was actually pull the trigger.

Irene emerged from the lodge, waving for us to wait, a canvas bag in her other hand. "Lunch for the flight out," she said and handed me the bag with a genuine smile. Her hand lingered, holding mine for a moment. With a determined gaze, she said, "Be careful." I thanked her with a smile.

Once again, I climbed into the passenger seat, making Dalton sit in the back. I wasn't in the mood to sit next to him.

If we couldn't go out with Townsend, why couldn't we have gotten assigned with cute Jack? He seemed kind, personable even. Or the mysterious Bob. Rocky went about his work without notice that actual humans were part of the equation. He kept his head down, didn't make eye contact.

Maybe I'd gone too far with my dismissal of him and he'd taken it personally and felt insulted. I *had* called him a clown. I'm sure they'd dealt with arrogant clients before, though. Oh well. There was nothing to do about it now.

Rocky climbed into the pilot seat.

"Good morning," I said, trying to lighten the mood.

He paused, looking ahead as though he might turn to stone if he dared to look me in the eye. "Mornin'." He went through all the motions, flipping switches, pumping levers, and the propeller started spinning. "Buckle your seatbelt. The weather's supposed to turn. It'll be a rough flight," he said, an edge to his voice, more threat than warning.

Well, I guess that answers that question.

He scanned and rescanned the dashboard. Not like Mark had done, checking and double checking all the controls. Rocky seemed impatient, like waiting for the engine to warm up created an unbearable time gap of inaction.

"Is something wrong?" I asked. "With the plane?"

He turned to me, his gaze a gray stare. "Don't you worry your pretty little head. I'm quite capable."

Something about his stare made me back down. "That's not what I meant," I said. The last thing I wanted to do was insult the guy any further. "I just, you know, don't like flying." That was a good lie.

He pushed the throttle lever forward, the engine fired up, and we were in motion. He turned his steel gray eyes on me again. "Everything will be all right. You're with me now. I'll take good care of you."

Somehow that didn't feel comforting.

The rain came while in flight. Water droplets hit the windshield and slid off leaving tiny trails, making the view muted and blurry. The whir of the engine and the steamy warmth inside the cockpit pushed me into a drowsy state.

We flew south-southwest. Right toward the park. We'd either be within the boundary, which was illegal, and risky with a plane, which was easily seen, or, more likely, just outside of it, to lure a bear out of the refuge.

And there was nothing we could do about it.

Rocky pulled back on the throttle and we started to descend toward a small lake tucked in among what appeared to be rolling hills, but I was coming to realize that what they said was true: everything's big in Alaska. The landscape was so vast, it was hard to judge distance and size. Those hills were probably considered mountains back home.

He banked the plane sharply, dipping hard to the right, then made a full circle as he descended, scanning the surface of the lake for any obstructions before touching down.

We taxied to shore, leaving a ripple that slowly crossed the silvery water, disrupting the perfect reflection of the birches and diamond willows that grew at the water's edge.

Two ravens swooped down, landed on the shore, then hippety-hopped along toward us as if in greeting.

Rocky left the engine running while he and Dalton unloaded all our gear, then took off his raincoat, then his shirt and boots, and threw them onto the pile, then waded into the water, pushing the plane out from shore.

"What's going on?" I asked.

"Wait here," he said and climbed into the cockpit.

"What's he doing?" I asked Dalton.

Dalton was scanning the hillside. "I assume he wants the plane where he can see it."

"What's he so paranoid about?"

He shrugged. "Beats me."

I wore a rain hat and rain coat, but the rain was really coming down, cold and misty. Fall in Alaska. Fog enveloped the forest, but hints of treetops poked through on the hillside. I pulled my coat closer, slid my gloved hands into the pockets.

Dalton turned to me. "Hey, listen about last night—"

"Forget it," I said. "Let's just do this thing and go home."

I snugged my coat up closer around my neck.

Dalton looked away. "Hey, look at that."

A blur of brown feathers dropped from the sky—an eagle, its feet stretched out beneath, talons ready to grip. Below, a squirrel darted behind a rock. The eagle arched its powerful wings, slowing its descent, just as the squirrel burrowed in, but its tail was still hanging out, vulnerable. The eagle snatched ahold and flapped, once, twice, and lifted into the air again, the squirrel dangling in its grasp.

The squirrel let out a shriek and twisted and dropped to the rocks below. With a flip, it was running again for a larger rock to hide behind and hunkered down.

The eagle, trying to change direction at such low altitude, fluttered and spun before landing, its sharp eyes fixed on the location of the squirrel.

The squirrel made a run for it. I winced. *You were safe where you were!*

With a whoosh of his enormous wings, the eagle lifted and pounced, this time snatching up the squirrel about the belly. He didn't have a chance. His little feet swayed, lifeless in the eagle's grasp as it flapped hard to get airborne again, then flew back to its perch among the treetops.

An incredible silence descended on us. Rocky had set an anchor and cut the engine. The sounds of the forest—the glock-glock of a raven in the distance, the patter of raindrops hitting leaves—were all enveloping, like being wrapped in a blanket of nature.

We turned toward the lake and watched Rocky swim back to the gravel beach.

"That water is ice cold," I said as he trudged over the pebbled shoreline in bare feet, water sloshing down his camo pants.

"It's okay," he said through clenched teeth, then paused long enough to look me right in the eyes. "I'm fierce. Really. You'll see."

Dalton and I exchanged a glance. *Uh...weird.*

He put his shirt back on, slid his raincoat and boots on, slung his duffle bag over his shoulder, his rifle case strapped to it, then from a canvas bag, he pulled out a modern, compact crossbow outfitted with a hefty scope. It looked like something The Green Arrow would carry.

"Sweet," Dalton said, admiring the weapon. "Is that the new Carbon Express?"

Rocky nodded, barely acknowledging Dalton.

"You use carbon fiber arrows?"

Rocky ignored him altogether.

"Whew," Dalton continued anyway. "That thing is accurate as hell. Dude, you could put one right between a bear's eyes."

Rocky paused, looked at Dalton, resigned, as though dealing with him pushed Rocky to the edge of his patience. "Ptarmigan. For dinner," he said, annoyed. "We don't need to draw any unwanted attention firing a gun."

"You're going to shoot birds with that?" Dalton said with awe.

Ptarmigan are large grouse that provide an exciting challenge for hunters. They lift off abruptly and fly erratically.

Rocky turned to me. "Let's go," he said and took off, pushing through the alder-brush like he had something to prove.

Suddenly I was glad Dalton was with me. He was right. Something was off about this guy.

I hefted my backpack. "I guess we follow him."

Rocky led us through the thick tangle of alders that lined the lake, branches scrapping at my jacket and snagging at every seam, until finally we emerged in a forest of old growth trees. The terrain reminded me in some ways of the steamy jungle in the Philippines, though the temperature here was seventy degrees cooler. Beneath the dark canopy of spruce and juniper, willow and birch, the rain still found a way in.

We slowly made our way over deadfall covered in moss and slick with water, pushing through blueberry bushes and devil's club and many kinds of ferns, the rain pitter-pattering on my hat, drowning out the sounds of the forest.

It was rough going with the heavy pack, but Rocky never slowed, never even looked back. Usually, I wouldn't bother to try to keep up. Pacing is important and being in the elements, especially rain, presents risks that otherwise wouldn't be an issue. If I hiked too fast and got sweaty underneath my raincoat, I'd get cold later when I stopped. If I unzipped my coat so I wouldn't get too warm, I'd get wet anyway from the rain.

But today, I didn't want to lose sight of Rocky. So we climbed upward at a pace that, I admit, made me winded. Dalton stayed with me and I could tell he wondered why Rocky forged ahead without checking on us, but neither of us said anything.

Finally, I emerged from the trees at an abrupt drop-off. Thirty feet below, a river gushed through a narrow gorge, then widened, tumbling over rocks and around boulders, making its way to the lake. Rocky waited near a log that had fallen over the gorge and lodged between stone ledges, forming a bridge that spanned the twenty-foot gap.

"Is this the only place to cross?" I asked. The log seemed firmly planted but was wet with the rain.

He nodded and held out his hand for me.

"Oh, thanks, but—" I held up my hands "—I need to balance." With my arms spread out to either side like an airplane, I shuffled across.

As soon as I stepped foot on the other side, Rocky was right behind me. I swung around, my eyes wide.

"Good," he said and passed me by, continuing on at the previous pace.

Good?

Dalton came along side me. "What'd he say?"

I shrugged. "Good."

"Good?" He shook his head. "This guy's something else."

I grinned. "Maybe he's the Kushtaka."

"The what?"

"It's a Tlingit legend. Kushtaka is a half-human, half-otter shapeshifter, a deceptive spirit that lures unwary adventurers to their doom, kind of like the sirens of Homer's Odyssey. He melds with the fog and snatches souls from the wilderness."

"I buy that."

I smirked.

On this side of the gorge, the trees gave way to meadow with rocky patches covered in mosses and lichens of varied greens and textures. Red bunchberries stood out from their broad-leaved plants. This was terrain in which we could more easily keep Rocky in sight. The fog had lifted some as well and the rain had stopped.

Not far, we found him crouched in the grass, pointing to something on the ground.

"Bear," he said and I realized it was scat he was pointing at. Next to it, in the wet soil, a platter-sized footprint remained. "Not long ago. Maybe an hour."

Dalton and I scanned the hillside.

Rocky laughed. Actually, more like a sarcastic huff. "You make so much noise, any respectable animal is already miles from here." He stood back up, adjusted his pack on his shoulders, and continued on.

Dalton let him get several yards away before leaning in to whisper to me. "Which is it? Is he trying to impress us or insult us?"

"I'm not sure *he* knows."

Dalton crouched down and held his hand to the print. The bear's track was nearly twice the size of his hand with his fingers spread wide.

A draft of cool air whispered over the hilltop. "Let's keep moving," he said.

I agreed.

Over the next rise, we came to a halt. Rocky was up ahead. He'd dropped his pack and had the crossbow in hand, stalking something in the bushes. *Whoosh*—a flock of birds took flight. Ptarmigan. Rocky let an arrow fly and one dropped with a thump. He had a second arrow loaded and drawn so fast, the birds were still in range. He fired and a second bird fell from the sky.

"Holy crap," I said to Dalton.

"Holy crap is right. I've never seen anyone shoot like that."

"When Townsend said he was the best, I guess he meant it."

"The man's got skills," he said, genuinely impressed.

Rocky pulled the arrows from the birds, wiped them off in the wet grass, and carefully placed them back in the quiver. He held one of the birds by the neck, ripped it open at the wound site, peeling back its skin, shoved his thumbs inside, tore the breast meat out and tossed what was left on the ground. He did the same with the second bird, tucked the meat in a plastic sack, then hefted his pack once again and set off. Without one word to us.

"Hey Rocky," I shouted after him. "That was pretty amazing. How'd you learn to shoot like that?"

He came to a halt, slowly turned around, stood tall with a smug pride. "I could show you."

"Would you?" *Whatever, dude.*

He set his pack down and held the crossbow out for me.

I dropped my pack and approached him, but as I took hold of the bow, he kept a firm grasp on it and eased beside me. "Here, like this," he said, placing his hand over mine, making sure I held it properly.

"I get it," I said.

The thing had two grips on the bottom like an assault rifle. I positioned the butt against my shoulder, my right finger on the trigger and looked through the scope.

"It's just like shooting a gun. Just as accurate too. I keep an arrow loaded all the time."

"May I?" I said, gesturing toward a rotting, moss-covered stump about thirty yards away.

He hesitated. It might damage an arrow. Then he smiled. "Sure. For you."

I raised the weapon, both hands on the grips, bringing the sights in on the stump. I eased back the trigger and twang, the arrow released with the force of a bullet. A split second later, smack, it lodged in the soft stump.

"Wow, that is accurate," I said, genuinely impressed. "Dalton, you should give it a try."

"Well, it's not a toy," Rocky said, snatching it back from me. He stomped away, pulled the arrow from the stump, then continued on without looking back.

I shot Dalton a look. *What'd I do?*

Dalton shrugged. This guy was an enigma.

Another five hundred yards, we reached the top of a rise where he'd set up the spike camp. The area, about fifteen by twenty feet, was surrounded by an electric fence, a necessity in bear country. The fencing consisted of four wires, each about twelve or so inches apart, stretched between wooden posts, the top wire at eye level.

I dropped my pack and breathed hard to catch my breath.

"Don't tell me that little stroll got you winded," Rocky said, his eyes challenging me. "Maybe I've misjudged you. The bear I was planning to—"

"I'm fine," I said. I pointed to the fence. "That's quite the corral. Is that really necessary?"

"If you want to sleep."

The entry gate was simply the spot where each of the four strands of electric wire had a plastic handle to grab ahold and unhook from where it connected. He unhooked each, motioned for us to enter, then followed us through and set down all his gear. Without a word, he turned right around and headed down the hillside toward a copse of alders in the valley, leaving the gate open.

This lack of communication thing was annoying. "Where's he going?"

Dalton shrugged with a look of resignation. It was what it was. We were here, with this guy, for a hunt. We'd smile, act our part, then go home.

Moments later Rocky appeared pulling a wagon with a plastic storage box mounted on top. *Smart.* The electric fence was probably not visible from the air, if there was even air patrol of the park here. I'd have to check on that. But hiding some gear and not having to carry it in every time made it awfully convenient.

He wheeled the cart into camp, then snapped the electric lines back into place to reconnect. "Can't be too cautious in bear country," he said with an actual grin. He flipped open the lid, reached in, and pulled out a box. "This here's the battery. I'll get that hooked up right away, then we'll get a fire going and grill up your dinner. That sound good?"

I gave him a smile. *Sure, now he's all chatty.*

Dalton pointed at the battery. "Do you need a hand with that?"

Rocky gave no response, as if Dalton wasn't there at all. His eyes on me, he said, "Can you pitch a tent?"

"Of course," I said. I think I liked him better as the sulking, quiet type.

Dalton and I got to work setting up camp. There were only two tents, so that meant Dalton and I would be together. In the same tent. *Don't think about it.* Lying next to each other—*don't think about it!*

We stashed the guns and ammo in the plastic storage box to keep them dry and the rain had let up in time for us to get a fire going, though fresh ptarmigan wasn't something I thought I could stomach.

Rocky skewered the ptarmigan breasts and propped them over the fire. Then he stood a flimsy tripod over that, hung from it a pot he'd pulled from the storage box, filled it with water and a packet of soup from his bag.

We sat in the wet grass around the fire on our rain jackets, eating the warm soup from coffee mugs in silence as the sky grew darker and the meat slowly browned.

The plane looked tiny, resting on the placid lake. The shoreline where we'd come ashore was hidden from this view, far below us, but why would that be a problem? Why was Rocky concerned about the plane being out of sight? Bears wouldn't bother it, would they?

The fog had completely cleared and I could make out part of the route we'd taken up the hillside. A line of trees marked the gorge we'd crossed, now a dark slit amid the lush green. The rest of the hillside, yellow and green, muted into gray.

If it weren't for Rocky, I'd be content to be here, camping in the great outdoors, even though rainclouds lingered on the horizon, hiding any hint of the sunset.

When I finished the last of my soup, Rocky rinsed all the mugs in a small plastic tub, then walked several yards outside the fence to dump the rinse water. When he returned, he tucked everything away in the plastic storage box, then plopped back down by the fire, turning the meat. "We have enough daylight for one hunt a day. We'll set out at first light," he said. His eyes fell on me. "Are you ready?"

My throat started to constrict. "We already flipped a coin. My brother gets to go first."

He shook his head, his gaze locked on me like a tiger's. "I made a plan and you'll follow it."

An awkward moment passed before Dalton shrugged. "Fine with me."

"What the hell was that?" I whispered in Dalton's ear as we lay in the tent.

He shifted to whisper in mine. "I don't know. He's odd, that's for sure. But we have to play this out. Remember what you told Joe."

"I know," I said and pulled away from him. *What am I going to do?*

He moved closer. His breath hot on my neck, he said, "I'll be right there with you."

"He could be right outside the tent, listening to us," I whispered.

Dalton pressed his lips right to my ear. "I know. That's why I'm so close."

His warm body next to mine, snuggled up like a spoon, made me shiver.

"Are you cold?" he asked and inched closer to me.

"No. Yes. I mean, yes I'm cold." *Dammit.*

He put his arm over me and snugged me closer, all warm and strong and...*too close.*

I stiffened and tried to control my breathing. This thing with Dalton was getting too—

"Are you all right?"

"Yes, yes." *No! Get your head on straight, McVie.* I drew in a long breath. Maybe Dalton had a real thing for me. Maybe not. But he was a professional. He wasn't going to cross the line. Ever. He and I both knew what that would mean. The end of our careers. Yep, he was off-limits. End of story.

So why did I want so badly to roll over and—

"I know it's your first time. But we talked about this. It's part of the job."

"Huh? Yeah, I know." *Shut up about the hunting already.*

"And I've got your back. Remember? Partner?"

I nodded. *Partner.* That's what we were. Partners.

"Just get some sleep," he whispered and smoothed my hair across my ear.

Sleep? Are you kidding? With your body pressed against me? Poaching I could handle. But hiding my feelings for Dalton, well, that was another story.

CHAPTER 7

"Gear up," Rocky said after I'd scarfed down an energy bar and half a mug of coffee. He tossed me a bag of trail mix. "We've got a hike to get there."

"I'm ready," I said, stuffing the bag in my pocket.

A clear sky promised a warm, sunny day even though I could see my breath as I got my things ready to go. The sun was already bathing the landscape in pastel orange and there was no rain. The air was crisp and puffs of vapor rose from the surface of the lake. A dusting of snow had fallen on the mountain tops in the night and the highest peaks stood out like white beacons on the horizon.

Dalton handed me my rifle and slung his over his shoulder. We both had daypacks with water, snacks, and emergency gear.

Rocky had repacked his own gear and now carried a backpack, I assume with the tools to skin a bear, a knapsack, his rifle and crossbow, and now, a sidearm on his belt. He looked at me, said "Keep up," and set out.

We trekked over the hill, down into a ravine choked with knee-high brush bearing yellow leaves covered in tiny, shimmering beads of dew that soaked our pants and socks. The smell of wet moss—that distinct scent of autumn—was in the air. After we climbed another rise, we finally stopped for a break. Rocky gave us about forty-five seconds to gulp from our water bottles before pushing on again.

I thought of myself as being in pretty good shape, but this man was inhuman. With all the gear he carried, he didn't break a sweat.

Finally, he slowed as we approached an open valley, wide and dotted with patches of alder. He moved to a moss-covered boulder that stood to my waist and dropped his backpack beside it. "Stay here, armed and alert," he said and disappeared down the slope.

"What the hell?" I said to Dalton once Rocky was out of earshot.

"The guy thinks he's Rambo." Dalton crossed his arms and shook his head. "He's probably going to crawl into a bear den and wrestle him into submission."

"Rambo is right. Damn, he's fit. He moves like a machine."

"Ex-military maybe? Did you notice how he blouses his pants? And the way he wears his cap?" He smirked. "I bet he was a Ranger wash-out."

"Why is that?"

"Well, he wouldn't have made it as a SEAL."

"Right," I said, shaking my head. "Men."

Dalton shifted his stance, standing a little taller. "Hey, it's not that. SEALs have a code. You're part of a team, something greater." His eyes scanned the area where Rocky had gone. "That guy's a lone wolf."

I stared at Dalton. Wasn't that what Mr. Martin had said about me? A lone wolf? I was a problem because I go my own way, make my own decisions? Well, not this time. I was going to do my job, just like I was supposed to. Rocky was tracking the bear. Like Dalton said, he'd find it. He'd do anything it takes. There was big money at stake. And when he came back, I'd have to cross a line I never thought I would.

My throat thickened and my hands started to shake.

Dalton was watching me. He didn't say anything. He didn't have to.

I held the rifle in my hands, ran my finger along the trigger. My dad's voice came to my mind. *Sometimes we have to do things we don't like.* In the vision that came with it, I was sitting in front of a plate of broccoli. I smiled at the memory.

"What are you thinking about?" Dalton asked.

"It's funny, the things that pop into your head. My dad, he..." My hand went to the bracelet my dad had given me.

"Poppy, I know you believe your dad was killed by poachers and we're here—"

"I don't believe. I know."

He held up his hands. "I understand. I'm not saying he wasn't. My point is, being here, well, how are you doing?"

The weird thing was, I hadn't thought of my father again until now, what with my job on the line and the fiasco on the plane. But now all those feelings rushed in. "You don't know the whole story. That file, it paints a picture of my dad that isn't accurate. Like he just happened to be in the wrong place at the wrong time. It's not true. My dad had a purpose, a reason. He was passionate about what he did. Maybe he didn't know the extent of the danger he was in, but that doesn't make him an idiot."

Dalton nodded in understanding.

"An idealist, surely, but—" I sucked in my breath. My gaze locked on Dalton.

He stared back at me, his eyes filled with compassion.

I turned away. *Dammit.* "I'm not my dad."

"Okay," Dalton said. A whisper.

I spun back to face him. "It's not the same anyway."

"I know."

I can't shoot a bear.

Dalton nodded, acceptance in his expression as though he'd read my mind.

My gaze shifted to the horizon, away from this conversation, these thoughts. "Where is that guy, anyway?"

"God knows," Dalton said with a shake of his head.

About twenty awkward minutes or so passed, me pacing, Dalton examining his cuticles, before we spotted Rocky coming over the hill.

Once he got within earshot, he said, "No sign of him in that direction. But I'm going to find him for you, darlin'. You'll see. I'm going to check to the west. You just sit tight. Be ready."

"Okay," I said.

As soon as he was gone again, I turned to Dalton. "Darlin'?"

Dalton stared after him, a look of concern on his face.

"Dalton?"

"Huh?" He turned. "Yeah?"

"Darlin'?"

He just shrugged and shook his head. As soon as Rocky was out of sight again, Dalton said, "Check it out," pointing to a spot along the ridge.

"What is it?" I asked.

"I'll be right back."

"Great," I said as he moseyed away, leaving me alone with my thoughts.

As Dalton wandered away, I followed his backside, that nice, tight—*knock it off!* I spun around and looked out over the landscape in the other direction, took a deep breath, then slowly turned back toward Dalton.

About two hundred yards away he'd come to a halt. He gave me a wave with a nod. Whatever that meant. Then he seemed to be picking leaves from some bushes. No, he was picking berries.

About ten minutes later, he came back with a handful of blueberries.

"There's a whole patch of them over there," he said with a boyish grin as he took my hand in his and filled it with plump berries.

At his touch, I felt my cheeks turn pink. *Dammit!*

I tossed a few of the berries into my mouth and squished them against my tongue, enjoying the sweet and tangy taste. "Thanks," I managed, facing the other way so he couldn't see my cheeks. How embarrassing. You'd think I was ten and he was my first crush.

"I don't know where Rocky went, but any self-respecting bear in the area will be by to hit that patch of berries," Dalton said. "The branches are drooping with them."

I could only nod. That grin had left me tongue-tied.

Another four hours passed as Dalton and I leaned against the boulder, talking about nothing, my nerves on a razor's edge, before Rocky appeared again. As he approached, he didn't have the same vigor in his stride.

"I know there's a trophy bear in these parts. I've seen him. I've tracked him. I ain't lyin'." He paced, wringing his hands. "I'll find him for sure tomorrow."

Relief flooded over me, but I did my best to look disappointed.

"I won't let you down. I swear it. I'm gonna get you your bear, ya hear me?"

I managed a reassuring nod. "It's all right. We've got several more days, right?"

"Yeah, yeah. But I'll find him tomorrow. You wait and see. Tomorrow."

He was so apologetic, I almost felt bad. Almost.

Rocky marched back to camp without another word. Once inside the fence, he dropped his pack and weapons in a pile, flipped open the lid of the box, and stomped back and forth, hanging his head as he built a fire.

He hung the pot over the flames and attacked the soup packaging, ripping it open with his knife, then shook the contents into the pot, crumpled the bag and tossed it to the ground.

Dalton and I watched in silence, avoiding any interaction, fearing it might irritate him even more.

Once the soup was ready, he dished it out, handing us the mugs without eye contact.

Pushing his issues from my mind, I wrapped my hands around the mug of soup, enjoying the warmth, and inhaled the Asian-spiced scent of the broth. When I drank it down, nothing had ever tasted as good. Something about being out all day in the fresh air, the physical exertion, that makes anything with nourishment and extra salt taste heavenly.

While we ate, Rocky poured over a map and journal, his notes, I assumed, from his scouting expeditions to find bears. He probably kept accounts of every sighting, every direction, time of day, trying to understand the habits of any particular bear. Like Dalton had said, there was big money on the table.

After Rocky had rinsed our dishes and packed up camp for the night, he headed for his tent. He unzipped the fly, and without turning to face me, he said, "Tomorrow. I'll prove myself to you tomorrow," and crawled in.

The next morning, we set out again for the same boulder. With the same strategy, Rocky left us alone to track the bear.

Dalton whispered to me. "I hope he brings in a bear today. I'm not sure what he'll do if he doesn't."

"I was thinking the same thing," I said, but if I was honest, I'd rather have had to deal with a disgruntled Rocky than have to kill a bear. I was content to lean against that rock next to Dalton, the sun on my face, and let the day slip away in uneventful bliss. But deep down, I knew it wouldn't. I was going to have to face it. There was no crawling back out of the rabbit hole.

I leaned my head back and closed my eyes. *What the holy hell am I going to do?*

About an hour later, Rocky appeared, coming up over the bluff, heading for us at a pretty good clip, shouting and gesturing for me to raise my weapon.

Dalton turned toward me. "It's time. You ready, Poppy?"

My heart thrummed in my chest. I nodded and placed my rifle on the boulder, using it to steady myself.

"Get ready," Rocky said as he approached.

No! No, no, no. "I was born ready." My nerves buzzed up and down my arms.

He looked at me from under his cap. "I mean be alert. Ready. He's coming." He said it in a creepy voice like we were in a Stephen King film. Man, these guys were all about the drama, the thrill.

From his knapsack he pulled out some kind of remote control box that had a fancy joystick and a video monitor.

A surge of anger rushed through me. This asshole had a drone.

"Dude," Dalton said with a full-fledged, dumbass-grin. "That is kick ass."

"Be ready," Rocky warned, fiddling with the joystick.

As soon as I heard the whir of the drone, the bear emerged on the hill across from us, about four hundred yards away, running full speed toward me, all muscle, fur and teeth. He could cover the distance between us in twenty seconds. My heart went into overdrive, sending adrenaline coursing through my veins. I swear I could hear my heartbeat vibrating against my eardrums. I gripped the rifle handle and told myself to breathe.

Rocky worked the drone, steering it to dive-bomb the

bear. The bear spun on it and reared up, swiping at it with his monster-sized paw. Rocky managed to work the drone just out of the bear's reach, making him swat at it again and again, getting him frustrated and angry. All for the excitement, so a poacher could shoot a charging bear.

"Ready?" Rocky said.

I managed to nod, my finger on the trigger, shaking.

The drone swooped downward and the bear started to chase it, but then turned. The drone zoomed upward, then swooped back downward toward the bear, making him run again. The bear took three strides, then dropped to the ground, spun around again, and roared. The bear's rage rumbled down my spine.

"C'mon, you bastard," Rocky said, working the controller. I wanted to yank it from his hands and slam it into his face.

The drone dipped and buzzed, spun around the bear's head like a giant bee, until it pushed him into a run again.

"You got him now," Dalton said with a whoop.

"He's a trophy, girl," Rocky grunted. "Get ready. All nine hundred pounds of him are headed this way."

The drone zoomed from left to right, keeping the bear on a path straight for me. The poor thing didn't have a chance. What the hell kind of hunt was this? How could anyone think this was fun?

"Get him in your sights," Rocky growled.

I leaned over the gun and looked through the scope, my heart pounding. The bear was moving closer, and fast.

"Shoot!" Rocky pushed. "Hundred fifty yards, take him."

All fur and muscle, bearing down on me. Brown eyes, enraged and angry. I aimed, blinked, holding my breath. I pulled to the side and above his head, and fired.

The sound of the rifle ricocheted off the hills, echoing in the distance.

The bear skidded to a stop fifty yards away.

Rocky dropped his hands to his sides. "You missed? Really?"

The bear huffed and snapped his jaws, swinging his head from side to side, white froth dripping from his mouth.

I tried to reload, but my hands were shaking like crazy.

The bear lowered his head and charged. Dalton stood up to his full height, raised his arms, and shouted at the bear. About twenty feet from us, the bear threw his weight and turned away.

I let out my breath. It was a bluff. *Run, bear, run! Run away!*

Kaboom! Boom, boom, boom! Rocky was beside me, his sidearm raised, unloading the clip into the bear. The big bruin staggered sideways and collapsed on the ground with a grunt.

I was shaking so hard I couldn't get words out.

Dalton was there. "What the hell, dude? He turned. You could have brought him back around again."

Rocky holstered his gun, swung around and locked on me. "You choked." He shook his head, disappointed, then something shifted in him. His demeanor changed, the way he stood. His eyes turned glassy and seemed to pass right through me.

Dalton got in his face. "Hey, give her a break, man."

Rocky took a step closer to me, not just ignoring Dalton, but passing him by as though he didn't exist. "It's too bad," he said, his voice like gravel. "I hoped you'd be different than all the rest."

Dalton stepped between us. "Hey, I'm talking to you. What the hell is your problem?"

Rocky lifted his eyes to meet mine. They narrowed and shifted into focus. "What a disappointment." He curled up his lip in disgust. His eyes traveled down my body, then slowly back up and I felt ripped bare. "You don't even realize it," he growled as he took a strand of my hair in his hand and twirled it through his fingers. "If it wasn't for me, you'd be dead." His eyes darkened. "Out here, it's kill or be killed."

CHAPTER 8

Dalton wedged himself between me and Rocky. "Dude, back the hell off already!"

Rocky blinked his eyes and blinked again, then hung his head, the shy outcast returning.

While Dalton and I exchanged uncomfortable glances, Rocky rummaged through his pack for tools to skin the bear. "The scent of blood will bring 'em running," he said to Dalton, shoving his rifle at him. "Cover me. I'll be quick about it."

He warily approached the bear, then kicked it with his boot to make sure it was dead. I turned away but couldn't escape the sounds as he sawed at the skin and ripped open the hide.

"It's all right, Sis. You'll get one next time," Dalton said, his eyes scanning the hills. "You got buck fever, that's what you done. Happens to lots of people." He grinned. "Except me of course."

One thing about Dalton: he could stay in character.

He gave me a reassuring wink. "I bet Rocky here can keep a secret," he went on. "We don't have to tell nobody you choked."

"I didn't choke," I said. "I just—I just missed. Okay."

Rocky's hands were covered in blood. He had the two front paws sawed off of the bear and was working on a foot.

I glanced at Dalton, my head still spinning from Rocky's bizarre behavior. I managed to get my thoughts in order. We were poachers. Unethical, greedy poachers. "I guess that'll still make a nice rug."

"Now you're talking," Dalton said with a nod.

Rocky paused, but didn't look up at me. "Too late," he muttered and went back at it.

"Well, what, that's it then?" I said. "Will I get another shot? Will you find another bear?" *God, please say no.*

"Dunno," Rocky said, dropping the severed leg and lifting the last one to remove the paw.

"What are you doing there, anyway?" I asked even though I knew. Bears paws were worth a fortune on the black market. In Korea, they have been considered an exotic delicacy since the ancient dynasties, reserved only for the elite. A bowl of bear paw soup can sell for as much as one thousand dollars.

"Taking my pay," he said. He plunged his knife into the bear's gut, made a slice, then reached into the entrails and pulled out the gall bladder. He didn't have to fish around. He knew exactly how to get to it. He'd done this many times before.

A gall bladder was worth more than the paws on the black market. Some believe the bile can cure all kinds of ailments, though modern science proves otherwise.

"Open my pack and get some water to rinse my hands," he said to me. There was no please.

I doused his hands, trying not to look at the gall bladder. He stuffed it into a Ziploc bag, along with the paws, hefted his backpack, and said, "Let's go."

"That's it?" I asked. "What about the carcass?" The bear lay there, his blood soaking the ground, his vacant eyes staring at nothing.

He jerked his head toward the forest. "Something'll eat it," he said, turned his back to me and walked away.

Once we arrived back in camp, Rocky got a fire going and hung a pot of water to boil for coffee. The guide once again.

A cold, drizzly rain fell like mist. I sat down on the tarp next to the fire, holding my hands to the flame, trying to get rid of the chill and at the same time keep them from shaking.

Rocky dumped a spoonful of coffee grounds into the pot, then slung his rifle over his shoulder. "I'll be back to get dinner going. Gotta check in."

"What? You're leaving us here?" I said, getting to my feet.

"You'll be fine. The fence is on." He looked at me from under his cap. "I just forgot the satellite phone in the plane is all."

Something about his tone was off. He was trying too hard to be cordial. "Oh, yeah, okay," I said with a smile. "We'll be here."

Dalton and I watched him in silence as he trudged down the hill, then disappeared on the other side, then reappeared as he crossed the river on the log bridge.

"I've got a bad feeling about this," I whispered to Dalton, even though Rocky was more than five hundred yards away by now. "He didn't leave the phone in the plane. I'm sure he's had it with him all along. Shit, what if we're blown?"

Dalton, calm as can be, said, "We stay the course."

"And what the hell was that all about after he shot the bear? This guy's a serious head case."

Dalton nodded in agreement, concern in his eyes.

"I know this is an important case, but I don't think I can spend another day out here with him. He's giving me the creeps."

"I don't like him either. That's why I'm not going to leave your side." He flashed me a smile and his gaze dropped to my chest, ever so briefly. "So try to enjoy it." He turned away abruptly, as though catching himself. His eyes swept over the landscape. "It's gorgeous out here."

I took the opportunity to enjoy his backside, how his hiking pants fit snugly over the nice curve of his ass. As he turned back, my eyes snapped to the lake. "It is beautiful, but Rocky's ruined it all. Do you think he's really calling Townsend and he just didn't want us to hear the conversation?"

I could see Dalton's mind turning over the possibility. "Maybe."

"We're blown. That's what it is. I blew it."

Dalton looked me in the eyes, strong and steady. "We stay the course." He waited for me to nod confirmation. "There's nothing to indicate our cover is blown. People choke and miss all the time."

I nodded. "You're right. He's just so…weird."

"Well, there's that. But Poppy—" he gave his full attention to our conversation "—we're going to stay the course. You with me?"

I inhaled and blew out my breath with a sigh. "Yeah. I'm with you."

The campfire popped and crackled. Dalton used a stick to give it a stir and stuffed another log under the hanging pot. He stood up and ran his fingers through his hair, all curly from the misty rain.

I chewed on my fingernail. Yep, I needed to figure out what to do. Being with Dalton like this, damn, it was going to get me in trouble. But then again, maybe it wouldn't matter. I was probably going to be fired anyway. This op was going nowhere, and as soon as I got back, I had to face an investigation. There was nothing I could do now but power through this and keep my cover—

"Shit, Dalton." I threw my hands up. "He's suspicious. That's what it is. He's going to tell Townsend. I should have—"

"We don't know that." He shook his head as though something wasn't adding up. "Listen. If he suspected us, why would he still take the paws and gall bladder? Right in front of us?"

"I don't know. Maybe he's cocky and thinks the evidence to corroborate our story is being devoured by ravens and wolves right now."

Dalton rested his hands on his hips and stared in the direction Rocky had gone. "But being caught with the bear parts would be enough for a conviction. He'd know that. So why's he going to the plane? To stash the goods? And why did he anchor the plane out where he could see it instead of leaving it on shore? What's he worried about?"

"Good question." I scanned the landscape around us. All hills and forest. No sign of humans save for the aroma of our fresh coffee in the air. "We are literally in the middle of nowhere. No one is going to come along and steal the plane. They'd have to arrive by another plane to do it."

Dalton spun around. "The radio."

"You think he's using the radio on the plane? To call another plane? Maybe to pick up the bear parts?" I looked out at the plane floating on the lake. Rocky should be almost to it by now, but it was getting too dark to see anything on the surface of the lake.

"I don't know," Dalton said, hands on his hips again, his eyes traveling to the storage box. "It doesn't really make sense." He turned to face me. "Maybe he's planning to make a call on the sat phone, but not to Townsend." He shrugged. "Or maybe he really forgot the phone. Maybe it's legit."

"I don't believe anything's legit with that guy." All I could think about was the bear, charging toward me, then turning, scared, and him firing away. I gnashed my teeth together. "Kill or be killed. What an ass. That bear turned away. It was running away."

"He had it pretty aggravated." Dalton's attention was on me now. "We don't know what it would have done."

"Don't tell me you're defending him. There wasn't an

imminent threat. It was clearly a bluff. The bear had turned."

"I know," he said, holding his hands up in mock surrender. "I'm just saying that it was a dangerous situation, like we talked about. If it would have turned back again, and headed toward you, we would've had only seconds. If that happened, I would've—"

"But it didn't." I pressed my lips together, trying not to get emotional. "That bear had already backed down. To kill it like he did was..."

Dalton smiled at me, his eyes lingering on mine.

I frowned. "What?"

"You."

His expression changed, unexpected. He wasn't arguing with me or trying to convince me. He was—I don't know. "Me what?"

He stepped toward me. The way his eyes held mine made my pulse jump. "That bear was twenty feet away, in a rage, and you still believed, right up 'til the last second that it was a bluff charge. You truly are an optimist."

"Optimist. Ha!" I turned from his gaze. "That's what gets me in trouble."

"I wish I could be more like you."

"Don't mock me." I didn't need another lecture right now.

"Never," he said, putting his hands on my shoulders and gently pulling me toward him. "Look at me."

Something in his tone, a softness, made me give in. I turned toward him and raised my eyes to meet his.

"Don't ever lose that. You don't see the predator, like everyone else does, as a mindless killer." He took my hand and held it between his warm hands. "You see the beautiful being within."

"You think I'm naive." I pulled my hand away. "Don't talk to me like I'm a child."

"No," he said, shaking his head and taking my hand again.

This time, the feel of his hands on mine, the look in his eyes, stirred a fire inside me, one I ached to give in to. "Not at all. I'm saying I'm trying, trying not to always see the bad, the dark, the evil in everything. I wish I could see the good, the beauty in things, like you do. But when you've seen what I've seen, you think only in terms of survival, how you'll live to breathe another day." He smiled, a soft, resigned smile. "Then someone like you comes along." His eyes were clear, honest. "And you make me feel like life's worth living again."

"Well, I…" My cheeks flushed pink. *Damn cheeks!*

"I mean it, Poppy. Honest. It's what I…it's what I love about you."

My insides tingled. *Did he just say what I think he said?* His eyes on me felt so comfortable, so right.

The fire sparked. The pop made me pull back with a jerk, but Dalton held onto my hand, gentle yet strong. A warm electricity radiated from his hand to mine. He wasn't letting go.

A tiny dimple creased his cheek, enhanced by the light from the fire, as he smiled at me, his eyes locked with mine. He leaned toward me. A little closer. My heart raced and my hand felt tingly.

"Dalton, I don't think—"

"We have time."

Standing so close to me, I could feel his desire, like sparks shooting through the air between us. But he was off-limits. But god, he would be so worth it. But no, he was off-limits.

"We need to be careful. This op, my job—"

"Yeah and I could get fired just for what I'm thinking right now," he said with a mischievous grin that made my insides flush with heat, firing up places that shouldn't be fired up.

He stepped closer to me, so close I could feel his breath on my face. Our clothes were the only thing between us, the only barrier. Wow, it was hot out here. Like the heat stirred up from a tropical hurricane. And I was in the center of it, in the eye of the storm.

He cupped my cheek in his hand and his gaze lingered on my lips as his finger traced my jaw. I couldn't breathe. His eyes made their way back to mine as the tip of his finger lightly brushed my lips.

Then he paused. Was he having second thoughts? Pulling back? The corner of his mouth was still turned up into that irresistible grin. Was he amused? Already feeling regret?

Shut up, brain!

He'd dropped his gaze back to my lips and his breath came in short puffs.

I couldn't take the anticipation anymore. I surrendered to it. I reached around his neck, pulled us closer, and kissed him. He responded to me with the same passion, slipping his hands from my hips to my lower back, pulling me tight against him. His lips, his warm tongue, the feel of his stubble, rough on my face, sent shivers of desire up and down my spine. I pushed my fingers through the curls at the back of his neck, holding on.

I couldn't get enough, couldn't get close enough. I wanted him. Passion rippled through me like wildfire. I tugged at his shirt.

"Ah, well, isn't this interesting." A voice behind us.

I flung myself away from Dalton, my chest heaving.

Rocky stood there, a strange grin on his face, his sidearm in his hand, pointed at Dalton.

"Well, well, well." He moved toward us.

Shit! Our situation, the op—Dalton's supposed to be my brother. *We're blown! Oh shit! Oh shit!* I tried to move but my knees turned to rubber, like I was fighting quicksand. How did he get inside the wires without us noticing?

Dalton side-stepped away, putting space between us—textbook procedure for one assailant. At least he had his wits about him.

Rocky's eyes were locked on me, but he managed to keep the weapon trained on Dalton. "I admit, I wasn't expecting that." His eyes narrowed. He was thinking, considering some idea. The firelight flickered on his face, making him seem even more menacing. "Can't blame you," he said to Dalton. "She is one hot little tomcat. I plan to have a little fun with her myself." He turned his head toward Dalton and raised the gun to aim. "But you'd be in the way."

No! I lunged forward and kicked the boiling pot into the air. Hot coffee splashed in his face. He reared back, yelping, stumbled and fell. As he hit the ground, flat on his back, he fired blindly into the air.

"Run!" I yelled.

CHAPTER 9

I spun toward the gate. It was open. I ran so fast I couldn't believe my legs kept up with me. Dalton was right behind me, hollering, "Go, go, go!"

Shots fired in the air. I ducked. Adrenaline surged through my veins and spurred me on. I zigged left, heading for a copse of alders for some cover. One stride, then another, then another and I plunged into the brush, my heart hammering in my chest, branches slapping me in the face.

"Get down," Dalton was saying, right on my heels. "Get down!"

I dropped to my hands and knees, pushing through the brambles.

"Hold up," Dalton said, grabbing my ankle.

"Are you crazy?" I dug my elbows into the ground, pulling myself along.

"He's not following us."

"What?" I halted, listening.

"Damn. He's smart," Dalton said. "Just sit tight a minute."

"Sit tight?" I gasped, catching my breath. "You can't be serious."

"Shhh. Listen."

I held my breath. A wolf howled, a long mournful note. Then a yip-yip-yip, followed by another long, drawn out yowl. It was coming from the camp.

"Is that—?"

"The crazy bastard knows he's got us."

At once, I realized Dalton was right. Rocky had no reason to chase us down. He'd lose his advantage. In the camp, he had food, fire, shelter. He had all the weapons.

We had nothing.

And it was dusk already. Soon it'd be pitch dark. "Shit, Dalton. What were we thinking?" *How could I be so stupid?* "How did we let him sneak up on us like that? I thought he was half a mile away."

"Me too." He pushed back some branches, shifting to get a better view. "Me too."

"But now he knows we're agents!"

"We don't know that."

"He just caught us kissing! Seriously, Dalton? You think the brother-sister tryst is the most believable story here?"

Dalton's eyes never left Rocky, who stoked the fire, calm as can be. "It doesn't mean he thinks we're agents. Never assume."

"He pulled his weapon." I shook my head. "We're screwed." *Shit!*

Dalton turned to face me. "Maybe it was—" His eyes fixed on my forehead. "You okay?" With his hand on my chin, he turned my head to examine my face.

I wiped at a trickle of blood on my forehead. "Just a scrape from a branch."

"It sliced your skin pretty good," he said, concerned.

"I'm fine."

He frowned and turned back, his eyes trained on the camp, on making sure Rocky was still there. "Maybe it was a knee-jerk reaction. Maybe he had already planned to confront us for some reason. We don't know."

"Well, what's it matter? We screwed up. Big time. And now we're out here and he's back there. With all the guns."

"It matters because it will help us anticipate his next move."

"His next move? Seriously? You think he's already got a strategic plan?"

"I don't know." He rubbed his chin. "Depends." He turned to me again. "What'd he say exactly?"

I pushed up next to him so I could get a better view of the camp. "When? When he pulled the gun?"

"Yeah."

"I don't know. Something about me being a wild cat. Some crap about taking his turn."

"Exactly."

"Exactly what?" What did that have to do with it?

Dalton patted his pants, front and back, then sorted through his jacket pockets. "I've got a jackknife," he said. "What about you?"

I smacked him on the arm. "Earth to Dalton. Exactly what?"

"That's not what a poacher would say when he realizes you're an agent."

"Well, maybe…" The memory rattled around in my brain. The look on Rocky's face wasn't surprise. It was…amusement? "I guess you're right. What do you think it means?"

"Don't know for sure. I'm just trying to assess the situation. Did he say anything to you back at the lodge? Anything at all that might make sense of this?"

"Not really. No. He probably said a total of three words to me before we got into the plane with him. He was always with Townsend, standing behind him and—oh crap."

"What?"

"Do you think he's angry that I complained about having to hunt with him? So angry he'd shoot at me?"

Dalton cocked his head to the side, considering this. "You did a pretty good job of dismissing him."

"But to shoot at me for it?"

"I don't know. You challenged his manhood, his skills as a hunter. People have killed for much less."

I shook my head. "But that doesn't make sense either. He had the gun pointed at you."

Dalton nodded, concern etched across his face. "Yeah. I know." He puzzled a moment, then gestured toward my pockets. "What do you have on you?"

I unzipped my coat pockets, one at a time and produced a baggie of trail mix with about one handful left, a tube of lip balm, and some tissues. That was it. Our daypacks, with all our emergency survival gear, were back at the camp, inside our tent. I patted my coat for any forgotten pockets and my hand fell on the necklace around my neck and the tiny compass pendant that hung there. *Oh Chris, I really screwed up this time.*

A melodic whistle came our way from the camp. A lazy, ho-hum kind of tune, as though Rocky purposefully wanted us to know how cozy he was back in camp.

"He's a nut job. That's why this doesn't make sense." I shivered, suddenly realizing how cold I was. My pants from my knees down were soaking wet. I pulled my jacket tight around me and snugged the collar up over my face. The pungent scent of woodsmoke filled my nose and made me feel even colder.

Dalton moved closer to me and I thought he was going to put his arms around me, but then he didn't. "We need to stay warm. As soon as it's good and dark, we'll move to a new location. Not far. Where I can keep an eye on him."

"What do you mean, not far? I vote for getting the hell out of here."

"And go where?" Dalton said. "There's nothing for hundreds of miles in any direction. Glacier-covered mountains to the south and west, open ocean to the east, and marshy bog to the north. The odds are pretty good we'd die out there."

"What about the plane? Don't you know how to fly it? You were a SEAL. Doesn't that stand for sea, air, land? Air as in fly?"

"They taught us how to jump out of an airplane, not how to fly it." He ran his fingers through his hair, his tell. He was frustrated, trying to sort this out.

"Don't ever play poker," I said.

"What?" He pulled away to look at me. "Poker? What are you—"

"Nothing. Sorry." I pulled the jacket tighter.

"Are you cold?" he asked. "You're cold." He put his arm around me, hesitated as if waiting for me to object, then snuggled me tight to him. "We need to keep warm," he said.

"I know," I replied, wondering why it felt so awkward all of a sudden. He had just kissed me. Or rather, I'd kissed him. I was sure he'd wanted to—*oh hell, what a mess*.

"I want to know what he's up to," Dalton said. "See if I can figure out what he's planning. I bet, at least for now, he'll stay where he is. He'll protect the weapons and gear and let us get cold and tired. If he comes out, he risks one of us circling back and taking possession of the camp."

"You know, maybe being agents is an advantage. Maybe we should threaten him with jail time, tell him how much more trouble he'll be in when they send a team out looking for us. Encourage him to go in peacefully. Right now, we could promise a misdemeanor charge, which would probably get thrown out anyway."

The whistling came again, this time with long, sorrowful notes.

Dalton shook his head. "I don't know. I don't think this guy…"

"You don't think this guy what? It could work. Maybe he doesn't know the law. Maybe he'll believe us."

"I bet he knows the law better than we do. No"—he shook his head again—"if we admit we're agents, we put Joe at risk. All Rocky has to do is call Townsend."

"How do we know he won't do that anyway? Or that he hasn't already?"

Dalton frowned. "Good point." He turned to me. "Doesn't matter though. First rule of undercover work—"

"Never reveal your cover. I know," I said.

"We need to move."

"Are you sure?" I didn't want to let go of Dalton and the relative safety I'd felt for the last two minutes. "For all we know he has night-vision binoculars."

"He might. But right now, he knows where we are for sure. If we move, at least we'll have some advantage."

He was right of course. He was a SEAL. Trained by the best military in the world. If he had a plan, it would be a good one. Maybe it was time to trust. Like Mr. Martin said, *be a team player.* "Okay," I said. "You're the SEAL."

"What's that supposed to mean?"

"It means I'm being a team player. You're trained in strategic combat tactics, reconnaissance, et cetera, et cetera, right? I'm just saying, I'll follow you."

"Right," he said, pausing a moment as if he thought there was a catch, but then seemed to accept my explanation and moved to a crouch. Hunched over, he slipped through the alders, quiet as a cat. I followed, trying not to make a sound. We pushed through the back side of the copse and ran up a rise, then circled back to a spot with downed trees and a pile of brush and hunkered down behind a log where we could see Rocky's campfire.

The darkness enveloped us like a protective cloak. My hands shook. I blew on them, trying to get them warm, then shoved them in my pants pockets. My gloves lay on the grass, back in camp, next to the fire. The warm fire.

Dalton leaned against a stump and took my hand and pulled me down to sit between his legs, his arms around me. "We need to stay warm. It's important," he said. "Our worst enemy out here is hypothermia."

"Not the guy shooting at us?"

Dalton smirked. "Yeah, other than that." He snugged me tighter. "I'm serious. The rain and wind are not our friends. If we get soaking wet, we'll lose body heat twenty times faster than just in cold air."

He was right. In an instant, we'd been plunged into a serious survival situation. If Rocky didn't get us, and we weren't careful, the wilderness would. We had to think of every move in terms of life and death.

Snuggling with Dalton, though, felt a lot like heaven.

After I got situated where I could see the camp as well, I asked, "So what are you thinking?"

"He's smart. If he didn't leave camp before, he's not going to in the dark, but we should take turns on watch, just in case."

I nodded. "That's fine, but come morning, what's our plan?"

"I'm thinking."

"We're going to have to lure him out and subdue him on our own. I don't see any other option."

"But how? With what? He's got all the weapons, remember. This terrain is mostly open hills. There aren't many places to hide for an ambush and he'd never fall for it anyway."

I gritted my teeth together. "Well, what do you suggest?"

"I'm still thinking." A long moment passed, then he said, "We need to better understand the situation."

"You just said yourself, he's got the guns. We have none. He's got the food. We have none. He's got my warm, snuggly sleeping bag. And I've got—"

He pulled me closer. "I mean his mindset."

"His mindset is he doesn't want to go to prison. I say we try to make a deal."

"Maybe." Dalton wasn't convinced. "We'll see. In the morning. Maybe he'll talk."

"I'll take the first watch," I said and leaned into Dalton. Even with his arms wrapped around me, there was no way I was going to get any sleep. My mind was spinning in too many directions but mainly...*what the hell just happened?*

Denali's peak rose out of the northern horizon and seemed to join the stars. The moon shimmered across the lake and, despite the cold rain that fell earlier, the air had a hint of warmth and was filled with the scents of autumn. This could have been a perfect night.

If it weren't for that crazy man with the guns.

CHAPTER 10

The sun rises slowly in the northern latitudes, but today it felt like an interminable wait before it was high enough in the sky to confirm Rocky was sitting on his camp chair, not just a silhouette figure we'd assumed was him. He lounged, drinking a cup of coffee as though it was just another day camping in the great Alaskan wilderness.

Nothing had changed all night. But at least, after we'd moved, we were farther away and on higher ground if he would have left the camp and come after us. Dalton was adamant that we move back into the stand of alder before sunrise. He said being there would make us look less skilled, like we'd stayed there all night with no vantage point, and added that it was a better place to hide my location if I was going to try to talk to Rocky.

I couldn't argue with that logic. We didn't have a lot of choices.

I rubbed my hands together, trying to get warm. I drew in a deep breath and my nose filled with the aroma of fresh coffee and frying bacon. My stomach rumbled. *Geez, buddy. Nothing like enjoying your stay.*

"Here's what I want you to do," Dalton said. "When you speak to him, no matter what, I want you to keep your head down. Stay hidden from sight. Do you understand? I'll be the eyes."

"Sure, I guess. But won't he be able to pinpoint my location by my voice?"

"Maybe. He'll know the general area you are anyway. But if you stay hidden, he'll be watching for you. That's what we want. Him looking for you, not for me."

"What? Why? What are you going to be doing?"

"Assessing the situation."

"Right." I nodded. "Wait, what? Where will you be?"

"I won't be far. Just far enough where he won't spot me while he's looking for you."

"Okay," I said. That made sense. I supposed.

"Are you all right?" Dalton asked.

"Yeah," I nodded. "Yes." Trust your partner, that's what I was doing. What was that old saying, too many chiefs? I was going to do my best.

"Give me two minutes," he said, then belly crawled away from me through the brush.

I waited. Then waited some more, listening to Rocky whistle that same damn lazy tune while I plucked some twigs from my hair.

Maybe Dalton was right. Maybe Rocky hadn't called Townsend. Maybe this wasn't about us being agents. I shook my head. Of course it was.

Enough time had passed for Dalton to get into place. It was now or never. "Rocky!" I shouted.

Nothing. Certainly he could hear me. There was no doubt. I could hear his whistling from here. Which had stopped. What was he doing?

"Rocky!" I shouted again, into the cold air.

No acknowledgment. I wanted to crawl over to Dalton to see what was going on, but I'd promised to stay hidden.

A raven called in the distance, breaking the eerie silence.

"Listen, this is crazy. Let's talk about the situation."

Nothing. I stared at the tangle of alder branches surrounding me, keeping me hidden, yet keeping me from seeing what was happening. I felt like a sitting duck. What if Rocky was coming for me right now?

This wasn't working. We were getting nowhere. *No. Trust Dalton. He's watching.*

The whistling started again, a strange tune, like a New Orleans funeral dirge. I imagined him cleaning the weapons, part by part, and reassembling them, a creepy grin on his face.

Well, what the hell, here goes. "Look. I know you can hear me. I want you to know, we're not upset. Things just got a little out of hand. There's no reason we can't forget the whole thing. What do you say?"

The whistling stopped. What was he doing now? Dalton had completely disappeared in the brush. Too far away. *Dammit.* What was going on? Something wasn't right. I could feel it.

I rose, just to get a peek, make sure Rocky was still in the camp. I took one step to the right and bang—a shot fired, then a burning sensation seared though my upper thigh. I looked down. Blood was soaking my pant leg. I dropped to the ground and the pain hit me full force, like a hot ice pick had been shoved into my leg. I tried to breathe. Then Dalton was there, hovering over me.

"I told you to stay hidden," he said, his voice urgent.

"I… you…I just…" My breath returned in a rush. "God that hurts!"

He ripped my pant leg open and took my hand. "Squeeze my hand."

Breathe. Breathe. The pain.

"Squeeze my hand."

Oh my god, he shot me.

"Squeeze my hand!"

I clenched his hand with all my strength.

"Good." He moved my hand to my thigh. "Now squeeze

here and don't let go."

I did as he said and hot fire shot down my leg. My body clenched and I was in his arms and he was running, pushing through the branches.

"It's all right, I've got you. I've got you," he kept saying.

Blurry. Everything a blur. I clamped my eyes shut. My entire being flushed in agony, radiating from my thigh. Waves of dizzying nausea hit me, then the pull of sleep. Oh to escape to the bliss of peaceful, painless sleep. Darkness on all sides.

"Stay with me," Dalton said, shaking me. "Stay with me."

I was lying on the cold ground. Dalton knelt over me, his chest bare. Why was his chest bare?

He tugged at my thigh, a tightening, and the pain shot to my head, jolting me from my grogginess. I screamed out.

"That. Hurts," I managed, my hands going to my thigh.

"Good," he said, putting his coat back on over his bare torso. "That means you're not in complete shock."

Was that relief I saw on his face? I tried to sit up and the blood drained from my head.

"No, no, no," he said. "Stay right where you are."

"But, Rocky, he shot me. He's—" I blinked my eyes, trying to focus. "We have to get out of here."

"It's all right. He hasn't left the camp."

"I didn't think he'd actually—" I looked down at the bloody mess of my thigh. Dalton had tied a tourniquet above the wound. "I should've listened to you. He tried to kill me."

"I don't think so," Dalton said.

"What?" He wasn't making any sense. "He shot me."

"I know."

I got my hands underneath me and pushed myself up.

"Easy now. You're safe right where you are. Sit back."

We were on the bank of a tiny stream that trickled down the hillside with a lazy gurgle. Pieces of Dalton's shirt lay on the ground in torn, bloody hunks.

"I think I got it cleaned good. The bullet went right through. Brushed you really. You're lucky." He ripped a clean piece of the shirt and tied it around the wound for a bandage.

"Lucky? He shot me!"

Dalton grinned. "Welcome to the club."

I looked down at the bloody bandage. "Damn that hurts."

Dalton winked. "You need to rest. And don't move that leg. I don't have any way to suture it."

He took my hand and dumped the trail mix into it. "Eat that."

"No." I protested. "It's all we've got. You need some."

"You eat it all," he said. "I'm fine." Then a pause. "You said you'd follow me. Right? I say you eat it."

I did as he told me, crunching nuts between my teeth.

He dunked the baggie into the stream and brought it to my mouth. "Take a drink."

"But is it safe?"

He shrugged. "We'll worry about giardia later. You need to drink."

I sipped the ice cold water and glanced around. "Where are we?"

"Out of sight," he said. "For now." He looked over his shoulder as he gathered the bloody rags and tossed them into the stream. "But we need to move. Too much blood scent here."

"But you just said—"

"Bears. One gets your scent, he won't look so cuddly." He rinsed his hands in the stream, then turned to me. "I want to head uphill. We'll have to see if you can make it. I might need to carry you."

"Carry me? No," I said, trying to get up. Fresh agony brought me back to my seat.

He reached down and swooped me up in his arms like I was a toddler.

"I'll take my chances with a bear," I said, half meaning it.

"You'll change your mind when he bares his teeth."

I might have been delirious, or in shock, but something was bothering Dalton more than concern about a bear. "What is it?" I said. "Something's wrong. I can tell."

"I need for you to listen to me is all. To trust me." He pulled me close to his chest and headed up the hill. "We could die out here, you know."

I nodded. I knew the trouble we were in. "I'm sorry, Dalton. I misread him. Honestly, I thought we could talk to him. I didn't think he'd really try to kill me."

Dalton grimaced. There it was again. Something he wasn't telling me.

"Just hold on to me," he said, and headed for higher ground.

"No, you tell me. What's the matter?"

He pulled me a little tighter to his chest.

"Dammit, Dalton. I promise I'll listen. I'll follow. I'll do as you say, from here on out. But don't you dare keep me in the dark. What is it?"

He slowed, looked down at me. "The distance. With that weapon. He could have killed you. Easily."

"What are you saying? That he's not a killer? He's just trying to warn us? Scare us? That's a good thing, right?"

"I'm not sure." He shook his head, pulled me back tight to his chest, and started walking again. "I'm not sure."

CHAPTER 11

Overhead, an unkindness of ravens circled. An odd term for birds. A group of crows is called a murder. But ravens are even more sophisticated, more intuitively clever. An unkindness seemed appropriate right now, as they circled, seemingly uncaring of our plight.

Would they let us know if Rocky was on the move? Would they side with him? If he's as good a tracker as he claimed, would he pop up and slit our throats before we even knew he was there? Perhaps the ravens would swoop in to pluck our eyes out while we were still warm.

Dalton found what he was looking for, a protected spot where we could hunker down and he could see in multiple directions. The sun had already moved to the west. It was late afternoon. I must have been out of it for longer than I thought.

He put me down on the moss, then sat, his back against a rock embankment, and gestured for me to snug up against him. "We need to stay warm," he said, opening his jacket so I could lean against his bare chest.

Yeah, you keep saying that... "But you won't be able—"

"Just do it, McVie. You're at risk of hypothermia. No arguing."

I scooted between his legs and leaned against him and he wrapped his arms and coat around us both.

The coat didn't quite cover me. "Closer," he said.

I shifted on my thigh, sending sharp spines of pain into my hip. I panted, trying to endure it.

"Easy now," he whispered.

Leaning against his chest, finally able to relax, I could feel the tension in him. He was scanning the hills, watching, waiting.

"So before, when you said he could have killed me, but he didn't, you meant that he chose to shoot me in the leg when he had a clear chest shot. You think he missed on purpose." It was a half question, half statement.

Dalton nodded. "I do."

"That's good news then. He doesn't want to kill us."

"Not sure."

"You said that but—"

"Listen," he said, carefully shifting to get a better view over my shoulder. "Let's focus on what we know for sure. That he knows he hit you. We need to use it to our advantage."

"Okay. How?" I swallowed. My mouth was dry and my head felt like an orange that had been juiced. "I admit. I'm not thinking as clearly as usual."

"It's all right," he said, nearly a whisper. "You can count on me."

"I know." I leaned my head back, relaxing into him.

"The longer he's in there, with the food, all the weapons, and we're out here with nothing, the more advantage he gains. By shooting you, he thinks he's shortened that timeframe."

I was nodding, as though I were following, but really my head was banging like the bass at a Metallica concert.

"We need to go on the offensive right away."

"Offensive?" I sat up and spun around and looked at him. My vision blurred for a moment then refocused.

"How's your leg feel?"

"Like I got attacked by a meat grinder."

"Right," he said, his mind somewhere else.

"Dalton, you've got a plan already. I can see it in your eyes. What are you up to?"

His eyes met mine. Focused. Serious. Dalton the SEAL. "We need the satellite phone or a weapon or both. He's not coming out of that camp, but he's got to sleep some time. When he does, I'll slip through the electric fence and—"

"Wait," I said. "Why don't we get to the plane and call on the radio for help?"

"I thought of that." He frowned. "Remember how he wanted the plane in sight of camp?"

I nodded, following his train of thought. "He's got a long-range rifle. We try to get to the plane and he's got us. That and I suspect he's disabled the radio anyway."

"Really, why would—" *Damn*. I closed my eyes. *Damn!* "You think he already suspected us when I didn't shoot the bear."

"I'm not sure." He turned to face me. "I don't see how he could have gotten to the plane and back in time to catch us—"

"Yeah, I know. What were we thinking?"

He winced, turned away. "We can talk about that later. Right now we need to—"

"You think he disabled the radio when he anchored the plane then?" That seemed a stretch. "But that would mean—no, it had to be the kiss that gave us away."

"Anything's possible. I'm not sure what to think."

"But you're saying that the odds are, if you took the risk to try to swim out to the plane, in the dark, slowly so as not to be seen, if you actually made it without being hypothermic or getting shot, you'd find the radio disconnected."

He gave me a nod, satisfied I was following his logic. "That's what I would do. My gut tells me he didn't pull his weapon on a whim. He planned this. I'm not sure for how long, but when he left camp for the phone, he had something in mind."

"You think he planned to confront us? Get us to talk?"

"I don't know," he snapped. He stared down at the ground. "Like I said, what I do know is you're injured. The longer we let this go, without food, shelter, first-aid, the more vulnerable we'll be. Assuming the plane radio is disabled, that leaves only one option, infiltrating his camp. Tonight."

I nodded in agreement. He was right. We had no other choice.

"I want you to stay right here until I get back."

"Oh no," I said, shaking my head. "You're not going without me. Besides, your plan will never work. Look at you. You can't fit between the fence wires. It's got to be me. I'm small enough and flexible enough."

His eyebrows went up. Was that a hint of a blush? "Your leg isn't—"

"I'll be fine. Just"—I fiddled with my bandage—"tighten this thing up."

"You're not fine. You can't even walk."

"I can and I will. Besides, you said use it to our advantage, right? He won't suspect this. Maybe you should even let yourself be seen sneaking toward camp, keep his focus on you in case he's awake."

"It's too risky," Dalton said.

"Or what? It's not like we've got a lot of choices."

"We do have a choice. You stay here where you'll be safe. I'll wait until I'm sure he's asleep."

"Really? And what if something happens to you? Then what?" I whipped my hand into the air, blocking his rebuttal. "We work together. We're partners, right? That's how we get out of this. My strengths and yours. That's it."

He set his jaw. "You're wounded."

"I'm fine. You said it yourself, merely a flesh wound."

He stared at me a moment, a thoughtful expression in

his eyes. He was weighing the options. "You're going to be stubborn about this, aren't you?"

I gave him a grin.

"Fine. We'll do it just before dawn. But you need to show me you can walk on that leg before we go."

"Fine," I said and leaned back into his chest. "So what's the plan?"

"I'll approach the camp directly, on this line." He held his hand up, slicing through the air in the direction of the camp. "You'll circle around and approach from the backside. That's where you'll breach the perimeter. If it appears that he is alerted to your presence in any way, I'll create a distraction, rustle some alder branches or break some twigs, yell to him if I have to. If that happens, you run downhill, toward the lake and the cover of the pines, then at daybreak, circle back to rendezvous with me."

It was a good plan. Except for the running part. If I could actually walk on this leg, it would be a hobble. But I would make it work. I had to.

"Got it. Rustle, then rendezvous. But if not, once I'm inside the fence—"

"Once you're inside the fence, get to the plastic storage box. That's where the weapons and phone should be. Don't rush it."

I turned to look up at him. Our faces were inches apart. "One tip-toe at a time."

He grinned, that half-grin, the one that makes my tummy tingle and suddenly I wanted him to kiss me again.

"What is it?" he asked, his grin disappearing.

"What's what? Nothing." My eyes lingered on his lips. *Stop it.*

"Are you sure you want to do this?"

"Yes, of course. I just...yes. Go on."

His eyes held mine a moment, but then his expression

changed back to the serious SEAL. "If he hears you, duck behind the box. That way he can't be sure whether you have a weapon in your hand yet, which will buy you time. If that happens, or even if I see the slightest twitch, I'll clear the fence and—"

"I won't let it come to that."

He nodded, but I could tell, he wasn't convinced. "Once you've got something, weapon or phone, either one, get out of there. Don't get greedy."

"Hey, what's that supposed to mean?"

"It means we get in, get out, unnoticed, unharmed."

"Right," I said. Unharmed.

"What we're planning is risky. It could go south in an instant." He flashed a look of concern. "Are you sure you can get through the wires with that leg injury?"

I thought a moment. *No.* "Yes. I'm sure."

"Then all we do now is wait."

I leaned back against him and we sat in silence for awhile, listening to the sounds of the forest.

"Dalton?"

"Yeah?"

"You think I should have shot the bear."

Dalton pulled away from me, turned do we were face to face. "What? I didn't say that."

"But you did. You warned me about it."

He thought for a long moment before he answered. "I think you need to do what you think is right. Maybe shooting one bear to catch a poacher would save many bears. Maybe not. Maybe not shooting it made Rocky suspicious of us. Maybe not. Maybe it made no difference at all." His gaze shifted to the distance, the direction of Rocky. "The bear died regardless." He turned back to look at me, more intense now. "An unfortunate casualty."

"Is that what they teach you?"

He cocked his head to the side, confusion on his face. "What?"

"In SEAL school. In Afghanistan. Casualties are *unfortunate*, but an acceptable outcome of war. Is that the lesson I'm supposed to learn?"

"I don't know," he said, guarded.

"Is that what it means to be part of the team? To be a wildlife agent? I have to be a soldier? Why? Why does it have to be that way? Why do I have to compromise my values? Why can't I do it my way? Who makes the rules anyway? Who? Stan Martin? Maybe I don't want this job anyway. The hell with it."

"You don't mean that."

"I do. If it means what you're telling me. To save animals from harm, I have to become a killer myself. That's what you've been saying, right?"

"There's a difference," he said. "Sometimes it's justified."

"No," I said, shaking my head. "That's what people tell themselves. It's never justified. There's always another way."

"Not always. Unless you've been there, in that situation"— his voice changed, defensive—"you don't know."

"Sure. It's always about naive little Poppy. I don't play along. I don't follow the rules. All because I can't possibly *know*."

His expression turned dark and his eyes locked on me. "You don't know." There was pain in those eyes, the pain of regret.

Suddenly I realized I'd gone too far. I could see it clearly. "I'm sorry."

He narrowed his eyes at me then turned his face away from me.

"Was it in Afghanistan? Tell me what happened."

"We're not going to discuss my time in Afghanistan." He still wouldn't look at me.

"Okay," I said. "But you told me we're partners, that you

needed to be able to trust me, to know what I'd do. Well, I don't know about you. I don't know what you've done, what you're capable of. Where would you draw the line? What do you feel about—"

His head snapped back toward me. "What do you want me to say?" His stare held me in its grip. "I'm not you." He paused. "I'm a SEAL. Always will be."

I nodded. In a whisper, I said, "Kill or be killed."

The sky in the east was still dark, no hint of dawn. It was time. Now or never. My hands shook. Would my leg hold out?

As Dalton and I crept toward the camp, moving in an awkward crouch, I gripped my thigh, keeping pressure on the wound. It seemed to help with the pain, but I couldn't let Dalton see. He'd turn us back around. No way was I letting him take the risk alone. All this was my fault. And if he got shot, then where would we be?

This was my responsibility. I got us into this mess. I had to get us out.

Problem was, I wasn't sure how I was going to pull it off. The plan relied on Rocky being asleep. But he would have figured out this was our only option. He'd be waiting for us. But what else could we do?

With no cover but the dark of night, we pushed through the wet grass toward the glowing embers of the campfire. My heart beat a rhythm in my ear, the tempo increasing the closer we got.

Just get the phone. Or one gun. That's all I had to do. Get in, get out. Unnoticed, unharmed.

Rocky slouched in the chair, a long gun lying across his lap. Without binoculars, we couldn't be sure his eyes were closed, but, like Dalton said, everyone has to sleep sometime. Once you sit down, sleep will come, whether you want it to or not.

You could fall asleep standing up if you were tired enough.

Sitting in a chair, in the dark, in front of the warm fire, would put Rocky out at some point. At this hour, the odds were with us.

Once Dalton hunkered down in place, I crept around to my entry spot. My best approach was from behind Rocky. He might be a trained woodsman, even military, but he didn't have eyes in the back of his head.

My leg was beyond numb from all the walking, but it was still working, though I had to place my feet carefully, taking my time. One bad step, even a tiny stumble, might give me away.

The electrified wires surrounded the camp, four of them strung about ten to twelve inches apart. The lowest was about eight inches off the ground—too low to get under. I had to slip between that one and the next higher one, which meant I'd have to straddle it, putting my weight on my wounded leg. I drew in a breath. I could do it.

One last look at Rocky. He hadn't moved. He was asleep. He had to be.

I knelt in the cold, dewy grass and kicked my wounded leg back, swung it over, between the bottom two wires, kept my body long, then reached with my right arm and placed it on the ground inside. No problem. Easy yoga. I was straddling the wire. So far so good.

Now for the hard part. I leaned inward, shifting my weight to my bad leg, and lifted my other leg. Pain shot up my backside, but I held me leg in the air, breathing. *Okay. You can do this.* Getting my arm through first would be better. Then lean and roll. That should work.

Slowly, I lifted my outside arm. Almost there. As I pulled my arm through the wires, my coat shifted and my compass necklace dropped and hit the wire. Kazap! A jolt zipped through my body, seizing my muscles. I jerked upward and smacked the upper wire. Kazap! A groan of agony escaped my lips.

I froze, stuck between the wires, my eyes locked on Rocky in the chair, my heart jackhammering inside my chest.

I huffed, trying to settle my nerves. *Breathe. Breathe. You can do this. Just stay still.* Maybe I hadn't woken him. I waited, my back arched, between the wires, one leg in, one leg out. The necklace dangled from my neck, inches from the wire. Slowly, I shifted my weight to my good leg, reached up and tucked the charm into my mouth to get it away from the wire.

I turned my head back to check on Rocky. "Well, whaddaya know," he said, calmly looking over his shoulder. "The brave little rabbit's come right into the fox's den."

Shit! I rolled out of the wires, hitting the back of my hand on the upper one, giving me one more jolt. I pulled myself to my feet and stumbled into the dark night.

"Run, little rabbit. Run!" Rocky shouted after me followed by a laugh that sent a shiver through to my bones.

CHAPTER 12

I ran into a veil of pitch dark as fast as my bum leg would take me, down the hill, into the pines. I kept running. The laughter faded behind me, but no gunshots. He didn't follow. But still, I had to get away. Something about that laugh frightened me to my core.

Finally, I came across a fallen log and slumped down next to it. Running in the dark was dangerous. I would catch my breath, wait for dawn, then circle back to the rendezvous location.

Adrenaline zipped through my veins—the ultimate drug. My leg didn't hurt, I didn't feel the cold, and my brain shifted into overdrive.

I snugged my coat tight around my neck. *That laugh.* He wasn't alarmed or worried. He was amused. I don't know what I'd been thinking, trying to talk to him. When he caught us kissing, he could have kept up the guide act, keeping it legal, without risking anything. We had no hard evidence against him. Yet he pulled his gun. It didn't make sense. What was Rocky thinking?

Put yourself in his shoes, my dad would say. Why would Rocky pull his sidearm on Dalton, then shoot me in the leg, but not shoot just now, when I was right in front of him again? None of this made any sense. Had I startled him awake and he didn't think to shoot until I was out of sight? No, he'd shouted for me to run. As if he were actually cheering me on, wanting me to get away. But why?

The eastern sky showed no sign of the sun, so I hunkered down. Wandering in the wilderness in the dark was not a good idea. Everyone worries about nocturnal predators, but no one thinks of the more common dangers, like getting stuck in the eye by a branch. Yep. Better to stay put until dawn.

In autumn, the Alaskan woods are quiet, peaceful. So unlike the jungle, where the night sounds are louder than the day. If Rocky decided to follow me, I'd hear him coming.

When the sun finally arrived, a light rain started to fall. *Great*. The bandage around my thigh had come loose. Fresh blood oozed down my leg, mingling with the dark, gooey dried stuff. My thigh was swollen and red. I winced as I tightened the bandage then got to my feet. I had to get back to Dalton.

I pushed through the thicket and a patch of devil's club, avoiding the spiny barbs that line the stems and undersides of their massive leaves. There was a rustle ahead. I dropped to my knees. Waiting, hidden. There it was again. Rocky wouldn't be that careless. Not to make that kind of noise. Easy now, I slowly rose to my feet.

About twenty yards away stood a bull moose, staring at me, stone-still save for the sideways slide of his jaw, crunching branches with his teeth. His rack must have been at least a sixty inch spread with sharp tines. The massive antlers looked like thorny paddles. Absolutely majestic. He sized me up as I sized him up, two beings meeting unexpectedly in the woods.

I've seen moose before, but to face off with one, alone, made my knees weak. God he was huge. A half ton of muscle and, this time of year, oozing with testosterone. At the shoulder he stood taller than me, probably six feet. He took a step, shifted his gaze, turning slightly to the side, showing his flank. The flap of skin hanging from his chin, the bell I thought it was called, swung with his movement.

"Okay, moose. I'm backing away," I said in a calm, soothing voice. "I'm backing away."

His ears perked up, twitched. One of them turned to the side. His tongue flicked in and out, licking his lips like a cow. He took a couple more steps toward me, a moose mosey, tilting his head back and forth, ever so slightly, causing his huge antlers to swing side to side.

"Look at you," I said, letting my mouth spit out whatever words came to mind as I slowly stepped backward. "All handsome, big boy. I'm going to back away, okay? I don't want any trouble."

Drawing his head back, he snorted, his breath a tiny cloud of mist in the cold air. He looked like he was posing for a National Geographic photo, though his fur was matted from the rain.

"That's okay. I'm having a bad hair day, too, my friend."

I took another step back, my foot caught on a root, and my bad leg gave. I stumbled and crashed into some brush.

The moose jumped backward and spun around, his hind side facing me now.

I managed to get back to my feet, but not without a scrape across my face. Warm blood ran down my cheek.

The moose watched over his shoulder with wary eyes. My eyes fixed on the massive hump on his back, pure muscle to power his front legs. He could run thirty-five miles an hour, knocking down half the forest as he went. He might not have the sharp canines of a bear or wolf, but that rack on his head could gouge with the force of a bulldozer.

His eyes intent on me now, he slowly turned and walked toward me, one carefully placed hoof at a time.

"Nothing to see here, Mr. Moose. Just a klutzy woman with a bum leg. Nothing to be alarmed about. I'll be running along now. See you later, then."

He came to a halt, his fur standing up, ears pinned back, and his head dropped low. With a snort, his front legs slapped at the ground and he charged.

Holy shit!

I ducked behind two trees as his antlers rammed the trunks. *Crash!*

I stepped right. He reared back and plowed into the trees again. I shifted left and staggered to another tree, spun around it, turning in another direction. He was right behind me. The crack of his antlers smacking the tree ripped through the forest. I lunged toward the next tree, thrashing through a patch of devil's club, and spun around. The moose backed away and took off into the brush.

My heart hammered in my chest. I huffed and huffed, trying to catch my breath. *Damn, that was close.*

My head spun. I sat down in the moss. "Damn," I said out loud.

All right, McVie. You're all right.

My face burned, all the way down my neck. I reached up and felt the thorns stuck in my skin from the devil's club. *Great. Just great.*

Fresh blood soaked my pant leg. The bandage had come loose again. I tried to tighten it, but my hands were shaking. *Dammit!*

Deep breath. I worked the ends of the bandage and managed to get the bleeding to stop, but I'd ripped it open and made it worse.

I looked around. Nothing but the forest deep.

Dalton's voice echoed in my head, *Bear gets your scent, he won't look so cuddly.*

I got to my feet again. Now, which way was north? I hobbled downward, toward the lake. From there, I'd get my bearings.

It's this way. No, that way.

I sat down. My head dizzy. I needed to rest. Just for a minute. It was cold. So cold. My teeth were chattering.

I need to keep moving.

The rain was coming down harder now, feeling like pellets stinging my face. The pattering turned to a steady whoosh as it penetrated the canopy. Droplets ran down my neck. My rain hat hung on my back, the cord tight at my throat, rubbing on the rash where I had fallen against the devil's club. I slung it up atop my head, cinched down the chin strap, and drew in a long breath. *Which way?*

The forest in every direction was dark and misty. I couldn't see the sun to gauge direction. All right. The downward slope headed for the lake. That meant I needed to stay at this level for five hundred yards or so. Not go up or down. That would take me on a course to circle back to Dalton. I could do this.

Putting one foot in front of the other, over moss-covered logs, through the blueberry bushes, across a patch of skunk cabbage, I went. What was a little dizziness? I could see. I could find my way.

I could do it on my own. Alone.

Alone.

Maybe Martin had been right. This alone crap was overrated. My hand went to the compass necklace at my neck. *Oh Chris. I'm so sorry. I didn't mean to make things worse. I'll make it up to you, I swear.*

I laughed out loud. I was holding a fake little compass. *Oh Chris. If you only knew. I* have *lost my way.*

Every part of the forest dripped water. My pants were soaked. My socks sloshed in my boots. My hair was heavy on my back. I should've been freezing. But I wasn't.

Is that what happened when you became hypothermic? You no longer felt cold. Yes. I remember. Then a feeling of well-being, euphoria even. Was I shivering? No. Wasn't that what happened?

My leg must have been dragging. It caught on a stick and I collapsed to the ground.

Must get up.

Dalton can't be far.

I planted my hands on the earth and pushed myself upright. One step. Another step.

I was back on the ground again, my face in the moss. It felt soft. Nice.

I could sleep.

"Thank God I found you." A face, inches from mine. "I've been worried sick."

I tried to open my eyes.

"Are you all right? Poppy? Talk to me."

The throbbing of my head brought me around. I was in Alaska. In the woods.

"What happened?" he asked.

Dalton. That was his name. I tried to sit up, but my head spun. A wave of nausea came over me and I leaned over and retched.

He held my hair back, then pulled me to him. "You've gotten too cold," he said, wrapping his arms around me. "Dammit, I shouldn't have let you go."

I remember. The bush plane. The lodge. Joe smoking that cigar.

"No cigars."

A bear. Charging toward me. *I won't shoot. I can't shoot.*

"Poppy. Poppy! C'mon, stay with me."

Dalton. A kiss. "Rocky gun. Run. Run."

"Here, drink some water."

He held a plastic bag at my mouth. I drank.

"There now," he said. "Just rest. Get warm."

Dalton. Holding me. Warm now.

I blinked my eyes open. Dalton was holding me tight.

"You feeling better?"

I nodded. "Did I sleep?" My arms felt heavy.

"Yeah." His hand went to my forehead. "How are you feeling?"

"Better, I think."

He smoothed my hair back from my face, plucked a couple twigs from it. "What the hell happened?"

Was it dark already again?

"Poppy? Tell me what happened."

"You wouldn't believe me if I told you."

"Looks like you got into the devil's club."

My hand went to my neck. "Yeah. I could use some tweezers."

"I'll help. I didn't want to do it while you were asleep and risk waking you."

I nodded in understanding.

"Let's see that leg first." He pulled back the bandage and winced.

"That bad, huh?"

He gave me a reassuring smile. "I've seen worse. A little bleeding is good. Flushes it out."

"Right," I said. He was a bad liar.

He took hold of my chin to turn my head and get a good look at the thorns in my neck. "You just can't keep yourself out of trouble, can you?" He was trying to sound funny, keep it light, keep my spirits up, but it fell flat.

"Just get them out."

"All right. Hold still."

With the patience of a neurosurgeon, he carefully plucked away while intermittently scanning behind me for any sign of Rocky. "So who made the first move? You or the plant?"

He said it with such a serious tone, a smile crept across my face.

"It was a moose, actually. I tried to back away, but he charged."

Dalton sat back, his eyebrows up. "You're kidding."

I nodded. "Scared the living shit out of me."

He pulled another thorn. "I bet."

"Nothing more badass in these woods than a bull moose all doped up on testosterone."

He gave me a frown. "I don't know about that."

"Ow!" I pulled away.

"Sorry," he whispered.

"Seriously, a moose in rut can—"

"Rocky," he said, serious now. "He let you run away."

"I told you. I knew it. He doesn't want to kill us. We should try talking to him again."

Dalton was shaking his head before I finished the sentence. "No. Don't you see? He let you go. All the while he was scanning for me."

"What? You think he sees only you as a real threat? I'm going to try not to be insulted by that. But it only makes my point. *I'll* go talk to him."

"No," he said, more sternly than usual. "Listen to me. He could leave. He could go get in the plane right now and go. Leave us to die. Why hasn't he?"

"Because, like I said, he's no killer. He's got to make a point." I couldn't possibly sound convincing. I wasn't sure myself.

"Okay, but he could send someone else to get us later. Leave us out here for a while. That would make a point."

"He could I suppose, but he'd be vulnerable getting to the plane, leaving the camp. We could ambush him."

"Not really that risky. He has all the weapons. We have none. We've been out in the cold for two nights. We're tired. You're wounded."

"Okay, so maybe he's scared. Maybe he's not able to assess the situation as rationally as you can."

"No. He's smart. And arrogant. Didn't you hear him laughing?"

I nodded. That was some creepy laughing.

"No,"—he shook his head—"there's another reason." He examined my neck. He'd pulled the last of the thorns. "Wait here," he said and went into the woods. He came back with a leaf from the devil's club plant, crushed it in his hands. "This should soothe the burn," he said. "As ironic as that may be." He gently rubbed it on my neck.

"Dalton, what are you saying? What other reason?"

"It's not me he's focused on. To him, I'm a dopey boy from Oklahoma. Boring. Inconsequential. But you. Little Miss Sharpshooter. All cocky and capable and sexy as hell." He paused. "I mean, what man wouldn't want to—"

"Are you saying this is all about him having the hots for me? About him trying to impress me?" No way. That didn't make sense either.

"I'm saying he isn't your everyday trafficker, selling buckskins out of his trunk. Who knows what he did in the lower forty-eight. Maybe he's a felon. Maybe he didn't fit in. Maybe he just couldn't quite get his shit together. Snubbed by the ladies. Couldn't keep a job. Who knows. But I do know one thing. We shouldn't underestimate how dangerous he is. This isn't like Ray Goldman."

"What? Ray Goldman was on our most-wanted list."

"Yeah, because orcas are high profile animals. But Ray was a fisherman. Yes, you saw him as a kidnapper, a killer. But in his own mind, he was just another fisherman." Dalton looked around, over his shoulder, then back at me, frowning. "With Rocky, it's different." His face took on a shadow of concern. "For him, it's all about the hunt."

My stomach dropped and the cold air seemed to envelope

me. "Are you saying—?"

"I'm saying that out here, for Rocky, it's a whole different world. Out here he's in his element. Out here, he's the apex predator." Dalton looked me square in the eyes. "And you're a little rabbit."

My whole body went cold. Dalton was right.

Chapter 13

My palms got sweaty and my head light. "This isn't good," I said. "Not. Good."

Dalton watched me, letting it sink in.

"I can't believe I got us into this. I should've known. I should have seen. Back at the lodge. He heard us talking that night. Or, I don't know, what I said to Townsend about him. He seemed so meek, so nerdy. Who would've thought? I mean, he wouldn't even make eye contact. I figured he—or maybe he...maybe he didn't suspect us at all." I looked Dalton in the eyes. "If I hadn't kissed you and—"

"What? No." He sighed. "This isn't your fault." He turned away, his jaw tight. "It's mine. I should've known better."

What? You mean you didn't want—

Dalton jerked his head to the left. He'd heard something.

"What is it?" I whispered.

"Dammit," he said, his eyes now on the sky.

Then I heard it too. The drone.

"Get him to focus on you," Dalton said.

I had a pretty good idea what Dalton was thinking. I got to my feet and stormed toward the drone, my fists in the air, shouting at it. A crazed woman was not a character I had to fake right now.

The drone dropped nearly to my level and hovered about twenty yards away.

I stumbled, for effect, then bent over and propped my hand on my hip as though I were trying to catch my breath.

Bam! A rock slammed into the drone, knocking it sideways. The propellers made a grinding noise. Another rock flew by my head but missed the drone this time. It sputtered and shot skyward, tilting to the side, but managed to stay airborne.

I swung around. "Hit it again!"

Dalton threw another rock, but the drone was too far away.

"You damaged it," I said with a whoop.

"C'mon," Dalton said. "Let's get out of sight anyway. It'll be dark soon."

I limped after him, into the cover of the pines.

Dalton found a dry patch of moss under a rocky overhang. "Right here," he said and gestured for me to lie down.

"But we're barely a hundred yards from where he saw us."

"It's all right. He'll assume we ran."

I eyed Dalton, skeptical.

"Trust me."

I nodded and dropped to my knees to crawl into the mossy bed.

"What do we do now?" I asked once he sat down.

"We give him what he wants." He frowned and looked me in the eye. "At least make him think it."

"What he wants? You mean use me as bait." I closed my eyes. I didn't know if I had the energy to hear his plan, let alone enact it.

"No," he said, shaking his head. "Like I said, he doesn't find me so...intriguing."

My head was in some kind of fog. "I don't understand."

"I need some things from the plane."

"The plane? You're going out there? To the plane? But you said—"

He gave me the I'm-doing-this-no-matter-what look. "We wait for darkness. Then I'm going to the plane. There were some things in the back. I'll check the radio too, but you and I both know he's disabled it."

"What do you mean, things? What are you planning to do?"

"You stay here. Keep warm and try to get some sleep."

"What? You can't be serious."

"Listen to me. You need to rest. That's the best way. I know you. I know you'll fight until you collapse. But right now, you need to trust me. We're a team. Partners. Do you understand?"

I crossed my arms. "You're planning something and keeping me out of it."

"It's not that. We need to know what resources we have. The plane might give us some options. It's worth the risk. I need to see what is there, then we'll work out the details. For that, I'm going to need you at your best. That means rest now." His eyes pleaded for me to consent. "Tell me you will."

He was right about needing to rest. My leg throbbed. My head throbbed. My neck burned. I was cold and wet. And I was pissed. Was I even thinking clearly? But for him to swim out to the plane? Alone? In the dark? What did he think he'd find that was that valuable? Was he not telling me something or were we that desperate?

I held my hand to my head. I wasn't sure. Somehow I couldn't concentrate. "Okay," I said. "If you think it's our best option, but...Dalton?" Man, I was tired. "Do you really think we'll get out of this alive?"

His eyes shifted to his hands. "We're smart. We're well trained."

"But?" I could feel it. There was definitely a but.

"There's something about this guy. This doesn't feel right. This whole thing. It's not about him being a poacher."

I nodded. "In Costa Rica, we knew what we were up against. In Norway too. This feels..." I shook my head.

"Yeah."

"In Costa Rica, when Chris—" I sighed. *Oh Chris.* All the feelings of guilt rushed in. "He risked his life for me, my job. And now I don't know if I'll ever..."

"Don't say it."

"I put his job on the line. He could get fired for what I did. That was stupid."

"You were sticking up for him."

"Yeah, but he was right. You were right. I wasn't thinking. And now...this."

"You've been friends all these years. He knows who you are. I'm sure he's already forgiven you."

"You're probably right. Because he's Chris. That doesn't mean it's forgivable."

Dalton squeezed my hand. "When we get back, you'll call him, tell him how you feel."

I nodded. "If we get back."

"We'll get through this. You got me?"

My stomach ached, my leg hurt like hell, and we were stranded in the center of the wilderness with nothing. Nothing but each other. I nodded.

"You should get some rest," he said.

"Yeah, right. There's no way I'm going to be able to sleep."

Dalton nodded in understanding. "Tell me about Chris. How'd you two meet anyway?"

"Well, the first time was in sixth grade. My mom was stationed in the Philippines. Up to that point, I'd been homeschooled by my dad, since we moved around so much, but she'd decided I was old enough to go to school with the other kids at that age, I guess.

"For several months, I endured it, bored. Then Chris showed up in class one day, sat down beside me, and the first words out of his mouth were, 'Hey, wanna be best friends?' Kids were always coming and going. The nature of being a Navy brat. If you wanted a friend, you connected quickly. I said sure and that was that.

"I think at the time, what I liked so much about him was that he seemed exotic. It was his skin, his hair. All the other kids were so plain. And boring."

I chewed on my lower lip. "I know it sounds awful, but I always had a hard time getting along with other girls. All they ever wanted to talk about was boys. How they should wear their hair, for the boys. What clothes to wear, to attract the boys. Which girls were dating which boys. With Chris, it was different. I didn't have to deal with all that stuff because he was a boy. We worried about world politics, about the environment, about national debt. We'd stay up all night talking about religion.

"Then one day, at lunch time, a couple of boys cornered us. Bullies. They started in calling me Pippity-poppity-poo and—"

"What?" Dalton grinned. "They called you Pippity—"

"Don't even," I said. "Do you want to hear the story or not?"

"I do."

"So these boys, who I wasn't exactly fond of, get us in this corner and start in, calling Chris names. Well, I wasn't having it. I realized, in that moment, that I'd started thinking of Chris as my boyfriend." I smiled at the memory. "And they were calling him names like...well, you know.

"One boy, Tommy was his name, I'll never forget, he got right in Chris's face. I grabbed him by the shoulder, spun him around, and punched him right in the nose. Blood everywhere. 'You don't talk to my boyfriend like that,' I shouted.

"The boys ran away. I thought I'd really done something, all proud of myself for sticking up for him. But Chris stood there, shaking his head, tears in his eyes. He was angry. With me.

'I'm not your boyfriend,' he said and stomped away, leaving me there with bloody knuckles."

"Wow," Dalton said. "Then what happened?"

I stared at him, into those eyes. Is that what was happening now? Did I completely misread Dalton's intentions? Was he just trying to be a kind partner and then I went and kissed him? I turned away. What had I been thinking?

"What happened next?" he nudged.

"My dad lectured me on why he'd gotten me all those Kuntaw lessons in the first place. You know, the Filipino martial art I used to knock you on your ass that day we first met."

"Yeah, I remember," he said with a frown.

"He said I was supposed to learn discipline. Not beat up the boys."

Dalton laughed. "Right. Guess you haven't mastered that one yet."

I grinned.

"I meant, what happened with Chris."

"He wouldn't talk to me. Two months later, my mom got transferred. I thought I'd never see him again. Then, several years later, he walked into my high school classroom in California. By then he'd come out and everything was clear, as if it had sorted itself out. We've been best friends ever since.

"Oh Dalton, what if I never see him—"

"You will." He squeezed my hand again. "You will. Trust me."

Dusk had descended on the forest, taking all color, leaving nothing but darkness.

He took off his coat, pulled me tight to him, then wrapped the coat around me like blanket. "You need to stay warm. Right now, the most important thing is that you get a good night's sleep."

I melted into his chest. I might have misread that kiss, but I could trust Dalton. With my life.

I awoke with a start. Someone was near.

"It's me," Dalton whispered. "It's all right. It's just me."

I glanced around. Daylight had filled the forest once again. "What happened? I must have—"

"Slept, yes. You needed it."

"But I, you—" Dalton stood next to a pile of things—things he'd gotten from the plane. "You've already gone?" I shook my head in disbelief.

"Did you know you snore?"

My mouth dropped open.

"I'm just kidding." He winked at me. "I made sure you were safe. You needed the rest. And I got some things."

There were parts of the airplane seat, straps and cords, a duffle bag, and an old iron bear trap lying in a pile.

"You swam to the plane? You must be freezing." He'd left his coat wrapped around me. I got to my feet and held it out to him. "Get your coat on."

"I'm fine."

"You're naked." From the waist up, which was enough to distract me. "We don't need you getting hypothermic too. Now put it on."

He took it from me, but first held his hand to my forehead and checked my pupils, giving me a nod of approval.

"So what's your plan? What are you going to do with all this?" I pointed to the trap. "Do you think he'll just step into that?"

"No. You're going to have to lure him into it."

"Lure him? *I'm* going to lure him? And what about you?"

"Oh, I'll be dead."

My head felt a little better, but did he just say—"Come again?"

"There's only one way he's coming out of that fortress he's built. If I'm dead." He held a seat cushion he'd pulled from the plane up to his chest and knocked on the metal backing. "This ought to do it."

"You can't be serious. Your plan is to use a seat cushion for a bullet-proof vest? Are you nuts? He has a high-powered rifle. You can't be sure that will stop the bullet."

"You're right. I can't be sure. But it's the best we've got."

"No, no." I sliced at the air with my hands. "No! We'll talk to him again. We'll find another way."

Dalton put his hands on my shoulders. "Poppy, there is no other way." His eyes held mine. "You know it."

"The radio?"

"Disabled. Just as we thought." He looked at me with those eyes. "He planned this. From the beginning."

"But you can't—"

"Listen to me. We have one shot at this. One. Do you understand?"

I spun around and sat down. This couldn't be happening. Dalton was going to put himself in the line of fire, with a seat cushion for protection. This wasn't happening. I shook my head. "It's too risky."

"I know. Just like in Norway and Costa Rica. Only this time I'm taking the lead." He gave me a gentle shrug. "It's my turn, right?"

I shook my head.

"It's our only chance. We've got to take him by surprise. A full-on, frontal attack would be suicide."

I nodded. I knew he was right. But, what if—?

"We're going to set the trap. Then go down by the log that crosses the river. It's the only place to cross and he can see us from the camp. He'll think we've gotten desperate. That's where he'll shoot me."

I was shaking my head again. "No. No."

"As soon as he sees me fall, he'll come out. He'll want to verify the kill.'"

"What if you really get shot? What if he shoots you in the head?"

"He won't. SEALs are trained to take a chest shot."

"But you said he wasn't really a SEAL. What if—?"

"You don't worry about me. Think only of taking care of yourself. Do you understand? And stick to the plan. Like the SEALs, live and die by the plan."

"Exactly!" I shook my head. "I can't believe this is our plan."

"When you get to the trap, don't hesitate, don't look at it, run over it, as fast as you can. Go way beyond it. If you hesitate, if you check, you'll give me away."

"What do you mean?" He'd lost me.

He picked up the trap. "It's broken. I'm going to have to trip it. That means you've got to keep him busy until I can circle back around and get into position."

"Are you kidding?"

His stare was heavy.

"What if he doesn't step into it? How will—?"

"We are going to put it in a place where he'll have to step in it. You'll step in it. He'll follow."

"How do you know he's not going to just shoot me?"

Dalton's eyes turned dark. He looked away. "I don't."

My stomach dropped. "This is crazy."

"It's a good plan." A beat. "Considering the circumstances."

I ran my fingers through my hair, tried to make my brain settle down and think.

Dalton stared at his hands. "He wants to hunt you. I feel it. In my bones. He's going to track you."

"What if you're right and he shoots? What if you actually get shot? What if he kills you? Then what happens?"

Dalton stood, picked up the trap. "Then let's hope I'm wrong about him."

CHAPTER 14

Dalton chose a muddy spot in a tiny stream to hide the trap. He tied a cord to the broken lever that tripped it and ran it into the tall grass on the edge, then crawled on his belly into the weeds. "Can you see me?"

"No. Not really."

"Is that a no or a not really?"

"It's good. He'll be running right? It's good."

Dalton crawled back out. "All right, then. It's showtime." He held the seat cushion to his chest and had me help him strap it tight, then the other on his back. He'd stuffed a pair of pants he'd found in the plane with pine needles. "This is going to work," he said. "He'll think I'm floating face down. You'll keep him busy for at least an hour. Time for me to get out of the water without being seen, then back here and hidden. You can do that, right?"

"I don't know." I shook my head again. I couldn't let him go out there with only a seat cushion for protection. This was crazy.

"We've been over this." His eyes locked on me. "Promise me."

I couldn't.

"Listen to me. This will only work if we're both all in, one hundred percent. And it will work. You just have to trust me."

What could I say? What could I do? He was right. We were out of options. I nodded. "I promise."

He gave me a smile. "It will be all be over soon."

"I know, I—" That's what I was afraid of. "Dalton, I…this whole thing…and you and me…I can't go without knowing…" I looked into his eyes and the words fell away.

With a gentle smile, he said, "Knowing what?"

"I need to know…" *Damn.* My cheeks were on fire. *You kissed me and then—* He was staring, waiting. "Your first name." *Oh geez. I'm a total dope.*

"That's what you want?" he said with a hint of disappointment. He shook his head to blow it off.

"I just thought, you know, since we've been working together, and then all this, that we'd, well, you know, you're my partner and I don't even know your name, so I thought that, you know, in case everything—"

He grinned. "You're babbling."

"What?" I drew back, thrown off. "I don't babble."

His eyebrows went up.

"It's just that I don't understand. You don't want me to know because you're embarrassed?"

"No, that's not it. I just—" He gave me a resigned grin. "It's Garrett."

I smiled. "Garrett. That's a fine name."

He rolled his eyes and turned away.

"What? I mean it. Really. What's wrong with Garrett?"

He shook his head. "Nothing. Except when you were named after your mom's favorite movie character and your mom was—well, how lame is that?"

Obviously there was a lot more to it, but now wasn't the time. "I'm still going to call you Dalton because—"

"Yes,"—he nodded—"yes, you are."

Our eyes locked in an uncomfortable moment. "That is, if I still have a job," I managed. "And, you know."

"Don't worry about that now," he finally said. "Focus on our mission here. On the plan. Okay?"

I nodded. Staying alive. I could focus on that.

He smiled. "Okay, let's get going."

"Hold on," I said. "I need one more moment." I drew in a deep breath.

He took hold of my hand, pulled me closer to him, and looked into my eyes. "It's all right," he whispered. "It will be all right."

I wrapped my arms around him and didn't want to let go.

"It's a good plan," he murmured in my ear.

Ak-ak-ak rattled behind me.

I pushed away from him with a start. Spun around. A raven. It was a raven.

My chest heaved, trying to get my breath to return. I came back around to Dalton. Our eyes met for a brief moment then he continued scanning. His muscles pulled tight, on full alert.

"It was just a bird," I said.

He nodded. "Still," he said. "We should get moving."

I drew in a breath, then another, trying to get my racing heart to settle. "Yeah."

We moved along the ridge, keeping at a low crouch, until we came within about a hundred yards of the log bridge. From there, we let ourselves be seen, a head up here, a push through the branches there, as though we were trying our best to stay hidden. Dalton stayed clear. Mainly I was the one exposing myself, betting that Dalton was right and Rocky wouldn't shoot me. Shoot to kill anyway.

Dalton came to a halt and peered through some brush. I crawled up next to him. "Has he noticed?"

Dalton nodded. "He's got the binoculars sighted on us."

"And he hasn't shot me again. That's a good sign I guess."

"You ready?" he asked with an encouraging nod.

Deep breath. I nodded.

Dalton took off at a quick pace, running for the log. I was right on his tail, staying between him and Rocky, blocking any chance of a shot until he was out on the log. He had to be directly above the river before we allowed Rocky an opening. Five more strides and we'd be there.

One, two, three. Dalton was on the log. I feigned a stumble, making a space between us. Ca-rack! The shot reverberated across the distance, then the clang of a bullet hitting metal. I dropped to my knees. God, I hoped Rocky hadn't heard it at that distance.

Dalton crumpled into a heap, then slumped over.

"Dalton!"

He didn't turn. Didn't say anything. Didn't give me any sign he was okay.

"Dalton!"

He slid from the log and plummeted to the river below. I spun around. Rocky already had the binoculars to his eyes, watching. I looked back to Dalton. He floated in a froth of white water, face down. Had he really been hit? *Oh god!* I couldn't see his face, couldn't see if he was conscious. "Dalton!"

Could he hear me over the rumble of the rapids? With his ears in the water? "Dalton!" His body bobbed in the rapids like a fallen log, farther and farther away from me. "Dal-ton!"

Oh my god! What if he was really shot? I couldn't breathe. Couldn't think. *What were we thinking?*

Okay. Deep breath. Of course he wouldn't give me a sign. Rocky might see it. He had to play it out. Be convincing. To the end. Dalton always, always stayed in character.

He's all right. Stick to the plan. The plan.

The white rush of water carried him toward the lake. Part of the plan.

I spun back around. Rocky was wasting no time. He had the

lid of the plastic storage box flipped open and was gearing up. Dalton had been right. Rocky was leaving camp to confirm the kill.

I bolted from the log and ran for cover, back to the spot from which Dalton had been watching Rocky. I burrowed in and crawled on my elbows to get a view, my chest heaving.

This is happening. My hands shook. I had skills. But that man was fully armed, well fed and rested. I had to keep him occupied, on my trail, but not let him catch me. All that, exhausted, wounded, recovering from hypothermia. It was going to take everything I had.

Dalton, you better be at the trap when we get there.

I drew in a deep breath and moved to higher ground.

CHAPTER 15

Rocky passed through the gate of the camp fully loaded—handgun at his belt, pack on his back, rifle slung over his shoulder, and the crossbow in his hand. He covered the ground from camp to the river's edge at the speed of a cheetah, I swear. How was I going to stay ahead of him?

He went straight to the log, then followed the rim of the gorge downhill, his eyes trained on the water, scanning. I saw before he did. Dalton's body—or fake body—floating out in the lake. Even from where I was hidden, I could see his coat spread on the surface, the legs floating behind. He'd made a good, believable dummy. *Unless?—Don't go there.*

Rocky moved double time toward the lake. By now, the dummy was nearly a hundred yards out from shore. Rocky came to a halt, set down his crossbow, and dropped his backpack. He slowly turned around, scanning the hillside. I dropped down, my heart racing.

For a moment, I thought he was going to strip down and swim out to the body for confirmation. If he did, he'd have to leave all his weapons unattended on shore. Could I get there in time? Grab his gun and this would all be over?

He stood there, as though seriously considering the swim, then pulled the binoculars from his pack. A flush of nerves made me shiver. Would Dalton's pine needle-stuffed pants hold up to scrutiny?

Rocky held the binoculars to his eyes for too long. Surely he saw it was a fake. *Oh, what if it isn't?* Then he lowered the glasses and turned back in my direction. I swear his steely eyes zeroed right in on me and my breath caught in my throat.

"Where are you, little rabbit?" His voice thundered across the distance with a rough edge to it. Different now. Heavy with thirst. "Where have you run?"

I set my teeth. *Game on, asshole.*

I leapt to my feet, sure he'd see me. *C'mon. I'm right up here, you creep.* I limped along the ridge, glancing back to be sure he was following but still some distance away. Whatever it took—circling back, zigzagging, staying uphill—I needed to keep track of where he was and not let him get too close while I killed the time needed for Dalton to get to the trap and be ready.

If he was alive.

This is a bad plan, a terrible plan—no. Dalton was alive when he went into the river. Wasn't he? *Knock it off. Just stick to the plan. Lure Rocky to the trap. Dalton will be there.*

At the far side of the ridge I pushed through a thicket. A covey of ptarmigan lifted off with a clatter, wings thrashing through the brush. My heart leapt into my throat.

"Careful, there, little rabbit," Rocky shouted.

I spun around. He was much closer than I'd thought. How could that be?

"You'll give yourself away," he warned.

Shit! I dropped my head and ran, bounding over the rocky terrain, dodging bushes. Tiny twigs slapped me in the face as I headed toward the pines and the deep forest. I needed the cover, where I could get ahead of him, then I'd circle back.

I leaped over a rock, my leg faltered, and I went down, slamming my chin into the ground. The fall knocked the wind out of me. I pushed up onto my hands and knees, my chest heaving.

Rocky's laughter rumbled after me, so close it felt like he was breathing down my neck.

I got back to my feet, stumbled forward, but managed to get going again. Maybe I could hide. I could duck under a bush, let him pass me by, then turn and head back the way we'd come. His speed and mine, in opposite directions, would put more space between us. Yes, that was what I'd do. Leave a false trail, then circle back.

He might be a good tracker, but I had some skills too. But did I have time? Was he too close?

As I entered the thick of the forest, I snapped a little sapling in two with my boot, then four paces later a pine branch, then in another ten feet, I left a scuff in the wet soil. I crept sideways then, making sure to leave no sign and circled back and got down on my belly in the mud and crawled under a moss-covered log.

As I lay still, my heartbeat thrummed in my chest sending pulses of throbbing pain through my leg. I focused on my breathing, trying to settle it as I waited.

Then he was there. Without a sound he appeared like a ghost. *God he's fast.*

My heartbeat thundered in my ears, racing back up to double time.

Through the foliage I could see he'd stopped to examine the sapling. He sniffed the air, like a dog, then turned to scan the forest behind him. As he came around, his eyes cast on me. I shrank back, holding my breath, sure he'd seen me. But his eyes kept scanning at a steady pace.

He moved forward a few steps, holding the crossbow up at the ready. He took the broken pine branch in his hand and twirled it between his fingers. A few more feet and he stopped. He squatted down, pushed back the plants around the scuff I'd left, then rose, looking in the direction I'd intended for him to continue. He paused, scanning again.

Go on. That's the way.

His feet planted, shoulder width apart. *Oh crap. He sees me.* Then I heard the zip of his fly. Then the patter of urine hitting the forest floor.

His feet swiveled as he tucked himself back inside his pants and zipped up again.

He finally moved forward, without a sound.

I let out my breath. Another thirty seconds passed before I slipped from under the log and hobbled back toward the river.

It wouldn't be long before he'd realize I'd fooled him. Once he'd walked a bit without seeing any sign, he'd circle back. By then, I'd be over the hillside and headed toward the trap.

I ran along the same path I'd taken down, where he'd followed, so that my tracks would be somewhat hidden amid his. I didn't need him finding me again so soon.

I pushed through the brush, staying low, moving as fast as I could with my hand on my leg and careful not to twist an ankle over the rocky ground.

When I got to the thicket where I'd flushed the ptarmigan, Rocky's voice stopped me dead in my tracks. "You are a sly one."

I spun around, my heart racing. Where was he?

Up, to the left? On the ridge above me? How had he made it that far back already?

I dropped to my hands and knees. A groan escaped my lips as searing pain shot through my hip. I gripped my wound and crawled through the thicket.

"He had to go, you know." His voice made me duck lower. "I couldn't let him get between you and me."

How far was he? Too close. *I let him get too close.* My pulse hammered away in my ears.

He's going to kill me. I'm going to die. Out here. Alone.

No. Stop it. He's taunting you. That's good. Part of the plan.

He was confident he'd killed Dalton. Good. All was going as Dalton had planned.

So why am I shaking like a…like a little rabbit?

"It's just you and me now, babe."

He'd moved. Circling me. But how far away was he now? I could make a run for it. Maybe.

"And we're going to have us a little fun."

Into a patch of devil's club I crawled. It was good cover, if I didn't scrape every inch of skin from my face. I crept forward. Easy. Quietly.

"Arr-oooooooh!" he howled, the call of a crazed wolf, echoing across the hillside.

I got to my feet and pushed through the alders to a stand of spruce. He might hear me, but he couldn't see me. It was too thick. It would buy me some time. Maybe I could slip out the other side. With enough cover—

"What I want to know," he shouted after me, "is why couldn't you just shoot the bear?"

What? I felt his beady eyes on me, taunting. Somewhere behind me. I stumbled, caught my footing and kept moving.

"You had me going for a while there. I admit. I was sure you were the real deal. But then you didn't shoot the bear."

He was moving. Which way now?

"That's when I saw you for who you really are."

I came to a halt. What did he mean? What was this all about?

"All your talk about being Little Miss Sharpshooter. Typical. Just like all the other women. All mouth. Running with the boys, just to be a tease. You think this is a game. A two week holiday from your otherwise boring life. You come out here for a little excitement. Act like a big hunter, but you're no hunter. You're a tease. You're all talk and you're only interested in boys with big guns. Like those brothers. They stroke their guns, pump up their egos, get off on pulling the trigger.

"But you didn't get to hunt with John-boy, did you. So you could bat your eyes and shake your little ass."

I dropped to a crouch. I had to get a bearing on him.

"They're not real men. They know nothing about being a man." He moved closer to me. "*I'm* a real man,"

Is that what this was about?

"Sure, Jack would have coddled you, helped you hold your gun, told you what a great hunter you are. But he wouldn't have brought in a bear like I did."

There was a long pause. I held my breath, sure he was listening for me to move.

"Mark, Jack, Bob—they don't know shit. I'm the best tracker. I'm the real hunter. You didn't know it, but I was the one you wanted. And I proved it. But you had to go and do what you did."

What? Not shoot the bear? Kiss Dalton? What?

"You don't deserve a real man," he said, his voice a growl. My hands started to shake again. Dalton was right. This wasn't about poaching. This guy was a madman.

"If you ain't the predator, you're the prey. It's a brutal world."

I shrank back, tucked into the pine boughs. He was only a few feet away. *Don't let him get to you. Stick to the plan, like you promised Dalton. Live and die by the plan. Get out of here.*

"What's it feel like being the one hunted?" I swear I heard him lick his lips. "You are feisty though. I was hoping for a feisty one."

Feisty is my middle name. He'd moved again. Closer. I ducked. Where was he?

"I bet you miss your daddy, don't you?"

The image of my father, my real father, flashed before me, hiding in the bushes, poachers surrounding him, moving in for the kill. *You leave my dad out of this.*

"He's not here to protect you, sweetheart. You're all mine to do with as I want."

I sucked in air. Rage churned in my belly. *You son of a bitch.*

"You're not going to disappoint me and give up without a fight, are you?"

Oh, I'll show you a fight. Adrenaline pumped through my veins.

"Oh, yes," he moaned. He was right behind mc now, his voice husky. "I can smell your fear."

I'm not afraid of you.

"You're heart's thumping away in your chest. You're shaking. Why don't you run, little rabbit. Run!"

No more running.

"You're just a scared little girl."

I'll show you what this little girl can do.

Chapter 16

I dropped to my belly and wrapped my hand around a stick that was lying on the ground.

Every sense alert, I propped myself up on my elbows under the pine tree, waiting.

The subtle wisp of misty rain, accumulating on needles, then dripping to patter on the ground was the only thing I heard. Where was he? I turned my head to hear. Drip. Drop. Nothing.

The sound of my own breathing drowned out everything else. The beating of my heart thudded away—*thump thump, thump thump*.

I inched forward. Then I heard something. The snap of a twig. Which way? The whoosh of his pant leg against the brush. I kept hidden, scanning the forest floor. Then it was there, his boot. Five feet away.

He took another step. Then another, creeping toward me.

Just a few more steps. One, then another. His boot settled on the moss, two feet away. I drew back and thrust the stick into his calf. *Take that!* He reared backward. I grabbed his other foot and he toppled, landing flat on his back.

"You bitch!"

I sprang on top of him, my hands at his throat.

He bucked and shoved me, but I hung on. We rolled in the brush, slammed into a spruce. I closed my eyes as the branches scraped across my face.

Rocky's chuckle made me open them again. His hands were on my hips. "You wanna play do you?"

I drew back and slapped him across the face.

He laughed louder. Then his eyes narrowed. He shifted and flung me on my back, knocking the wind out of me. *Damn. How'd he do that?*

Then he was on top of me, pinning my arms back. I pivoted on my hip, shoved my arm out farther to break his balance. As he collapsed, I rammed my elbow hard against his throat. He fell over, hacking, surprise in his eyes.

I was on my knees and had one hand on the rifle when he swiped me with his left hand, right across the rash on my neck and hard on my ear.

"Ow!" I shrieked. I still had a hold of the rifle. It came free from his shoulder. I gripped it with both hands and struck him in the crotch with the stock.

On my feet, I ran, my arms pumping, my heart pounding, my lungs burning, my wounded leg moving faster than I thought possible. I barreled through thicket, plowed through bushes, up a ridge and down another, getting as far away as I could.

I couldn't beat him at hand-to-hand combat. He was well-trained, stronger. I was wounded, too. But now I had the rifle. I had the rifle! *Hallelujah! You're going down, you crazy son of a bitch!*

Ahead, there was a natural ledge. I climbed to the top, pushing my limits, then spun around to where I could see the path I had come before I stopped to catch my breath.

My lungs couldn't settle down. So I paced, puffing out the air, watching for him to chase, the rifle still in my hand.

I grabbed the bolt and racked it back. Empty. No bullets. *Dammit!* Of course he wouldn't carry it loaded, for this exact reason. It was for long distance. He had his sidearm, which was more securely fastened to his belt. *Dammit! What was I thinking? Why hadn't I grabbed that?*

Was there more ammo back in the box in camp? Dalton's and my guns were there. But would Rocky have left all the ammo there too once he left the camp? That's probably what he carried in the backpack. Or, if he was smart, he would have hidden it somewhere in the woods.

Dammit!

He'd be on my trail soon.

Settle down, McVie. The trap. Dalton will be there. Stick to the plan.

After a quick scan, I realized I'd run back in the direction where we'd hunted yesterday. Or was it two days now? Three? My hand went to my head, as if I could steady my thoughts. I needed food, water.

The rain had stopped, thankfully, though I was soaked through to my skin. The sun beat down from directly overhead, giving a hint of warmth. In the sky, further east, ravens circled with two vultures, their broad wings tipping on the wind. A sign of carrion below. Was I that close to the bear kill? If so, what other animals were gathered for the feast?

I didn't want to find out.

I needed to keep moving and lead him back around to the trap without running into any more trouble. If there were any animals feeding on the carcass or even in that blueberry patch that Dalton had found and— blueberries! The branches drooping with them, he had said.

Which way was it? That way. I pushed through the brush and there they were, bushes loaded with little, luscious spheres of blue. I dropped to my knees and grabbed at the branches, stripping them of handfuls of berries, and crammed them into my mouth. Oh so sweet! I didn't know blueberries could taste so good. I slumped to the ground and shoved berries into my mouth, eating as fast as I could pick them.

My brain signaled alarm bells. I had to be careful, move on.

Rocky couldn't be far behind. *Just one more handful.* Then back toward Dalton and the trap. Had it been enough time? Was he in place by now?

I got to my feet. From where I stood, I had two choices: head upward, through the open hillside, then drop back on the downward slope to the trap or head toward the lakeside now, push through the woods and the thick understory that lined the lake, then make my way back upward.

Either way had disadvantages and—whoosh! The ground at my feet exploded, spraying mud at my pant legs, and a split second later, the shot echoed inside my head.

I dropped to the ground, my full weight coming down on my injured thigh. I retched with pain. A patch of berry bushes burst into pieces beside me. I pushed and rolled as the second shot rang out. Then a third.

You're supposed to chase me! Not shoot at me!

Crawling on my hands and knees, I managed to get cover under a spruce. Wet branches let loose their droplets, soaking my head. Then I felt a burning sensation. In my arm. My coat sleeve had a rip in it, a hole. Blood oozed out. My left arm. *He shot me in my arm!*

With my right hand, I clenched my bicep, squeezing to suppress the blood flow. *Damn that hurts.* A few short breaths. *Shit.* I had to get to the trap. To Dalton.

What had I been thinking? Believing I could take on Rocky on my own. What have I done? I started to shake uncontrollably.

"You *are* a feisty one." Every one of my muscles tightened at the sound of his voice. Panic rumbled in my gut and threatened to spread. "More fun than I thought you were going to be."

Where is he? Which way?

"And looky there. Under the tree, like a Christmas present."

Shit! I rolled, got to my feet, and ran, my hand gripping my left arm, my head down.

Toward the trap. My foot caught. On a root. Something. I slammed to the ground, face down, knocking the wind out of me. I lay there, a quick moment to catch my breath, then got to my knees, to my feet, and I was running, fear carrying me forward.

I couldn't underestimate him again. He'd slept. Eaten. And he was bigger and stronger and more fit than I was. He could've caught me by now, if he hadn't been toying with me.

What if he was tired of that already? What if he decided to shoot at me again? Get it over with?

I needed cover. Downhill, into the forest that lined the lake. That was the way.

His laughter followed me—the wild, primal, blood-curdling shrieks of a hyena.

Chapter 17

Somehow I got to the woods. My leg on fire, my arm screaming with sharp jolts, the rash at my neck burning where the devil's club had done its work. But I'd made it. I'd made it this far. I gulped in air, trying not to think about how thirsty I was.

The forest here was white and black spruce, quaking aspen, and paper birch. Not the best cover, but better than being out in the open. I pushed forward. I had to get as much space between me and Rocky as I could. Without him losing my trail. He'd shown that wasn't likely.

I followed the shoreline, uphill from the water's edge, concentrating on putting one foot in front of the other. Wait— wasn't this where I'd encountered the moose? No, that was old growth. I had to get ahold of my dizziness, get focused.

"There you are, little rabbit."

I spun around.

Rocky stood thirty yards away, his crossbow trained on my chest.

My lungs seized, catching my breath in my throat.

"Thought you were getting away, did you?"

His eyes glowed with satisfaction in startling me.

There was thicket to my left, downed branches to my right, if I could—

"Don't even think about it. I'll shoot. Enough running."

He took a step closer to me. Then another. "Don't worry. I

wouldn't make a fatal shot. Just one to slow you down." He grinned, a wicked, sleazy grin that made bile stir at the back of my throat. "You're wearing me out. And we haven't even got to the fun part yet."

He took another step. "Don't get me wrong. I like the feisty ones. Full of spice." He opened his mouth slightly and his tongue flicked at me. "Maybe you'll buck like a pig in heat."

I shuddered, the taste of bile in my throat making my stomach flip-flop.

"Tell me you won't lie there like a dead fish." He cocked his head to the side, scrutinizing me, his reptilian eyes darting up and down my body. "No. You wouldn't. You've got too much fire in you. I knew I liked you. The moment you walked in the lodge, trying to hide your disgust for the place."

You knew? You saw right through me?

"Righteous little cowgirl princess." He closed the distance between us. "I'll take pleasure in taking you down off that pedestal." He jerked the crossbow downward. "Get on the ground."

I froze in place. No way was I getting on the ground.

He stomped toward me, grabbed me by my hair, and yanked my head down to his knees. "I said get on the ground, Bitch."

My knees collapsed and I was on my belly, my face in the moss.

"You better learn to listen. To obey. Do you hear me? No girl of mine defies me."

I nodded, trying to pacify him.

"That's better. Now look at me."

I turned my head, looked up at him, into those colorless eyes, eyes reflecting years of anger, pent up, twisted into a calculated rage. His hand rubbed at the bulge in his pants. "Oh yeah, that's it," he said with a grunt. "You're going to be my best yet. My finest trophy."

I fought back the nausea. If I showed any sign of revulsion, he'd kill me. I knew it, in my gut. He had to believe I felt beaten, that I'd given up.

He grabbed the back of my pants, and with an amazing strength, lifted me in the air and flipped me on my back. He dropped down on the ground between my legs, shoving them apart.

I shrank back, crawled with my elbows, trying to get away from him.

"Now, now," he said, grabbing my belt. "Enough playing hard to get." He set down the crossbow so he'd have both hands now, yet he still fumbled to get the buckle undone. I bit my lip, trying not to react. Not yet. "You'll do as I say." A pause. He cocked his head to the side. "Well now, we can't have that."

At first, I didn't know what he meant, but he took hold of my arm and examined the gunshot wound. With his other hand, he flipped off his pack, reached into it, and took out a first-aid kit. He ripped my coat open and without a word, doused my arm with hydrogen peroxide, then wrapped it with a bandage.

I kept still.

Once he taped it off, he leaned down. His lips to my ear, his hot breath on my neck, he said, "I want you alive and kicking." Slowly, he drew back, running his lips along my cheek. "Until I'm done with you."

Don't react. Wait for the right moment. Wait.

His hands squeezed my breasts.

Son of a bitch. "What are you waiting for?" I spat.

"Oh, now you want it, do you?"

I made myself look up at him, look into his eyes. Saw his dilated pupils. The sign of excitement. Of lust. Of reveling in his conquest.

"Tell me how you want it," he moaned.

I calmed my voice, my breathing. *This could work.* "Since I walked into that lodge and saw you across the room." I steeled myself. "I've been wanting you. I was hoping it would be out here. In the wild." I looked him in the eye. "Take off your pants."

There was hesitation in his look. Had I gone too far? Did he know what I was trying to do? Either way, he would lose. If he kept his pants on, he'd have a hard time doing what he wanted. If he pulled them down, he'd be vulnerable. *Go ahead. Pull down those pants.*

He reared back and slapped me across the face. The sting fueled my rage. I swung and clipped him in the jaw. He caught me by the wrist and slammed my arm back, pinning me to the ground. "I knew you'd be a scrapper," he said as he brought his knee up, ramming it into my thigh to keep me in place.

I screamed out in pain.

"That get you hot?" he growled.

The man was built like a tiger, all sinewy and quick, with the same dangerous unpredictability. But he'd underestimated me. I was counting on it.

"You gonna be a screamer, too?" He said it like that's what he wanted.

He fumbled at his belt with one hand, unsnapped his pants as he held me down with the other hand. "I'm going to give you something you'll never forget."

He underestimated me. I had one hand free. The moment his pants were lowered, I reached down, grabbed his balls, and yanked as hard as I could. Like starting a lawn mower, my self-defense instructor had said. *Pull!*

Rocky reared back, his face bright red, and let out a yowl like a speared pig. He fell back, right on top of the crossbow. *Dammit!*

I reached for his sidearm, but it was gone. Where? In his pack?

"You bitch!" he roared, his hands at his groin. "I'm going to kill you."

I rolled, got to my feet, and ran, one foot in front of the other, as fast as I could, my heartbeat thumping in my ears. Through the trees, up the hillside. Ignoring the throbbing pain in my leg, in my arm. My light head. I wasn't stopping until I got to the trap.

I could hear him behind me, crashing through the foliage, his footsteps thudding on the ground. *That's right. Follow me, you son of a bitch.*

My head down, I focused on nothing but speed. My chest heaved with my breath, lungs burning. I couldn't fall down. If I fell, he'd be on me again. Stay upright and run, run, run.

Behind me was a loud thump, then a curse. He must have fallen down. I kept running. Any distance I could gain, I needed.

I broke from the thick woods, ran up a ridge, my arms pumping, feeling nothing but adrenaline. The stream was ahead. Not far now. The stream. And the trap. And Dalton. He'd be there. He had to be there.

One stride. And another. And another.

There was the stream. Straight ahead.

Two more strides and my foot fell into place, right where I knew the trap to be. Another stride and I was past, running. Rocky right behind me.

What if he didn't step where I had? I slowed and turned. Rocky was there, almost at the edge of the creek, his eyes on me. He hesitated.

"What is it?" he said.

Run. Keep running.

Rocky looked down, around. "Why'd you hesitate? What is it about this place?"

Dammit. I dropped to my knees. "Just shoot me! Do it now. I'm tired of this!" I shouted.

A grin crept across his face. He raised his index finger and shook it at me like a father scolding a little child. "Oh no, little rabbit. You've been up to something. Haven't you?"

He raised the crossbow to put me in his sights and took a step toward me, his foot right on the trap. Or was it? Wasn't this the spot where we had hidden it? Nothing happened.

My heart stopped. Where was Dalton? Was he really dead? Shot back at the river? *Oh god! Dalton!*

Another step, and another. My body shook with anger and fear. Then Dalton reared up from the bushes and tackled Rocky, knocking him over. The crossbow flew out of his hands as the two tumbled into the bushes in a mass of grunts.

Dalton! Thank god! I scrambled toward them on my hands and knees, reaching for the crossbow. Dalton pummeled Rocky with his fists, but Rocky took it like he was jacked up on something. He didn't wince or pull away like a normal person would. It was as if he wanted it, welcomed it. When Dalton rose up, Rocky landed a punch in his kidney. Dalton doubled over.

"No!" escaped my lips. I grabbed hold of the crossbow.

Then they were wrestling again, arms and legs enmeshed, crashing through the brush. I couldn't make out one from the other. No way could I shoot.

Rocky was encumbered by the pack, but it didn't seem to slow him down. Rage was a powerful motivator. And Dalton was getting the brunt of it.

Then Rocky had a knife in his hand—or was it Dalton? No, it was Rocky. He sliced and red blood streamed down Dalton's arm. He jabbed again and Dalton slapped his hand away. Rocky flipped the knife in his hand and sliced back. Dalton blocked with his forearm but took a knee to the gut.

They were on the ground, rolling downhill again.

I pushed through the brush, keeping up.

Dalton broke free and kicked Rocky square in the jaw,

sending him backward, stumbling, trying to stay on his feet.

I raised the crossbow, tried to hold it steady to look through the scope, but Rocky had gained his balance and pounced on Dalton.

Dalton came up from the bushes with Rocky's sidearm in his hand, but Rocky lunged, sending it flying. Could I get to it? I had a weapon in my hands. A lethal weapon. A more accurate weapon. But a gun was a gun. I headed for it.

I pawed at the ground where the gun had fallen, scrambling through the bushes. *Where could it be?* I searched left, then right. *Dammit! Dammit all to hell!*

I popped my head up. The men were tumbling down the hill again. I took three strides before they came to a stop with a distinct moan. Dalton lay motionless, Rocky on top of him. I planted my feet and raised the crossbow, my whole body shaking.

"Get off of him!" I shouted.

Rocky's eyes slowly raised to focus on me.

"Get off of him right now!"

Slowly, measured, he rose, sitting atop Dalton, his chest facing me, fully exposed. Thirty yards away.

Holding the crossbow trained on his heart, I said, "It's over."

His eyes held mine, cold and hard. In an instant, he raised his knife and thrust it downward. Toward Dalton.

I pulled the trigger and let the arrow fly.

Chapter 18

Rocky fell backward, the arrow stuck in his chest, rage and shock in his eyes.

I raced down the hill toward Dalton as fast as my leg would take me.

The knife protruded from Dalton's thigh, his hand wrapped around it, his face white. Blood. There was too much blood.

I reached for the knife.

"No!" he grunted. "Don't take it out."

"What?"

His chest was heaving. "I'll bleed to death if—" he drew in air "—if you take it out." He panted to hold back the pain. "Make sure," he managed, nodding toward Rocky.

Rocky lay on the ground in a heap, his leg twitching. Dead. I'd killed him.

"I...I..." My stomach flipped. "I think I'm going to—" I leaned over and retched, vomit heaving from my stomach and onto the ground, the bitter, nasty taste of bile making me spit and gag.

"Breathe," Dalton was saying. "Stay with me. Just breathe."

I sat back, closed my eyes and drew in a long breath. Then released it, slowly, trying to find calm.

"I killed him." I puffed. "I shot a man."

"Poppy, focus. It's okay. Everything's going to be okay."

I nodded. My heart rate was slowing.

"Listen to me. You have to check. Make sure. Do you hear me?"

Nodding, knowing he was right, I stretched my reach as far as I could, not wanting to get any closer than I had to, and placed my index and forefinger on Rocky's neck. No pulse.

"He's dead," I said.

"Well it's about goddamn time," Dalton croaked and lay back.

"Yeah," I said, not knowing what else to say. I'd just killed a man. A man trying to kill me, trying to kill my partner, but still…I'd killed him. My stomach pulled tight, the acid bubbling back up.

"Take a breath," Dalton said.

I did.

"You look like hell."

My attention snapped back to him. "You don't look much better." Sweat beaded on his forehead. His hand that clutched the knife, holding it in place in his thigh, was white. "Let me take a look at that."

Blood oozed around the knife blade where it entered the skin, soaking his pants around it. "Do you think he hit your femoral artery?"

Dalton's lips were pursed into an O as he concentrated on his breathing.

"I'll take that as a yes. Okay." *Okay. Shit.* I stood to look. We were at least a quarter mile from the camp, maybe farther. "Okay," I said again.

I dropped to my knees next to Rocky, rolled him over onto his side, and ripped open his backpack.

All his daypack emergency gear was inside, but not the sat phone. *Damn.*

A tourniquet. That's what was needed.

I pulled a strap from the pack and quickly wrapped it around

Dalton's thigh, higher than the wound, and pulled it tight. An arrow was the best I had to cinch it. I tied one into the knot and twisted. Dalton winced.

"Too tight?"

He shook his head.

"Good." I tied the other end of the arrow just above his knee to keep the tension. "Here's what we're going to do. I'll run back to the camp and call for help. You—" I choked back my fear "—you stay alive. Okay?"

With gritted teeth, he nodded.

"I'll be right back, Dalton." I leaned forward and kissed him on the lips. "Don't you die on me, do you hear me? I'll be right back."

"Enough drama," he said, the muscles in his neck pulled tight. "Go already."

I got to my feet and ran. And ran. I had to get help. Now. A severed femoral artery was life threatening.

If Rocky had pulled the blade back out, Dalton would be— my hand went to my mouth. I couldn't say it. I couldn't think it.

Keep running. Keep running!

I came up over the ridge and saw the camp over the next rise. There I would get the phone, call in the calvary, then race back to keep him stable.

The gate was closed, the electric fence still energized. I gripped the plastic handles to unclip the wires as fast as I could, then moved right to the storage box. Our guns, boxes of food stuff—*food!* I shoved the crackers and bananas into a pack then continued sorting through the box, tossing the contents on the ground—cast iron skillet, box of matches, can of coffee, utensils, two blankets, camp chairs, the tent bags, a first-aid kit. No phone.

I spun around. "Dammit! Damn him to hell! Where's the phone?"

I raced to Rocky's tent. His sleeping bag and pillow got shaken, tossed out. Extra socks. Nothing else. Nothing.

What had he done with it?

The only place left in camp was our tent. I rummaged through it. Nothing there. As I'd thought, all the ammo was gone too. I scanned the hillside. Where would he have hidden it? There was no way of knowing. It might as well have been on the moon.

I grabbed the bag of food, a jug of water, a sleeping bag, and the first-aid kit and headed back to Dalton.

His eyes were closed but he was conscious when I got back.

"Do you want the good news or the bad news?" I asked, bent over, heaving to catch my breath.

His pupils looked a little dilated. Not good.

"Food," I said, holding up a rucksack. "How about a banana?"

He didn't make a sound or move.

"Okay, let's start with water," I said. I unscrewed the top of the jug and held it to his lips. "C'mon, just a sip."

He tried to drink, his hand tightening around the knife in his thigh.

As he lay his head back, his eyes met mine. "No phone?"

I shook my head. "And Joe won't be expecting us back for at least, well, a few more days, assuming—" I looked over at the body, at Rocky, lying there in a heap and my throat constricted—*don't think about that* "—he checked in, which I'm willing to bet he did."

He nodded and drew in a deep breath.

I pried open the first-aid kit. "I don't suppose there's a field technique for—" I stared at the knife sticking out of his thigh "—for that?"

He gave me a sideways grin. "Yeah. You order a body bag."

"No way. Not on my watch," I said. If the knife had to stay in, well, we'd make sure the knife stayed in.

I packed mounds of gauze around the blade, then used the entire roll of tape, round and round his thigh, to keep it in place.

"I'm getting you out of here." I risked a glance at Rocky's body one more time, lying there dead, and down at the plane, floating on the lake. "You watch me. Sit tight."

"What are you thinking?" Dalton managed.

"The plane. It can't be that hard to fly."

His eyes grew wide. "You can't be serious."

"You need a hospital. Now."

"Build three fires. Lots of smoke. Someone will see."

"Like who? We haven't seen another soul, not a plane, nothing, since we've been out here."

"Someone will come. Eventually. You have the supplies now. You'll be fine."

"But you won't."

He shook his head. "It's not worth the risk."

"Not worth the risk? Your life is not worth the risk? You listen to me, mister. You keep pressure on that leg. You stay awake. And you live. Do you hear me? We're taking that plane and getting the hell out of here."

His eyes focused on the plane. I could tell he was contemplating the distance, how he'd get to it.

"You leave that up to me," I said. "I'll get you there."

"Your arm," he said, noticing my bandage for the first time. "How'd you—"

"It was Rocky actually. Don't worry. Another flesh wound. Nothing serious."

In a stand of alders I found two downed limbs, long enough for what I needed. This had to work. He couldn't die on me now. It had to work. It would work.

With the two branches laid out parallel, I stretched the

sleeping bag between them. From Rocky's pack, I found some nylon cord. Using Dalton's jackknife, I cut holes in the sleeping bag at intervals where I could lace the cord, tying the bag to the branches.

I laid my makeshift travois next to Dalton. "Let's get you on here," I said. He was too exhausted to argue when I rolled him on his side, pulled it up under him, then rolled him onto it.

With a push of sheer determination, I took hold of the branches and lifted, and with one step, then another, I dragged him down the hillside.

Chapter 19

At the edge of the lake, I dropped to the ground, exhausted.

The sun was behind the trees. It had to be at least three o'clock.

Dalton must have been reading my mind. "It's too late. Even if you do get that thing running, and up in the air without killing us, it will be dark. Trying to land in the dark is suicide."

I stood up and shoved my coat off, then my shirt and pants. "I'm getting that plane," I said. "I'm getting you in it. Then we'll see."

"That water's ice cold. You're already exhausted."

"It'll revive me," I said. "Stop arguing."

He closed his eyes, resigned.

"You just sit tight," I said and waded in.

It's amazing how quickly legs can go numb. By the time I plunged full in, my breath came in short pants and my muscles threatened to seize. But I had to get there. To the plane. Back to Dalton.

I kicked and threw my arms forward, pushing through the icy water. One stroke. Then another. Then another. And I was there, pulling myself up onto the pontoon. I half-expected the door to be locked but it flung open when I grabbed the handle. I crawled inside and went straight for the radio. Dalton had said it was disabled, but I had to check. The knob turned, but nothing happened. Was there a wire I could reattach?

Something?

Forget it. Dalton would have checked all that. I went for the flight manual in the side pocket.

How to start the engine. It had to be in the first pages. I flipped page after page, shivering. Drawings. Specs. Lists of equipment. *Oh crap*. Maybe this was just a maintenance manual? No. There. `Start Engine`.

`Battery master switch - ON`. I peered at the dash, all buttons and switches, knobs and levers. *Crap. C'mon!*

I flipped back through the pages to the diagram of the dashboard, ripped it from the book, then opened back to the page on how to start the engine.

`Battery switch`. Okay, got it.

`Fuel selector to fullest tank`. Got it.

`Mixture lever - AUTO RICH`. What did that mean? There was no setting for auto rich. I pushed the mixture lever forward, half way. Would that do it?

My hands shook, my teeth chattering. "Can we get some heat in here!" I shouted to no one. *Where's the damn purser when you need her?*

I could do this. I had to do this.

`Throttle lever - 1/4 to 1/2 in. OPEN`. Ok, got it.

`Build up pressure with wobble pump to maximum 5 psi`. *Wobble pump? Seriously? There really is a wobble pump?*

Right there on the page. Wobble pump. Fuel pressure. The lever was in the center, between the seats. I gave it a few pumps up and down. It made a whoosh, whoosh noise. Definitely gas in the lines.

`Prime 4 strokes`. *Prime what? How?*

I scanned the dash schematic. Nothing. Was there an index in this thing? I flipped to the back. No index. A shiver took over and I shook uncontrollably, rubbing my arms. I bounced in the chair. Get that blood flowing.

What was I thinking? I don't know how to fly a plane. *I'm going to get us killed.*

No. *You can do this. You have to do this.*

Back over the schematic again. It had to be there. My finger shook as I dragged it across the sheet, checking each word. There. Primer. *There it is!* On my left side, a small knob next to the seat. I worked it up and down until it got harder to push. *That must be enough.*

`Both ignition switches to ON position.` Switched on.

`Hold starter switch to STARTER position.` Okay.

The starter whined, but the engine didn't turn over.

`Hold Booster Coil switch to BOOSTER COIL position. As soon as engine fires, release the switch.`

"Here goes," I said aloud and held the switch. With a rattle, the engine fired to life. The propeller started turning. I let out a whoop.

Quick. Off with the starter and booster coil switches.

The plane rattled and shook as the engine huffed and sputtered, then quit.

"Dammit!"

What? More throttle? More priming? More wobble? Wobble. *Oh my god. It comes down to a wobble.* I giggled. Then I laughed. My eyes started to well up with tears. *No! Dammit! We are not going to die out here!*

"Listen to me, bitch!" I slammed my fist on the dash. "You're going to fly. You're going to fly me back to that lodge. Do you hear me? Me and Dalton. Right now."

I shoved the throttle lever forward, then back. Cranked on the wobble pump a few more times, then flipped the starter switch on. She whined, the starter turning. I pushed the booster coil switch again. She shook and sputtered to life. Up with the throttle. "Don't you quit on me!"

She reached a steady hum. *Yes!*

Okay. Now to get her in motion. Next page. Next page. There.

`Taxiing.`

`Flaps at CRUISE POSITION.` What's cruise position? Does it really matter? I'd fiddle with them once I got her moving.

`Propeller lever - full INCREASE rpm.` Got it. I pushed the lever and the engine got louder and the plane started to move. Excellent.

`Watch oil and cylinder temps.` Ah, sure.

`Operate rudder pedals to steer airplane by means of steerable tailwheel.` I placed my feet square on the pedals and pushed one, then the other. Okay, got it.

The plane jerked to a halt. *Crap. The anchor.*

I pulled back on the propeller lever, flung the door open and jumped out onto the pontoon. How was I going to pull up an anchor? Wait. I wouldn't need it again. I untied the line and let it go.

Back in the cockpit, I shoved the propeller lever forward, moved the foot pedals back and forth, and got her pointed toward shore. Toward Dalton.

"Wake up." I slapped him across the face. "C'mon. Wake up."

Dalton's eyes fluttered.

"Wake up, damn you!"

One eye opened.

"C'mon. I got the plane. Get in."

I'd managed to get the plane turned and stopped in about two feet of water, rather than bring her nose right up on the beach. I wasn't sure if there was a reverse and didn't want to risk getting stuck now.

The plane was floating without any tether, the propeller slowly turning.

"C'mon. Now." *Before she floats away.* "Get on your feet, soldier."

With a shove, I got him sitting upright. He saw the plane then. His eyes narrowed then flicked toward me.

"All you have to do is get in the passenger seat. I'll do the rest."

With a groan, he shifted his weight to his good leg and slowly pushed himself upward.

"I'm right beside you, holding you steady."

He raised himself to his full height and focused on the plane. "Just my luck," he mumbled. When he put his weight on his bad leg, the pain must have been unbearable, but he didn't show it. SEALs.

I got up under his arm. "Lean on me," I said.

He didn't slow. Into the water and up onto the pontoon he hobbled. With those strong arms, he pulled himself into the cockpit and swung into the seat, panting to abate the pain. It had taken all he had.

In the pilot's seat again, I thrust the throttle lever forward, worked the foot pedals, and pointed her toward the middle of the lake. The sky was clear, but the clock was ticking.

"McVie."

"What?" I turned. "Did you say something?"

I reached over him, grabbed his earphones from the hook and snapped them over his ears, adjusting the mic.

His voice raspy, he said, "Have I ever told you—" he drew in a needed breath "—you're incorrigible?"

"Yeah, I think so," I said with a smile.

"Well, in case—" A cough. "—in case we don't—"

"We're going to make it, Dalton. I can do this."

He nodded, his eyes closed. "I know. I just—" His eyes

fluttered back open. "I just want you to know—" Those eyes held mine. "Thank you, partner." And he was out again.

I reached over his chest, pulled the seatbelt down and clipped it into place. Then I put mine on too.

Holding the manual in my hand, I flipped to the page titled, "Take Off."

All levers in place.

`Flaps - TAKE-OFF position.` What position is that? I shuffled through a few more pages to the diagram. Okay, got it.

Face into the wind. The manual didn't state that, but I knew it. And I needed lots of lake.

`Mixture at full rich.`

`Open throttle smoothly to maximum permissible take-off power. See figure 4-1.` Figure 4-1 showed the gauges. Green good. Yellow caution. Red danger. Simple enough. *Maximum it is.*

`Allow aircraft to fly itself off at 55 to 65 mph in a tail down attitude and climb at 65 mph.` *Tail down attitude?* Did that mean nose up? We were going to find out.

Easy now. The voice of my father in my head. Nothing drastic. *Easy touch.*

Deep breath.

"Hang on," I said to Dalton as I grabbed hold of the throttle lever and shoved it all the way forward.

The propeller started spinning faster and faster, the hum rising in volume as the plane moved through the water, building speed.

We were doing this thing.

The mph gauge needle rose, up, up. 45mph. Then 50. 55. 57. 60. We were still on the water, the pontoons slapping in the waves. Then it happened. We were airborne. But the plane veered drastically to the left. I shoved the rudder right and she corrected, still climbing, leaving my stomach on the lake.

I took hold of Dalton's hand and squeezed. "We're going to make it. Stay with me now. We're going to make it."

The plane climbed, smooth as can be, like I'd been flying one for years.

`Slowly increase airspeed to 80 mph and re-trim.` Throttle forward.

"We're flying!"

Once we got to 500 feet, the manual said to set flaps to climb. Did I want to continue to climb? This seemed high enough for me. The higher we flew, the more we'd have to descend. I quickly read through the section on climbing and cruising. Nowhere did it say what altitude to fly. 500 feet felt right to me. I set the flaps to cruise position and the plane leveled. Good.

The flight out to the camp had been about forty-five minutes on a south-southeast path. Using the rudder, I turned to head north-northwest. Back to the lodge. Trying to fly all the way to Anchorage wasn't an option. We'd have to take our chances that Joe hadn't been compromised.

Getting a feel for the flaps, the rudder, the trim, was a priority. They'd be needed for landing. Back to the manual, I read through the section on landing.

Caution. Notes. Fuel tank capacity. Airspeed correction.

Finally, a section titled "Descent." There were three lines:

`Reduce airspeed and power as required.`

`Fuel selector to fullest tank.`

`Instruments in correct ranges.`

What? That's it? What's required? What are the correct ranges? I looked at Dalton, passed out in the passenger seat. *Oh shit.*

Under "Landing," the same. `Trim as required.`

There were sections on cross-wind landing and minimum run landing. Then the post flight checklist.

What have I done?

We were flying. Committed. But flying was one thing. Landing was something else. This plane was coming down eventually. One way or another.

Okay. Don't freak out!

Landing was just a controlled descent, right? Slowly, take her down, until the pontoons touch the water. Easy. The lodge was on a river, so I had all the distance I needed. That was a plus.

First, I had to find the lodge.

I reached over and placed my fingers on Dalton's neck to check his pulse. Slow, but there.

Blue sky spread before me. Green and yellow hills below. A beautiful landscape. Would it be the last I'd see?

Stop thinking like that.

My mom. Would I see her again? And Chris. I had to call him. First thing and plan that trip to Mexico like he wanted. What if I didn't—*McVie. Cut it out.*

I checked the clock. Only fifteen minutes in the air. Thirty to go. *If* I had the right heading. I should be able to see the river though. Then follow it until I spotted the lodge. Then circle back for landing. That's what I'd do. That was the plan.

Double checking the manual for landing tips seemed like a prudent thing to do, so I scanned the table of contents. Description of the aircraft. Procedures. Operating limits. Special installations. Data charts.

Nothing helpful.

Info on the propeller, the rudder, trim, flaps. All there. But what to do with that information? What angle was right? What trim?

I took hold of the yoke, my feet on the pedals, and slowly made adjustments, easy now, feeling the plane dip and turn. That was my best option. Feel it.

Dalton moaned. Sweat beaded on his forehead. I took his hand in mine. He'd risked his life for me. And it wasn't the first time. Now, were we going to die together? Without me telling him how much I—his eyes opened.

"Are we there yet?" he said.

"Almost. Make sure your tray table is in the upright position," I said, trying to manage a smile.

The way he looked at me made my stomach flutter. Then it clenched with dread. "I'm sorry I got you in to this."

He closed his eyes. "Don't be sorry." He opened them again. "We're in this together."

My stomach fluttered again and I turned so he wouldn't see the tears in my eyes. Deep breath. I turned back. "I'm going to land this plane."

"I know you will." His eyes winked shut.

"I mean it," I said, squeezing his hand, making him open his eyes and look at me. "I'm going to land this plane and get you to a hospital. I swear it."

"I know, Poppy. I know." And his eyes closed again.

I let go of his hand and gripped the yoke. *I will land this plane.*

The landscape stretched before me, a blur of fall colors. There, ahead. The river. It had to be the one.

I sat up straight. This was it. The plane seemed to putt along, taking its sweet time. Finally, the river was nearly below us. I turned the plane, easy now, to follow. The lodge had to be here somewhere. A mile. Another mile.

There it is! That's it. That's the lodge. That big old eye sore. Was I glad to see it, standing out like a beacon.

I went past, then turned the plane in a big, easy circle and lined up with the river. Throttle back. The engine hum slowed. Flaps set to landing. Throttle back some more. Slow. Dropping.

My hands gripped the yoke. We were coming down. Was it too fast? Throttle back some more. Glide in. That's the way. The trees got bigger. Closer. Dropping.

"Keep the nose up."

"What?" I turned.

Dalton's expression was adamant. "Keep the nose up!"

"Right."

I pulled back—easy—on the yoke. We were level with the treetops. Throttle back. Easy now.

Dropping fast. Maybe more throttle? *Shit!*

The pontoons slapped hard on the water, whipping my head forward.

We bounced up, the nose pointing to the sky, slamming me back in my seat. Then dropped flat, the floats crashing into the water, pitching us forward. I yanked the yoke back, but it was too late. The nose dove. The propeller rammed into the shallow water and hit bottom, breaking off with a bang as we rolled. Glass shattering. Metal crumpling. Over and back up again, everything spinning. Then the plane tipped backward and the tail hit the water with a sploosh.

Then all was still. Quiet. I let out my breath.

Dalton stared at me with that half-grin. I burst out laughing.

Chapter 20

We sat in the cockpit, staring at each other, my heart thrumming in my ears, my hands shaking.

Dalton gazed out the broken window, a contented smile on his face.

"You seem awfully calm," I said.

"I knew…" His voice shook, strained. "I knew you…could do it."

The whir of an outboard engine grew louder. The pontoon boat coming closer.

I unclipped my seatbelt, took my headphones off, then Dalton's before pushing the door open and stepping out onto the plane's float, which was bent at an awkward angle.

I had to be cautious. If Rocky had called and given us up…

Irene was at the helm, some man beside her. The other guide? I couldn't remember his name.

"Are you all right?" she shouted as they approached.

I shook my head, pointing to the passenger side. "Dalton! He's hurt!" They pulled up alongside. "He needs a hospital, right away."

The other guide—Jack, that was his name—stepped off the boat, onto the plane float, opened the door on Dalton's side, and peered in at Dalton. His eyes came to a halt on Dalton's leg and the knife sticking out of it. "What the hell happened?"

he asked, alarm clear on his face.

"Help me get him out," I said, crawling over the pilot's seat. "Don't move the knife."

His lips pursed in a sympathetic owe, he didn't hesitate. He took Dalton by the arm. "You awake, buddy? Can you move?"

Dalton nodded, a subtle, but determined nod.

Irene had the boat tied off and got on the other side of Jack. One under each arm, they heaved Dalton up and onto the pontoon boat where he slumped onto the bench chair.

I followed, sliding onto the chair next to him. "Go, go, go!" I hollered.

Irene obeyed, understanding the severity of the wound, the importance of expediency. There'd be time for explanations later. The boat engine fired to life and she was on the radio, shouting orders to someone.

Jack knelt in front of Dalton, a first-aid kit in his hands.

"How long has it been? Has he lost a lot of blood?" he asked as he stuck a needle in Dalton's arm, then donned surgical gloves and started poking at the gauze I'd packed around the knife.

"A couple hours?" I said. "We were up on a hill. It took some time to get him down to the water, to the plane."

He nodded, taking in the information, but the expression on his face was grim.

"Do you think—" I couldn't say it. "Is he going to—"

He gave me an encouraging smile.

"Thank God we've got two planes," Irene said, setting down the radio. "Jack'll fly him straight to Anchorage."

My head was buried in Dalton's chest, holding him upright, holding him close. All I could do was nod. It was out of my hands now. If Dalton was going to live, it depended on others. On time. On the weather. On the—*oh god*. I sat upright. "Can you fly at night?"

Jack nodded. "We'll get him there."

When the pontoons hit gravel, I looked up. Joe stood on shore. In two strides he was onboard and had me in his arms. "Oh my sweet daughter, what's happened?" His eyes landed on Dalton and the knife in his leg, then back to me, full of questions. "What happened?" He looked lost, wanting to help, but Jack was there, tending to Dalton.

"Oh Daddy, it was awful." I collapsed into his embrace, his arms, as if he really were my dad, my real dad. Thankful he was alive. The op hadn't been compromised. And Dalton was going to be all right. He had to be.

The brothers appeared with a stretcher, easing Dalton down onto it.

I tried to help but the ground moved, the world spun. Joe was there, holding me upright. "Take it easy," he was saying. "We've got him. You take it easy now."

"But—"

"But nothing. Sit back down. Daddy's here now." He hugged me tight and stroked my hair. And I remembered. I was Poppy Pratt, spoiled daughter of a rich oil tycoon. In her Daddy's arms. I let the tears flow. "Don't let him die."

"Everything's going to be okay," he soothed, rocking me. "Daddy's here."

"I got Mark on the radio. He's in the air, headed straight here," Irene said. "Maybe twenty minutes."

"Twenty minutes!" I sat upright. "That's too long."

Jack patted me on the knee. "It's all right. You kept the knife in. That was smart."

I managed a nod. "But he's lost a lot of blood."

"Irene, did you call Anchorage? A medevac?" Jack asked.

"Too far out," she said, shaking her head. "We have to wait."

Jack tugged at the bandage on my leg, peeled it back. My thigh had turned purple and yellow and the wound site oozed some nasty stuff. "I'll take him to the hospital then turn right around and come back for you."

Dalton was white, passed out, but Jack stayed with him, keeping a close eye on the wound. I sat next to him on the gravel shore. Waiting.

"It's too long. It's been too long. Too much blood lost," I said. I'd failed. He was going to die.

"We're not giving up yet," Joe said.

Finally, the plane came into view, the steady hum of the prop like the sound of salvation. It pulled up on shore, the propeller left slowly spinning as the brothers joined Mark, helping him to remove the back seat, then the passenger seat. They dropped them on the gravel shore, then hurried to carry Dalton on the stretcher toward the plane.

I yanked out of Joe's embrace. "I've got to go with him."

"There's no room," Mark said. "Jack will be with him."

"But—"

"It's in God's hands now," Mark said. "You have to let him go."

I stared. Frozen. *In God's hands?* This, from a poacher. I wanted to scratch his eyes out. Rip his heart from his chest. Scream, *this is all your fault* as I bashed his skull against the gravel. Instead, I leaned into Joe's arms and watched the plane taxi down the river, then lift off into the darkening night.

Irene fussed with my leg wound, dousing it with alcohol. "We don't want that to get infected," she said, making a painful face as I winced. "This will have to do until Jack gets back for you."

They'd brought me inside, into the great room, with all the dead animal heads hanging on the walls. And the fireplace. Oh the warmth. I wasn't sure I'd ever be warm again.

Irene pressed some gauze to my leg wound and secured it

with tape as her eyes traveled to the wound on my arm. "You look like you've been to war."

I nodded, thankful for her kindness.

Mark sat down across from me. "What the hell happened out there?"

I glanced at Joe.

"You know what," he said, "let's just give her some space. She's had a shock."

Townsend frowned but got up from the chair. "I'll make some tea."

Joe nodded a thanks and took my hand, but Irene didn't budge.

"I knew it," she muttered. "I knew that Rocky was trouble."

"What did you say?" Joe asked.

"Nothing," she said with a sigh. She shook her head, her gaze shifting to the rash at my neck. "I've got some salve for that." She rose and left to go get it.

"Just relax," Joe said. "We've got nothing but time. We'll get this all sorted out later. Lay your head back and relax."

"I can't. Where's the plane? I have to get to Dalton, he—"

"Don't you worry about Dalton right now. Just try to relax. Close your eyes."

"No. I can't. I have to know about Dalton."

"I promise. You'll be the first to know. Trust me. Just close your eyes."

I lay back, every muscle complaining. *Maybe just close my eyes for a bit.*

Someone grabbed my arm. I sat upright with a jolt, my heart racing. "What?" Where am I? It was warm. My head heavy, groggy. Were we—"Dalton?"

"He's stable," Joe said, letting go of my arm and sitting

down next to me. "They got to the hospital in time. Jack is already headed back here to pick you up."

Relief rushed over me and I felt like I might collapse. My eyes turned misty. He was going to be all right. I drew in a long breath, tried to relax.

Townsend was sitting on the chair across from me, Irene beside him. Both wore expressions of concern.

"Are you ready to tell us what happened?" Mark asked.

I glanced at Joe. He nodded. "Tell us everything."

"Well," I said, hesitating. Everything? *Crap.* Dalton and I hadn't talked about our story. It didn't matter. The kiss—the kiss wasn't relevant. Unless Rocky had called. I looked at Mark, trying to read him. "I'm not sure, to be honest. We flew out to the spike camp. Got set up. Everything seemed fine. I guess. The next day, Rocky took us to look for the bear. He spent all day but didn't find it and he was upset about that."

Mark nodded. That made sense to him.

"He was more than upset. He was...distraught?"

"How do you mean?"

"Like he was embarrassed maybe? Anyway, the next day—" *Rocky shot the bear?* No, no need to mention that. "He found the bear, but I missed the shot. Well, after we got back to camp, Rocky said he forgot the phone in the plane and took off to get it." I paused. "We assumed he was going to call you. Did he call?" I watched his response.

"No," Mark answered. Innocently. "Not a peep since you headed out to the spike camp, not until Irene called me to come back with the plane."

I looked to Joe for confirmation. He gave me a subtle shake of his head. If Rocky called, he wasn't aware of it.

"When he got back to camp, he pulled a gun on us and started shooting. For no reason."

All three shared the same look of surprise and confusion.

"Dalton and I took off running. For the next two days,

he—" I closed my eyes. *Stay true to character.* "Daddy, it was awful. He had his crossbow and he—" I swallowed hard "—he hunted us."

"What!" Joe looked truly shocked. He couldn't be sure if I was telling the truth or making it all up to maintain my cover. Either way, he played along. "You're saying he, he—"

"He chased me and shot at me. He shot Dalton too, but…"

"I knew something like this would happen," Irene muttered, holding her head in her hands.

Mark shut her up with a glance.

I looked to Joe. "He was crazy. Like he went wild."

Joe turned to Mark. "What the hell kind of psycho did you have working for you?"

Mark held his hands up in defense. "I had no idea. Honest. I'm as shocked as you are. I mean, Rocky was a bit odd, but—"

"A bit odd?" Joe rose to his full height. "He shot at my daughter and stabbed my son! You sent my children out into the wilderness with this man, knowing he was psycho?" He had his chest puffed out in full papa bear mode. "What the hell kind of operation are you running here?"

Mark stood toe to toe with Joe. "I'll get to the bottom of this," he said, his jaw set with determination. He turned to me. "Where is he now? Still at the spike camp then?"

"He's—" My eyes went from Mark to Joe then back. "He's dead." A flicker of surprise showed in Joe's eyes. "He and Dalton got in a fight. The knife, he—" I left it at that. Too many details wouldn't be prudent right now.

"Why didn't you call for help?" Joe asked.

"We couldn't find the phone. I think he hid it somewhere. The radio in the plane was disabled. I tried to fix it, but…I had to get Dalton to a hospital. I had to—" Tears welled up in my eyes again.

Mark glared at me in disbelief. "So you thought it was a good idea to try to fly a plane?"

"That's enough." Joe sat back down and wrapped his arms around me. "She's been through enough. The damage to your plane is inconsequential."

"Inconsequential?" He shifted on his heels. "This is my livelihood."

Irene held out a hand to Mark. "I don't think—"

"How dare you?" Joe rose back up from the chair and faced him down, his eyes enraged with fire. "I'm going to sue your ass from here to the South Pole and back. As soon as I get to Anchorage and get my lawyers on the phone, I'll—"

Mark's hands shot up in defense, his expression quickly changing from anger to realization, then to a placating smile. Lawyers meant investigations. "Let's not get carried away. I see your point, of course. I'm sorry. I wasn't thinking. This has all happened so fast." He sat back down. "You're right. The important thing is you got your brother back here," he said to me. "You were very brave."

I nodded, accepting his apology, but Joe wasn't having any of it.

"That's enough. Now leave my daughter be. She needs rest."

Mark's gaze dropped to his hands and he nodded. Irene took him by the arm and led him out of the room, shutting the door behind them.

Joe's eyes followed them out, then turned to me. In a whisper, he said, "Is that what happened?"

I nodded.

"Was your cover blown?"

"No, we don't think so. That's the thing, he—" And the tears surged to my eyes.

"Jesus," he said, shaking his head. "I'm sorry."

"Oh my god. Oh my god. I killed him, Joe. I killed him."

He sat down next to me and took me in his arms.

"He stabbed Dalton and I did it. I shot him with the bow."

Sobs wracked my body and I shook.

Joe rocked me, stroking my hair. "It's all right," he kept saying. "It's all right. You did what you had to do."

Snot ran from my nose and stuck in my hair. Joe reached for a tissue box on the table and handed it to me.

"He chased me, hunted me, like a..." I couldn't bring myself to say it. "And then the trap, it didn't work maybe? Or maybe Dalton was worried because he was holding the bow? I don't know."

"The trap? What trap?"

"Well, there was this bear trap and Dalton, he didn't—"

"You know what. That doesn't matter right now. Listen to me," he said. "You defended your partner. You risked your own life to save his getting him back here. You're a hero."

I shook my head and more tears gushed from my eyes.

"We're officers of the law. We put ourselves in harm's way. We never know what that might mean. He was a very bad man. You defended yourself and Dalton." He wiped a tear from my cheek. "You did your job."

I snuffled, trying to get myself together. "What's going to happen? I mean, here? What about—"

"You let me worry about that," he said and pulled me back into his bear hug embrace.

Chapter 21

Next to his bed, bags of blood and saline hung from hooks, plastic tubes running down into his arm. The sounds of beeps and clicks, his steady breathing helped by a machine, the potent scent of disinfectant—all reminded me of being in this same position in Costa Rica.

Maybe I was a bad partner. Last time he got shot. Because of me. This time stabbed. Maybe I deserved to be investigated. Maybe I was brazen and...maybe I wasn't cut out to be an agent. Dalton deserved a better partner.

He lay there, asleep. My heart ached for him to wake, to tell me he was all right, to show me that half-grin, one more time.

I sat down on the edge of Dalton's bed, took his hand in mine. "You're gonna be all right," I said, wishing he could hear me. "For a while there, I wasn't sure, but they say—"

The nurse came in. "We're doing everything we can," she said, checking the knobs and fiddling with the tubes and wires in the machine next to him. "You're not supposed to be out of bed. You need to rest yourself, young lady." She gave me a motherly look, hands on her hips. "Let me help you back to your room."

"No. I've been sleeping too much."

"Oh my."

I spun around. Chris stood in the doorway. I sprang to my

feet and into his arms. "You got my message!"

"I was in Chicago and hopped a flight right away."

"Oh Chris, I'm sorry. I'm so sorry."

"What are you prattling on about?" He led me back to the chair. "Sit down. Take a breath."

The nurse smiled at us as she left the room.

"Your job. My big mouth. Chris, I can't believe I was so stupid. I don't know what I was thinking."

He grinned. "You never could hold that tongue."

I shook my head, filled with relief. "I promise, I'll—"

"All right. All right. Enough already. I forgive you."

I hugged him again, holding on tight, needing to feel his strength.

When he eased back from my embrace, he looked me up and down. "What the hell happened, girl? You look like shit."

"Yeah, well."

He turned toward Dalton, concerned.

My eyes got misty. "Every time I come in here to see him, he's sleeping."

Chris pulled me close with one arm, squeezing me to him. "What do the doctors say?"

"He lost a lot of blood, but they say he's going to be fine."

"Well, then. I'm sure he will." His eyebrows shot up and with his teasing voice, he said, "The most important question then is: did you get the bad guy?"

My eyes dropped to the floor. I couldn't talk about it. Not yet.

Chris nodded in understanding. He saw the bandages on my arm and frowned. "I don't suppose it would do any good to try to convince you to take a desk job?"

I shook my head, smiled. Then giggles bubbled up from inside and we both burst into laughter. It felt good.

"You are taking a vacation with me though," he said, feigning a stern father's voice. "I won't take no for an answer."

I raised my right hand. "I promise." No argument from me. I needed a break. Some time to think. Some time with my best friend, to talk and—"Oh Chris. You had something you wanted to tell me. What was it? Tell me. Tell me please."

He shook his head. "Right now isn't—it can wait. You come on vacation with me and I'll tell you all about it. Deal?"

I nodded. "Deal."

"Hey there. Welcome back," Chris said, his eyes focused over my shoulder.

I spun around.

Dalton's face was still pale, but his eyes were lit with vigor. Relief came upon me like the warm sun breaking from behind a dark cloud.

"You're awake!"

His eyes held mine. My teeth clenched together and my lip quivered. I wanted to hug him, hold him, tell him how scared I'd been.

Chris put his hand on my arm. "I'm going to go. I'll be at the hotel."

I gave him a hug and a kiss on the cheek.

Once he'd left, I wrapped my arms around Dalton's neck and squeezed him tight to be sure he was really alive. "You're here. You're really okay."

"Thanks to you."

I sat back and stared at him, holding his hand in mine. There were so many emotions swirling around in my head. But Dalton was alive. That's all that mattered right now. Tomorrow I could worry about the rest.

He gave me a smile. "I've been thinking," he said. "We should—"

"I'm sorry. I shouldn't have kissed you. It was—"

"What?" His eyes softened. His eyes traveled to my lips and held there. "I'm quite sure that *I* kissed *you*."

My breath caught in my throat.

He squeezed my hand.

I exhaled. "We should what?"

"What?"

"You started to say, we should…"

"You know. When I get out of here, we should go out and do something. Together."

I couldn't help but grin. "Are you asking me out on a date?"

He held my gaze. "Would you say yes?"

"I might as well." I shrugged. "I mean, since I'll be fired and we won't be working together anymore."

He stared at me for the longest time, that mind of his weighing something.

"Nice to see you're up and well."

I swung around toward the door and the source of the voice. A man. I blinked. Stan Martin? "Omigosh, sir." I yanked my hand from Dalton's and started to get up, but he held out a hand, gesturing for me to stay seated. "What are you doing here? I mean, all this way and—"

"Two of my agents have been injured on duty. I wanted to come myself, make sure you're taken care of." He yanked the chair out from against the wall, sat down, smoothed his tie against his shirt, then looked up at me. "I take it you're feeling better."

It all came rushing back. The investigative hearing. My job on the line. And now I was going to have to explain shooting Rocky. "I know you have concerns—"

He held up his hand. "Don't worry about that right now." He gave me a warm, genuine smile. "I understand that if you hadn't taken the action you did, Dalton wouldn't be alive today."

"No. He's the one who saved me. He—"

The hand again. "I'm glad to see you humble. But Joe's already told me the whole story." His eyes went to Dalton and mine followed. "In fact, he's been singing your praises. From the sounds of it, you're a candidate for a medal of honor."

I turned back to Mr. Martin, keeping it together. "I'm sure that's not—"

"Poppy," Dalton interrupted. "You saved my life. The doc said if you hadn't got me back to the lodge when you did, I would have bled out for sure. I wouldn't have made it through the night."

My stomach clenched. This was too—*get a grip*. I pasted on a cordial smile and said to Mr. Martin, "I can't believe you came all the way to Alaska."

"Actually, I wanted to talk to you two anyway. Give you the news in person."

I shot a glance at Dalton. What news? Dalton shrugged.

"The President has created a task force, an elite team, if you will," Martin said, "to investigate animal-related cases. Wildlife and domestic." He hesitated, as though what he was about to say he wasn't sure he wanted to share. "You're participation was specifically requested. In fact," he cleared his throat, " it was more like a demand."

He was looking at me. "Me?"

"You are the one who single-handedly apprehended Ray Goldman, our most-wanted, are you not?" His face looked like he was actually in physical pain as he spit out those words. Either that or constipated.

"Yes. I mean, Dalton and I did. Together. We're a team."

"Indeed. And I'm glad to hear you say that."

"Did you say the President, sir? Of the United States?"

"Yes, *the* President of the United States."

I turned to Dalton. He was grinning. "Your mouth is hanging open."

I snapped it shut.

"I reported that you two need some time to recuperate. As soon as you're up to it, you'll join the team. That is, if you want to?"

I nodded, then caught my head bobbing. An elite task force. I couldn't believe it.

"But sir," I said. "This op, there was an incident and—"

"Yes," he said with an exaggerated nod. "Joe told me about that. A hunting accident. Unfortunate, but, it happens." He straightened his tie. "We did a little digging. It seems the man in question was wanted in Iowa for assault, kidnapping, and multiple weapons offenses. I guess they can close the case."

Was that it? I'd killed a man and it would be scribbled in a report, stuck in a manila folder in the back of a file cabinet somewhere, as a hunting accident? Was that justice?

"What about Townsend?" I asked.

"Joe will be by later this evening to fill you in."

"Okay, but Irene, his wife, doesn't know about the poaching. I'm sure of it," I said. "She shouldn't be arrested."

"Put it in the report," Martin said, nodding in understanding. "But I don't believe Joe plans to arrest anyone just yet. The man's got a dead body on his hands. We'll see how he deals with that." He gave us an amused smirk. "Joe seems to really be enjoying making Townsend squirm. This Rocky fellow might have acted on his own trafficking in wildlife parts, but Joe's convinced Townsend was complicit in the poaching. The guy's already offered a two-week hunt, next year, opening day, on the house, to make it up to you." He winked. "Next year you'll have your trophy."

He rose from the chair, smoothed his tie, and straightened his back. "So, we're clear," he said, his gaze intense, "you've had an exemplary career so far, outstanding even. Not one blemish. And I can count on you both to represent us on the task force?"

I nodded, my mouth hanging open again. There'd be no inquisition? No investigative hearing? All swept under the rug because the President had called?

"We'll see you back at headquarters then." He nodded to Dalton and headed for the door. "As soon as you are up and at 'em."

"Thank you, sir." Dalton's words followed him down the hall, then he turned his attention to me. "Are you happy?"

I nodded. "You're going to be all right."

"Yes, but I mean about the task force?"

I couldn't help myself. The thought of being on that elite team filled me with excited energy. I bounced a little on the bed, grinning like an idiot. "I can't believe it. Can you believe it?" I was going to need to let it sink in. "A presidential task force. Think of what we'll be able to accomplish."

"Government work." He rolled his eyes, teasing me. "It's all the same."

"I wonder what we'll be called. Maybe we'll have special berets. You'd look good in a beret," I said, teasing him back. "Maybe they'll call us The Green Berets—oh wait, that's taken. Maybe we'll have to come up with our own, secret name. Like—" I thought a moment "—Righteous Animal Crusaders against Evil."

"If the government gives it a name," he said, "it will be dull and practical, like, Task Force for Animal Enforcement."

"You mean like the SEALs? Sea, air, land."

Dalton looked at me with those eyes, those irresistible eyes. "Whatever it's called, if you're in, I'm in."

I shook my head, the emotions rushing back in. I hadn't been a good partner to him. "You were right. About the plane. That was a risky stunt I pulled."

He smiled wide. "I'm glad you did."

I relaxed a little. "Order a body bag. Was that supposed to be funny?"

The smile disappeared. "No."

"Don't ever say that again. Ever."

"Okay."

"I mean it."

"Okay."

"Because I—we—"

"I know."

I swallowed the lump in my throat. "I killed him, Dalton. I killed him."

He squeezed my hand. "I'm so sorry, Poppy."

"You were right about me. About..." I lifted my head, looked him in the eyes. "I'd do it again."

His eyes held mine.

"But now, with this—" My thoughts followed Stan Martin down the hall and the new assignment, the new team we'd be on. Together. Working as partners. "On the task force. We can't—"

"Kiss me."

I hesitated.

His eyes. "Kiss me."

I leaned down, my lips met his, and everything else floated away.

I nuzzled my face against his chest, felt the comforting rise and fall as he breathed.

"We'll figure it out," he said, stroking my hair.

But I knew better. We couldn't work together. Not as partners. We had let our guard down. We'd damn near gotten killed because of it.

I'd have to choose.

Thank YOU for reading. If you feel as strongly as I do about the issues presented in these books and you want to help, PLEASE start by taking a moment to post a review on Amazon.com and Goodreads.com and tell a friend about the story. Help me spread the word. For the animals!

If you'd like to learn more and stay in touch, please sign up for my newsletter or follow my blog at www.KimberliBindschatel.com

Author's Note

In 2012, on a wildlife tour boat in Resurrection Bay, I first learned of the infamous Butcher Baker, Robert Hansen. Our captain was pointing out landmarks and mentioned the maximum security prison there, telling us the story of an escape and, of course, of the well-known inmate and his sick obsession with hunting women.

I didn't give it another thought until I read the book, *The Blue Bear*, by Lynn Schooler. I highly recommend this beautiful story (if only I could write prose like that) about friendship and living in the Alaskan wilderness. Mr. Schooler endured his own tragic experience at the hands of Hansen and his telling brought the idea to life for me. I had been struggling with the theme of hunting, what fuels a desire to hunt, and Hansen's behavior seemed to fit.

I hope you enjoyed the story.

If you'd like to learn more and stay in touch, please sign up for my newsletter or follow my blog at www.KimberliBindschatel.com

About the Author

Born and raised in Michigan, I spent summers at the lake, swimming, catching frogs, and chasing fireflies, winters building things out of cardboard and construction paper, writing stories, and dreaming of faraway places. Since I didn't make honors English in High School, I thought I couldn't write. So I started hanging out in the art room. The day I borrowed a camera, my love affair with photography began. Long before the birth of the pixel, I was exposing real silver halides to light and marveling at the magic of an image appearing on paper under a red light.

After college, I freelanced in commercial photography studios. During the long days of rigging strobes, one story haunted me. As happens in life though, before I could put it to words, I was possessed by another dream—to be a wildlife photographer. I trekked through the woods to find loons, grizzly bears, whales, and moose. Then, for six years, I put my heart and soul into publishing a nature magazine, *Whisper in the Woods*. But it was not meant to be my magnum opus. This time, my attention was drawn skyward. I'd always been fascinated by the aurora borealis, shimmering in the night sky, but now my focus went beyond, to the cosmos, to wonder about our place in the universe.

In the spring of 2010, I sat down at the computer, started typing words, and breathed life into a curious boy named Kiran in *The Path to the Sun*. Together, in our quest for truth, Kiran and I have explored the mind and spirit. Our journey has taken us to places of new perspective. Alas, the answers always seem just beyond our grasp, as elusive as a firefly on a warm autumn night.

Most recently, my focus has shifted to more pressing issues — imperiled wildlife. With the *Poppy McVie* series, I hope to bring some light into the shadowy underworld of black market wildlife trade, where millions of wild animals are captured or slaughtered annually to fund organized crime.

IT. MUST. STOP.

If you'd like to learn more and stay in touch, please sign up for my newsletter or follow my blog at www.PoppyMcVie.com

The adventure doesn't end for
Poppy and Dalton

Join them in Mexico as they pursue turtle poachers in